DEMONS OF DESIRE

HALF-BREED SERIES, BOOK 1

DEBRA DUNBAR

Demons of Desire
By
Debra Dunbar

❀ Created with Vellum

CHAPTER 1

$\mathcal{M}$ost people don't think of sex when they're sweating in an airport baggage claim, but most people aren't half succubus. I tried to keep my eyes on the endless parade of identical black bags, but my gaze kept drifting toward the three virile college boys staring at me. They'd been on my plane, and I'd been all too aware of their testosterone-fueled fascination for the entire two-and-a-half-hour flight.

Pick one, my naughty half urged.

Actually, she wanted all three of them, but I'd bartered her down to one. Not that I had any intention of screwing anyone in an airport. I'd eventually have to give in to her, but it would be on my terms. I was picky, where *she* most definitely was not.

Perspiration rolled down my back, gluing the light-blue tank top to my skin. The heat had hit me the moment they'd opened the aircraft doors, and the baggage claim wasn't much cooler than outside. It was hot enough up in Maryland, but New Orleans was like being submerged in a hot tub. Of course, I would have braved the fires of hell to get away from Maryland — and away from *him*.

"So, what brings you to New Orleans?"

One of the college boys had finally worked up the courage to approach me. His friends stood back, watching and obviously holding their breath in anticipation of a smack down. Little did they know, my succubus side would never give a prospective partner the cold shoulder, and my elf side couldn't tolerate rudeness in any way, shape, or form.

Did I mention I was also half elf?

I smiled. It's not like I could help it. He was just so darned cute, and his attention so very flattering. "I'm here to visit an old college roommate. She transferred to Tulane a couple of years ago."

"Cool. We go to Maryland — 'Fear the Turtle'." He gave a fist pump to emphasize the college's sports slogan. "We're here to party. Airfare is really cheap right now."

Yeah. It was a million fricken degrees and hurricane season. If I hadn't been escaping . . . no, I wasn't going to think of *him*. Instead of replying, I turned to watch the bags circle by, concerned that I may have missed mine. Even my elf etiquette had its limits.

"We're going to be down on Bourbon Street tonight. Maybe we can meet up?"

Of course they were going to be down on Bourbon Street. But even a first-timer like me realized the futility of trying to vaguely "meet-up" with someone on a street filled with hundreds of bars and wall-to-wall people.

"Sure," I replied, watching the bags circle by. "I'll look for you all." My succubus side was irritated that I wasn't already dragging this guy into the nearest alcove and having my way with him. I stalled her again with vague promises, well aware I wouldn't be able to hold her back for long. I'd need to get laid in the next few days or she'd take control and I'd find myself with a less-than-desirable partner.

College Boy seemed to realize that the odds of actually running into me on Bourbon Street were the equivalent of winning the Powerball lottery. "We'll be at Saints and Sinners."

Channing Tatum's place. It was on my short list of places to check out. I gave him another smile. "Okay. I don't know what my friend has planned, but I'll try and be there."

That seemed to delight College Boy beyond all reason. He grinned and walked backward to join his friends. They hooted and slapped him on the back, casting quick glances at me as they walked toward the big glass doors. I waved good-naturedly then turned to see my bag coming down the line.

"Excuse me. Oh, crap!" I squeezed between two other travelers and reached for the handle, but my fingers slipped off. The bag dropped back onto the belt of the luggage carousel, firmly wedged between two black suitcases. I watched in irritation as my bag moved away. Now I'd need to wait for it to make a whole circuit before I had the chance to grab it again.

"I've got it."

A tanned arm sporting a gold watch shot out and grabbed my bag, yanking it from the belt with a practiced grip. I followed that arm upward with my eyes. Trim guy. Fifties. Mostly bald with close-cut light-colored hair. Lemon-yellow polo shirt paired with khaki shorts. Business man, perhaps? Here for a convention or on vacation? He had nice, friendly blue eyes.

I reached out a hand to take the bag from him, and his eyes darted downward, lingering on my tank top, or, rather, on the breasts it barely covered. The succubus within me awoke, fixing this man with a hungry stare. Desire stirred, surfacing and arcing out in invisible tendrils.

No, no, no. I tried to rein her in. This man probably had kids my age. Either way, I could tell he was a nice guy. He deserved better than this, but my baser self didn't agree. She was hungry.

The man's eyes left my breasts and rose to meet mine. I saw the lust in them, along with confusion, and a bit of shame. I was ashamed too, but that emotion was drowned out by the thought of his mouth on mine, his . . . .

Married. Married. It was like an alarm bell, bringing my rational-self back into control. I didn't care how hungry the monster living inside me was, I was *not* going to be responsible for this man breaking his wedding vows. Besides, he deserved better than a mind-blowing fuck in an airport bathroom that would yoke him to me for the rest of his life. He deserved better, and so did I.

"Thank you."

I snatched the bag from him and nearly fell in my haste to get away. For Pete's sake, I was in an airport, surrounded by people, and I was on the edge of having sex with a stranger who had been kind enough to grab my luggage off the conveyor belt. My face burned with embarrassment at the encounter, but I would have felt worse had we wound up naked in a public restroom stall.

I *was* out of control. Irix had been right, but his solution wasn't something I could live with. I envisioned his mocking voice, his raised eyebrows when he gave me the I-told-you-so speech. I'd heard that speech all too often over the past month, but that wasn't why I'd left. I could handle bossy; what I couldn't handle was the way I felt every time he was near.

"Amber!"

There. By the doors. A young woman waved at me, her black hair pulled back, highlighting perfect cheekbones and warm, dark-brown skin. She bounced up and down on strappy sandals, all long legs and slim hips. I waved back and hustled myself toward her, shrieking as I grabbed her in a tight hug. Darci and I had kept in touch even after she'd transferred to Tulane, but I'd really missed her — my freshman roommate, my best friend. If anybody could help me find the Amber I used to be, it was Darci.

"Hurry, I'm double parked." She disengaged and looked around for my luggage.

I grabbed the bag I'd dropped to hug her, grateful to be getting out of the airport. The heat and excitement of my escape had stirred up the monster inside, and the guys at baggage claim weren't the only ones I was beginning to have lurid fantasies about. I hadn't had sex in four weeks. This was New Orleans, a town of indulgences. I'd indulge, then hopefully the desperate hunger would taper off, and I could just relax and enjoy myself — like the old Amber.

We crammed my bags in Darci's Jetta and took off, blasting the AC. Darci chatted on about college, a guy she was desperate to go out with, and what was on the agenda for today. She hadn't been able to get the whole week off work, but I assured her I could manage on my own. My anticipation built thinking about po-boy sandwiches, Cajun music in the French Quarter, and a hot new dance club in the warehouse district. Already I felt the monster grow tame, distracted by the prospect of nice, normal *human*-type activities.

"So . . . tell me about this guy you're running away from."

Darci's inquiry jolted me out of my happy space. Irix. Thick sable-brown hair that fell to his shoulders in back and brushed his jaw in the front, dark, golden eyes that seemed to see right under my clothing. He moved like a large cat on the prowl, and his smile held a promise of wicked carnal delights.

"He's bad for me. And if I'd stayed, I would have wound up in his bed."

"Oh, those are the best ones, aren't they? Bad for you how? Because I've never known you to walk away from something bad."

Only when it was something I couldn't truly have. "He's one of those guys who is completely addictive. I'd take it far more seriously than he would. I just don't need that kind of emotional damage, thank you very much."

Darci shot me a knowing look. "Oh, the tables have been turned! Amber, the queen of love-them-and-leave-them is in danger of losing her heart to a world-class womanizer."

What? I was *not* that sort of girl! Well, I hadn't been that sort of girl up until recently.

"I'm sorry I ever told you about that Zumba instructor from the gym. One guy does not make me a player."

That's when the problem began. I'd been so crazy about him, wanted him so bad. One date, one night of torrid passion, and it was all gone. I didn't care if I ever saw him again. I couldn't even remember what his name was. What I did have was the thin trickle of energy he'd supply me with for the rest of his life. And guilt. A whole lot of guilt.

I thought Darci was going to wreck the car from laughing. "One guy? *One* guy? Seriously, Amber, once you get them in the sack, it's 'adios my friend'."

"I'm not . . . no way," I sputtered. How could she *think* that? I'd had plenty of relationships. Yeah, none had lasted very long, but that wasn't *my* fault.

"Oh, let's see . . . Darius, Nick, Brent, Jason."

"Jason dumped *me*," I protested.

"Zac, Scott, Theo."

"Hey, I dated Theo for a month. That's not a one-night-stand!"

Darci made a "pffft" sound and waved her hand at me. "It

took you that long to sleep with him. Remember, finals? Then he had the flu. Then you went on that ski trip. Once you guys did the nasty, Theo was yesterday's news."

My head whirled, and I stared at Darci open-mouthed. She was right. This problem of mine had been going on longer than I'd thought; I just hadn't realized it. She glanced at me, smiling fondly.

"It's okay, Amber. Doesn't make you a bad person. Actually, I always thought it was kind of funny. Guys are usually the ones that do this; it was refreshing to see the tables turned."

No, it wasn't funny. It was just as shitty as when guys did it to girls. These were nice boys that I'd screwed over, that I'd hurt. I hadn't realized it back then, but now the thought of it devastated me. I'd hidden some things from Darci — things she would never believe anyway, but I needed to let her know how terrible this made me feel, how I didn't want to be that sort of person.

"It's not okay. There's something wrong with me, Darci. I want to have a long-term relationship. I want to meet someone nice, fall in love and commit to them. I'll never have that, and it hurts. It hurts almost as much as how I treated all those guys."

"You *will* fall in love. You'll find the right guy, and it will all click into place." She gave me a quick, mischievous look. "Now tell me all about this sexy scoundrel you ditched up in Maryland. I live vicariously through your tales of sexual conquest, you know. What's his name?"

"Irix." I didn't want to think of him, let alone talk about him, but I knew Darci would never give up until she'd heard all the details.

"Oooh, exotic! Is that his first or last name?"

It was probably one of many names. I'd been told demons

have quite a few and are very cagy about letting anyone know all of them.

"I'm not sure. It's the only name he goes by."

"Like Madonna, or Sting? How did you meet him?"

Now this was the tricky part. I couldn't really say my demon parent had sent an incubus to teach me how to deal with my succubus side.

"My family contracted him as a sort of life coach for me. That's why I can't just avoid him. He's there every day, following me around, pestering me to do this or do that. I told him to go home and leave me alone, but he won't until he feels I've learned what I need. It's his job." And I got the feeling he was getting quite a kick out of it too.

Darci scrunched up her face. "Ugh. Totally hot does not outweigh bossing you around. That sucks. What happens if you just tell him to kiss off and do whatever the heck you want?"

Heat roared through me. I felt my face redden.

"Oh!" Darci chuckled. "You bad girl, you! Well, no need to worry. You're safe here from Mr. Sexy Life Coach, and I've got all kinds of fun activities planned."

CHAPTER 2

"Fun starts now." Darci grinned as she parked.

A wide expanse of green spread as far as I could see on the opposite side of the street — the manicured lawn dotted with ancient, sprawling trees. My breath caught at the sight.

"My friend, Jordan, works for the Department of Parks and Recreation. I conned her into giving you a tour of Audubon Park."

Jordan was short with an athletic build, dark red spirals of hair and a café au lait complexion. She grinned and pumped my outstretched hand enthusiastically.

"Darci tells me you're an environmental biology major? I graduated last year, and I'm working on my Masters down here. You've no idea how glad I am to meet you. Darci is bored to tears with my ramblings about trees and wetlands."

"Just biology," I corrected with an apologetic smile. "I haven't decided on a specialty, but I'm leaning towards botany."

"Kindred spirits," Jordan exclaimed, raising both hands.

"New Orleans is heaven to us plant lovers. Let me show you around Audubon Park."

There was a serene majesty to the place that captivated me in an instant. Gray Spanish moss draped from the trees. Instead of mown, manicured lawns, the foliage was a mix of indigenous plants. Water flowed throughout the park — as it did all over New Orleans. Ducks and other waterfowl loudly pestered visitors for food, waddling along as they begged. I was enchanted.

"Audubon Park was once a plantation. In addition to the usual trails and play areas, it harbors a huge selection of indigenous birds. Named for the famous James Audubon. . . ."

Jordan's voice faded away, and all I heard was the sound of the trees — a low, soothing hum. Huge oaks, some over six-hundred-years old, spread thick, moss-draped branches low to the ground. Lagoons wound their way through the park, a reminder of the city's below-sea-level elevation. The ironwork bridges and fountains irritated me by their presence. This was a place for earth and water, not human-wrought embellishments. Reaching out, I placed a palm against the thick bark of an oak, feeling its song through my skin. Something inside me shifted, and I felt myself sing back to the tree, achieving that sense of peace and alignment that always came when I worked with plants.

You may be old, but I'll outlive you, I thought. *I'll watch your seedlings rise and fall, watch the waters nurture countless generations of your saplings.*

Jordan had fallen silent, and I looked up to see the woman watching me, a quizzical expression on her face. Darci was over by a fountain, texting into her phone.

"Beautiful, aren't they?" Jordan asked, walking close to put her palm on the bark alongside my hand. Her energy merged with the oak's, strong and rich. "Wisdom and protection. The old gods whisper in their leaves."

"Fertility and prosperity," I replied, giving the tree one last caress. I had a few Wiccan friends in college and back home and recognized the reverent tone. Maybe Jordan was simply poetic in her passion for nature, but I got the sense her dedication delved into the spiritual.

"Do you practice?" she asked, confirming my suspicions.

"No, but I have an affinity for all things green."

It was a weak explanation. What I felt wasn't in the realm of religion or belief — it went into my very bones, into the blood that flowed through my veins. When I was in a forest, everything came together. I felt like I could lie upon the moss and melt into the earth itself. It was the one place where my crazy succubus side relaxed and stopped pestering me with her incessant needs. It was wonderful to know this place existed right here in New Orleans — a spot I could retreat to when I felt out of control and needed to center.

Jordan and I continued the tour while Darci lagged behind, still fiddling with her phone. I didn't mind if she was playing Candy Crush or posting on Instagram. All this tree stuff wasn't really her thing. It was a testament to our friendship that she was enduring this for me.

There was a parade of oaks, cypresses and other trees. I loved the Live Oaks the best — how their horizontal spread was nearly twice their height. They were the largest tree species east of the Rockies, from the red oak group of trees.

"Unfortunately, this one isn't going to make it. We're scheduled to take it down tomorrow, although there's no real guarantee the disease won't spread to the others."

I felt it before I turned to look at the tree — a thick, sickeningly sweet aura. Black spots, like burns, dotted the bark of the Live Oak, and its leaves showed similar brown and black marks. It was as if someone had held a torch to the tree. I placed my hand on the bark — it confirmed what my eyes told me, and I jerked away in horror.

"Phytophthora ramorum."

Sudden oak death. The plant pathogen was fungus-like in how it spread, covering the tree with cankers that bled thick sap. Under the bark would be discolored tissue and black lines. It was a death sentence, and the bane of every arborist. Removing the tree and surrounding soil was the typical response, but it often didn't halt the spread. I worried for the old grove, but my greatest sorrow was for the sick oak.

I reached a hand toward the oak then hesitated. My supernatural green thumb had its limits — or did it? All I'd done so far was correct mineral imbalances in soil and adjust absorption rates. I'd never removed disease. I'd never cured. The oak was dying before my eyes, forgiving me my limitations. Noble. Accepting of its fate.

I couldn't turn my back on this tree. My hand touched the damaged bark. A sensation of black sludge rocketed through me, twisting my stomach into a knot of pain. I pushed back, fighting my way through the haze of death, into the heart of the tree. The blight fought back, angrily defending its prey and stealing my breath with a smoky scent. A faint shout barely registered in my mind, along with the sensation of something on my arm. It felt strange, as though my body were coated in layers of wool, or as if I were buried deep inside another. Gold pushed back the black, expanding with a flash of light and heat.

"Amber!"

I was on my back, staring up at Darci's dark brown eyes, her face framed by a cerulean sky. Jordan stood to the side with her hand covering her mouth. She wasn't as concerned over my horizontal position as Darci was; she was too occupied staring at the Live Oak. Emphasis on "live".

"Low blood sugar," I told Darci as I tentatively sat up. Her eyebrows shot up, but she held her tongue. Jordan wasn't so circumspect.

"You cured it! I've never seen a magical working have such a quick result. Wow, if you can do that for a tree, I can only imagine what you could do to help rebuild the swamp areas. Centuries of damage could be corrected in one day. You *must* meet my coven."

"She *must* get a sandwich." Darci's voice was stern as she helped me to my feet.

"What kind of magic do you practice?" Jordan continued, undeterred.

"The low-blood-sugar kind."

"Let's get you some lunch," Darci chimed in.

"But the tree. . . ."

"Yep. Looks like a tree to me." Darci's voice was cheerful as she waved a dismissive hand at the oak. "Exactly the same as all the other trees."

"I know. It was sick — dying. Now it's healed. She cured it."

Darci pursed her lips, eyes giving the tree a quick sweep. "Huh. Looks exactly the same as it did before Amber fainted."

Jordan turned toward me in mute appeal.

"It's a lovely tree. Perhaps you were mistaken about the Phytophthora ramorum. It's an easy mistake to make." It wasn't, but I'm not the greatest at thinking on my feet . . . or lying.

Darci grabbed my arm and hustled me to the car, away from Jordan and the inquisition that probably wouldn't have ended until I'd confessed all. Low blood sugar. What a crappy excuse. I was feeling shaky and weak, but part of me realized it wasn't from lack of food — at least the kind that went into my stomach. Healing the tree had drained every last bit of energy from me. The monster inside me, the succubus, crossed her arms in smug judgment.

I told you so. Now go find someone — anyone — and fuck their brains out.

CHAPTER 3

We were tucked away in a dark booth at the rear of a busy French Quarter restaurant. Aromas of peppery spices and sizzling cooked meat filled the place, and my stomach growled in response. Under all the tempting food aromas was a faint air of age — like the heat and humidity of centuries had seeped into the very brick and beams of the building.

The Zydeco band was a perfect complement to the atmosphere. The drummer was inexplicably behind a wall of clear plastic, while the keyboard and guitar players stood just outside the enclosure. The man on the accordion danced close to the door to draw in passersby, but my eyes couldn't stray from the woman front and center. She played a metal washboard that hung over her shoulders and across her chest. Her dark eyes flashed as she stomped her cowboy boots in a hopping, swirling, fast two-step that was so typical of Cajun dancing.

It was like I'd been transported to another world, where centuries melded together in the passionate embrace of scent and sound. The people, the buildings, the food and music —

it was rich beyond words, larger than what I'd ever imagined. I knew immediately why Darci loved this city so, why she'd left the excitement of a different state and college to return here when that big scholarship had come in. It had hurt to lose my best friend to a city a thousand miles away, but now I understood her choice. It was about so much more than funds or a wise career move. This was a place that seduced your heart. I'd been here only a few hours, and I longed to make it my home, too.

The waitress plopped two pints and several dishes in front of us. The glasses wept drops of condensation, but the significant appeal of the icy beer was outweighed by the bowl of red beans and rice in front of me. The thick, savory red was filled with shredded pork and chunks of beans. Garlic and cayenne gave what would have been bland food a bite of flavor and mild heat. I closed my eyes and murmured my appreciation at the first mouthful. This was the kind of food I could happily eat every single day.

"Okay, spill it. What the heck was that all about?"

I'd barely taken two bites when Darci launched into an interrogation. She'd been squirming across from me in the booth, casting me impatient looks as we ordered and waited for our food. The time had come to tell her everything I'd held back over the last few months. Still, I hesitated, worried that what I was about to confess would cost me my best friend.

"I healed that tree, but it took too much out of me and I passed out."

Darci's eyes bored into mine. "I've seen you bring back a wilted gardenia with some water and TLC, but I've never seen you do that before. There was light everywhere, then the tree just turned green, and all the black spots went away. Seriously, Amber — what the heck was that all about?"

I swallowed hard. "I'm part elf. I have this thing with plants — a kind of magic."

"Elf?"

I nodded, and Darci let out a whoosh of breath, shaking her head toward the ceiling. "You're joking me, right? People aren't elves, they're . . . people. How long have you been an elf? Did this occur after some sort of head trauma? Have you suddenly taken to hallucinogenic drugs since I came back south?"

"Elf. I was born this way. And no, I haven't turned into a druggie or suffered a concussion."

Darci stared at me, her expressive face disbelieving as she tried to make sense of what sounded ridiculously impossible. "So where are the pointy ears and the toy-making skills? You're not the Keebler kind of elf, are you? Last time I checked, you were struggling to boil water."

"No cookies. No toys. No pointy ears." I did have the pointy ears, but my demon half worked to ensure I blended in with the human world. I'd been told it was some kind of self-preservation genetic thingie.

"This sounds like total bullshit, but I can't think of any rational explanation for what I saw you do to that tree." She still looked like she didn't believe me.

"I swear I'm telling you the truth."

Darci drained her pint in one long pull then slammed the empty glass onto the table. "Plants are it then? You're not going to surprise me with any rings of invisibility that an evil sorcerer misplaced? You're not escorting any hobbits and dwarves on a quest?"

"Plants." I squirmed on the hard wooden bench, hoping the waitress would hurry with more drinks. "But I'm only half elf. The other half is demon."

"Demon." There wasn't even a questioning note at the end of the word. "So, should I be researching exorcists? This *is*

New Orleans. We could probably find someone to help you with the demon possession. I don't know about the elf thing, though."

I wish someone could help me with the demon thing. The elf, I was okay with.

"It's not a possession; it's just part of who I am. One of my parents was an elf, and the other was a demon."

Darci looked about the room. "Where is that woman with more drinks? I need another drink. I really need another drink."

"Me too," I muttered.

We sat in uncomfortable silence, Darci refusing to meet my eyes. I was on the verge of tears. She was my best friend. If she couldn't accept who I was, then no one could. I saw a lonely future before me, one full of lies and shallow friendships. My succubus self would forever deny me the joy of love, but the loss of hope for any sort of friendship hurt even worse. Was this life really worth living?

"Why does your supposedly best friend not know these things?" She finally burst out, her voice full of hurt and anger. "I *lived* with you for a year. I know that you pick out all the orange jelly beans, that your first boyfriend was Jeff Henrick in Kindergarten, and you got in trouble for kissing him in the coatroom. I know that you spent most of your childhood in therapy after your father died before your eyes when you were five, that you were convinced you'd killed him."

I *had* killed him. No one believed me. Five-year-old children don't get angry and shoot a lethal stream of electricity into their father. At least, five-year-old human children didn't. I'd begun to think I'd imagined it, that the therapists were right, until the skill returned this past spring.

Darci took a deep breath. "I know all these things, and

more, yet I don't know that my best friend, the one I tell *everything* to, is a half-elf/ half-demon."

"I didn't know either!" I dashed the back of my hand across my eyes to wipe away the tears. "Darci, I swear I didn't know until a few months ago. I wanted to tell you — I was desperate to tell you. Can you imagine how I felt finding this out? But how could I share it with anyone, even you? Would you have believed me, telling you this sort of thing over the phone? Heck, you hardly believe me now, and you saw what I did to that tree."

The waitress arrived with another round of drinks, and Darci sipped the beer, staring intently at her bowl of red beans. I waited for her to speak, dreading what she might say.

"What kind of demon are you?" Darci asked, her voice tremulous. "Are you killing humans? Causing war? Taking souls?"

"Sex. I'm half succubus." I wasn't about to kill again — never, ever again.

Darci's shoulders relaxed, and she finally looked at me. "Why does that not surprise me?" The beginnings of a wry smile twitched at the edges of her lips. "If that's all, then I guess we're good. I can deal with a tree-healing elf and nympho demon. Basically you're the same Amber I've known for the past three years, only with different labels."

"Being a succubus isn't one big happy porno." I didn't want Darci to make light of this. I wasn't the same Amber she'd known for years. Even I wasn't really sure what I was. "I have sex with people and take energy from them during the act."

"Does it hurt?" Darci leaned forward, elbows on the table.

"No, but my partners are linked to me for the rest of their lives. Every time they have sex, or masturbate, or even get turned on, I get a hit of energy from them."

Darci shrugged. "Doesn't sound too bad. If it doesn't hurt them, and they have a fun toss with you, then what's so wrong about that?"

"I'm a parasite. That's what's wrong.

"Parasites kill their hosts." A smiled played around my friend's mouth. "I'm thinking this is more like a symbiotic relationship."

"I may not kill my host, but it's hardly symbiotic. That would mean my victims actually got an equal benefit out of the deal. A lifetime of obsession and me getting a free ride on their energy isn't actually a benefit."

Darci rolled her eyes. "Girl, if Zac Efron came waltzing through the doorway and gave me one night of mind-blowing passion, I wouldn't say 'no'. And trust me, I'd be thinking of him every time I did the deed for the rest of my life. He'd be welcome to any energy in exchange. Seriously, what makes you think these 'victims' don't benefit?"

"Yeah, but how would you feel about a husband that saw another woman's face every time you made love? One who constantly fantasized that he made love to me as he rocked the bed with you?"

Darci grimaced. "Okay. Point taken. That would suck big-time. So it's all or nothing then? Every time you have sex, you leave the guy totally obsessed?"

"Yeah. But that's only half the burden. I'll never marry, never have a real relationship. I'll never love. The moment I have sex with a guy, it all fizzles to nothing, and I never want to see him again."

That was what troubled me about the whole circum-stance of my birth. Yes, the predator thing was bothersome, but I'll admit that, selfishly, the denial of any future with a life-partner hurt the worst. Darci extended a hand to pat mine and clasped my fingers tight. Her eyes were full of sympathy as they met mine.

"I love you. Maybe you'll not have the white dress and picket fence, but that doesn't mean you can't have caring relationships. Redefine love, Amber. And stop freaking out about this. It's who you are — you can't change that. Find a way to live with it that's acceptable."

I *was* freaking out. I always did, except I usually buried it deep inside under a calm, composed exterior. What I didn't understand was how *Darci* wasn't freaking out even more so than her initial disbelief and brief anger. She'd watched me perform magic — something that defied all logic. I'd confessed things that should have put me in the hospital with an IV full of anti-psychotic drugs. All that, and she'd shrugged it off. I couldn't ask for a better friend.

"Thanks." I gripped her fingers back.

Darci released my hand to raise her beer in salute. She had that narrowed-eye look that she always got when she was up to something. I clinked glasses with her, wondering what my friend was plotting.

"So, this sex demon thing might not be so bad after all. I've got an idea."

Uh oh. Darci with an idea was scary. The woman was an unstoppable force when she got something in her noggin. I should know — I had been her freshman roommate.

"You're not happy about draining energy and creating an obsession in your partners, but what if you target only bad guys — you know, sociopaths, con-artists, rapists."

I choked on my beer. "Jesus, Darci! I'm not making a naked version of a citizen's arrest. What I do involves intimacy. I'm not having sex with sociopaths and rapists!"

Darci grimaced. "Okay, so having sex with crazies and criminals wouldn't be my choice either, but how about those hot guys who treat women like a nameless piece of ass? They're fun to bang. You don't care about seeing them afterward, and it would be a karmic kind of revenge. Yeah, you'd be like Batman for all us jilted women."

I might be half demon, but at times like this, I truly wondered about Darci's parentage.

"You're really hung up on this vigilante-with-license-to-fuck thing. Don't get me wrong, it's a decent idea, but it would take me forever to research my 'victims'. I wouldn't want to nail some blameless guy just because a bitter ex-girl-friend made up an ugly story."

"True." She pursed her lips, tapping the edge of her glass with a finger. "Okay, let's forget about the whole crime-fighting succubus thing. How about guys who like one-night stands? Cute, non-criminal ones."

That gave me pause. There were plenty of men out there who didn't want a relationship, who would relish a fleeting moment of passion. Maybe I just needed to narrow down my candidate pool to those who were looking for what I was best suited to give.

"And don't think I'm not connecting the dots between this revelation of yours and that sexy 'life coach' you're running away from. Spill it, girl."

Damn Darci. Nothing got past her. I took a long swig of the beverage and rubbed my temple — a combination of the cold drink and topic change giving me a sudden headache.

"He's a full sex demon sent from Hel to help me better control my 'urges'. I'm not willing to turn into the amoral succubus he wants me to be. He's pissed that I won't go all Mata Hari on every guy I see, so we're at a bit of an impasse."

"And you want him," Darci prompted, her dark eyes gleaming with vicarious excitement.

I rested the cold glass against my suddenly feverish fore-head. "You should see him. Zac Efron would look fugly next to him. Damn . . . he's just. . . ."

"Pics? Why have I not seen this sexy demon on Instagram yet?"

I grimaced. "He's got an ego the size of a house. I'm not going to let him catch me snapping his picture with my phone, or include him in a selfie. I'd never hear the end of it."

Darci leaned closer. "Okay then, describe him. If you're this worked up about a guy, he's got to be a god."

He was. Everything any woman or man ever wanted. Either the way he looked now, or otherwise. A flash of light and he could be anything — man, woman, blond, dark, tall, thin, muscular. Dream, and he would oblige. This was the magic of a sex demon — an ultimate fantasy in the flesh.

"Demons can change form like an outfit, but for me he's always appeared to be a Mediterranean playboy – high cheekbones, sharp jaw and chin, with olive skin. His eyes are very light brown — like a tiger's-eye gemstone, and he's got the darkest brown hair. It's so soft — like silk, like mink. I just want to bury my face in it, to fist it in my hands all night long."

That was a huge admission. I was on a roll, pouring my entire obsession across our table, knowing that Darci would sympathize. She was like my confessor — a voyeuristic confessor.

"Oh. My. God."

I couldn't stop. "We fight, and when he's angry with me, he's even sexier. It's all I can do to keep from jumping him. His eyes glow like molten gold, and his lips — oh, his lips. So full and soft. To lick them, to bite them, would be a little bit of heaven."

My imagination ran wild envisioning kissing Irix. He'd taste of rum and bitter-sweet chocolate, and the skin across his chest and down would have a tang of salt and sun. A trail of soft, light hair would lead the way toward his hips. My hands on his ass would feel the solid tightness of his muscles. He'd be rock against me, urging—

"Amber."

Darci's voice was raw, full of need, and I looked up to realize I'd been releasing my pheromones in a tide across the room. Most of the occupants of the restaurant were looking my way with intent, and my own friend was seriously turned on. Shit. How could I do this without even intending to? I had only to think of Irix and *I* was halfway to orgasm.

I ratcheted it down a few notches and grimaced. "Sorry."

My friend shook her head, and the look in her eyes made me feel like everything would be okay — not just today, but for the rest of my life.

"Good Lord, girl. Anybody that does that to you isn't somebody you should be running away from. Take this week to get your head on straight then go back home, or to hell or wherever, and reel that man in like a fish on a line."

CHAPTER 4

The line stretched all the way down the block and around the corner. Women in absurdly high heels and scanty bits of fabric chatted or typed numbly on phones. Further up the line, there were slumped shoulders, shoes draped over wrists, and sweat stained dresses. The men were worse off. They were drenched in perspiration.

I eyed the building with its graffiti-covered block walls and rusted sign proclaiming the club to be "Nations". Hard to believe from the exterior that this was one of the hottest new clubs in the city. It didn't seem all that impressive, but the music booming from the door was a siren song.

"Let's go somewhere else," Gabriella urged. "I don't want to spend half my evening standing in line."

I'd been introduced to Gabriella and Erica — Darci's friends, who, after glaring at me suspiciously for a few moments, were finally making tentative overtures of friendship. I was used to it. Women were so competitive. Most I met were reserved until they realized I wasn't a diva and wasn't hell-bent on stealing their boyfriend material. There was no honor among sex demons, but I was only a half-breed. If a friend was interested in someone, I wasn't about to go poaching. Plenty of fish in the sea.

"It probably won't take that long," Jordan argued.

I was a little concerned to see her among the group that met us at Darci's tiny shotgun apartment. Outside of watching me like I was an exotic circus animal, she'd kept mum about this afternoon's events.

"Hey," she shouted to a couple, about twenty from the door. "How long have you been waiting?"

The man turned dead eyes towards us. "Two hours. Probably another one before we get in. Those at the back won't be in before sunup."

Shit. That was just insane. I was ready to agree with Gabriella when I caught Darci giving me an odd look. Oh no. No way. I'd done this before, but not before I'd known what I was.

"Amber, can you get us in?"

The three other girls turned to me in surprise. "What, are you a celebrity?" Erica asked. "Is the owner boning you or something?"

Not if I had anything to do with it. Still, I felt the monster stir inside me at the thought. *Yes, please.* No. No, no, no.

"Amber has a way with these things. She totally got us out of that speeding ticket this winter, and that time we were drinking beers in the park, the cop let us go. He even let us keep the beers!"

I squirmed. That had been before, when I thought I'd just inherited the Lowry sweet-talking skills. Now that I knew what was *really* going on, I was reluctant to use my special abilities. Darci should have known better than to ask me after my revelation this afternoon, but she'd been rather blasé about the whole thing. This was evidently just a perk, in her opinion.

"I don't really think it will work this time. . . ." Lame. Of course it would work. It always worked. And my friend knew it, too.

"Oh, just give it a shot. What's the worst that can happen?"

I knew the worst that could happen, and even though I tried not to think about it, visions of me fucking the doorman flashed through my head. Great, now the monster really was awake and wanting to come out and play. No. Absolutely not.

I took a deep breath and walked up to the front of the line, determined to do this like the human I'd always thought I was. Darci and her friends followed me, whispering encouragement. The doorman's back was to me, facing some altercation beyond the roped area. As I approached, I saw two bouncers wrestling a short, stout man from the bar, his friends protesting loudly. I waited until the evicted guy and his buddies had staggered down the street before turning on the charm. No sense in trying to compete with a pot-bellied man so drunk he could hardly stand. I might be a half-succubus, but I'd stand a good chance of losing that competition.

"Hi."

He turned, eyebrows rising as he saw me by the rope. I put on my brightest smile, and the doorman's eyes did the usual male tour. Start at the top and work their way down, pausing significantly at the cleavage. I gave him plenty of time to take it all in while the elf in me preened. I was pretty. More than pretty. That alone should be enough to open doors.

Nope.

"End of the line is way back there. Around the end of the block."

At least he sounded like he regretted it. His eyes snagged

again on my lips before dropping back to the boobs. I sighed dramatically, and he was riveted by their movement.

"Are you sure? I'm from out of state and really wanted to come here."

The monster inside me took that statement all wrong. I felt her banging on the cage. *Yes, I do want to come here. More than once. With several partners.* I pushed her back and smiled at the doorman, raising an arm to brush back my hair, fully aware of what that did to the breasts barely contained within the plunging neckline of my dress.

"I . . . I can't. Fire code only allows so many in at a time. I'm sorry, but you'll have to wait."

Well, I tried. I turned to the girls and shrugged. Then I caught Darci's expression. Right before she hid behind a perky smile, I saw the disappointment. I actually *felt* it. There was something here — *someone* here that she really wanted to see.

Don't let your friend down. I can help.

Dratted monster. Would it hurt if I just let her out a little? Not much. Not enough to wind up naked on the pavement with the doorman. I gave a raised index finger to the girls, silently asking them to wait just a moment, and turned back around. The cage doors opened just a crack, and the monster emerged, meek and compliant.

"My friends and I would really like to party here. Won't you please let us in?"

I felt tendrils snake from me, undulating as they encircled and caressed the doorman. Too much. It was too much, but I couldn't help myself. I felt them roam across his skin, filling every sense, suffusing his very pores with need. He gasped and staggered back a step, his pupils so large his brown eyes appeared black. A nearly undetectable flush crept along his cheekbones, and his pants tented painfully outward. I should know, I was looking. And I couldn't avert my gaze if my life depended on it.

He was gorgeous, I suddenly realized. Ebony skin with a shaved head and muscles on top of muscles. My eyes roved as his had done, and I liked what I saw. No. No, that wasn't right at all. My monster liked what she saw. She wasn't especially discerning. Yes, he was attractive, but not my type. No, not my type. Okay, he was my type, but I wasn't going to seduce this man. What was I doing drowning in his eyes, envisioning his hands caressing my breasts?

You're admiring your latest conquest, that's what you're doing. The monster was indignant. I'd insulted her, but I didn't care. I was desperate to get her back under control, even if it meant we didn't get to go to this fantastic club. Even if it meant I disappointed Darci.

"Yes. Of course. All of you. I only ask . . . please, please . . . "

His voice trailed off, and I realized that he didn't really know what to ask. Some bit of his brain must realize how crass it would be to beg me to suck him off right here in front of everyone, but another part desperately wanted me. Maybe I wasn't the only one with two warring halves within.

"Later," the monster purred. And as impossible as it seemed, the man's erection got even larger.

No. Not happening, I scolded the monster. It had only been four weeks, and she was already acting like I'd denied her for centuries. I'd give in, but not with a stranger minding the entrance of a dance club. If I had to live with some kind of weird sexual addiction, I'd do it on my own terms. The monster pouted, but thankfully didn't push the issue.

He opened the door, wincing as if it hurt him to move, and I walked in followed by the four girls. They whispered behind me, and when I cast a quick glance over my shoulder, I saw Darci grinning in excitement. I led the way down a long hall, and Jordan jogged up on her four-inch stilettos to whisper in my ear.

"Sex magic. Holy cow, that was electric. How did you do it without any incantation? Without any spell components?"

I ignored her, pretending that the thumping music spiraling down the hallway had rendered me deaf. Great. She'd witnessed me bring an ancient tree back from death's door and thought I was a kindred spirit. Line-jumping at a trendy club had clearly moved me even further up in status. Hopefully she'd get drunk and not remember anything.

"The tree thing was just amazing. A-*maze*-ing. Light everywhere, and I actually felt the energy pulse through me. What you did to that guy at the door was subtle. Don't get me wrong; I'm impressed. That guy will be jerking it to thoughts of you for a week."

He was lucky. If I'd actually slept with him, he'd be jerking it to thoughts of me for the rest of his life. I picked up the pace and tried to wedge myself past Gabrielle in the narrow hallway. My auburn-haired nemesis blocked my progress with her shoulder and craned her neck at an impossible angle. It was a real feat of agility on her part to remain upright, given her sky-high heels and twisted posture. I sent a pleading look toward Darci, using the silent communication best friends had when they were trying to get rid of a clingy, unwanted guy. With a skill born of years of field hockey practice, Darci body-blocked her friend, and I darted past Gabrielle to safety.

If the only thing I had to deal with all evening was Jordan's dogged questions, I'd be thrilled. It was my succubus side that worried me. All that hunger and desire had been newly awoken at the club door, and I wasn't sure how much control I had over that increasingly demanding part of myself. For a brief moment, I missed Irix. He scolded and nagged, awoke feelings in me that threatened to send my future over the edge of a cliff, but around him I felt safe. My succubus half trusted him, obeyed him. But he wasn't here, and the monster was loose. Had I learned enough from him to control her on my own? I hoped so.

We crowded at the ticket counter, shelling out the astronomical fee and getting both hand stamps and neon wristbands in exchange. We'd agreed ahead of time to fork out the extra for the VIP area, which would give us a reserved table and chairs, and some assurance that no one would be doping our drinks while we danced. The table and chairs were completely worth it, since most of these clubs had no seating available for general admission.

I managed to keep one of Darci's friends between myself and Jordan as we negotiated the entrance process and headed into the club. So far so good. The hot doorman was far behind me. Surrounded by Darci and her friends, I felt more human than I had in months.

My monster seemed subdued. She'd retreated. I was completely in control. This might not be so bad. I'd let her out briefly at the door, and nothing disastrous had happened. Maybe I didn't need Irix after all. I could control that side of myself.

Nope. We sailed past the huge cement-block doorway and into the bar proper. The bass hit a chord that vibrated everything in my body. Heat shot through me, right down between my thighs. My monster broke her bonds and soared — free and unfettered. I could do nothing but go along for the ride.

"What do you want to drink?" Darci shouted, careful to position herself in front of me so I could read her lips over the deafening music.

It all ground down into slow motion — Darci's elation, the flash of colored lights reflecting off her glittered makeup. The music vanished, leaving only the thump of bass, like a heartbeat in my ear. Men all over the club turned their heads, as if in some synchronized dance, and focused their attention on me.

No. Not me. Them. My other, saner half asserted herself, and the men returned their gaze to their dance partners.

"Captain and ginger."

It was Irix's drink. Longing hit me like a fist in my stomach, nearly doubling me over. I was here, in New Orleans, out of control. I needed him, but it was more than his guidance that I missed right now. I missed him — his rakish smile, his sense of humor, the way he looked at me as if I were the only woman in the world. I know it was all part of his charismatic act, but I really wanted to believe otherwise. Even though he teased and tormented me, pissing me off more than any man had ever done, I missed him.

I'd left him. Told him to go back to Hel, that I didn't need him anymore and was just fine without him. And here I was wishing he'd appear from nowhere like a genie from a story book. It was just as well. Good riddance. All he wanted me to do was screw random strangers and discard them like yesterday's news. I didn't need him. I was completely in control, in a dance club with my friend, about to have a wonderful evening.

Darci shoved a drink into my hands, and I took a sip, appreciating the carbonated sweetness like I never had before. This would all be okay. I'd dance with the girls, get a bit tipsy and enjoy myself. *The monster wasn't attracted to women,* I lied to myself. So as long as I hung with the girlfriends, I'd be fine.

"We're going to dance," Gabrielle announced, dragging Erica with one hand and Jordan with the other as she headed to the dance floor. Darci snatched my drink, plopping it down on our table, and pulled me along.

Squeezing past half-naked bodies, I gripped Darci's hand.

She was a vanishing lifeline in the closing press of flesh before me. Silk and lycra slid along my side, the music lending itself to a writhing seduction of movement. It was a succubus' dream, and six months ago I would have lost myself in the caress of music and motion, letting it take my soul to a dark and carnal place. But now . . . . I held back, only allowing a small piece of myself to fly free. I'd need to find a partner soon, but not now — not my first night in New Orleans. I hadn't seen Darci in over a year. I'd just revealed my deepest secrets to her. I didn't want her to think I was some crazy slut, picking up the first guy I laid eyes on. Tomorrow. I'd find someone then. Quick. Discrete. Someone who wouldn't make me wracked with guilt as I fucked his brains out.

We were hip to hip on the dance floor, practically wiggling our bodies up against each other in time to the music. I tried hard to focus on Darci and to stay safely surrounded by her friends — her very off-limit friends. My monster may have been sex-starved, but so far she hadn't been the slightest bit interested in the girls I'd arrived with. Or any of the women in the bar. Now, that guy rubbing his thigh up against my ass was another story.

I turned slightly, hoping the contact was accidental. Nope. Now some other body part was rhythmically rubbing my buttocks. I couldn't exactly tell which part, but from the narrowed gaze his dance partner was sending my way, I had a good idea. Sorry, girlfriend. I wasn't doing it on purpose. Or was I? How much of the attraction was natural, and how much of it demonic? Was the guy just a player, or was I inadvertently pulling him toward me?

Stop freaking out. Darci had been right. I needed to just chill and refrain from assuming every guy that looked twice at me was under my spell. I stepped backward, crunching a sharp heel onto a foot, and heard a yelp behind me.

"Sorry!" I shouted, giving his dance partner a quick wink as I moved away. If the guy wanted to feel me up, he'd need to do it on my time, not someone else's.

Darci grabbed my hand, pulling me into the middle of a cluster of incredibly hot guys. "These are my brother's friends," she screamed in my ear.

The rest was lost in the deafening thump of the music. I eyed the three guys, quickly eliminating the one Darci had her arm around as off limits. The other two . . . mmmm, two. I quickly slid my way in between them, making myself the middle of their sandwich. It was more like a Panini. The dance floor was wall-to-wall people, and these two men were pressed against me so firmly I could feel every muscle under their clothing. Some muscles were more prominent than others. I fell into a mindless rush of pleasurable sensation, where the only thing that existed was the feel of our bodies against each other, the warm scent of men surrounding me. Reaching around, I grabbed a handful of tight ass. This was awesome. And judging by the aroused state of both men, sex was as much on their minds as it was mine.

But where? I could hardly bonk two guys in Darci's apartment. Having sex in some out-of-the-way spot in the club seemed kind of slutty. Normally that wouldn't bother me, but I didn't want Darci's brother thinking I was one of "those" kinds of girls. Of course, having a threesome with two of his buddies would give me the same label.

What was I thinking? I couldn't do this with Darci's brother's friends. Letting go of the one guy's butt like my hand was on fire, I excused myself and wiggled free of their bodies. Air. I needed air. And a stiff drink. All these half-naked men and women, the seduction in the air, the heady beat of the music — I was going to be in real trouble if I didn't slow it down.

I staggered over to our table, where Jordan had returned

to sip a beverage as dark red as her hair. I hesitated, reluctant to be alone with her, but my need to get away from the dance floor trumped. Trying to ignore her, I grabbed my drink and took a sip.

Jordan gave me an odd look. "You okay?"

My glass clinked empty except for the ice. How had that happened? Taking a deep breath, I tried to convince myself that I was fine. More than fine. The girls could dance. I'd just stay here and watch. Later, when I was more in control, I'd find some guy and arrange a one-night stand. Not tonight. Tonight was for girlfriends. My succubus self would have to be satisfied with an appointment for sex in the next twenty-four hours. I smiled at Jordan and waved her toward the dance floor.

"Yep. You go. I just need to catch my breath a bit."

I stood beside the table, not trusting myself to slide into the upholstered seats. Darci and her friends danced, hips gyrating, hair flying. I'd just watch them. No one else. Just them. But my eyes drifted to a couple nearby. Her leg was between his, thighs rubbing against his crotch. He bent down to wrap his hands around her waist and pull her close, mouth sealing to hers. Everything exploded with the beat. Hot pulsing waves that flowed along the room like a tide. Soft skin, the musky scent of arousal, shared breath, fingers nudging apart thighs and reaching for the sweetest of spots. It all blurred together, but somehow I remained standing and remembered to breathe.

Hands touched my waist, smoothing down to rest at my hips, and a voice like dark chocolate whispered in my ear.

"Whoa there my little half-breed. Steady, steady, or we'll have an angel down on our heads. There's one permanently assigned to New Orleans, and although they usually don't bother with hybrids, you're a bit different. Take the pheromones down a notch, and don't pull so hard on the energy."

Irix. Was I hallucinating? Did someone slip something into my drink? I'd dismissed him. I'd left town. How had he found me? Why was he here? My wild monster suddenly tamed, aligning herself with his wishes. She was overjoyed to have him here, and the elf part of me was equally thrilled. Traitors, both of them.

The dancers continued their very inappropriate dance moves, but it was slow and purposeful, less frenzied. I leaned back, into a hard chest. Arms came around to clasp at my waist. With a gentle tug backward, I felt myself being pulled down onto a lap.

"Do you feel it, elf-girl?"

His voice rolled over my skin, and I leaned my head back against his shoulder. Yes, I felt it — an erection like steel against my ass. The man could pound nails with that thing. I squirmed in appreciation.

"Not like I could miss it."

He chuckled. "No. The energy they're generating. Take it. It's yours."

Sex. It flowed from the dancers, from the D.J., from the people at the bar. Darci danced with her brother's friend. The other girls had attracted a group of men and were now pairing off. Their lust sparked into me. I nearly purred. Perhaps I could make do with this. I wouldn't need to run around like some crazed nympho. I could just hang out in dance clubs, enhancing the natural sensuality, and refuel that way.

"It's only an appetizer, little one. Look around and pick out someone for the main course."

No. I'd planned on doing just that, hooking up with someone tomorrow, or even tonight if I just couldn't wait, but suddenly none of the men on the dance floor appealed to me at all — even the two guys I'd been gyrating in between just a few moments ago. I was still turned on as hell, but I wanted none of them. Not the doorman, not the bartender, not any of these men.

Irix's hand slid up the inside of my knee, bunching up my skirt and halting a tantalizing inch away from the apex of my thighs. "You haven't had anyone since I arrived from Hel, Amber. You're hungry. That man at the door is yours for the taking. Anyone here is yours for the taking. Why do you deny yourself?"

How do I explain to a sex demon that I hated what I was? Eternal fascination might fuel my power, but it made me feel like a cruel, selfish monster. A trail of broken hearts wasn't worth it. The other part of me, the part I'd always thought was human, wouldn't allow it. But there was something else that kept me from picking out a "main course".

I'd resigned myself that I'd have to give in to my needs occasionally, and there were plenty of guys in this club that would meet my criteria, but when Irix was around, all the other men became as sexually interesting as a piece of cardboard. I might be contributing to the sensual atmosphere of the dance club, but the incubus whose hand caressed my thigh was the sole occupant of my very lustful thoughts.

"I don't want any of them." And for once, my demon and my elf both agreed.

Irix sighed. I thought for a second it was in disappointment, but then his hand ventured north to run along the strip of my thong.

"Liar."

I was wet. Soaked. And his accusation only increased the throbbing moisture between my legs. My mind scrambled for something to say as I felt my face heat up.

"I . . .uh, spilled my drink."

Yeah. Only on the crotch of my underwear and nowhere

else. I should have claimed incontinence. It would have been more plausible.

"Amber."

The word was drawn out, like I was an adorable, naughty child. Irix shifted me on his lap and I looked into his face. Light golden-brown eyes, like caramel, like whiskey on ice, like the amber I was named for, stared back at me. Thick sable hair brushed his collar. A lock hung along his face, curling right at the corner of his lip. And, oh his lips — generous and sculpted, the cause of so many of my restless nights. Those lips turned up in a smile, and his hand left my thigh. Slowly he brought it up and slid a finger into his mouth, pursing his lips as he withdrew it.

"A drink this wonderful should never be spilled."

His voice was husky. I suddenly didn't care if it was pheromones, or some trick of incubus magic. Heat shot through me, and every nerve ending quivered. There was no argument between the various parts of myself. I was of one mind as I leaned forward and claimed his lips with my own.

They were better than I'd dreamed of — soft and firm, tasting of rum, and the darkest chocolate. The hint of my own musk on his mouth only increased my desire. It was as if I'd marked him, imbedded my scent onto his. I bit his lip, demanding entry, and squirmed on his lap, desperate to straddle him and ease my ache against his hard cock.

He held me firm on his lap, but obliged my other request, opening his mouth. I explored every inch with my tongue before he captured it, sucking it deep inside. Pulling away, he placed his forehead against mine. His eyes were calm and thoughtful, revealing none of the inferno I'm sure mine reflected. It brought me back to sanity, made me remember that as much as I wanted him, I'd never be more than just another fuck to him. Sex was like eating lunch — he might enjoy it, but ultimately it only served to fuel his body. I'll be damned if I was going to be in the same category as a ham and Swiss on rye.

"You're losing control of the dancers, Amber."

I was. Clothing was beginning to slip off, some had completely stopped dancing and were groping each other with desperate hunger. My twosomes were beginning to blur into foursomes and more. Struggling, I turned my attention from Irix and reined in the pheromones pouring from me like a fire hose. It wasn't easy with Irix's hands roving over my bare legs and his lips feathering across my neck.

"Better. I'm all in favor of orgies, but I know you'd have a hard time facing yourself in the mirror tomorrow if you caused one — especially one that included your friend."

Darci. I barely knew the other girls, but Darci would not want that. I glanced over at her dancing, her partner bending nearly in half to hear her above the music. Irix's lips traced a line across my jaw. I shook with the sensation. The desire flowing from the dance floor, the warmth of Irix's body against mine, it was like a little slice of heaven, but he was right — it was only an appetizer. And it would have to suffice.

"Let's dance. You'll absorb more out there with them."

I hesitated. Out there, pressed up against Irix, I'd have little to no control. The orgy he'd mentioned earlier would surely come to pass if I didn't manage to hold things in check. Standing up, Irix slid me off his lap to my feet, rubbing a hand up the back of my dress to squeeze my ass. I gulped air, feeling more stable now that there was a little distance between us. His hand on my rear felt good, but it was nowhere near as disruptive as when it was caressing the inside of my thighs.

"Come on. I'll help you. If you're going to continue on this absurd course of self-starvation, I might as well ease your pain as best as I can."

The dancers parted, creating a small passageway for us as we worked our way toward Darci and her friends. As we reached them, Irix turned, pulling me against him. I loved the way we fit together — my nose nestled into his neck, and his cheek against my temple. My arms circled his waist, and I breathed him in, content to just stand there in his arms.

Irix had other ideas. His knee nudged between my legs as he guided me forward and backward in a three point step pattern. I didn't recognize the dance, but his hand, firm at the small of my back, guided me, and I soon fell into the rhythm. The movement was like a drug, and I found myself kissing his neck, my breasts rubbing against his chest.

With a sudden movement, he spun me around, hands holding me tight against his chest. "Here?"

He knew how much I wanted him. I hesitated, needing to feel him inside me, but a tiny bit of my sanity remained. There was no way I was going to have sex in public, especially in front of my friends. Especially with Irix.

"No. " My voice was thick with frustration.

"I know a place."

He nuzzled my neck, his hand skimming across my waist to splay against my stomach. I was drunk on him, so very lost. A night of passion in his arms was tempting, but it would be only once. In the morning, he'd look at me with dispassionate eyes and I'd carry the cravings for him all my life. I was only half a succubus. He'd bring me to my knees without a second thought then leave me, not because he was mean and cruel, but just because it was his nature. No, I wouldn't be his ham and Swiss.

"I'm not having sex with you."

His soft laugh was warm against my ear. "I know. My complaint exactly. Let's go somewhere and remedy that situation."

I stepped forward, trying to put more space between us.

The dance floor was crowded, so I only managed a few inches. "Irix, I'm not going to have sex with you. Not tonight. Not ever. Now go away. I came here to get away from you. Go back to Hel. Or at least the next state over."

The hands on my waist and stomach tightened, curling painfully into my flesh. I felt his sharp intake of breath against my neck, and a punitive nip of teeth. It hurt. It would leave a mark, but I held still and silent, refusing to turn this into a fight. Irix's anger was just as much an aphrodisiac as his passion.

"I won't leave. You're barely holding on here. If I go, this whole place is going to fall apart into a mess of sexual activity — consensual and non. Personally, I don't care, but I promised Leethu I'd guide you, promised I'd keep you out of trouble. I can't return to Hel and tell her that her daughter went crazy in a dance club and was executed by an angel before sunrise."

Neither of us was really sure what an angel would do to me. I wasn't the typical hybrid. They might not overlook my existence as easily as they did the others. Angel or no, if Irix kept this up, I'd be screwing *him* on the dance floor before sunrise. I'd rather take my chances with the angel.

"I've got it. You helped me, and now I'm fine. Leave." It all came out through clenched teeth, because, in spite of my words, I wasn't fine. "Just leave."

He must have heard the wobble, the unsaid "please" in my voice because the hands gripping me relaxed and caressed with an apologetic gentleness. His mouth moved over the bite on my neck, licking and sucking. I leaned back against him, all resolve slipping away.

"Please." And now I actually said it, although at this point I wasn't certain what I was begging him for.

"I will give you a chance to do this on your own," he murmured, moving his lips back up to the edge of my ear.

"I'll stay in the club, where I can watch in case you need me. Deal?"

"Deal." My heart thudded in gratitude.

Just like that, he was gone. Vanished, leaving me cold and shaking in the middle of the dance floor. The only thing keeping the crashing feeling of loss at bay was the knowledge that he was somewhere close by.

I glanced over to make sure Darci and her friends were still dancing then stumbled back to the table, flagging down a waitress for another drink. With Irix gone, the energy flowing off the dance floor seemed thin — a watered-down version of what I'd had earlier. I struggled to keep it going, my enthusiasm flagging. The sparks sputtered, died, and the only thing left was a group of humans doing the bump and grind to Trap. The waitress brought my rum and ginger ale, but nothing cleared the sawdust taste in my mouth. I was starving, and the one thing I wanted was the one thing I'd sent away.

"I was wondering when you'd run out of juice." It was Jordan, picking up her beer and edging up beside me. "I owe you a big thanks. That was the hottest guy that's ever looked twice at me. Too bad he ditched me as soon as your spell ended." Her eyes focused to a spot behind me. "I see yours did the same."

I refused to look, and I refused to rise to the bait. Unfortunately my silence didn't deter her.

"I can't believe what you did at the park this afternoon. That's when I really knew. I mean, you've got that vibe about you, but Darci never said anything about you being a witch. Not many have that talent with plants *and* can rock the sex magic too. We could really use your energy in our coven. I'd love to introduce you."

This had to stop. Now.

"I'm not a witch. I'm not even human. I was born in Hel

and smuggled here when I was an infant. I'm half elf/half succubus."

Jordan made a sputtering noise, choking and coughing as beer poured out her mouth and nose. I gave her a half-hearted slap on the back and walked away. It didn't matter whether she believed me or not; hopefully it would stop her from pestering me.

"Hey, how's it going?"

Darci's eyes were wild with excitement, her face flushed as she leaned in close to me. A fine sheen of sweat coated her dark skin, setting the glitter aglow in the lights. The boy she'd been dancing with trailed after her, a cocky grin on his face.

"Good." I looked pointedly at the boy. "I didn't catch the name of your brother's friend before. It's too stinking loud on that dance floor to hear a thing."

Darci nodded. "Totally. I think I've lost hearing in one ear. Gavin, Amber. Amber, Gavin."

The way she said his name approached reverence. The big brother's friend — I'd been there many times before. Gavin reached over to shake my hand, using the movement as an excuse to rub against Darci's hip and shoulder. Things definitely looked promising for her.

"I'll get more drinks. Be right back," he shouted before working his way to the bar. Darci didn't waste any time grabbing me and pulling me aside.

"Where's that guy you were dancing with? Wow. Just wow. Leave it to you to score the hottest guy in here."

I felt my stomach twist. "We danced. He left."

Darci's eyes grew huge. "No way. You were practically devouring him. He had his hand up your skirt. I swear smoke rolled off you two. There's no way that guy 'left'."

"I don't want that, Darci. I came here to get away from that, remember? This is a week for me to hang with friends."

She gave me The Look — the one only best friends can pull off. I squirmed, but was unable to resist.

"That's Irix," I reluctantly admitted.

Darci made an unsophisticated noise that sounded like she was choking on a chicken bone. "Your life coach? Holy cow, no wonder you fled the state. I wouldn't be able to keep my hands off that if my life depended on it."

"Yeah, well tonight proves that I can't keep my hands off that either."

My friend shot me a shrewd glance. Uh-oh. Here we go again.

"I think you need to go for it. Hit that thing. From what I saw on the dance floor, he's more than willing to go there."

I sighed, because I sooo wanted to go there. "It would only be one night, though. He'd do the 'just friends' thing, and I'd want more. Remember?"

Darci shrugged. "Who's to say you wouldn't feel the same? You were crazy for that Zumba instructor, and the next day you felt nada. Maybe you need to jump this guy, get it out of your system, and move on. You wouldn't need to feel guilty either, because he'd want the same thing."

But the way I felt about Irix was different than that Zumba guy, or any of the other crushes I'd had over the years. The craving I felt for him went beyond my need for energy, beyond my desire for physical pleasure. Every cell in my body sang when he was around; every part of my being wanted him next to me. One night would never quench my thirst for him.

"Maybe, but not tonight. I need to think about things and get my head on straight before I make that sort of decision. Tonight I'm going to do my thing, and he's going to do his. Separately."

"Okay." Darci's voice wavered and her eyes focused behind me, just as Jordan's had done.

I will not look. I will not look. I was practically gritting my teeth with the effort. Whatever Irix was doing, I knew I didn't want to see it. *Just put him out of my mind and go dance with my friends.* I needed to pretend he wasn't here, needed to keep my eyes in my friends' direction.

Oh, fuck it. I turned my head and scanned the crowd behind me. There had to have been a hundred people on that side of the club, but my eyes zeroed in on one. Irix. A redhead was plastered to him, rubbing the entire front of her body along his backside in a rhythmic motion. At his feet was a brunette, wrapped around one of his legs, practically dry-humping his foot. A blond stood in front of him. He dribbled his beverage down the front of her dress then bent his head to chase the drops.

I whipped my head around, holding back the urge to rip his head off. My mind stupidly replaced the three girls with myself, and before I could stop my thoughts, they spiraled into lust and jealousy. In my mind, I could feel his back against my breasts, his foot rubbing between my legs, his tongue teasing down into the hollow between my breasts. . . but it wasn't me he was with on the other side of the bar. I tried to calm the fury that warred with a resurgence of desire. This was who he was, what he did. No sense in getting resentful about it.

Darci looked at me sympathetically, taking in my flushed face. She put an arm around my shoulders. "It's always the fish that tries to get away, isn't it? Maybe the problem isn't that you can't connect with men, it's that easy conquests don't capture your heart. Amber, every guy you crook your finger at falls at your feet. You need a challenge. You've got one. Go get him."

It wasn't that simple. I'm sure I could have him, it was the keeping him that would be the problem. I tried to force a cheerful smile and gave Darci a quick hug.

"I'm just a player that doesn't like to get played, I guess. Yeah, I want a challenge, but not one that has three women licking his boots."

"Got it. Let's dance and show your sexy life-coach what he's missing out on. Gavin can join us when he gets back."

She yanked my arm, dragging me to the dance floor. I found myself in a big mess of friends, all dancing together and swapping partners. It was fun and light. I laughed, and every few moments slid a quick glance at Irix. It was practically a porno on his side of the room. I couldn't quite see with the crowd of people, but the blond was half seated on top of the bar, with her head tossed back. The brunette was on her knees, most of her body blocked by Irix's. Lord only knows what the redhead was doing. I know this was a pretty permissive club, but how the heck could he get away with this stuff?

I wanted to retaliate, to entrance one or more of the guys dancing near me and show Irix that he wasn't the only one who could inspire this kind of sexual adoration. I'd done it with the doorman; it should be easy to do it again. But it wasn't. Sure, plenty of guys gave me appreciative looks, rubbed various appendages against me, but I couldn't manage to spark a fire. So I just smiled, danced and mentally counted down the hours until closing time.

I felt Darci elbow me in the ribs. "He's coming this way. Mr. Sex-on-a-Stick. Look lively."

She didn't need to warn me. Even if I hadn't been watching him, I would have felt him approach.

"What's wrong?"

I'd yanked my hair up because of the heat, and his breath tickled across the nape of my neck. Sensation fluttered down through my body, and finally a spark caught — a tiny flame in the kindling of his presence.

"Nothing. I'm just having fun with my friends."

He sighed, turning me around to face him. "Amber, pick someone. Anyone. Male, female, bovine, I don't care. Just pick someone."

"I'm not here to get laid, I'm here to have fun with my friends. I might be half succubus, but that's just half. The rest of me actually enjoys activities that don't involve having something shoved in an orifice."

Crude, but I knew I'd made my point when his jaw tightened and his eyes narrowed. "You're ignoring that half of yourself, starving it out. I won't allow it. If you don't choose someone, then I'll do it for you."

My temper flared. "Oh like a pimp? I'm not fucking some guy because you tell me to. You don't have that kind of power over me, and you never will. Go back to your little harem over by the bar and leave me alone."

A slow smile spread across his lips, like a predator who knew he had his quarry cornered. My heart skipped a beat. He knew I'd seen him with those three women, and now he knew it bothered me enough to mention it. Crap. Me and my temper. He leaned in close, his breath stirring the loose hair around my ear.

"But the whole time it was your sweet mouth I wanted on my cock, your taste on my tongue, your velvet softness wrapped tight around my fingers. I want to splay you naked on the bar and explore every inch of you. I could be yours, Amber. Yours for all eternity."

The noise of the club faded into background buzz; the only sound was the thud of our heartbeats. I turned my head, lips so close to his. His breath smelled of rum, of dark chocolate. Mine.

But he wouldn't be mine for all eternity. It would be one night, and I'd be enslaved. I already was enslaved. I knew what he was doing. He was trying to jump-start that succubus instinct in me, the one that longed to occupy a man's thoughts for the rest of his life. Every time he dreamed, when he made love to his wife, when he jerked off to naughty magazines, it would be my face and my body he saw. He'd forever relive the memory of one passionate night, and each time I'd be given a bit of his energy. But I'd never get that from Irix. All I'd get would be one night and a lifetime of heartache.

"I'm not going to have sex with you, Irix. Never."

My voice was weak and shaky. Heck, even I didn't believe myself. Rather than laugh at me, or call my bluff, he closed the tiny distance between us and brushed my lips with his — soft, gentle, and fleeting.

"Then pick someone. Or you *will* have sex with me. I won't see you starve, and if you won't feed yourself, then I'll share my energy with you."

Well, if that wasn't the most romantic thing I'd ever heard. Still, his words stirred something deep within me. A demon shouldn't care if I starved or not, and certainly not enough to "share" anything with me. Could his offer be spurred by something beside the obligation he had to my demon parent? Or was I a fool, head over heels and grasping at straws?

"Not tonight. I'm enjoying an evening out with my friends. I'll go back to Darci's house tonight, go to bed alone and sleep."

Nope. I'd toss and turn all night, dreaming of him and all the things I wanted to do to him — what I wanted him to do to me. Still, he didn't have to know that.

His hands snaked around my waist, pulling me against him. We swayed in time to the music, his leg between mine. I couldn't help but angle my hips toward him, riding his thigh, and he cupped my ass, tilting me into optimal position.

"Twenty-four hours, Amber. That's your deadline. Find

someone by this time tomorrow, or it will be me warming your bed. Understand?"

I closed my eyes, letting everything fall away except for the friction of his jeans against me. The thought of him rolling naked with me across the sheets turned that tiny flame into an inferno. I felt things ratchet up again on the dance floor, felt the energy course into me. Twenty-four hours was an eternity. I'd deal with that tomorrow. Right now, all that mattered was the feel of Irix against me.

"I understand."

CHAPTER 5

I woke up to the smell of coffee and the sound of Darci snoring beside me. We'd crashed on her bed without removing either our dresses or makeup. Mascara was smeared across my pillow, and I'm sure Darci's was covered with glitter. At least I wasn't hung-over — one of the advantages of my succubus side. I was pretty sure Darci wouldn't be so lucky, so I slid out of bed as quietly as possible and showered before heading into the kitchen.

Darci somehow had the forethought to set the coffeemaker on automatic and put out a store-bought coffee cake before we'd headed to the club. I need more than a pound of sugar to start my day, so I dug through the fridge and went to work. By the time my friend staggered out of the bedroom, I was ready for her.

"Oh my God." Darci covered her mouth as I pushed a plate in front of her. "You can't seriously expect me to eat that."

"Yep." I handed her a big glass of water and two aspirin. "My brother swears by it. Biscuits and sausage gravy — best hangover cure ever."

She sat and gulped down the pills and water, staring at the food like a convict facing the hangman. "Is that why you're so chipper? You were sucking down those rum things all night."

"I don't get hangovers. A quirk of genetics."

"I hate you." She took a bite of the food and swallowed. "Although, this is really good. You made it from scratch?"

I had. Both the biscuits and the gravy. "Yep. Wyatt taught me. He can cook all sorts of things."

She grinned. "And is he single? I've seen pics, and he's pretty hot."

'He's dating Satan' didn't seem like a good response. "He's got a girlfriend. Besides, doesn't your heart belong to Gavin? Hmmm?"

Darci shoved another forkful into her mouth. "I can't believe that. Last night was magic. I've been trying to get him to look at me for months, and suddenly he's like flypaper. He barely left my side. We've got a date tonight." She looked up at me guiltily. "I hope you don't mind. I can see what the girls are doing, and maybe you can hang with them."

My heart nearly stopped, and it wasn't from my friend ditching me to go out on a date. I'd remembered last night, Irix's deadline, and the repercussions of not meeting said deadline. Last night, in his arms, the punishment sounded pretty good to me, but in the cold light of day, I panicked. I needed to find someone to have sex with. I glanced at the clock. Noon. Oh crap. It was noon, and I had a little more than twelve hours to get laid. Normally, that shouldn't be a problem, but I had hoped to be a little pickier than just grabbing someone off the street.

"I'll fly solo tonight. I've got some needs to take care of, if you know what I mean."

Darci gave me a quick grin. "With Irix, the life coach, I hope?"

"Nope." I took a quick swig of my coffee. "It's going to be a stranger-in-the-night for me this time."

"Be careful; some of the places in the French Quarter can get a bit crazy. Stay off the side streets and watch your drink."

I couldn't help but smile. I might not be a black-belt in anything, but I did have some special self-defense skills. And I always watched my drink.

"Will do," I promised.

"Well, I'm going back to bed." Darci pushed the empty plate across the counter. "Come join me."

If only. I could use more sleep, but I needed to strategize how I was going to find and seduce someone who wouldn't result in my feeling like a horrible monster the next day. I waved Darci on, promising to wake her by four, and opened the laptop. Dating sites? Craigslist ads? I wanted someone attractive enough that I would actually enjoy this, but not someone I'd feel guilty about. Not married. Maybe a bit of a jerk, so I could justify it by thinking he'd had it coming. Or should I go for a backward, socially inept guy — a virgin who could be happy with fond memories the rest of his life? One night stands had never been so much work before, and I grumbled to myself, regretting that I'd ever found out about my weird parentage.

The doorbell rang. I answered the door to see Jordan with a backpack that looked like it weighed three-hundred pounds.

"Darci's sleeping," I told her, closing the door. She stuck her foot out, blocking it.

"Good. I came to see you."

And here I thought I'd gotten rid of her. Instead, she pushed past me and deposited the backpack on the sofa, pulling out what seemed to be an endless quantity of notebooks and photos.

"I know you said you're not a witch, but you've clearly got some powerful magical stuff going on. I did some research last night, and there's not much out there on what elves can do. Still, I'm hoping you can help us."

Help them do what? Revive dying petunias? It's not like I'd ever been able to do much with my elf side. It's not like I even knew what my elf side was capable of. My mother was dead, and there hadn't been an elf outside of Hel in millions of years to ask.

"I don't have any magic. I've got a bit of a green thumb, and I can make a room full of people want to have sex. I'm sure most of your coven can do that too. Just light a few candles, break out the oysters, and open up a bottle of wine."

She paused, giving me the raised-eyebrow look before continuing to pull stuff from her backpack.

"You nearly dropped that doorman to his knees. I'm sensitive; I can *see* the way the energy circles around and loops into you. When a witch does sex magic, we channel the energy into our spell — but the energy comes *from* us. You don't do that. You jump start the energy in those around you and absorb it. You're like a giant battery."

I'd never heard it put that way. She could actually see it? Jordan might be a pain, but I was thinking she could give me some insights into what made me tick. More than Irix's "it is what it is" speech.

"What did your research say about demon magic? Succubus magic, specifically?"

She paused again. "Nothing good. Thankfully it's your elven magic we need."

I plopped down on the sofa. "Well then, you're out of luck. My elf side doesn't seem to do much except keep the monster in check. I'm good with houseplants. That's about it."

Jordan picked up a notebook and waved it at me. "We've got some serious problems here. The city has grown, and the very things that kept our fragile bio-system sustainable have been damaged. Levees keep the flooding at bay — good for the residents, bad for the replenishment of nutrients in our soil, so the plant life is changing. That means our fish and wildlife industries are struggling, and so are the people that rely on them for their livelihood. Worse, logging and draining of the bayous along with rising sea levels mean we're increasingly vulnerable to hurricanes. Isn't it ironic that the two activities are countering each other? Less wetlands means hurricanes hit us with a force the levees can't hold against."

I shrugged. It was just another example of Mother Nature swatting at flies. Once pesky humans bothered her too much, she'd wash them away with hurricanes, earthquakes, or volcanoes. Such arrogance to think they could stand against the forces of a planet. And yes, it was the ultimate irony for me to be referring to "humans" when less than a year ago I'd counted myself as one.

"So what is it you think *I* can do? Protect the city from hurricanes? Rebuild the wetland forests? Fertilize a million acres of ground? No problem. I'll just cure cancer and solve world hunger while I'm at it."

The look on her face made me feel like a complete jerk. Crushed. Hurt. Her shoulders slumped, and she slid the notebook back into the backpack like a robot.

"Jordan, I'm sorry. It's no excuse, but I've been a bit edgy lately. I honestly think you're overestimating my abilities, but tell me what you want, and I'll let you know if it's something I can help with."

She looked up, and I saw the tears in her eyes. Great. Now I really did feel like a world-class asshole. What had happened to me? I'd always been the peacemaker, the one who got along with everyone, but lately I was so irritable and snarky. I'm surprised I had any friends left.

"I don't know. Maybe accelerate the growth in the bald cypress trees that are part of the forested swamps? Soil regeneration would be great too, if you could do that. Do you have any skills with water? Between the weirs and sea level rise, the brackish wetlands are becoming saline."

I sighed. Might as well be honest. "I think for those sorts of things, you'd need a full elf. Probably a group of them. I might be able to help a few trees along, but what you're proposing is too large scale for my abilities." Her face fell, and my heart went out to her. "You have to understand, I'm only twenty years old. That's young in human years, but in demon and elf years that's practically an infant. If I were back in Hel, I'd still be in a nursery. I've been told the only reason I have the abilities I have now is that being in the human world has accelerated them."

"I understand." Her voice was soft, like I'd been her last hope. "It's just . . . I've never seen anyone like you before. Lots of local covens have tried, but we can't channel the kind of energy we need to make any kind of significant impact."

"I'll tell you what. Why don't I talk to the head of your coven? I can go out with you to look at the affected areas and see what I can do. Hey, one healthy tree is better than none, right? Maybe we can figure something out."

She smiled, and I felt bad for being so annoyed by her last night. "I'd appreciate it. I know you're only here for a week, and it's your vacation and all, but maybe you could manage to do a little bit while you're here."

An idea was forming in my mind. "I'll try my best. I've got a favor to ask of you, too. Darci's going on a date tonight, and I'm wondering if you'd go out with me. To a club or something. I could really use a local so I don't wind up in the wrong neighborhood or something."

Her eyebrows shot up. "Me? I mean, I guess. I'm not usually anyone's first choice when it comes to turning it up, but I know a few places. What kind of club do you want to go to?"

She knew what I was, so I figured it was time to be completely honest. "One where I can pick up a guy in a relatively short time for quickie sex."

Jordan's jaw came close to hitting the floor. "You could just walk down the street and do that, from what I've seen."

I squirmed. "There's a problem. I'm half succubus, so anyone I have sex with is kind of attached to me for the rest of their life. I won't want anything to do with them afterward, but I'll overshadow pretty much every sexual experience they'll have from that point onward. Their obsession transfers energy to me."

"Wow. That's. . . ."

"Terrible. I know. I've been putting it off, denying myself for as long as possible, but I need to find someone by midnight tonight. I just want it to be someone I won't feel too guilty about. Some kind of player-type that's used a lot of girls. Someone who will probably spend their life in a string of one night stands anyway."

Jordan nodded knowingly. "Like the hot guy last night that you were practically inhaling? You should have done him. He certainly fit the profile."

I winced. Yes, he did.

"I can't have sex with him. He's an incubus — a full-on sex demon. He's kind of my mentor, and if I don't close the deal with someone by midnight, then he'll make me have sex with him."

The notebook bent in Jordan's fist. Her eyes flashed. "He'd *rape* you? Not in my city, he won't. I've got spells. I've got amulets. If he thinks he's going to force you, then he's got another thing coming."

"Trust me, it would *not* be rape." I told her, in what I hoped was a soothing voice. "I've never wanted anyone the way I want that guy. Sex with him would be the highlight of my life — and I'll most likely live tens of thousands of years."

Jordan frowned. "Then why not do it? I'd give a limb to have one night with someone that looked like that. Is it because he won't provide you with the energy you need, or something?"

"No, he said he'd transfer some of his energy to me. It's just. . . ." I hesitated, my face heating up. "It would be like a charity fuck. He doesn't like that I've been denying myself, in essence starving myself, so he'd have sex with me to ensure I had the energy I needed. Like a feeding tube for someone who can't eat. But I don't . . . I can't. . . ."

Realization dawned on her face, and she nodded. "Sex with him would mean more to you than that, and you need him to feel the same way."

It all came out in a rush. "I'm scared that *I'll* be the one who spends my life measuring every partner against him, pining for him. I'm scared that in the morning, I'll mean nothing to him, that he'll be completely uninterested in ever repeating the experience. Right now, he wants me. If I give in, he might never want me again, and what little we have now will be gone."

"You're in love with him," she added softly.

"No! Not at all! Not love, but a friends-with-benefits thing. Although we haven't gotten to the benefits part, and I really don't want us to."

It sounded lame. Jordan tilted her head, and her eyes were warm as she patted my hand. "I know the perfect place. There's a Goth club I go to. The guys there are really nice, but these 'others' come in sometimes. They basically do the pick-up-and-dump routine. You know, take someone outside for twenty minutes, then they're back for another? You wouldn't have to worry your conscience one bit."

Sounded perfect to me. "They're guys, right? Because pretty much any guy will work for me, but for some reason I'm only attracted to one in a hundred girls."

"Usually it's a mix, but there are always at least two or three guys. Don't worry, you'll have your pick. And if you want more than one tonight, now's your chance."

Perfect indeed. I'd prove to Irix that I could take care of myself. Hopefully that would be enough to convince him his job was done, and that he could leave me in peace and return to Hel — the prospect of which left me seriously depressed.

"Here's the tree. It had phytophthora ramorum and was due to be removed today. It's a severe blight and always fatal, but she cured it."

I stood by the side like a second grader awaiting judgment of my science fair project while Jordan and an older woman, who had been introduced to me as Bev, examined the tree.

The High Priestess of the Bon Nuit coven had short silver hair, and a neat figure in olive pants and a gauzy top. She looked like she should be volunteering at the historical society or trimming heirloom roses in her prize-winning garden, not running an eighty-person Wiccan coven in New Orleans.

"Are you sure, Jordan?" Bev reached out a hand to touch the bark, frowning first at the tree, and then at me. I tugged at my shorts, suddenly wishing I'd worn a longer pair today. Her expression pegged me as a stereotypical college coed — all looks and no brains in clothing just a few inches from indecent.

"Totally." Jordan looked at me pleadingly. "Amber, can you show her? Heal another tree, maybe?"

This meeting wasn't going as planned. I was supposed to have a lovely sit-down with Jordan and Bev to discuss their needs and my significant limitations. Instead, the whole meeting veered into doubt over my abilities. Now I needed to prove myself, perform like a circus dog.

"I'm low on energy, remember?" I'd passed out healing this tree, and although I felt better after all the smoky seduction of the club, I was still far from fully charged.

"Oh . . . that's right." Jordan looked away in embarrassment, obviously thinking about our mission this evening.

Bev did not look away. She stared intently, like she was trying to bore right through my skull and into my thoughts. "If you don't have enough energy to heal another tree, what makes you think you can do a magical working on an entire section of bayou? Where do you plan on getting the energy for that?"

That was the question on my mind too, along with the doubts that I could even do what they were asking of me.

"I'm planning on having more energy after tonight. It's rather personal how I do that, so I'd rather not say."

The woman's eyes narrowed. "We don't work with anyone practicing black magic of any kind. If you're killing something for your energy, then you can just get right back on the plane to Maryland."

This woman was seriously looking at me, all blond and blue-eyed in short-shorts and a skin-tight lilac crop top, and thinking I was merrily sacrificing goats or small children for power? It was a ludicrous idea.

"You okay with fucking?"

She recoiled in shock from the crude word, and I had to bite back a smile. Deliberately offending her probably wasn't the wisest choice, but I couldn't help it. I *was* half demon, after all.

"Yes. Sex magic is an acceptable source of energy for spell workings."

"Oh good. Now, let me see if I can find something to do that will prove to you that I'm not a fraud, but not put me in a coma."

I looked around. Reviving some trampled grass probably wouldn't suffice. I could increase the size of the bougainvillea blooms, but that might be discounted as an illusion. Blooms!

"Watch that azalea over there." I pointed to the bushy plant with thick dark green leaves. The two turned toward it.

Walking over, I lay a finger against a leaf, feeling the pulse of the plant, vital and healthy. *Sorry, sweetie*. What I was about to do wouldn't hurt the azalea, but the poor thing would be terribly confused. With a steady stream of energy, I adjusted sugar levels, slowed sunlight absorption, and triggered changes in the plant that mimicked six months of seasons in five seconds. Buds appeared and burst into bloom, covering the azalea with a blanket of white. They wouldn't last long. Once the plant realized it was far too hot for this sort of thing, the flowers would drop off en masse.

"Wow . . . just wow!" Jordan gushed, coming over to inspect the flowers.

"You'd make a good florist," Bev countered.

Some people were just really hard to impress. Luckily, Jordan wasn't one of them.

"You didn't just force a bloom, you tricked a cold-weather plant that flowers here in January into flowering in August! I can't even begin to imagine the subtle environmental and chemical changes you had to make to do that!"

It was good to have a fan. Of course, now I felt like I was going to puke. Or take a sudden, unexpected nap.

Bev walked over and stared down at the azalea with her arms folded tightly across her chest. "Okay. I'll arrange for a ritual tomorrow night. What do you want to target, Jordan?"

"Either the bayous directly south of the city, or the marshes farther toward the gulf. I'll take Amber out there, and we'll decide whether to concentrate on the tree growth or indigenous plant volume."

The high priestess nodded. "Let me know and I'll choose an appropriate spot based on energy flow. Hopefully, combined, we'll be able to have some impact." She turned to leave, calling back over her shoulder. "Make sure she knows ritual etiquette. I don't want everyone going to all this trouble only to have her going around the circle widdershins or knocking over one of the four-quarter candles."

Bitch. It's not like I'd never been to a sabbat.

Jordan sighed, watching the head of her coven walk away. "Sometimes I wish Kristin had stepped up to the plate. Bev can be really inflexible."

Ya think so?

"Who's Kristin?" Wiccan covens generally had a male and female lead, with one assuming primary responsibility. Although, if they were Dianic and strictly female, this Kristin might be the second in charge.

"A member. When she moved down from Minnesota, we thought she might make a bid for high priestess, but she insists she doesn't want to lead. Don't get me wrong, Bev does a great job and has really grown the group, but she's polarizing, while Kristin is more about compromise."

This Kristin sounded more my type. Maybe I'd get lucky and Bev would get run over by a bus or something. We headed for the car, and I stumbled, nearly falling into the grass.

"Here." Jordan was extending a granola bar and a soda

toward me. "You okay? We can grab some barbeque before we head out of town if you need to eat."

It would help, but I needed a different kind of food. "Thanks." I took the granola bar and munched on it. "Now, if you could just masturbate a few times, I'll be good as new."

I laughed at Jordan's horrified expression. "Just kidding," I told her.

But I wasn't. Irix was right. I was starving. If I didn't get laid tonight, I was going to be in serious trouble come tomorrow.

CHAPTER 7

"I guess this is as good as spot as any," Jordan said, parking her car on the side of the road. We'd crossed the Mississippi and jumped off the highway south of the city to travel down a long, flat country road. Eclectic wasn't quite the right word to describe the landscape. Expensive new homes were flanked by neat ramblers and not-so-neat trailers. Signs for fishing charters, swamp tours, and crawfish boil dotted the roadway. The only consistency was in the land itself — flat as an ironed bedsheet with stretches of trees and rushes broken by canals, inlets, and small lakes.

We'd driven as far south as the road went, to a narrow strip of sand that would have looked like any other inland beach if not for the lacy network of grassy marshes right behind it. Huge shallow lakes were divided by narrow strips and patches of green that became thinner and sparser as we journeyed further south from the city. It reminded me of southern Maryland, where the Potomac River joined the Chesapeake Bay. Wide bodies of water lapped against the shore. Half-submerged grasses waved in the breeze. Egrets screamed as they flew across the horizon. People stood at the edge of the docks, casting their lines into the water and hoping to take home redfish or pompano.

"Pretty," I commented as Jordan and I got out of the car and walked along the short pier. It was pretty, and I couldn't see anything wrong with the area — at least by my eyes. Rushes and grasses thrived, and the water appeared to be reasonably clean of pollution.

Jordan got right to the point. "Remember when I said that the levees kept the river from flooding and spreading soil nutrients to the areas along the shore? Well, this is where all the nutrients go — out to sea. It's causing algae blooms at the delta basin, which creates a dead zone for fish and other plant and wildlife species."

I grimaced. "So I'm assuming you want me to increase depleted oxygen levels, and kill the algae blooms in a way that won't result in the release of neurotoxins or biotoxins?"

"Exactly!" Jordan clasped her hands, spinning toward me. "You can do that?"

"Uh, no." I'd never killed a plant before, and wasn't sure how to do it without further damaging the water chemistry. Then there was the tricky fact that the bloom was far enough away that it was out of sight. I'd need to take a boat down the inlet to the gulf to be close enough to do anything at all to the algae. I couldn't work my magic on it from this distance, especially when I didn't even have a good solid idea of where it was. This Bev woman disliked me enough already; she'd truly hate me if I killed off a few miles of marsh grass instead of the algae bloom.

"Hmmm." Jordan chewed her lower lip.

I had a bad feeling that everything she was going to suggest today would be a "no". I appreciated her enthusiastic optimism, but I just wasn't all that skilled when it came to my elf side.

"It's probably just as well. I'm not sure if Bev would allow it."

Why the fuck would Bev not want me to kill a lethal algae bloom? If she was that worried about my skill, or lack of, then why didn't she just tell Jordan "no"?

"Do you need more grasses? I could try that." I ran a hand over the tops of the blades coming up to the height of the pier. Surely Bev wouldn't doubt my ability to grow some grass after my azalea display.

"No, that won't work. The bank drops off here to a depth that won't support the plants, and I wouldn't want to mess up the outline of the bay." She shook her head, dark red spirals of hair bouncing around her face. "Bev *really* would throw a fit if we mess with the water flow."

"What is that woman's problem?" I got the feeling from Jordan that it wasn't just me on Bev's bad list.

Jordan shifted from foot to foot, staring out into the tranquil bay. "There's a reason our coven is so large. Bon Nuit claims the southwest section outside the city as ours — for rituals and to draw energy. Over the last few decades, the energy streams have shifted, and we have the lion's share."

She didn't have to say anything else. Bev might care about the environment, but her primary interest would always be in maintaining control of the energy sources that gave them, and her, power.

"And you still stay with her?" It was a shitty thing to say, and I wished I could take it back the moment it came out of my mouth. Jordan's eyes jerked to mine. She looked like I'd stabbed her in the chest.

"I know, I just. . . . We get things done. Good things. The other covens, heck even the other paths, are losing members to Bon Nuit. There aren't many other alternatives if I want to make a difference."

"I'm sorry. I'm not judging," I patted her on the shoulder.

"Well, *I* am. I hate that we turn a blind eye to things we could do outside our territory." She gestured toward the wide mouth of the bay. "I hate that we suffer a massive algae bloom to exist, that we don't address the nutrient issues in the river because it might jeopardize our near monopoly on power."

I held my breath, unsure what to say. Back home, my Wiccan friends had always seemed to be free of such politics and selfish motives. Perhaps these undercurrents ran there too — I'd just never taken the time to see them.

Jordan sighed and shrugged, turning back toward the car. "Let's head back, closer toward the city, and see if there isn't something you can do in the bayous."

We were silent as we drove. The large stretches of water began to narrow, grassy marshes becoming crowded with an explosion of green, broken here and there by the gray skeletons of dead trees.

I frowned at the silhouettes. "What happened to them?"

Jordan glanced out the side window before returning her eyes to the road. "Rising sea levels are turning the brackish wetlands into saline ones. These trees just can't exist in a saltwater marsh. There's nothing that can be done for them now. In a few years, this area will look like the marshes toward the south. It's the freshwater bayous that worry me. Trees there are dying, and I can't find a natural cause for it. If they die, New Orleans is more vulnerable to hurricane damage."

"Three miles of wetland can reduce the height of a storm surge by a foot," I added, remembering the fact from one of my textbooks.

The woman beside me nodded. "The cypresses especially provide a natural storm barrier. They're our last line of defense before the levees."

We pulled off the main road onto one of crushed gravel.

Dwarf palmettos stretched their palm fronds toward us. Behind them, prickly bushes vined around the plants and low-lying tree limbs.

"Dew berries," Jordan commented, noticing my interest in the thorn-covered vines. "They're in the blackberry family. Too bad you're here so late in the summer. In April or May you'd see flowers in bloom, and be able to pick some of the berries to eat."

A strange longing coursed through me. I'd pegged this to be a rare visit. As much as I'd love to visit Darci more often, my scant finances wouldn't allow it — especially after graduation when my massive student loan debt became due. Maybe I could find a career here. The prospect was exciting — rooming with Darci once again, surrounded by the diverse plant life that fueled my elven soul. Heck, if I could withstand a week in the heat of August, I could manage the rest of the year.

"This is as good a spot as any," Jordan announced, pulling the car off the side of the road. I'd need to scoot over and out her side, since my door would open into knee-high vegetation.

I scrambled out, thankful that I'd worn shorts and sensible shoes today, and not a miniskirt and heels. I followed Jordan down a narrow path of wood decking, raised a few inches off the ground. Green closed in around me, and the sound of crickets and tree frogs drowned out the noise of our footsteps. It was rather claustrophobic, the press of life around us, reminding me that the steady, persistent power of flora and fauna was far more everlasting than any magic I held. Surrounded by nature, hubris melted away.

"There." Jordan pointed ahead where the wall of green gave way to an algae-speckled swamp.

It was picture-perfect — the bayou of my textbooks. The wooden decking widened to a five-foot by five-foot square; a few feet of black ground separated the raised surface from the still water. Trees rose majestically from the swamp, ornamented with silvery Spanish moss that draped the sprawling limbs. I started at the sound of a splash and watched a long-legged egret take flight, its feet trailing a line in the still water as it flew by.

I stepped tentatively onto what I thought was firm ground, only to sink past my ankle into thick, brownish-gray water. Yikes. With a backward leap, I returned to the wood decking, my shoes covered in mud

"There's a drier spot up further, but this is the area I'd want you to target. See how the trees over there are stunted and yellowed? I've checked water samples, looked at everything, but can't figure out why they're dying. The loss of these groves will have a significant impact on both storm protection and bayou stability."

And on Bev's precious energy source, no doubt. I had a feeling this project would get the green light, but could I manage it? Moving around as best as I could on the small deck, I tried to get a good visual on the trees.

Baldcypress — taxodium distichum. The nearest was about ten feet from where we stood, ridged bark rising into a lacy canopy of brownish-black leaves. Most of trees in the grove were young — less than two feet in diameter. Nearly all the old growth had been harvested by loggers, the soft, durable wood coveted for its resistance to rot. Left on their own, the trees became massive — with a fifteen-foot diameter to their trunk. They could live thousands of years, their dead branches serving as nursery logs for seedlings to take root in the water of the bayou.

There was something definitely wrong with these trees, but from this distance I couldn't tell what. I looked down at my discolored sneaker, weighing whether more than my footwear would suffer if I waded out for a closer look. But that wasn't the only problem on my mind.

"I've never healed a plant without touching it. I'm not sure what I can do from this distance. Is there a way we can get closer? I'd hate to have your coven go to all this trouble only to have me fail to make any impact."

Jordan frowned. "I don't have any problem with mucking out there, but I'm not sure we could cast a circle in a foot of water. And that's assuming the rest of the coven would even agree to conduct a ritual with the possibility of snakes and alligators swimming about."

Snakes and alligators. Well, that put the kibosh on any ideas of sloshing out to see the trees. "Is there a Plan B? This is a possibility, but if you've got another location where I can actually get my hands on the plants, that might be a better choice."

"The other two wouldn't deal with plants; they'd be water or earth. A dam breach caused the release of a large volume of salt water into a group of freshwater wetlands further east a few days ago, and we'd need to restore the original water salinity."

There were plenty of fresh, brackish and saltwater wetlands in Louisiana, but the balance between the three was crucial to the overall health of the area. You couldn't just flip a switch and turn a freshwater marsh into a saltwater one — all the plant life would die, and it would take years for appropriate replacements to grow. In the meantime, the loss would only add to the erosion and flooding issues that were plaguing the lower part of the state.

"So that's water. What's the earth one?"

"All the man-made canals, levees, and dams do a great job of keeping the Mississippi River from flooding the city and surrounding areas, but no flooding means no fresh, nutrient-rich sediment is being spread across the land. If we can restore nutrients to the soil, we'll help native plants thrive, and natural storm and flooding controls will be strengthened." Jordan shot me a tense look. "Of course, I doubt Bev would approve that one."

Probably not.

This was all very complicated. I had a new respect for Jordan's passion for her career. There were so many variables at work, so many beneficial actions that caused harm in another direction that it was difficult to know what to do. Which would be the best course of action? I looked once more at the sickly trees in the distance. Trees I could do, water and soil . . . I wasn't sure.

"I think I could do the water one — the marsh to the east." Changing the chemical content of several bodies of water would be a challenge, but I'd done something similar with tree sap, and I might be able to use the water as a medium to reach the plants themselves.

The extent to which I could do anything, though, would depend on how much energy I could accumulate. One goth boy tonight might have to turn into two or three. My mouth scrunched downward at the thought of banging guys assembly-line style behind a bar. Not exactly dignified, but I wouldn't be in this state if I hadn't become a sexual ascetic over the last few months.

Jordan watched me, her brown eyes shrewd. "Let's check it out before we get seventy plus people out here for a ritual."

We drove east, the forested swamplands becoming increasingly broken by long strips of lawn with neat houses on blocks. As we veered south, the buildings rose, some twelve feet up on concrete stilts. Driving over yet another bridge, I noticed the green ahead fading into yellow and brown.

"That's the affected area."

I'll say. We parked, and I looked in horror at acre after acre of suffering plants.

"What happened with the dam? Equipment failure, or excessive flooding?"

Jordan shook her head. "Neither. It's a fairly new dam, but a section of it just crumbled like rice paper one day. Everyone is pointing fingers — contractors, cement manufacturers, engineers. They're still inspecting the incident."

I knelt down and dangled my fingers in the water, feeling the familiar glide of molecules across my skin. Water and, of course, sodium, but also traces of chloride, magnesium, potassium, sulfate, calcium and more filled my mind. I reached out, just to see if I could change the concentration of salts in the area around my hand. The resulting shock flew up my arm and knocked me backward onto my rear.

"You okay? What happened?"

I took a few deep breaths to slow my heart rate and stared at the water. "Has your coven attempted any magical workings on this water already? Or maybe another group?"

Jordan tilted her head to the side. "No. The dam breach only happened a few days ago. Besides, this is our territory. Anyone else doing magic here would need to get Bev's permission."

"Well, someone did something. I can clearly feel the residual magic. It's diluted, but the original spell packed a serious punch."

A frown furrowed Jordan's brow. She leaned down to drift her palm across the top of the water. "You're right. There *is* magic here. It's odd, though. I don't think it's Wiccan magic."

A shiver rolled through me. "Demon?"

"I have no idea what demon magic would look like, beyond the sex thing you did at the club. This is . . . different. Maybe Scarlet Moon?"

"Huh?" I had a vision of our satellite, blood red as it sometimes appeared in the fall, rising over the newly mown hay fields. "So it's a planetary effect? Astrological?"

Burgundy spirals swung from side to side, and Jordan glanced up at me, her face grim. "No. They're a ceremonial magical organization that follows the old alchemical traditions. Their rituals are full of numerical calculations, exact incantations, and spell components. We're all about the feeling — the energy and purpose behind the spell. With them, energy goes nowhere if the slightest thing is off in their ritual."

"So, like Golden Dawn or other Hermetic groups?"

Jordan stood, wiping her hands on her pants as if to rid herself of the magical residue. "Sort of. What I don't understand is how they could have done this sort of thing."

She'd totally lost me. "Done what? Tried to fix the damage the dam breach caused?"

"No. Caused the breach."

CHAPTER 8

I tapped my chin and squinted at Darci. "The ecru. Definitely the ecru."

"Seriously?" Darci blew out a puff of air. "My skin is so dark. Doesn't it make me look like a shadow in a dress? Too much contrast?"

"Your skin is flawless. And the contrast makes you look exotic, especially with your hair pulled up tight on top of your head like that. Besides, your legs seem five miles long in it. Gavin is going to take one look at you and imagine those legs wrapped tight around his waist while he's inside you."

She was too dark to show a blush, but Darci glowed at my comment, a silly smile springing to her face. "Oh wow, what a visual! What are you getting into tonight with Jordan? Or should I say 'who' are you getting into?"

Ha ha, very funny. "A goth club where I'll be seducing a wham-bam-thank-you-ma'am guy. And possibly a few others. Jordan has talked me into joining her coven for a ritual, and I need the extra energy."

Darci paused, a necklace in each hand. "I'm glad you

warmed up to her. She's brilliant, and a total hoot once you get past the awkward introductory phase."

And that brought me to something that had truly puzzled me for the last two days. "How the heck did you guys meet? No offense, but she hardly seems like the rest of your friends."

"As the future governor of Louisiana, I make it a practice to associate with all of my constituents." Darci gave a regal wave of her hand, and I couldn't help but giggle. "Seriously, I went to a talk she was giving on the future of the fishing and fur industries in the western part of the state, and we got to talking afterwards. Like I said, she's brilliant. Her area of study jibes with my poly-sci major, and she can be a lot of fun once you get her out of the swamps and into a club."

I thought while watching Darci try on ten different pairs of shoes with the ecru dress. Darci's family had been in New Orleans for five generations. She'd always had great pride in her roots. The governor thing might have sounded like a joke, but it was more than a bit of truth. Darci had brains and plenty of ambition. If something concerned the welfare of the state and the people here, she'd know about it.

"What do *you* think happened at the Little Neck Reservoir Dam the other day?"

"Sabotage."

There wasn't the slightest hesitation in Darci's voice. Her hands, in the middle of switching navy blue pumps for wine-red sandals never faltered.

"Why?"

I was stunned. Jordan had suggested a variety of possible causes that were all innocent, stemming from poor workmanship and accidental quality control problems, until she identified the residual magic present in the water. Why would *Darci* suspect sabotage?

"The cement company contracted in the construction was

from North Carolina, and very reputable. The dam was regularly inspected. There's no reason for that portion to fail. The whole thing has been controversial from the get go. Some environmental groups feel all the artificial water controls are doing more harm than good." Darci shot me a knowing look. "And a few magical groups take issue with the effect dams and levees have on ley line energy that courses along the waterways."

"Whoa. Why would a radical environmental group sabotage the dam and send saltwater into a freshwater marsh? It seems against their overall mission."

"Exactly. But it wouldn't be if they were more concerned with the magical power transmitted in the ley lines than the health of the wetlands." Darci surveyed her appearance in the mirror, turning left and right. "When you're born and raised in New Orleans, you learn to keep an open mind to the supernatural. We've got voodoo, rougarou, vampires, and more ghosts and ghouls than you can shake a stick at. We're a hothouse of the occult down here."

My jaw nearly hit the floor. Darci had always been pragmatic, scholastic, driven. She went to Mass every week — even when hungover. Her family was solidly middle-class — normal, average humans, hard working and energetic. They had the two-point-three kids, dog, and the white picket fence — or the New Orleans equivalent. But this . . . this part of her upbringing I'd never realized.

"So this is why you weren't as freaked out about my elf/demon revelation as I'd thought you'd be?"

Darci shrugged, examining a variety of lipsticks for the evening. "New Orleans is thrumming with power. You don't have to be 'other' to sense it. I grew up exposed to traditions and folklore that would send most people running away in terror. It's our heritage, our birthright, and I'm proud of it. I don't take an active part in it, but I'd be a fool not to notice and watch these things with a careful eye."

An it harm none. "But Wiccans would never do that. Someone could have been killed in the dam breach, and the damage to the marsh — that sort of thing would violate all they work towards. It must have been another magical group." Such as that Crimson Moon Jordan had all but accused.

Darci nodded. "Not every magic user in this town is Wiccan. And not everyone has the same interpretation of their creed. There are those that believe the end justifies the means, and those who feel a temporary setback is worth a longer-term gain. This is a town full of secrets, Amber. Only God knows what's in a person's heart."

My thoughts shot to Bev. I'd need to watch carefully for anyone more interested in personal power than the welfare of the people or the environment. Long term, this was their problem to take care of — Jordan, Darci, and the good citizens of New Orleans, but if my actions were at cross purposes with a mage, I might become the target of some ugly stuff. Best keep my eyes open.

"Lover boy stopped by today," Darci commented, grinning as she slid gold hoops into her ears.

"Gavin?" It seemed rather early in their relationship for Darci to have that sort of pet name for him, but she always did fall hard and fast.

"No, Irix."

My brain screeched to a halt. He'd called while I'd been out with Jordan, but I'd sent him to voicemail. Just talking to him distracted me, and I was sure he only wanted to pester me about my looming deadline.

"He said to tell you 'midnight tonight'."

Yep. I was hardly going to forget his ultimatum. As if we

were linked by telepathy, my text alert went off, and I glanced at my phone. *Remember. Midnight.*

"I like him." I stared at Darci in amazement. "Once you pry your eyes away from the incredible, sexy good looks, and smile that would melt the polar ice caps, he seems like a nice, sincere sort of guy."

"He's a demon." Was I really hearing this from my best friend? Maybe Irix's seductive powers went beyond sins of the flesh and he could convince people he was a "nice, sincere sort of guy".

"Well, you're half demon, and you're nice. We humans can be pretty horrible sometimes. I figure he can't be worse than most of us, and probably a lot better than some. What's the most awful thing he's done, anyway?"

I opened my mouth to protest and shut it with a snap. I really didn't know anything bad that Irix had done, besides the love-em-and-leave-em that was part of being a sex demon. As far as I knew, he wasn't running around disemboweling people or setting apartment complexes ablaze. The most awful thing he'd done was insist that I face what I was and accept it.

Looking down at my phone once more, I typed in a response. *I'm on it.*

Well, I would be on it. Tonight.

CHAPTER 9

I felt a little ridiculous walking the street in a neoprene black mini-skirt that barely covered my ass and what amounted to a lace bra. The skirt was covered in huge silver grommets that matched the ones in my platform boots. My fishnet hose had holes big enough to drive a truck through, and the fingerless gloves came up past my elbows.

I'll admit that I went through a goth phase in high school, but that had ended before my first year in college. This was a bit too much like a stroll down memory lane for me — a flashback to a younger self. At least I still had my blond hair. Black had not been a good match for my complexion, and the need to color it every week quickly grew old.

"We're here," Jordan hissed in my ear.

As if I couldn't tell by the Victorian signage and group of black-clad individuals congregating near the doorway. The music flowing out from the doorway was promising, and the folks standing outside greeted Jordan by name, so I checked my attitude street side and waltzed on in, determined to have fun.

The moment I walked through the door, I saw why it was one of Jordan's favorite clubs. Heck, it would be one of my favorite clubs too if I didn't have to put on the signature outfit every time I went. The ancient warehouse had been carved out on the inside like a pumpkin, leaving nothing but an enormous room enclosed by brick walls. The brick had been painted black and faux stripped to look as if it had gone through centuries of wear. Dark stained-wood beams marked where a second story had been. The steel girders and piping high above were partially concealed beneath a suspended-coffered ceiling. The lighting was in cool shades of blue and violet, which gave an old romance feel to the place. Marilyn Manson blared from the speakers, and I couldn't help but smile. Some things never change.

Suddenly the DJ hit a switch. Black lights illuminated the dancers' neon makeup and the formerly hidden, intricate arcane symbols painted onto the brickwork.

"Wow."

"Cool, isn't it?" Jordan grinned as she took my hand and led me to the bar past a series of imposing gargoyles. She was in a burgundy leather corset that matched her hair to a tone and lifted her light-brown breasts into a shelf just below her collarbone. She looked hot, sexy — not at all the graduate student in environmental biology. Clearly that dark red hair hinted at a fire within. I eyed her in appreciation, realizing that Darci was a far better judge of character than I was. Then my gaze was transfixed by what lay ahead of us.

The bar was a fiery hell in the middle of a misty grave-yard. Here the blue lighting changed abruptly to orange, and everyone behind the rail wore red horns clipped to their hair. One bald bartender appeared to have his crazy-glued onto his scalp. We got drinks and waited. And waited. And danced. And waited some more. I was beginning to get anxious, glancing at my cellphone and noting the march of time toward midnight. I'd been scouting out guys as a backup plan, but no one was standing out to me as particularly deserving of the kind of painful passion I was about to deliver.

"There." Jordan nudged me and gave a sharp nod to my left. It was five minutes to midnight, and I'd expected Irix to waltz in at any moment. I'd never thought he had any particular homing instinct as far as I was concerned, but his sudden appearance in New Orleans last night, in the same club that I was in, made me wonder.

I turned, relieved to see that it wasn't Irix coming through the door, but two men and a woman. Not caring if they saw me checking them out, I stared. The woman was in a floaty Victorian-style dress minus the traditional under-skirts. A jaunty hat perched on her black hair. The men wore ripped t-shirts and tight leather pants. One had a multi-strand chain belt draped around his hips. In spite of the typical goth clothing, all three of them seemed weirdly out of place.

Don't get me wrong, they cast around like fishermen looking for the prime trout in the stream, but there was something off about all three. They reminded me more of shoppers in a grocery store than sleazy clubbers looking to get laid.

"I'd love it if you could manage the short guy with the chains." Jordan curled her lip. "He's here pretty much every night. The others vary."

"Got it."

I slid off the stool and made my way over. Might as well get this show on the road. With any luck, I'd have this guy in a back alley in ten, and be back to Darci's house before she returned from her date. Hopefully I'd be done before Irix decided to put in an appearance. Worry made me increase my pace. I wouldn't put it past the demon to interrupt me in the middle with pointers and suggestions. I'd better hustle and get this done before he showed up. Exaggerating my hip movements, I put enough of a bounce in my step to make my boobs jiggle in their black-lace bra. Eyes turned my way. It didn't hurt that I'd continued to work my special mojo, sending out enough sexual encouragement to get everyone's pulse racing. My three targets also noticed, and I tried not to laugh as they engaged in a violent jostling of elbows to see who could get to me first. Thankfully, dude-with-chains won out. I would have hated to have to plow through the others to reach him.

"Hey." I grabbed a fistful of chain with each hand and yanked, jerking his hips toward mine. "Dance with me?"

His eyes traveled downward, lingering on my considerable cleavage before he moved his gaze upward with an embarrassed flush.

"Umm . . . how about I buy you a beer?"

I thought this guy was supposed to be a Don Juan, a quickie-Casanova? He should have been leering at my ta-tas and had his hand halfway down my pants by now. Why would he turn down the opportunity to rub up against me on the dance floor and offer to buy me a drink instead? Puzzling over the incongruity, I decided not to judge. I was on a tight timetable here.

We worked our way to the bar, and I ordered a beer while Jordan gave me a stealthy thumbs up. Chain-guy paid, and watched me intently as I took a sip. This was a little creepy. I wasn't exactly inexperienced when it came to creepy men, but this guy was really giving me the willies.

Maybe he was just going to sit here and stare at me all night while I guzzled beers. I had a moment of panic, thinking that he'd drugged my drink as part of his one-night-stand M.O., but I'd seen the bartender open it and hand it to me. I doubted Anheuser-Busch was in on that sort of thing, so the drink had to be clean. Still, his silence and intense stare were really unnerving. It's a wonder he got laid at all if this was his approach.

"Don't you want something to drink?" I asked.

His eyes made a tour of my exposed flesh. "Yes. You."

His voice was raspy, full of need. I felt warmth come over me. This would be a lot easier now that he'd expressed interest. Yeah, he was still a bit over the line into weirdo territory, but I could deal with that. I set my beer on the bar with a thump and leaned toward him, putting out every lure my succubus self had to offer.

"I'm all yours."

He drew in a huge breath and held it, pupils dilating as I watched. Just to seal the deal, I licked my bottom lip and worried it gently between my teeth, dropping my eyes to stare at his mouth. I'd never seen a man move so fast. I was on my feet and out the door before I could bat an eye. With his arm around my waist, he rushed me into a side alley and pushed me against a brick wall, slamming his mouth against mine.

Not cool. The faint interest I'd had at the bar faltered with the rather violent kiss grinding the back of my head into the jagged bits of mortar. I was sure it would be a bloody mess in the morning. Still, this was a bird in the hand, and I just wanted to get it over with. I cranked the pheromones up to eleven, and kissed back, pushing against him to try and turn our positions around.

It was like trying to move a Toyota Corolla. Uphill. In the snow. I felt a tickle at the back of my head. Great. I was bleeding. This was going to go down as the worst sexual experience ever.

The guy went into a frenzy. His hands were all over me — breasts, waist, ass. After some significant tongue action, he jerked his mouth free and I gasped for air. I'd thought the guy was going to suffocate me for a moment there. An unexpected benefit was that my head was now free to pull away from the painful brick. Sexual interest began to return on my part as he pulled me against his body, his mouth licking and nibbling its way down my neck and across my shoulder.

"No. Can't. Shouldn't. Wrong," he moaned as he dipped his head down to kiss the top of my breast.

"Right. So very right," I replied.

Finally my desire was getting with the program. I grabbed the top of his head, digging my fingers through his thick dark hair and pushed him into my chest. His fingers fumbled with the clasps of my bra-top. The mechanics of the garment were clearly beyond him, so I yanked his head upward.

"Ear. Lick my ear."

It had always been one of my erogenous zones. I remembered the feel of Irix's mouth from last night and ground my hips against Chain-guy, hoping his caresses would come within a mile of what the incubus' barest touch could do to me.

He missed his mark, instead kissing and licking my neck, pausing to suck one particular spot. It wasn't my ear, but damn it felt good. I angled my head to give him better access and snaked a hand downward. The guy's boner was nearly tearing a hole through his leather pants. I figured I'd help him out by liberating this very important part of his anatomy and giving it some loving hand attention.

I'd barely gotten the zipper halfway down when something pinched my neck. It felt sharp and quick, like a sting. The pain lasted a fraction of a second before vanishing. I jerked, and opened my mouth to exclaim . . . something. What was I going to say? My brain felt like it was swimming in thick molasses, and a thrill went down my spine and into my extremities. Floating. I murmured something un-intelligible and leaned my weight against Chain-guy. This was very nice, his kissing my neck and all, but my monster was screaming frustration in my ear, and my elf was on the verge of panic. What was her problem?

The monster seized control, yanking down Chain-guy's zipper, and pulling his cock out, fisting it in a slow but firm slide. He moaned against my neck, hands cupping my breasts. I increased the tempo. It didn't matter if I came or not, all that mattered was him — giving him the ultimate, mind-blowing sexual experience of his life. I felt him sucking firmly against my neck, his penis thickening in my grasp. I reached down to cup his balls, rolling them in my other hand.

My elf screamed in my ear. *Run! Run, run, run!*

I jerked to the side, feeling a tearing sensation in my neck. Fuck, that hurt! Giving Chain-guy's dick a retaliatory yank, I turned to voice my complaints. And froze.

Chain-guy had fangs. Fangs like the pictures I'd seen of saber-toothed tigers, only in a human mouth. They were coated in blood – no doubt *my* blood, and dripped a clear liquid at the tips. I couldn't tear my eyes away from them, and the fuzzy drunken chill I'd felt vanished in a breath. I wish I could say that I punched him in the face, put a knee into his balls, twisted the cock I held in my hand, but I did none of those things. Instead I did the most embarrassingly girly thing I could. I screamed.

Chain-guy jerked backward, his eyes widening in alarm. "No! Hush. It's okay. Calm down."

Calm down? Right. The guy was a vampire. The elf in me thrashed in terror, and the part I'd always thought was human agreed. *Run, run!* My monster didn't seem to see what all the fuss was about, but for once she got onboard, throwing a charge of electricity into Chain-guy. I was holding onto his dick and his balls, so I'm ashamed to admit that's where the charge went.

Now he was screaming with the same pitch and volume that I had been. Giving him a hard shove, I blindly dashed from the alley and down the street, not caring where I went as long as I was as far away from Chain-guy-with-fangs as possible.

"Wait!"

The words were pain-laced, but I still heard his footsteps close behind me. I'm fast. And agile. It's an elf thing. I took off like a formula-one racecar, knocking pedestrians aside and darting dangerously across traffic. I had no idea where the hell I was going, I just knew I needed to get away from this guy. The sound of his footsteps retreated, and I turned a corner, running into an all-night convenience store to hide.

The dark-skinned man behind the cash register gave me a sour look as I ran through the door and bent in half, heaving air in and out of my lungs. Checking to make sure no one else came through, I headed to the back, pretending to check out the available snack food options.

Where was I? I'd completely lost my bearings in my mad dash across the city. Plus my feet were killing me in Jordan's borrowed boots. Eyeing the cashier, I unzipped them and eased them off, stretching my poor, mangled toes. What a complete cluster-fuck this evening had turned out to be. My easy score had wound up being a vampire. Yeah, he seemed as willing to fuck me as he was to drink my blood, but my elven half had objected mightily. I reached up a hand to rub my neck, and it came away streaked with red. Hopefully the cashier wouldn't notice and call the cops.

"Shoes," the clerk commented, pointing to the sign on the door.

It was a clear testament to my distress that I couldn't charm my way out of that rule. I picked up my boots and limped out, carefully looking both ways before walking aimlessly down the street. I had Darci's address on my cell phone in my pocket. I was completely lost, but with modern technology, I should be able to find my way back with just a few clicks.

Setting my boots on a bench, I pulled out my cell phone and felt a hand on my arm.

"Wait. Just wait. Don't run off again."

There was something needy in his voice, and his eyes shone with sincerity. Still, I had blood trickling down my neck, and he had the tips of fangs peeking out from beneath his lip. I threw my cell phone in his face and frantically tried to wrench myself from his grasp.

I may be fast and agile, but I'm not physically strong. I twisted and pulled, screaming at the top of my lungs. He held on, trying to drag me behind a grouping of magnolias, out of the view of passing traffic. I dropped to the ground, hoping my dead weight would prove to be an impediment. Evidently not. He dragged me with ease across the sidewalk, adding road rash to my other injuries.

"Hey! Let her go! I'm calling the cops right now!"

Thank heaven for good Samaritans. Someone had pulled their Prius over to the side of the road and was jumping out, cell phone in one hand and what appeared to be a tire iron in another. Psycho-chain-guy dropped my arm, and without a word of thanks, I bolted.

Ten blocks later, cowering behind a parked car, I finally convinced myself that I'd lost him. I'd also lost Jordan's platform boots and my cell phone. My feet were bruised, my clothing was torn, and I probably had blood all down my neck. The few bars that I passed were not ones I felt comfortable walking into as a solo female. By the sky lightening on the horizon, I assumed it was early morning. My hope was to find a convenience store that I could ask directions, but I found myself wandering through a residential neighborhood. I was on the edge of tears when ahead of me I saw a familiar figure, perched crossed-legged on the roof of an old Cadillac.

"Way past your deadline, sweet cheeks."

The relief I'd felt upon first seeing him fled, replaced by anger. The thought of his ultimatum should have had me quivering with anticipation, but right now, not even Irix could put me in the mood. All I wanted was a hot bath, a warm blanket, and my pillow. I didn't want sex, and I especially didn't want to be berated for my procrastination and my failure to "get it done".

"I tried," I snapped at him. "Even had his junk out of his pants, ready to go. He was a vampire. A *vampire*! Fucker bit me, then chased me down and dragged me along the pavement. If some guy hadn't shown up threatening to call the police, I'd be dead behind an Oleander somewhere near the garden district."

I paused by the Cadillac, under a street light, and Irix must have finally gotten a good look at my disheveled state. His eyebrows went up as he looked me over — tangled hair, torn clothes and all. Then he laughed.

"Only you, elf-girl, would manage to pick a vampire for your target. Of all the red-blooded human males in this city, you somehow decide a stodgy old vampire would be a better choice? Babe, they want your blood, not your body. It would have been easier to seduce a dead man."

"Oh, trust me, he wanted my blood *and* my body. I think he was looking for a package deal."

That earned a look of respect from the incubus. "Good show! That's not an easy thing to do. Why didn't you finish the job?"

The anger fell from me, and much to my dismay, I started to cry. "He was going to *kill* me — suck all the blood out of me. I might have been able to finish the job, but then I would have been dead. You have no idea how strong those things are. I even jolted him with electricity and it hardly slowed him down."

My last words were barely coherent, because I'd begun to sob in earnest. Irix leapt off the roof of the car with the grace of a leopard and pulled me into his arms. I buried my face against his shirt, not caring one bit that I was smearing mascara all over it.

"Hush, hush. You're all right. He didn't kill you. Hush."

Irix's hands smoothed over my hair. It made me cry even harder. I'd expected him to laugh at me, make fun of me then haul me off somewhere to seduce me — not comfort me in this very un-demonic display of sympathy. When I'd finally calmed down enough, he pulled back and gave me his charming, crooked smile.

"Amber, vampires don't usually kill their victims. They'd quickly run out of food sources if they did, and they'd attract some very unwelcome attention from the human law enforcement. It doesn't hurt, and can be kinda kinky. You should have just gone with it."

I sniffed, wiping my nose on the back of my tattered lace gloves. "I'm part elf. We're mortal enemies. He would have killed me."

His smile deepened, adding a faint dimple to the equation. "They haven't had contact with elves for millions of years. I doubt any surviving vampires even know what elves smell or taste like. And even if this guy did, you have enough power to take him down. Unless you're facing a full demon, or an angel, don't doubt your ability to defend yourself. When it comes to predators in this realm, you're right at the top of the food chain."

"That might be so, but I'm not having sex with any vampires." My voice sounded much stronger. I actually felt better. Well, except for my feet.

"You have got to be the pickiest little half-breed I've ever had the misfortune of meeting." He shook his finger, scolding me, but his tone was teasing. I couldn't help but smile. "You won't have sex with vampires. You won't have sex with women. You won't have sex with me. This one's too young. This one's married. You don't like guys who wear socks with sandals. There's got to be someone in this whole city who will appeal to your discerning tastes."

There was. Right here in front of me. But there was no way I'd ever tell him that.

"Can I have one more day? I know that I agreed to this, but I'm tired, cut and bruised, and I'm lost."

To my surprise, he leaned over and kissed me on the forehead. It wasn't his usual sexy move, it was . . . kind.

"Yes. One more day, because I find I can't say 'no' to a barefoot half-elf who has smeared her makeup all over my shirt." He put an arm around my shoulders and urged me forward. "Come on, waif. I'll take you back to your friend's house."

He wound up carrying me, complaining that it would take us two weeks to walk there if we had to limp along at my pace. By the time we made it to Darci's, I was practically catatonic. Instead of leaving me at the door, Irix brought me inside and plopped me down on the sofa while he disappeared into the bathroom.

A few moments later he'd emerged with a first-aid kit and helped me clean up the worst of my cuts, even washing the smudged makeup off my face. While he put away the supplies, I slid onto the sofa, pulling an afghan over myself and drifting in that middle land between wake and slumber. Just as sleep began to claim me, I felt the couch sag and arms gather me up against a warm body. Was I imagining it? Did I dream that I drifted off in a demon's embrace, his lips brushing the top of my head as I slept?

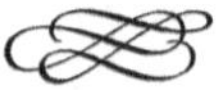

The smell of coffee penetrated my dreams, and I rolled over to find Darci sitting on the coffee table in front of the sofa, one cup in her hands, another beside her.

"Here." She extended the coffee toward me, her grin nearly enveloping her entire face.

"Good date?"

I didn't need to ask twice. Darci told me all about the virtues of Gavin while I smiled and nodded into my coffee. I was glad one of us had a good evening.

"And you?" she asked with a critical look at my snarled hair. Did you get the job done? Bury the sausage? Bump uglies?"

"Uhhh, no." I told her the whole story. Everything. Vampire right down to Irix snuggling up with me on the couch. Because from now on I was telling my best friend everything.

"Hmmmph." Darci eyed me over her coffee cup. "Told you he was a nice guy. That's what you should be tapping, not Dracula-with-a-hard-on."

"Okay, okay. So Irix isn't exactly what I thought. I've got

bigger problems than my love life, though. I'm supposed to do that ritual tonight, and I'm running on empty."

"There are about a hundred and seventy thousand men in New Orleans, not counting the tourists. Pick one."

I scowled. My best friend was beginning to sound a lot like a certain demon.

"I did, and he bit me." Reaching up a hand, I ran it over tiny scabs on my neck, wondering if I'd have to endure the hot discomfort of keeping my hair down, or face teasing over my "hickey".

"Let me see." Darci scooted over to sit next to me on the sofa and look at the marks. "Oh for crying out loud, you baby. They're barely noticeable."

I doubted Darci's opinion of the matter, given that I could actually *feel* the raised marks on my skin. I'd need to check them out myself and possibly apply some makeup over them. But first, to get a much-needed shower. No way I was going trolling for sexual partners filthy and smelling like a yak. The moment I could break away from Darci, I did, taking a re-filled coffee cup into the bathroom.

Surprisingly, the marks on my neck weren't all that bad. I could explain it away as a bad bug bite. Overall I looked and felt pretty good for a girl who'd been nearly exsanguinated and had run all over the city barefoot. I heard Darci over the spray of the water, shouting about someone at the door, and cut my shower short, throwing on some clothes and comfortable running shoes. Was it Gavin, come to take her to breakfast? Or Irix? My heart sped up at the thought. I'd been so disappointed to wake up alone on the couch, although with my one-day extension I should be thinking more about finding a suitable sex partner than sleeping in late with my incubus nemesis.

It wasn't Gavin waiting by the couch. Or Irix. It was a vampire holding a cell phone and a pair of platform boots.

Panic stole my breath, but then I remembered what Irix said and tried to compose myself. In a show of confidence I was far from feeling, I crossed my arms in front of my chest and glared.

"You've got a lot of nerve showing up here."

Darci's eyes widened. "Oh, is that . . . him?" Her gaze darted back and forth between us in glee, delighting in every last juicy detail.

"I'm sorry. I want to apologize. And talk. Can we please talk?"

The vampire's words came out rather muffled, and I noticed for the first time a fading bruise under his eye. From the speed at which he'd recovered from electrocution, he must have been beaten to a pulp to still have injuries. Score one for the guy with the Prius and a tire iron. I was tempted to just grab my stuff and kick him out, but part of me was curious. Apologize? If he was going to be forthcoming, this could be a great chance to get information on a species I needed to avoid.

Top of the food chain. Top of the food chain, I chanted as I scowled at him. "Okay. Let's take a walk. Maybe I'll even let you buy me a coffee."

"Are you sure, Amber?"

It was then I noticed Darci had picked up something that looked like a sharpened chair leg in one hand, and a bunch of coins strung onto a chain in the other. It reminded me of a weapon from prison movies, minus the sock.

"What the hell, Darci? Do you have a shank in your pocket or something? A Saturday night special in the coat closet?" It actually detoured my mind from thoughts about my own demise. This was too bizarre. Darci Beauville, vampire hunter.

"Silver coins," she commented, swinging the weapon in question to and fro with practiced ease. "Alligators, copperheads, and vampires — you live in Louisiana, you gotta be prepared."

I eyed the vampire, seriously considering letting Darci have a go at the man first, just to make me feel better, but the black eye he sported gave me pause. He'd clearly paid a price for his actions. Besides, he'd been nice enough to bring back Jordan's boots and my phone.

"I got this," I told Darci. "We're going to go get a cup of coffee, and you and I will discuss your supernatural readiness methods when I come back. Cool?"

My friend shrugged, dropping the coins-on-a-chain and the wooden stake onto the coffee table. "Cool. But if he pulls anything, you fry the balls right off his body."

The vampire eyed Darci nervously as he put the boots down, extending my cell phone toward me. He looked like a normal guy in the light of the day without his leather pants and chains. Still, I couldn't put the image of those fangs out of my mind.

I snatched my phone and stuffed it in the back pocket of my shorts, leading the way out and down the stairs. Having a vampire at my back was sending all sorts of uncomfortable prickles up my spine, but he seemed equally reluctant to have me at his back, and I didn't want to spend all day standing like statues in Darci's apartment.

We walked in awkward silence, grabbing coffee at the corner shop. He paid. He also grew increasingly anxious as we strolled, running hands through his dark, curly hair until it stood on end like a lopsided afro. Finally, just as we reached the edge of a park, he spoke.

"Look, I'm so sorry. I thought you were human. I would have never bitten you if I'd realized what you were."

And what exactly was he assuming I was? Plus it kind of pissed me off that he thought it was okay to go around biting humans, but that it was a terrible breach of etiquette to munch on *my* neck.

"I should have suspected," he went on. "I mean, when I felt *that* sort of attraction to you . . . that never happens with humans. I want their blood, but I *never* want to have sex with them. I wanted you so much. It was mortifying. So embarrassing."

What an ass. "So you wanted to fuck me and drink my blood?" I was purposely crude just to see him squirm. "And I take it you never want to fuck the humans you prey on and attack in dark alleys?"

He shot me an irritated glance. "Oh, that's rich coming from you. I'm so glad to hear you don't drink the blood of the humans you prey upon and sexually attack in dark alleys."

Touché. "I give them pleasure. I don't leave them befuddled, wondering what the heck happened."

"I don't do any lasting harm. You do. I may drain their blood, but you drain more than that, and you do it the entire rest of their lives."

He was right. We both needed to feed on humans in our own unique ways. His might be less enjoyable for the victim, but it was at least short term, and only a minor inconvenience. Once again I felt shame at what I was, at what I had to do to survive.

"Anyway," he took a deep breath. "I didn't mean to come out here and get into an argument with you. I came to apologize and thank you for not killing me."

"With the electricity?" I felt kind of bad now about shocking him through his genitals. That had to have been horribly painful.

"No, with your blood. There was a demon last summer going around masquerading as a human who would transform his blood once we began to feed from him. Four in my family spontaneously combusted before we got the word out in warning. Every time I went to feed that year, I was terrified it would be my last. So thanks for not killing me."

Yikes. His tale reminded me how horrible demons could be. Would Irix do something like that? I always knew there was a dark side under his playful, sensual demeanor. Clearly this guy thought I was a full demon too. Which was probably a good thing. I didn't need him questioning what exactly my other half was.

"No problem. Sorry about the electrocution. And sorry the dude with the tire iron beat the crap out of you."

He lifted a hand to his eye and gave a short laugh. "Nah, I got away from him with no problem. This was from . . . someone else."

He turned slightly, avoiding my gaze. I wondered who beat him up. Then I wondered how he managed to find me. I had Darci's physical address in my phone, but it was buried behind password-protected e-mails. I hadn't had a chance to type it into the GPS when he'd grabbed me. How did he know where I was staying?

"Well, I just wanted to return your stuff and tell you again how sorry I am." He shot me a quick grin, saluting with his coffee cup. "And let you know that you have the best tasting blood I've ever had. You've got the nectar of the gods running through your veins."

That was a bizarre compliment. I wasn't sure how to return it given that my experience hadn't been so pleasant — bitten and my head ground against jagged bricks.

"Umm, and your cock is very nice. Wish I'd seen more of it."

He paused in shock, and then threw back his head, laughter roaring out of him.

It wasn't what I expected, and I couldn't help but laugh

along. Vampires were kind of cool — at least this one was. How very different from the movie portrayals.

"What's your name?" I asked, putting out my hand.

"Ourson Delacrois." He shook my hand. He pronounced it like "arson", and I thought it was one of the most splendid names I'd ever heard.

"Amber Lowry. Friends?"

He grinned. "Friends."

An idea crossed my mind, so bizarre that I couldn't shake it. "Sit," I commanded, pointing toward the ironwork chair at an outdoor café. "I'll buy you breakfast, assuming you eat the traditional human stuff."

He hesitated, and I wondered if I'd crossed a line somehow.

"I doubt they have type A straight from the vein at this place. You could drink coffee and watch me eat brioche. Unless that would make you puke or something."

"No, it's not that." He shook his head, looking nervously at the horizon. "It's just . . . work. I'm still young enough that I get stuck with the dreaded day shift, and they keep close tabs on us. . . ."

I felt like a total shit. I'd stupidly assumed vampires did nothing more than run around at night sporting black capes and swooping down on unsuspecting humans. Of course the guy worked, and from his explanation I assumed it was a vampire-owned business.

"Sorry. Rain check?" I had no idea why I wanted to connect with this guy so badly. It wasn't my succubus half eyeing up prey, or my elf half who still regarded him with nervous resignation. It was me — Amber, who felt a connection with Ourson. I really did want him as a friend.

He hesitated, then plopped down into the uncomfortable-looking chair, pulling out his cell phone. "Give me a minute."

There was a hushed, rapid-paced conversation in a

language I didn't understand. I caught something that sounded like "guest" and "demand", then Ourson fell silent as a burst of muffled sound trailed from the phone. With a quick word, my vampire friend shoved the phone into his pocket and grinned at me.

"Brioche."

"Hope you didn't call in sick on my behalf."

I was prying. Ourson ordered more coffee and our pastries from the waiter, obviously buying himself time to think of how to respond. We both watched the man walk away.

"Your next victim?" the vampire asked. Seemed he wasn't going to answer my question after all.

"Nope. He's gay. Thinks you're totally hot and is a bit bummed you're with me. He's lamenting that the cute ones are always straight."

Ourson shrugged. "So turn into a guy and do him."

"What, and have the angels all over my ass?" I wasn't about to tell him that, unlike full demons, this was the only form I could manage — probably the only form I'd ever be able to manage. No changing genders or races for me. What you see is what you get.

"I called my boss and told him I had a VIP."

I had no fucking idea what he was talking about, so I remained silent and nodded knowingly. I have a feeling my "knowingly" came across as "clueless", because Ourson gave me a sharp look and leaned his chair back onto two legs.

"A potential demon alliance. Vampire families are very interested in fostering relationships with powerful demons that we can leverage in the future for favors."

I didn't like that word "leverage". And I seriously doubted I met the criteria for a "powerful demon". Unless the vampires wanted me to fuck someone, or bring their begonias into an early bloom, they were shit out of luck.

The waiter brought our coffee and presented our brioche with a flourish, his eyes darting over Ourson's broad chest. Poor guy. The vampire didn't give him a second glance, his eyes fixed on mine the whole time.

"You know what that means?" Ourson asked as the waiter walked slowly away with dejected shoulders.

"I owe you a favor?"

Irix had tried to teach me this stuff, but it had gone in one pointy ear and out the other. Stubborn resistance plus a brain entranced by his physical charms had rendered me deaf to his instructional lectures.

"No! Well, sort of. Is this your first time here or something? Exactly how old are you?"

The gig was up unless I could manage to talk my way out of this. Usually, not a problem, but humans were more susceptible to a beautiful pair of eyes and heaving breasts than vampires seemed to be.

"I've been here almost twenty-one years, but it's my first time."

I was rather proud of my prevarication. And I added some heaving breast action, just in case. It worked. Ourson's eyes nearly left his head, but it wasn't my ta-tas that swayed him.

"Twenty-one years? Sweet Moses, how have you managed to avoid the angels that long?"

I mimicked him with my shrug and tried to look mysterious. I think my lame acting blew the deal. The vampire's eyebrows rose, and he looked knowingly at me over the rim of his absurdly tiny espresso cup.

"Whatever. Anyway, I'll be your minder while you're in New Orleans, to ensure you don't get killed on our watch and to provide you with the ultimate in vacationing experience."

The time-share bullshit went right over my head. All I

heard was that ugly word "minder" — that hit my guts with the strength of a noro virus. "Leverage" was bad. "Minder" made me want to puke.

"You are not following me the fuck around. Got that?" I liked this guy, but I already had an incubus shadow, I didn't need a vampire one too. "I'm here to visit my friend and enjoy myself, not look over my shoulder every block while you stalk me. Screw that."

Ourson threw his hands up, alarm flashing across his eyes at my mild temper tantrum. "You won't see me, won't even know I'm there. I'll make sure you're safe from the angels — kind of a personal bodyguard, only completely stealthy. If you need someone — a human to satisfy your needs, I'll screen and provide the perfect partner. Think of me as a concierge."

Sounded more like a pimp to me. Not that I was averse to that sort of service. I was in a strange city with a deadline looming over my head, and very particular requirements.

"Okay, deal. But I need to ask you my first favor, as my concierge. I need sex. Male, unmarried. Someone who doesn't want commitment and only is looking for a brief encounter. Preferably someone in their forties or older who has made casual sex a lifestyle choice."

Ourson stared at me, his mouth open.

"In good health. I don't mind an old guy, but I don't want to have someone stroking out on me." I hated the thought of causing another's death, no matter how pleasurable the passing might be for the victim. Besides, the initial energy surge would be all I'd get if my partner left this existence immediately afterward. I needed a longer supply than that.

"I can do that." The vampire seemed rather breathless at the prospect. "Where will you be today?"

"South. A few miles out of town in the bayou." I needed to meet with Jordan's coven for our ceremony prep. The actual circle tonight wouldn't give me enough time to waste and meet Irix's new deadline, so I'd need to arrange an afternoon quickie. "Three in the afternoon good for you?"

He swallowed hard and nodded. "Marriott in the French Quarter. Room twelve twenty three."

"Awesome. Thanks, Ourson. I really appreciate this." I threw some money down on the table and got up. I had to hustle if I was going to squeeze all this into my schedule. "Oh, and no socks with sandals. That's a total deal breaker."

CHAPTER 11

"Thanks for loaning me your boots," I told Jordan as I stuck them in the back seat of her car. I was glad Ourson had returned them — who knows what they would have cost to replace. "I'll get the rest of the clothes back to you after I've had them cleaned." And repaired. I might need to purchase a new skirt for her after what it had been through last night.

"No problem. Did you take care of Mr. Quickie-in-the-Alley?"

Luckily I was turned toward the window, putting on my seatbelt or Jordan would have seen my grimace. I wouldn't call what happened last night 'taking care' of anything. Once again the two halves of myself warred with each other. Should I tell Jordan exactly what Ourson and his buddies had been doing in the back alley with their pickups? Although, at a goth club, a real vampire might be quite the draw.

I wanted to warn Jordan, but I didn't really want to out my new vampire friend. How shitty was that? Keeping his identity a secret so he could continue to prey on the goth club patrons. Where did my loyalties lie? Would it bother me if someone told my secret? Actually, no. I'd probably deserve being called out on my less-than-savory activities.

"I'm pretty sure he and his friends will continue their alleyway activities. They're harmless if you aren't looking for anything beyond twenty minutes."

There. Although that did sound a bit like an endorsement. Should I warn her that Ourson and his friends wouldn't exactly provide sexual satisfaction? Pretend that he was hung like a flea?

"Ah well. Once a player, always a player, huh? Hope he had a lot of energy, we've got a busy evening ahead."

Ugh. I hoped Ourson came through for me or I'd be lucky to grow a blade of grass this evening. I decided to keep my thoughts positive and turned to watch Jordan drive, her eyes sensibly on the road.

"So, what should I expect tonight? I've been to a few Beltane rituals, but I'm assuming this will be different."

Jordan shot me an appreciative glance. "I can only imagine how Beltane would be with a succubus in the circle. Wow."

I laughed. "Yeah. I didn't know I was half succubus at the time and just figured that the holiday always involved an orgy. No wonder I kept getting invited back."

"It's a wonder your mailbox isn't flooded with invites. This won't be anything like Beltane, beyond the usual method of casting the circle, calling the quarters, invoking the Lord and Lady. Bev and Jason will be designing the magic portion of the ritual, and they'll go over it when we get there. There's an energy raising — chanting, or dancing, then we'll direct it with intent, probably with a branch from one of the affected trees."

"Wait. I thought we were doing the water work. We're back to the trees now?"

Jordan shifted in her seat, her eyes practically glued to the road. "Yeah. Bev decided last night that the trees were more important. It's hurricane season, so I can't really fault her logic or priorities."

"You told her about my limitations?" Crap. Looks like I'd be in hip waders fighting off snakes and alligators tonight. Bad enough that the mosquitoes out here were the size of my fist.

"Yeah. . . ."

Uh oh. I didn't like that hesitation in Jordan's voice. I didn't press her, calmly looking out at the Mississippi River steadily flowing south under the tall bridge.

"Bev . . . she's a good high priestess in spite of some of our philosophical differences. Bon Nuit has grown and strengthened under her leadership."

"But?" I prompted.

Jordan shot me an inscrutable look. Her driving was smooth and even, but her hands flexed rhythmically on the steering wheel, and there were tense lines around her eyes. "She is very uncomfortable with the fact that you're half demon. Regardless of your demonic classification, it skirts the line, and she isn't fully supportive of working with you on this."

Great. Once again my monster was causing doors to slam in my face. "So why did she agree? I can't believe causing azaleas to bloom in late summer alleviated her moral doubts as to my motives or karmic baggage."

"*I* have no moral doubts on your motives or karma, Amber. I truly think you can help. Your magic is neutral in that it works for the overall balance of energy and environment. We need that — not just our coven, but all the humans living here."

"Yes, but we were talking about Bev." I had a sudden thought that her dislike of me might be more than my half-demon status. "She doesn't like neutral, does she? She fears whatever I do may not be in *her* best interests."

"The death of these trees could pose real problems for the coven. You're not loyal to us, and I think she does fear the neutrality of your magic. But in spite of that, she's willing to take a chance on you to save those trees."

This must be very important to Bev for her to go out on a limb like this. I watched Jordan carefully as she drove, feeling her doubts, her unease with the whole situation.

"Jordan, you're my friend. What do you suggest I do? You know my passion for nature, but I'll admit I've got a dark side. I don't really know what my abilities are and how to direct them. I don't really give a shit about Bev, but I don't want to go in there and screw things up. Maybe she's right. Maybe I shouldn't be messing around with this stuff."

Her hands tightened on the steering wheel as she glanced at me. "Let's see what Bev has to say today, and we'll go from there. As much as my loyalty is with my coven, I promise to be straight with you, Amber. I consider you a friend, and I won't be anything less than honest with you."

That was the most I could ask for. I continued to look out at the gray skies and highly populated areas that shifted from miles of retail strip malls to a dense landscape of trees and plants.

Five figures stood on a patch of reasonably solid ground about twenty feet from the road. Bev stood out, tall and thin with her silver hair plastered to her face in damp strands. She pointed into the distance, and the younger man next to her looked obligingly in that direction. They looked like Mutt and Jeff standing together, the man's short stature and round belly a sharp contrast. The others had measuring tape, compasses, and a plastic, wheeled item that dispensed a thin line of chalk.

"Marking the directions and the circle perimeter," Jordan

whispered. "Saves time later, and it's easier to do during the day."

Plus, I could imagine this sort of activity wouldn't be conducive to the state of mind necessary to raise magical energy. Jordan made introductions, and I was relieved to see that the others didn't seem to share Bev's unwelcoming attitude. We made our way to where the other two were standing, and I felt the curious but friendly stares of the other three on my back.

"Do they know what I am?" I asked Jordan in a low voice.

She nodded, giving me an apologetic look. "Bev thought everyone should know, in case they had any moral objections or felt their energy might not work well with yours."

"How many?" The heat in my face wasn't just from the sun broiling my skin.

Jordan patted my arm in an awkward sympathetic gesture. "Ten."

I should have been concerned with the fact that eighty strangers now knew what I was, but, instead, I was upset that a majority of them 'morally objected' to working with me. They didn't even know me. A pariah. A half demon. Even when I was doing something good, I was shunned.

"It's nothing to do with you. They're scared. They don't know you, haven't seen what you can do." Jordan halted me, stepping slightly in front of me. Anxious brown eyes searched mine. "I asked you to do this. I'm here, and so are ten other people. *We* want you here."

Well, everyone but Bev, although she seemed to have made her peace with me as a necessary evil. I guess, deep down, I really couldn't blame them. Last year if I'd been invited to a ritual that involved a demon, I would have probably refused too. Of course, last year I would have thought they were all off their rocker. Demons didn't exist last year. Neither did vampires, elves, or babies stolen from their cribs and replaced with monsters. It was like a curtain had been ripped away from a window, and my eyes were only now adjusting to the light. I couldn't blame those who were still blind and afraid.

"Thank you for having faith in me." I gave Jordan a quick hug, smelling the strawberry shampoo in her hair. "Let's go talk to the bitch and get this over with. I've got a hot date this afternoon, and I don't want to be late."

I'd frantically called Darci on my way back from the bayou, arranging to have dinner with her before Jordan picked me up for the ceremony. I hadn't seen my friend since this morning. This "vacation" was to spend time with her, and I felt guilty that I was constantly ditching her to hang with vampires and witches, not to mention all the time I was spending trying to score a sexual partner. Hooking up shouldn't be so damned hard.

Jordan dropped me off in front of the hotel, giving me a high five and a knowing look as I leapt from the car and raced up the stairs into the lobby. My Nikes squeaked as I dashed across the golden tiles, polished with such a high gloss they nearly blinded me. The man behind the reception desk helpfully pointed me to a bank of elevators, and I stood, impatiently waiting for the lighted numbers to work their way down to my level.

A guest played inexpertly at the huge grand piano in the lobby, and the smell of spicy seafood made my stomach growl. I hadn't eaten since the brioche with Ourson. First things first: sex, then food with Darci, then magic. After all that, I'd relax, comatose, on the patio of a bar overlooking the river, a mint julep in one hand as I listened to someone who played the piano better than the dude behind me.

Finally the elevator opened with a ding, and I entered, silently willing the thing to move faster as I glared at my reflection in the stainless steel doors. It didn't help. Elevators always seem to go slower when you're in a hurry. Eventually the stupid thing opened on my floor.

Twelve twenty-three. I knocked, my cheeks burning with embarrassment as Ourson answered the door with an impassive face.

"I'm so sorry I'm late."

The impassive face broke into shock. That's when I realized demons didn't give a flying fuck about being late. Everything ran on their timetable, at their whim. Oh well. I wasn't going to turn into a rude asshole and use my genetics as an excuse.

"Please forgive me. I'm not normally so inconsiderate about other people's time. I'm running on a stupidly tight schedule today and got held up south of the city."

The vampire nodded slowly. "No problem. We weren't waiting long."

Ourson opened the door wide, and I got an eyeful of white. White walls, white bed linens, white drapes, white lamps, white chairs. Even the damned carpet was white. I immediately wondered how in the world they managed to get bloodstains off anything. Or other bodily fluids. Hopefully there would be more of the latter and none of the former in this transaction. I felt bad enough about being late. I didn't want to saddle Ourson with that sort of cleanup, and there's no way I had time to squeeze it into my schedule. It was all up to the guy, though. I was his fantasy, and if that included blood, so be it.

I entered the room to see a man with black hair and olive

skin lounging against the mirrored wet bar, a glass of something amber on the rocks in his hand. For a second I caught my breath, noticing that the man bore a faint resemblance to Irix. Ourson grinned at my obvious approval of his choice.

"I hope you enjoy the tribute we have provided for you. Please feel free to spend as much time as you wish, and dial twenty-one on the phone if I can be of any service."

At least he wouldn't be hovering outside the doorway, listening in. My vampire minder discretely slipped out the door, and I faced the man. He was gorgeous — crisp shirt unbuttoned two from the neck. A gray jacket was casually draped across the end of the bed, and the man's left hand was in the pocket of matching gray pants. Expensive clothes. The fit form and beautiful face were more than compelling. I looked into the dark brown eyes and lamented for a brief moment that they weren't gold.

There was nothing for me to find fault with. He met all my picky criteria. Still, it was best to be sure.

"You know what I am?"

"You're a succubus." The look of confidence in his face never wavered. His husky voice made it quite clear that my demon side only heightened his desire.

"I will seduce you. I will be everything you have ever desired, and, in return, a part of you will always be mine."

His knees shook, and he swallowed noticeably. "Yes."

Well, that took care of the consent part. I needed him. He clearly desired me. There was no logical reason to back out now. No reason at all, except the image of sultry golden eyes that kept springing from my memory.

"Do you want me?"

I pulled off the tank top as I walked forward, revealing a lacy peach bra. The man held his breath, pupils dilating with need as he watched my progress. I may have been a bit sweaty, and not wearing the sexiest attire in the world, but I was rocking the pheromones, and my succubus side purred with satisfaction at the potential partner.

"Yes."

The word was guttural. Choked. As though he could barely force it from his throat.

I closed the distance and pulled him to me. He smelled of sandalwood and clove. Soft, full lips merged with mine, and I pressed myself against him. My partner for the afternoon wasn't shy. Hands skated across my waist and up to unclasp my bra. He leaned back a mere inch, sliding it expertly from my shoulders and down to the floor before encasing me in muscled arms. The feel of his silk shirt against my bare nipples was almost more than I could endure. I moaned against his mouth, rubbing myself along the silk.

"Mmmm." He shuddered against me, digging his fingers into my back as if he could somehow merge his body with mine.

I didn't need to ask him what he wanted, didn't need to awkwardly grope around. The succubus in me took over, and the elf half was surprisingly subdued. I took my time, extending the experience for my partner as I yanked the buttons from his shirt and pulled the ends from his pants. My hands skirted his fly and the bulge there, feathering along the sensitive skin of his waist and digging hard nails into flesh as I raked up his back. He gasped into my mouth.

"I want to see you naked before me. I want you on your knees." This was what *he* wanted, and therefore it was what I wanted too. Anything to lock him to me for the rest of his life.

He resisted. I snarled, biting his lower lip hard enough to hurt, but not enough to draw blood. "Down. Naked."

Lips left mine abruptly, and the man fell to the floor as if he were compelled by supernatural means. Tanned, muscled hands shook as he unbuttoned his pants and slid the zipper south. With a shimmy, my partner managed to wiggle himself free from the silk as I watched with cruel eyes. He was naked beneath the expensive pants. Naked. On his knees. Before me.

And I felt like a total shit.

Something hard lodged in my chest, and my stomach churned, but I was on autopilot. It didn't matter what I wanted, what I felt. The only thing that counted was being his ideal lover, fulfilling his deepest fantasy and securing my eternal link to him. I slowly removed my belt, sliding it through the loops as he watched my every movement. The supple leather folded easily in half, and I jerked both ends outward. His eyes widened at the whip-like crack of the belt. So much desire with just a tinge of fear. But what he wanted would have greater impact if I drew it out a little.

Unfolding the belt, I looped it around his neck and pulled him toward me, stopping as he teetered on the edge of falling forward. His wish would be my command, and the thought made me a little ill. Images of what he wanted filled my mind.

But there was nothing else filling me. I frowned down at him, wondering where the surge of energy was. Stepping forward, I gripped his chin with my hand and felt . . . nothing.

It was a like a bitch-slap to the face. There was no energy coming my way because it was all going elsewhere.

"Not your first time at this rodeo, is it?" I asked, unlooping the belt from his neck and stooping to pick up my bra and shirt.

He remained on his knees and stared at me, confused. "Huh?"

I hooked the bra around my waist and pulled the straps up and over my shoulders, waiting until I was fully dressed to respond. "Succubus. You've been with another succubus, or incubus. There's nothing for you to give me. You already gave it away."

His eyes grew frantic as I started for the door. "Please! You don't know what it's like, the torture of desire never fulfilled. No matter who I have sex with, I'm always empty."

I shook my head blindly and kept walking. His words were like hot knives tearing their way through my belly. Linked to a demon for life — this is what we did. This is what I did.

"Please! You're just like her. I've been searching for years trying to recreate how she made me feel, trying to find someone to fill this hollow need. I'll do anything. Please."

I paused. The sympathy I felt for this man was mixed with self-loathing. I'd leave the people I preyed upon like this — desperate and ravenous. *You're just like her.* I was. I remembered the Zumba instructor, his name forever lost to me, his image hazy in my mind. Did he troll bars late at night with haunted eyes, looking for someone to end what was an endless hunger? What had I done to him and all those boys I'd slept with once and dumped? I wished I could help this man, but I was just as much of a monster as the demon who'd done this to him.

"I'm sorry. There's nothing I can do to help you."

The door clicked shut as I left, instantly muting his sobs. I held it together all the way to the stairwell, and then I was the one kneeling on the floor crying. I'd rather starve than do that to another person, but it wasn't just revulsion that filled me. Relief. Relief that his prior commitment had kept me from going through with the whole thing. As desperate as I'd been to avoid Irix's ultimatum, this wasn't the solution. I just needed to stall the incubus until I figured out what that solution was.

Composing myself, I left the stairwell and took the elevator down to the lobby where Ourson waited.

"Would you like me to secure another partner for you?" He seemed very pleased with himself, and I didn't have the heart to tell him what had happened.

"No. That will be sufficient for my stay here." The moment I said the words I wanted to retract them. My tone was all wrong, as if he were a butler and I were some entitled aristocrat. The tears welled up again, and Ourson's eyes grew wide.

"What's wrong? Are you . . . *crying?*"

I choked a bit on a laugh, realized that demons probably never cried. "I hate what I am, Ourson. I hate having to do these things. And I hate that I just spoke to you like you were my flunky. Can we stop with the whole concierge thing and just be friends? Can you treat me like I'm not a demon?"

"What should I treat you like?" He was looking at me as if I'd gone completely insane. I felt like I had.

"Human? No, that won't work, will it?" I choked on a laugh, envisioning Ourson constantly trying to bite me. "How about you just pretend I'm one of your vampire friends."

A smile lurked around the edges of his mouth. "Sure. Wanna grab a bite later at the club? I get dibs on any B negative."

Okay, so maybe vampire buddy wouldn't work. It was a start though.

"Nah. I'm meeting Darci in a few for dinner, then I'm off to assist a bunch of witches in fixing the swamps." And then I was going to try and avoid Irix and his ultimatum.

Ourson grinned, his brown eyes warm. "Rain check?"

"Rain check." I assured him.

"I doubt this Bev woman is going to make herself look like a fool in front of her coven by blowing the ritual. Jordan said she needs those trees to be healthy. Plus, she arranged the whole thing."

I ate a spoonful of gumbo, savoring the sharp, peppery flavor, and the burst of caraway as I bit a seed buried in the sausage. Darci was probably right. I was just being paranoid again. It was understandable — the woman clearly didn't like me and had picked the area where I was most unlikely to have success. She'd been coldly polite this morning at the bayou, asking if there was anything special I needed for the ritual. Unfortunately, the one thing I needed I didn't have. I doubted they'd volunteer a member to have sex with me during the ritual. In spite of their acceptance of sex magic, my particular form of it wouldn't be acceptable. I'd already scared off over half the coven. No need to frighten off the rest.

I looked around the restaurant in desperation, but there wasn't time for me to screen likely candidates. There was no time left at all.

"No, it's totally on me if it doesn't work. I've procrastinated, and I'm going into this with hardly any energy in my tank."

Darci eyed me sympathetically between bites of corn muffin. "There's always Irix."

I choked, spewing a fine spray of stew across the table. Darci pounded me helpfully on the back as I coughed into a napkin and struggled to regain my breath. Irix. The ritual tonight wasn't my only issue. There's no way I'd meet his midnight deadline. I'd be in a circle with ten witches then. Even if I hustled back to the city, overcame my significant moral objections and pounced on the first man I saw, I'd never make it in time. I wouldn't put it past Irix to drag me out of the circle mid-ritual, just to prove a point. He'd given me one extension; I doubted he'd give me a second. I just needed to avoid him until I could manage to resolve my little issue on my own. I'd gained energy from the dance club. Maybe I just needed to spend most of each day in one. Hopefully that would be enough to sustain me, and satisfy the incubus.

"I'm trying to delay having sex with Irix as long as I can," I croaked out, still coughing.

Darci rolled her eyes. "Yeah. Right. I give you two days, three max. Any day now, I expect to come home and find a hanger on the door knob."

I couldn't help but grin. That had been our universal signal in college that one of us was getting some action — kind of like a do-not-disturb sign. It worked great until Megan down the hall stole the hanger as a practical joke and Darci walked in on me and Craig . . . or was it Luke? She'd stared, openmouthed, for a few seconds, remarked that she hadn't realized I was so bendy, then left. We still laughed about it.

"At the rate I'm going, it will probably be before dawn." I

lay down my spoon and pushed the empty bowl away. "Who knew it would be so damned hard to get laid?"

Not that I intended to get laid, ever. After what I saw at the hotel today, I was firmly returning to my abstinence routine.

She shook her head, biting back a smile. "Well, if you'd make an exception about the sandals and socks thing. . . ."

No way. Yuck. A girl had to have standards.

"I wish I had a few days to hang out in that dance club. That would probably amount to one night of sex." Of course, I'd have to avoid Irix for that long — which would be impossible given the odd homing beacon he seemed to have on me.

Darci hesitated, her eyes big as she waved her spoon at me. "Wait. I've got an idea. How long until Jordan picks you up?"

I caught my breath. Darci's ideas were often spectacular — spectacularly bad. "An hour."

"Perfect." She looked around, judging the distance between us in our little booth and the nearest diners. Leaning forward, she mumbled something incomprehensible under her breath.

"What?"

Darci's face creased in irritation. "Fetish club only a block away." More mumbling followed that announcement.

"Fetish club!" I shouted in astonishment, wincing as several interested sets of eyes turned our way. This was New Orleans, though, so after a brief glance, everyone went back to their gumbo. Darci, on the other hand, glared at me, her lips in a tight line.

"Yes, fetish club," she muttered between clenched teeth. "A block away. I figured if dancers at a night club could give you a jolt of power, watching people actually screwing might help even more."

I was stunned — not at the idea of going to a fetish club, but that Darci had thought of it and actually knew the location of one nearby. I'd never been to that sort of thing before and felt a flutter of anxiety. I know — stupid for a half demon who can shoot a lightning bolt from her fingers to be nervous about walking into a sex club. Still, my stomach clenched.

"Can you go with me?"

Darci's lovely brown eyes bugged out of her head. "No. Way. It was one thing to walk in on you and Mike. Totally another to watch a bunch of middle-aged swingers getting it on. No way."

Mike. That's what his name was. "Please? This makes no sense whatsoever, but I just don't want to walk into a fetish club in a strange city all by myself."

I tried for a pleading look, and after an agonizing grimace, Darci shook her head, covering her face momentarily with her hands before smoothing them back over her neat hair.

"I can't believe I'm doing this." Darci threw a few twenties on the table and scooted out of the booth. "Let's go before I lose my nerve entirely."

Bliss seemed like any other club in the French Quarter, except the doorman was far more discriminating as to entrance requirements. At first, he'd insisted this was a members'-only club, but wavered a bit once I started working my special mojo.

"Come on," Darci pleaded. "My friend is here from out of state. She's a member of the . . . the Inferno Club up in Baltimore. You can check her references."

I shot Darci a horrified look before managing to control my expression. Was there even an Inferno Club in Baltimore, or did she just pull that one out of her ass? Terrified the guy would dial up this mythical club to check, I cranked the pheromones up all the way and gave him my most sultry, heavy-eye-lidded look.

"We're just here to watch," I told him, my voice husky. "That's my thing."

He took a ragged breath, and I saw fanged tips peeking out from his upper lip. Eyeing him suspiciously, I took a chance.

"I'm a succubus. Surely you would not deny a demon on vacation entrance to your club."

His eyes widened. "You're Ourson's demon?"

"Yep. He's been an amazing host, by the way. Procured a very nice human for me this afternoon. I'm afraid I've been a bad girl and slipped my leash, though. I ditched him a few hours back. I'm sure he'll be here soon."

I'll give Darci credit, she stood by my side calm as a sunny lake while I spouted all this off. The doorman, on the other hand, looked around frantically, pulled out his cell phone then gestured at me to enter.

"Go on in, you and your human. I'll call . . . contact . . . I mean, enjoy yourself. Eloise will ensure you have a night that meets all your expectations."

"Hour." I corrected him as I opened the door. He was too busy texting to do it for me. "I've got a witch friend picking me up in an hour, so I need to fit in as much viewing as possible in that timeframe."

The doorman grunted, clearly not hearing me in his messaging frenzy. Darci and I slipped through the door to be greeted by a platinum-haired beauty, nearly six-feet tall with skin so pale I could practically see the blue of her veins.

"And you must be Eloise," I commented, assuming that vampires had some sort of telepathic link with others in their family.

The beauty smiled regretfully. "No, I'm Helen. I overheard you mention that you're one of our VIP clients.

Welcome to Bliss. Please enjoy the club room, and Eloise will be with you shortly to escort you to more interesting activities. She'll also provide you with any refreshments or 'snacks' you may require."

I glanced over at Darci and grabbed her hand, thinking that "snacks" didn't refer to alligator bites and shrimp with grits. I'd need to keep a close eye on her, just in case management got the idea she was on the menu. I mouthed "vampires" at her as we followed Helen to a second set of doors. Figuring it would be terribly rude if my cell phone went off in the middle of a particularly hot and sweaty moment, I sent a quick text to Jordan on where to pick me up then turned it off and stashed it in my pocket.

The door in front of us looked like it belonged on a medieval castle — a castle for giants. Huge rough-hewn oak planks bound in thick black iron nearly touched the nine-foot ceiling. Helen swung the massive door open with ease, and I waltzed in to collide with a naked man.

ell, almost naked. He was wearing a lavender ribbon around his neck. Where the goth club had sported enough leather to single-handedly support the tannery industry, Bliss took a more minimalist approach to clothing. There was leather, as well as rubber and a variety of metals, but the tiny scraps were clearly decorative.

"Don't you dare leave me," Darci whispered, clinging to my arm. She nervously clutched her purse with the other hand, and I doubted all her unease was due to the mass of mostly-naked flesh in front of us. She'd faced Ourson with great bravado this morning, but she didn't have her weapons now, and who knew how many vampires were here.

"I won't. Don't worry, they won't touch you. They think you're my human for the evening, and I'm some sort of VIP when it comes to vampires."

As long as they didn't figure out that I was half elf, that was. Still, my words reassured Darci, and she relaxed her death grip on my arm and looked around.

There was a lot to see. Bodies churned about on the dance floor — twosomes, threesomes and more, all pressed against each other with intent. A trickle of energy spiraled into me from the dancers and those at the dimly lit booths doing "other" stuff. One man licked slowly along a woman's foot, her discarded shoe pressed between his legs. Two women stood by the bar, important parts of their anatomy covered by balloons. A man next to them lovingly caressed not their naked flesh, but the pink and blue inflated objects.

"What are the ribbons for?" Darci asked.

"To identify fetish, maybe?" I had no stinking idea. The guy worshiping balloons wore yellow, and Foot-Licker wore blue. There was a whole rainbow of ribbons, and some people wore several.

"You getting anything in here?"

I shook my head. I was, but not enough. This Eloise better hurry up.

"There!"

Darci pulled me through the crowd of dancers where I was experiencing more contact with naked flesh than I'd had in months. The crowd around us thinned at the edge of the dance floor, and I finally saw where my friend was headed. Another large door loomed before us, a copy of the one Helen had led us through, except for the word stenciled on the front in blood-red.

Revelry.

"Sounds like the action room to me," Darci announced with surprising cheerfulness.

She yanked on the door, nearly falling to the floor as it swung open easily. On the other side was a set of gauzy curtains, not quite hiding the rhythmically moving shapes behind it. Low moans came from a good percentage of the occupants, and the warmer temperature carried the unmistakable aroma of sex — lots and lots of sex. Action room, indeed.

Darci took a deep breath, evidently steeling herself for

whatever lay behind, and pushed her way through the curtain. I followed, and what I saw was precisely what I'd imagined on the far side of the gauze.

Naked bodies in various stages of copulation littered the floor, sprawled across the sofas, and leaning against the walls. It was intense, but what really got my attention was the people milling about, drink in hand. It was as if they were at an X-rated art auction, casually moving from painting to painting as they admired each in turn. I felt stupid just standing there, gawking at the sweaty bodies thrusting against each other. I wished I had a drink, if only to have something to do with my hands. I didn't, so I crammed them in my pockets and tried to appear nonchalant about what was going on.

"Good Lord," Darci choked out. "Is he ... what ... wow."

She hadn't descended to pointing, but I followed her eyes and saw a burly blond man in a sixty-nine with the woman on top. The remarkable thing was the dark-haired man straddling the blond man's head, his cock buried deep in the woman's ass. As I watched, the blond guy reached a hand up and fondled the other man's balls.

"Looking away, looking away," Darci muttered.

I was *not* looking away. My monster was like a feline rolling in a field of catnip, and my skin felt the sparks of all the sexual energy. I let go and basked in it, savoring the rush as I took it all in. My heart thudded. My skin sensed every tiny stirring of air. I took a deep breath and felt high at the scent of sex. Humans had their heroine, but this was *my* drug.

A man writhed in ecstasy as another rode him. Two women were covering every square inch of an ebony-skinned man with their tongues. A large woman sprawled on a couch, the man before her thrusting his cock between her huge breasts. I wanted to join them — wanted to join them all. My monster reared her head like a hydra, demanding that I take them all. Male, female, married — it didn't matter to her. I'd deprived her too long, and as delicious as the energy was, I knew she wanted to be a participant.

"I need to get out of here."

Bless Darci for being the friend she is. She grabbed my arm and practically dragged me through the door, back into the dance floor area. We didn't stop until we'd reached the bar, where she got me a glass of ice chips and a Captain and ginger.

Irix's drink. Damn. And I needed a shit-ton more ice than what was in this pint glass.

"Thanks. I was barely holding it together in there."

Darci grabbed me in a big hug, holding me tight. I fought back tears. She got me, really understood what I was feeling. My best friend. Finally she pulled back, smoothing a hand over my hair and smiling tremulously. Her eyes were suspiciously bright.

"Well, you can always fall back on the rapists and con men idea."

I laughed, although there was an edge of hysteria to my humor. Leave it to Darci. She always managed to yank me out of any pity party I might be indulging in.

"Excuse me."

I turned to see a girl behind me. I mean girl. She barely looked over ten years old, but her eyes held a weary knowledge far beyond that of a child. Even vampires wouldn't allow an underage girl in a sex club. This must be Eloise.

"I see you found the Revelry room. Was it not to your liking? You are welcome to pick any sexual partners of your choosing — as many as you wish."

It was disturbing, hearing such things from someone who bore a striking resemblance to a pre-teen Shirley Temple. I stared at her golden curls and bright-blue eyes in shock, unable to force even a polite response from my mouth.

She smiled, increasing my unease. "Normally we restrict demon access and choices, wishing to mitigate damage and any potential discovery by angels or human law enforcement, but sex demons are different. We welcome you and are pleased to provide you with anything you wish."

We were lesser demons, considered far less dangerous than others. I could imagine the vampires were relieved to find a succubus and not a plague-bringer, or a dreaded imp.

"Thank you." I finally managed to find my voice. "I did find the Revelry room to be very stimulating, but I'm afraid I have only a short time to enjoy myself. Is there somewhere I could watch, and yet be removed from the temptation to join in?"

Eloise tilted her head and regarded me. "Certainly. We have a peep-room and a show about to begin. If you see anyone you particularly desire, please let me know and I will detain them until you've completed your other business."

Peep show. Well, at least it was consensual on the part of the participants. And her invitation to return gave me an idea. I wouldn't be selecting anyone for a sexual partner, but I could return later. If I stayed long enough, perhaps I'd gain enough energy to satisfy Irix and put off what I so desperately wanted, but wanted to delay.

I glanced at Darci, and she shrugged. "Sure. Seen one room full of people bonking, seen it all. What's one more?"

We followed Eloise to a wrought-iron spiral staircase to the side of the bar, and up to a long hallway with a series of doors. Each one had a slot cut into the wood above the door handle that read either "busy" or "open". The vampire opened one of the "open" doors and gallantly ushered us inside. The room was tiny, barely four feet by four with two cushioned chairs and a small stand with chilled champagne, two glasses, and a plate of delicate puff pastry appetizers.

"I will return after the show. If you need anything, please move your slide bolt to "open", and I will enter to refresh beverages or provide you with any assistance you may require."

With a surprisingly deep bow for a vampire barely over three feet tall, Eloise closed the door behind her. I immediately noticed the sliding deadbolt above the door handle and moved it to the locked "busy" position. Less than two seconds later, Darci launched into a furious tirade.

"What in Christ's name was that? A vampire? Who would do that to a child? Someone turned a little girl!"

"Hush!" I waved a panicked hand at her. What if these booths were monitored? I could protect Darci now — they wouldn't retaliate against her if they thought she was my human, but I'd eventually go home, and I didn't want to worry that she'd offended a group of powerful creatures.

"A child!" At least Darci had lowered her voice to an angry whisper. "Bad enough they're going around the city drinking blood from us like a bunch of oversized mosquitoes, but turning a *child*?"

"She's got to be at least five-hundred years old," I whispered back. I really didn't know, but from the look in her eyes, I probably wasn't far off. "Things were different back then. Maybe she was dying and this was something she or her parents wanted. Maybe it was an accident."

Darci's face was red, and I could tell she was struggling to hold her temper in check. I didn't blame her; it was revolting to think that someone would have done this to a child, but I was in no place to condemn an action that had taken place hundreds of years ago. I doubt at this point she'd have chosen death over vampirism. She seemed fairly satisfied with her life.

"Look, if it will make you feel better, I'll ask Ourson. I'll find out what their criteria and methods are for turning humans, and I'll ask about Eloise's history. Just please don't offend them. I don't want anything to happen to you."

That sobered her up. Darci took a few deep breaths and loosed her death grip on the back of the chair. "Thank you; I'd appreciate it. This is my city, and I really want to know if there's someone preying on children this way."

At that moment, the front wall of the room transformed from dark, smoky glass to clear, as the room before us lit up. I'd seen these types of windows before. We could see everything, but those inside would only see their own reflections on the walls. I motioned Darci to sit and poured champagne, trying to put myself into the right frame of mind for the show. I needed to do this for Jordan, for her coven, for the trees dying in the bayou south of the city.

As if sensing my struggle, Darci took her champagne, her eyebrows arching as she nodded toward the room before us. "Now *this* is more my style. Heck, I might have to give Gavin a booty call after this."

I turned and sank into the chair, my legs suddenly unable to support me. The room was staged with a hard wooden chair, an intricate pattern of candles around the floor, and in the middle of it all, a naked man. He knelt, forced into position by manacles that bound his wrists and ankles to metal rings embedded into the floor. His head was rigid as he looked at the floor, a thick collar around his neck studded with silver. We watched him for a few moments in silence, then the music began. It was languorous, like smoke dancing across our senses.

A door on the far side of the room opened with a snick, and a pirouetting calliope of colored silk scarves entered. The man's gaze remained on the floor, but as the prancing feet came within his view, he lifted his head. Agony shot across his face, and a drop of blood pooled at the edge of the collar. As a reward, the dancing woman shed a scarf, teasing the silk across his naked back before she discarded it.

As long as the man kept his eyes on her, the woman continued to shed her gauzy garments. The moment he dropped his head to relieve the spikes digging into his neck, she stopped, dancing around him until he couldn't bear to keep his gaze from her any more. Blood streaked his neck, and his body shook as he watched the woman dance, entranced by the seductive swaying of her body.

Finally, she tore the last scarf from her hips, revealing only smooth dark flesh and a few strategically placed piercings. The kneeling man groaned, every muscle straining against the chains that held him to the floor. At this point, he was insensible to the pain at his neck, to the blood that trickled slowly from the lower edge of the collar. The woman dropped to her knees before him, and her pink tongue lapped at the stains of red, her hands busy with the cuffs that bound him. His hands released, she pushed him onto his back and worked at his ankle chains, her teeth nipping up the inside of his thighs.

Even with his legs free, he held completely still, his eyes riveted on the woman. Her eyes met his with the intensity of an inferno. On his back, the man's cock rose like an ebony tower between his thighs. It was an impressive erection. I was glad a thick glass wall separated us, because I had a desperate desire to join them.

"Holy cow," Darci breathed beside me. I could feel her arousal, sense it as her energy spiraled into me. It was exquisite— the couple, the observers in other rooms, Darci. Their energy filled me, and I stretched like a contented cat.

Holy cow indeed. The woman crawled over top of the man, keeping eye contact the entire way. Straddling him, she rose up on her knees, hovering above him, teasing, tormenting with the promise of completion.

With a swift downward movement, she dropped onto him, sheathing his entire length in one thrust. I gasped as the energy flooded into me. The man groaned and raised his hips, trying for an impossible depth of penetration. The woman's smile was almost cruel as she rode him, leaning back and then dropping forward onto her palms to change the angle. The man's face was rigid with tension, his eyes never leaving her face. The woman rose to her knees once more, increasing the tempo and driving the rhythm into an erratic frenzy. She tossed back her head, crying out as she slammed down onto him, rotating her pelvis against his.

Still he remained tense, his eyes on hers. Aftershocks trembled her body and finally she looked down, true affection on her face as she reached a hand forward to caress his cheek and unclasp the collar from his neck.

"Well done, my love. And now I will allow you to come."

The look in his eyes came closer to worship than anything I'd ever seen. "Thank you, Mistress."

Her tempo increased once more, purposeful and steady. It only took a dozen strokes before the tremors shook his body and he cried out his pleasure. I watched her caress his side with a firm hand, and the window closed.

"Good?" Darci's voice was hoarse, as if she'd smoked a pack of unfiltered cigarettes.

"Good." I wasn't surprised to hear my voice sounded the same.

The sultry heat outside felt almost chill after the intimate warmth of the peep room. Darci drew a ragged breath, rubbing her face with both palms as I looked for Jordan's car.

"Do you need a lift?" I asked, waving at Jordan in her Honda across the street.

"Uh, no. I think I need to walk that one off a bit. Then

take a really long shower. Then go visit Gavin. Don't expect me home tonight, okay?"

I laughed, giving her a quick hug. "Glad it wasn't a total bust for you. Thanks again for coming with me."

Darci tugged a lock of my blond hair. "Yeah, just don't tell anyone, okay?"

The city lights shone bright behind us in contrast with the dark shapes lining the road. Headlights only did so much to illuminate our way, and the sporadic flickering street lamps added to the spooky atmosphere. Clouds had moved back in with the setting of the sun. In the blackness, trees seemed like menacing creatures, waiting for us to turn our back on them before they attacked. Even Jordan sensed it, her knuckles white as she gripped the steering wheel.

"It's not a good night for magic," she said ominously. "I feel . . . something. It's like another force is pressing down upon the ground — something dark and foul."

What the heck was I supposed to say to that? If I was uneasy before, Jordan's doom-and-gloom speech did nothing to shore up my confidence. Yeah, I had enough energy from Bliss to heal a few acres of trees, but would it be enough? Something prickled like nettles along my skin, and I worried. Bev and her motives weren't my only concern. There was something very wrong in the air tonight.

The lights of the coven participants were a welcome glow,

holding at bay the menacing shadows of trees draped with Spanish moss. Jordan parked, and we made our way, lit by her cell phone app, to the circle. Bev welcomed Jordan warmly, and me with a more frosty tone, then did a quick count.

"Places everyone. Let's begin."

We had thirty minutes to raise as much energy as possible then direct it toward our target at midnight. I doubted I could use any of their energy, but I figured between us all, we should have some results. Although I'd attended Wiccan ceremonies before, and my sex magic seemed to work well with their Beltane celebration, I wasn't sure how compatible our spells would be. I only hoped that it augmented mine, or perhaps healed some of the trees that were beyond the grove I was targeting.

Speaking of which — I couldn't physically reach any of the trees, and it worried me. I'd never done this before. Not only couldn't I touch them, I couldn't even *see* them in the pitch black of the moonless night. The enhanced vision of my elf heritage was negated by the candles flickering around the edges of the circle, and the fire just behind the altar in the center.

I took my place beside Darci and watched with respectful silence as a man sprinkled a line of salt around the circle, murmuring an incantation as he went. As he completed the clockwise round, voices lifted in invocation, locking the perimeter as tight as a steel fence. A woman dressed in darkest green stepped forward and hailed the north quarter, lighting a candle the same color as her robe. Another came forward to summon the east, praising the element of air as she lit the candle. I could feel their energy, sharp and smooth, hot and cool against the part of me that dwelled beneath my skin. I couldn't absorb it, but I appreciated the power and beauty it carried.

Each direction and their complementing element was called to the quarter, honored and summoned to tighten the bonds of the circle. The ladies stepped back as Jason and Bev approached the altar. When I'd seen them earlier, I'd envisioned a sort of business partnership, but now the spiritual nature of their connection became clear. Short and tall, round and thin, young and old — it all balanced into a perfect equilibrium of energies as they lifted the goblet with joined hands.

"The deep well of our Lady I hold in my hands," Bev intoned, her voice ringing with power. "Life and death, comfort and pain, the pang of desertion, the embrace of the Mother. She surrounds us, the circle of seasons, the chaotic nature of the eternal cycle."

Jason removed his hands from the chalice and picked up the double-edged knife — the athame. "The Lord of the cycle, the one who is born each year and dies by its end. Child of the Lady, lover of the Lady, the one who dies by Her hand. He brings us balance and order, a promise of life eternal."

Slowly he plunged the athame into the goblet, holding it in the depths as he spoke. "Thus we are joined. Only through the union of order and chaos are balance and bliss achieved."

"So mote it be," Bev intoned.

"So mote it be," we all replied.

Jordan motioned me forward, and I stepped toward the altar. Both priest and priestess turned to face me. Jason removed the athame, and Bev extended the goblet toward me.

"May the blessing of our Lord and Lady aid you in your task. May the power we raise aid the earth to heal. Amber Lowry, you are the right hand of our energy. Harm none, and let the Lady guide you."

I nodded, unsure what to say and took the proffered

goblet, sipping the spiced wine. The Bon Nuit coven had good taste and deep pockets when it came to ceremonial beverages. I was momentarily tempted to take the goblet and run, but reluctantly surrendered it back into Bev's hands. She and Jason made a circuit to each member, giving them the blessings and charging them with the task at hand. The air grew thick and heavy with purpose. I felt the confines of the circle like a snug blanket tucked too tight under the mattress — warm and safe, but restrictive. The succubus in me was uneasy, and I hoped she'd soon get with the program.

Jason pulled a small flute from his pocket, and a haunting melody in a minor chord filled the air. Bev began the chant, and after the first line, everyone else's voices joined hers. Swaying and dancing in tempo, the entire coven moved in a clockwise direction, circling the altar.

Oh Sun, invigorate us with your light
Moon, bring us strength through the night
Wind carry truth
River bring youth
Your power from us unloose

I felt the energy of the group like an increasing amp of electricity, swirling in a vortex within the circle. My own power rose to the surface, my fingers tingling. How to get it to the cypress grove almost twenty feet away in standing water without leaving the circle? I had to hope that what I'd been planning would work. Slowly I absorbed the coven's energy, feeling slightly ill and off balance from its unusual signature. Thankfully, it began to mesh with my own, forming something that felt like heat on soft fur — just this side of discomfort.

Bev nodded, giving me the sign that the group had reached maximum potential, and I focused my mind on the cypress grove in front of me, visualizing it as healthy and strong — and about two feet taller with a complementary increase in width. Unbidden, a word came to my lips, and I made the sign of the horns with my left hand — index and little finger pointed toward the ground.

Fecundity.

An orange light shot from me to the circle, halting at the edge of the salt line and spinning around it with a fiery blaze. A few of the coven shrieked, jumping forward to avoid being set alight. Bev said something that sounded like "Dratted demons." Then nudged her foot into the salt line to break the containment.

Like a burst of orange lightning, the energy streamed outward and lit up the cypress grove in an explosion of sparks before vanishing and leaving all once more shadowed in the dark black of night.

My eyesight took a while to adjust, and I held my breath, terrified that I'd set the trees on fire. It wouldn't be the first time I'd done that, although, given the complete absence of light, I assumed there was no on-going damage. Slowly my eyes adjusted, and Bev turned on a flashlight. When the circle had been broken, everything had gone out in a rush of air. The fire, the candles — all reacted as though there were a sudden, airless vacuum. The humans gasped, and Bev weakly gave the intonation to break the circle and close the ritual.

Unsure of what to do, and feeling as though I'd been running for two days straight, I staggered back to Jordan at the edge of the now-open circle. Others milled about, chatting.

"How did I do?" I was half afraid to ask.

Jordan shook her head. "I don't know. I felt something, but I can't see the tree grove enough to tell what happened and if we had any success."

Jason left the group and drove his truck toward us, flicking on the high beams in the direction of the cypress grove. There stood a thick group of trees, dark green and noticeably thicker and taller. They'd multiplied, and there were twice as many trees spreading through the swamp as before, the nursery logs all showing significant growth. A cheer went up, and everyone hugged — well, everyone but me. Jordan, noticing my exclusion, gave me a congratulatory pat on the shoulder.

"You know, we couldn't have done it without you. Thank you, Amber."

It didn't matter if no one else thanked me. Jordan had, and I felt a deep sense of satisfaction through my exhaustion. I'd never done anything like this before.

"We're going to Maxwell's to celebrate," Jason said, giving me a warm smile. "Join us?"

"No thanks." I appreciated his offer, but I was exhausted. All I wanted to do was go back to Darci's and sleep, but my deadline from Irix was long overdue. No rest for the wicked. I planned to change clothes and head back to Bliss, where I'd hopefully not doze off while watching people have sex. With some luck, I'd have enough energy by the time Irix tracked me down to buy myself another day or two.

*L*uck is clearly not my friend. No sooner had Jordan dropped me off at Darci's apartment than there was a knock at the door. Not only did I refuse to answer it, but I frantically dove behind a chair and covered my head with a cushion from the sofa. Darci had her key, and I didn't expect her home from Gavin's until morning. It sure as heck wasn't the pizza delivery guy at the door.

"Amber, I know you're in there. Answer the damned door."

Nope. I cowered under the cushion and held my breath. He sounded really pissed, as if he knew that I'd failed yet again. A pissed Irix was a sexy Irix, and my willpower was shot to hell as far as he was concerned. I was not answering that door.

I heard a faint sigh, then some muttering about angels and stupid elf girls. Then I heard the click of the deadbolt and the whisper of a door opening.

Shit. Oh, shit. Damned demons and their supernatural lock-picking abilities. I should have taken other precautions

— asked Jordan and her coven for a can of demon repellant or something.

The floor creaked over by the kitchen. I held absolutely still, praying the huge, ugly second-hand chair was concealing me from view. Footsteps by the bedroom. Two more doors open and shut, and the sound of the closet door opening. The footsteps came closer, and I heard him do a quick tour of the room. And then, like a miracle, I heard the front door open and close. The deadbolt secured. I let out a careful breath and waited.

Mississippi one, Mississippi two. One whole minute I counted out in my head. Demons were notoriously impatient. There was no way one of them would have stood motionless in an apartment for that long. He was gone. But just in case, I lowered the sofa cushion to the floor and peeked around the edge of the purple chair.

And looked right into a set of golden eyes. Furious golden eyes.

The scream I let out could have woken the dead. It didn't phase Irix one bit. As I tried to scramble backwards, his hand shot out to grab my arm, and he dragged me from behind the chair. Literally dragged. I was going to have some serious rug burn from this encounter — if I survived, that is.

"Ow. Stop. You're bruising my arm."

I should have held my breath. Irix's grip tightened, and he lifted me up, tossing me onto the sofa like a bag of groceries. I bounced and sprawled in a very unladylike posture while he loomed over me, caging me in with his arms.

"I will do far more than bruise you, half-breed. When I tell you to meet me somewhere, you will be there promptly. When I call or text, you are to immediately respond."

When had he called? Oh shit — I'd turned my phone off at Bliss and had forgotten to turn it back on. Not that he gave me the slightest chance to explain.

"You are to *answer* me when I call. I won't have you ignoring me while I race all over the damned city looking for you. You are to do as I say without hesitation, without question. Do you understand?"

Having him so close was wrecking my concentration, but his fury over what had been a simple mistake, plus the ridiculous demands for obedience cut through the fog of desire.

"Should I be wearing a French maid costume and crawl around on the floor after you, too?"

I was positive the sarcasm conveyed, but the unholy light in his eyes seemed to indicate he thought I was making a valid suggestion. He leaned closer, and one hand left the sofa for my pants. My breath lodged in my throat at the thought of what he might do, but instead of popping the snap at the waistband, he dug into my pocket and pulled out my phone.

His eyes left mine as he turned it on and scrolled through the device. I dragged a ragged breath into my lungs, but I had only a momentary reprieve. With a snarl, he threw my phone across the room and again put his arms on either side of me, freezing me in place with his intense gaze.

"Messages. Missed calls. Texts. You will respond when I contact you. Immediately. There is no negotiation on this."

What was *wrong* with him? Why was this such a big deal? "I forgot I had it off. I've been busy and hadn't checked. Sheesh, settle down."

That was clearly not the right thing to say. Fury flowed off Irix in waves, and his eyes darkened like molten lava.

"I don't care how damned busy you are; nothing is more important than answering when I call. Nothing."

"Fuck you. I'm not your dog."

Irix wasn't the only one that was pissed off, although, looking back on things, it probably wasn't wise to antagonize him further.

"You're my dog if I say you are. You don't get to ignore me like that. When I tell you to meet me somewhere, you better fucking well be there."

He'd totally lost control of his temper if he was cursing. Irix prided himself on his verbal restraint, unlike most demons. But underneath all the rage was a river of fear, and that halted my runaway mouth. He had been worried about me. This asshole-in-charge routine was his way of handling it. I doubted demons had much experience in dealing with concern for others.

"I'm sorry." The words defused his anger. Two sincere words was all it took, but I added to them. "I know you think I was being rude and immature, but I truly didn't know you'd called. I'm sorry."

He stood up and took a deep breath, eyes still locked on mine. "There's an angel in town, and he's tracking someone through their energy signature. I don't know if it's you, me, or some other demon he's hunting. I called to warn you, and when I couldn't reach you, couldn't find you anywhere. . . ."

Shit. No wonder he'd been so upset. And here I'd been, just a few miles out of town, blasting magical energy all over the bayous. I was lucky. Very lucky.

"I'm so sorry." I felt terrible that I'd worried him and was kicking myself for forgetting to turn my phone back on.

"Why did you have your phone off?"

"I was at a sex club and thought it would be kind of rude if my phone went off in the middle of things."

"Understandable. And afterwards?"

"I promised one of the local covens I'd do some magic on the bayou groves south of the city. I literally raced from one thing to another and forgot to turn it on. Although, it probably would have been just as rude if my phone had gone off in the middle of a ritual."

Irix nodded then his eyes narrowed as they scanned me

from top to toe. "So . . . you went to a sex club, yet here you are just as starving as you were last night? You had all day to get this done. What happened?"

Well, here goes nothing. "I didn't manage to have sex. I tried this afternoon, but it didn't work out, and the thing with the witches didn't leave me enough time to do much at the sex club or find another partner. Jordan just dropped me off a few minutes ago. I was going to change and head out to remedy the situation." There. Hopefully he wouldn't notice that I'd left out the fact that my "remedy" didn't actually including having sex with anyone.

He glared, anger returning, but not to the crazy level of berserker rage it had before. "You didn't have sex? What happened with the guy this afternoon? Was he a killer gnome? Bad breath? Socks with sandals?"

"He'd already been claimed."

Irix made a choking noise. "Leave it to you. Do you know what the odds of that are? There are seven billion humans, and you pick the one among a hundred thousand in the city that has been spoken for."

Maybe there was a silver lining in all this after all. If I could just buy myself a little more time, I could gain enough energy from the peep rooms at Bliss to satisfy him. I could do this — become a sort of voyeur, draining off the excess sexual energy of others without any kind of physical contact or morally ambiguous behavior. It would be the equivalent of eating out of garbage cans for the rest of my life, but hey, it might work.

"Can you give me another twenty-four hours?"

Irix stalked toward me, again boxing me against the sofa with his arms. I wasn't trusting the gleam in his eyes.

"No."

His mouth met mine before I could protest. This kiss wasn't sweet or lazily seductive; it was hard, demanding. I could feel the edge of his anger when his teeth nipped along my bottom lip. The sofa sagged as his knees hugged the outside of my thighs, supporting his weight and freeing up his hands to bury them deep into my hair. His tongue explored mine, and I lifted my hips, arching up to meet him. I felt like he was drinking me in, swimming through every part of me.

With a smooth motion that surely was beyond the natural laws of physics, he stood, clasping me to his chest. I wrapped my legs around his waist and held onto his shoulders. We broke our kiss, and I knew exactly where he was taking me. I wanted to protest, but his mouth was so close to mine. I could feel his breath, taste it, see with my hooded eyes the beautiful lips I wanted against mine.

Through the doorway, Irix eased me down to stand, holding me so lightly against him, I could only feel his heat. His lips were now soft as they brushed mine, his tongue gently tracing the corners of my mouth.

"I'm not having sex with you, Irix."

I didn't sound very convincing, and I knew in that moment that I lied. His kisses feathered on my nose, then on my forehead. My resolve wavered, died, vanished. I *was* going to have sex with him. It would be the best night of my life. I leaned my face against him and breathed deep, my hands moving toward the fly of his jeans.

"No." Irix's voice was full of regret. He turned me around, my back pressed to his front by the strong arms across my chest. "You're having sex with him."

At the edge of the bed stood what I can only describe as a gorgeous cowboy. Rugged. Tanned. Shirtless. He came complete with the big belt buckle accessorizing the front of his torn jeans. A battered hat lay on the bed alongside a pile of fabric that was probably his shirt. I didn't pay too much attention; I was too busy ogling his impressive pectoral muscles. He shifted his weight to one foot and crossed his arms. Oh my God, those arms.

"Ma'am."

And he called me "Ma'am". This guy had to have been the hottest specimen of masculinity I'd ever seen, and he was eyeing me just as appreciatively in return.

"Does this meet your exacting standards?"

Irix didn't have to ask. I'm sure he felt every bit of my reaction, from the flushed skin to the pheromones flying unchecked about the room. He sucked a sensitive spot on my neck, worrying it with his teeth, and I realized he was just as turned on as I was by this whole thing. Normally with Irix in the room, other men disappeared, but this was different. There was more here than just a super-hot guy ramping up my libido. The majority of my reaction came from the fact that Irix was enjoying this more than either me or Cowboy. It was him I wanted to please — him whose desire I got off on. Would he watch? Join in? What would *he* like me to do with this man?

And then it all came crashing down as I thought of the guy in the hotel room. I couldn't do that. As much as I wanted Cowboy, as much as Irix wanted me to want Cowboy, I couldn't.

"I'm not having sex with him either."

Irix's disappointment was worse than the anger that followed. His anger I could take. I'd been on the receiving end of that for over a month now.

"Give me another day or two," I pleaded.

"No. It's me or him. Or both of us. Pick."

His arms were gentle around my waist in spite of his white knuckles. I appreciated his restraint and desperately wondered how I could get out of this one. He couldn't force me. Wouldn't force me. Or would he?

"One more day."

"What's wrong with him?"

I got the feeling he'd been about to ask "what's wrong with me?" I looked over at Cowboy, who didn't seem to mind that we were standing in front of him, discussing him as if he were a pork loin at the grocer.

"Absolutely nothing. It's me that's the problem."

Irix growled. "Yes, it is you that's the problem. I've never met a more stubborn, pig-headed, self-destructive idiot in my two-thousand years of life. If you don't tell me right now what is going on in that pea-sized brain of yours, I'm going to throw you on the bed and force feed you my cock while that human rides you like a pony."

Cowboy nodded enthusiastically, and I had to admit the idea had a lot of appeal. Irix reached down to un-snap my jeans as he nudged me toward the bed.

"All right, all right." Irix halted at my words. "The guy at the hotel, the one who was claimed, he was pitiful. Every ounce of sexual energy was going to the demon that marked him. He was desperate and crying, a total wreck of unsatisfied need. She ruined his life."

I felt Irix shrug. "So."

So? Bastard. Just when I started to think he might be more than what a demon was supposed to be, he pulled out something like "so". I yanked myself free from his arms and spun about to face him.

"It's wrong! Fucking wrong! I'd rather starve than do that to someone."

He looked . . . confused. "Then don't."

"I won't. Because I'm not going to have sex with anyone again. Ever."

It was a depressing idea. I thought Irix would be furious, but instead he started to laugh. Which made *me* furious. I punched him in the chest, which only made him laugh harder.

"Is that what all this is about? Some sex demon decided to wring out her victim like an old washcloth, and now you're going to be celibate for an eternity? What are you, an angel?"

"It's not funny." I went to punch him again, and he grabbed my arm.

"Yes, it *is* funny. It's like saying that you don't want to eat pork, so you're not going to eat anything ever again."

"Should I leave?" Cowboy asked.

"No."

"Yes."

We'd replied at the same time. Cowboy looked back and forth between us then sat on the bed to wait it out. Irix released my hand. I held back from punching him again since he'd finally stopped laughing.

"Have you not been listening to a thing I've said this past month? What I've been teaching you? Amber, you are the one who controls the experience. You. Some demons like a strong tie, others prefer a lighter touch. You determine your style. And yes, you can vary it from partner to partner. It's all you, elf-girl."

"Oh."

I was an idiot. I'd been so unnerved out by what I thought I was becoming, and unsettled by Irix's presence, that I hadn't done much but fight with him for the last four weeks. I looked up at him, into those golden eyes, and wondered why he hadn't bailed on me weeks ago.

He sighed. "It's my fault. I obviously didn't do a good job at explaining these things. Maybe you'll do better with a different instructor. Swendal, perhaps."

A demon apologizing? But it was his suggestion that he should go home and send another in his place that sent my heart racing with panic. He couldn't leave.

I shook my head. "No. I was too busy freaking out to listen to you. I'll do better, I promise. Please stay."

He stared at me, deciding, while I struggled to breathe.

"Please. I don't want you to leave." I was begging him, and I was on the verge of tears.

"Another day. Twenty-four hours." His voice was husky, and something unreadable flashed across his face. I thought maybe he'd hug me, soothe me as he'd done the other night, but he stood as if frozen, with that odd expression. I nodded.

Irix escorted the disappointed cowboy to the door, and the pair left without another word. I felt like my world had been rocked to the core. I could do this — have sex with only the lightest of ties, or perhaps even none at all. It might mean I'd need more partners than most other sex demons, but that was okay. As long as I knew I wasn't doing any harm, I'd be fine. I always loved sex anyway.

But now . . . . I glanced at the closed apartment door and felt depressed. I'd find at least one partner, and Irix wouldn't need to share his energy with me. He wouldn't need to have sex with me. Irix. The one being in this world that I'd come to realize I simply could not live without.

What had originally been an intense physical attraction was turning into something else. He was a demon, an incubus, but he was so much more. He'd shown me that he could be caring, considerate, even patient. These traits drew me in further. He might break my heart, but I was too far gone to hold back now. I took a deep breath and knew no matter what the future would bring, I was going to jump into this with both feet and no regrets.

I wanted everything he was willing to give to me, no matter what pain I went through afterward. One night might be all we shared, but what a night that would be. I just needed to dig in my heels and be a stubborn, pig-headed, self-destructive elf-girl for another twenty-four hours.

 stretched, feeling decadent to be hogging up Darci's entire bed. Irix's texts hadn't been the only ones I had missed last night. My friend had made good on her plans to head over to Gavin's, and the last text from her had indicated her intentions of spending the night. Poor guy. He'd be lucky if he could walk by the time Darci got through with him. I needed to take her to sex clubs more often.

Rolling over, I gloried in the soft feel of sheets, the feather pillow cradling my head, and the warm, hard body next to me. My heart froze and exploded into panicked action. There was a man in my bed, and he'd certainly not been there when I retired for the evening. Screaming, I launched myself off the mattress. I had no idea what I planned to do. I was naked with no weapons besides my demonic ones, and some instinctive part of my brain realized it wouldn't be wise to launch a lightning bolt into Darci's bed — strange male occupant or not.

My feet hit the ground, but before I could make a run for it, my toga-like attire tangled around my legs, dropping me to the floor in a heap of sheets and pillows. The figure on the bed stirred, and I shrieked again, brandishing a pillow as a naked man rose to his knees.

"Is this the way you wake up every morning? Screaming and rolling around on the floor in the bed linen?"

Irix. Demons have no concept of modesty. I'd seen him in the buff before, but still the sight rendered me speechless. His body was flawless. Silken hair just this side of black was loose from its usual tie and brushed along his sculpted, broad shoulders. His chest was well-defined without being absurdly huge. Toned abs were divided by a faint line of brown hair that led to . . . Oh my God. I would not look, would not look. Fuck it, I was looking.

Narrow hips, powerful thighs, and between them the most perfect specimen of male sex ever. Thick and long, but not so big that I worried about needing a shoehorn or a gallon of lube. Just right, and I was Goldilocks, eyeing it with intent. As if reading my mind, it twitched, beckoning me.

"If you're going to look at me like that, then you better get back into this bed."

This wasn't how I'd envisioned our first night — or day, together. No, I'd better stay out of the bed. Tearing my eyes away, I hitched the sheet up higher around my chest and tried to think of something to say.

"What are you doing here — in Darci's apartment, and especially in bed with me? I thought I had another twenty-four-hour extension."

Irix sighed, and that very intriguing part of his anatomy relaxed. I know, I peeked.

"I came over to take you to breakfast, but you sleep like the dead. Since I had no idea how long you were going to be in that state, I figured I'd get some shut eye myself."

Breakfast. My stomach rumbled at the idea. Irix climbed off the bed and strode to the closet, completely unselfconscious of his nudity. This afforded me a lovely view of his backside, which was just as pleasing to the eye as the front of him.

"We've gotten off to a rocky start, you and I. Part of that is my fault, and part of that is you being a thick-headed, stubborn half-breed. So I'm here, waving the white flag and offering to treat you to pecan French toast as a gesture of good will."

He pulled a blue sundress out of the closet and carried it over to me. I didn't have the heart to tell him that these were all Darci's clothes, and the sundress would probably rip at the seams if I tried to squeeze it over my curvy frame.

"So you want to bury the hatchet?" I took the dress from him. It was very unnerving having him standing naked, scant inches from me while I was sitting on the floor in a sheet. That put me eye level with . . . well, you-know-what.

"I would so love to bury the hatchet as well as other things, but I'm restraining myself from that impulse. So, French toast and a fresh start?"

He held out his hand, and I took it, purposely letting the sheet drop to the floor as he drew me to my feet. Yeah. Two could play this game.

"Fresh start. Now get out of here and put on some coffee while I shower and get dressed."

Irix's gaze wandered appreciatively, and I noticed his eyes weren't the only part of him that approved of my body.

"I can scrub your back," he suggested.

I swatted him playfully with Darci's sundress. "Out. And coffee. I'm going to be very grumpy if I don't have coffee."

He bowed and gathered his clothing from the floor. "Yes, my elven princess. Coffee it is."

* * *

THE FRENCH TOAST WAS HEAVENLY, smothered in pecans and

drenched in a sweet rum sauce. Irix had surprised me with his coffee-making skills, and then further surprised me with light, entertaining breakfast conversation. He asked how I'd met Darci then listened intently as I talked about various college classes and my plans for a senior thesis.

"And this Jordan, she's also very interested in plants and trees, you said?"

He sipped his coffee, heavily laced with cream and sugar, eyes on me the whole time. For a second I worried that this was part of his whole sex-demon appeal, but Irix had no reason to draw me in with false interest. I went on to tell him about Jordan and her coven, about the ritual last night, feeling a warm, tingling sense of pleasure at our easy conversation.

"Did you use the coven's energy to repair the trees?" he asked. "You couldn't have had enough of your own to do such a thing, but witch magic isn't usually compatible with demon magic."

I had wondered the same thing last night. "I had energy I siphoned off at a fetish club that I used. The coven's energy felt odd — scratchy and uncomfortable, but I combined it with mine and used it anyway. I don't think I would have had enough if I hadn't been able to do that."

Irix frowned down into his coffee cup, then looked up at me with a smile. "Ah, I'll bet it's the elf part of you that allowed you to use it. That's why elves enslave humans in Hel. Their magical abilities are compatible, and, in some ways, the humans are actually more powerful."

More powerful didn't seem to help them. The elves ruled over their slaves with an iron fist. Still, it was good to know that I could partner with humans. It made me feel less an outsider in this world.

"So? Can I go see it?"

"See what?" I was momentarily confused, still thinking

about the elves in Hel — my brethren that I'd never be able to know for fear they'd kill me on sight. Elves didn't like anyone mixing in their gene pool, and in their eyes, I was an abomination.

"Your trees. The ones you worked your elven magic on. Show me. I want to see them."

Seriously? He wanted to go look at a bunch of cypress trees in a bayou? Who was this man, and what had he done with Irix the demon?

"It's a bit out of town. We can't exactly walk there."

"No problem." Irix tossed some money onto the table and stood. "We'll drive."

I followed him down the street a block to a black Audi A4. He opened the passenger door and ushered me in with a flourish. It was a sweet ride, kept cool from the morning heat by some type of circulating air system that worked while the car was parked. Irix climbed in beside me, and, with a roar of the engine, we took off. We were leaving the downtown area behind when I realized that there wasn't a key in the ignition.

"You stole this car," I accused, turning in my seat to face him. "Some poor guy is going to come out of his house, or from breakfast, and find his car gone."

Irix's shrug was nonchalant, but his lips twitched. "Probably. I'll have it back to him by tonight. Or maybe not. I like this car a lot. I may decide to keep it for the duration of my stay."

So much for him being a kinder, gentler doppelganger of Irix the demon. "He'll file a police report. We'll be pulled over as soon as we return to the city, and they'll haul you off to jail. Hell, they'll probably haul me off to jail too."

And I was just as bad, more worried about us going to jail then some poor guy having his awesome car stolen from in front of his house.

Irix shot me an amused look. This time the smile on his

face was unmistakable. "Since when have the police ever hauled you into jail? Come to think of it, since when have they ever even given you a ticket? Tell you what; if we get pulled over, I'll shut up and let you do all the talking, just to prove my point."

He was right. I'd never had a speeding ticket, a parking ticket, even a jaywalking citation. His reassurances didn't make me feel any better; if anything, they made me feel worse.

"Okay, but it's wrong. You stole someone's car!"

He nodded pragmatically. "Well, yes. It's not like I had time to go out and buy one off the lot. Plus you would have probably had a fit over me using stolen credit cards and someone else's identity to buy it. Jacking one is quicker, and I get the same lecture either way."

"Wait." I was suddenly suspicious. "Where did you get the cash for breakfast?"

"The ATM, where else?" His tone was cheerful, but I knew better.

"I'm pretty sure you don't have a bank account, so you either stole someone's card and PIN, or hot-wired the machine into giving you the money."

"The latter. Don't worry, I changed forms. The police are looking for a short, fat, blond man with a beard."

"You changed forms. With an angel in the city." I might not know much about demons, but I did know that changing physical forms took a lot of energy — energy an angel could easily sense and track if one were nearby.

"I did it up in Maryland. I may need to start using one of the credit cards I acquired though. Chasing around after a certain half-elf has really depleted my cash."

There was no arguing ethics with a demon. Giving up for now, I sat back and navigated to the ritual site, keeping my eyes on the rearview mirror for any police cruisers.

"Here." I pointed to a pull-off spot, and we got out and picked our way carefully through the scrub toward where the circle had been. The air was thick and heavy under a gray sky, with wind that promised rain. I paused to tie my hair up and let the breeze cool the sweat on the back of my neck while Irix strode ahead through the short, dense brush.

"Are you sure this is the right spot?"

"Yep. Why?" I trotted to catch up with him, suddenly realizing "why".

Past the solid ground of the ritual site, across the stretch of half-submerged grass and algae-dotted water stood dead cypress as far as I could see. Dead. Not a leaf on the branches, they hunched over, stunted and twisted as if in pain.

"I . . . what the fuck happened? I *healed* them. They're . . . dead. Not just the ones I healed, but all of them. They weren't that way last night, even before we started."

Irix turned, his posture tense, as if he were wary of my reaction to anything he might say. "Maybe the result was only temporary. You really didn't have much energy, and human magic doesn't mix well with our own."

I felt on the edge of tears. Temporary? How could that be? Nothing I'd ever done in the past had been temporary. The Live Oak in Audubon Park was still fine. Temporary was bad enough, but these trees were dead — I'd made them worse. I'd killed them. The idea made me want to puke up my French toast all over the grass.

Irix took one look at my face, and his expression hardened. Spinning on his heel, he walked past the edge of the circle and right into the swamp.

"Be careful. There's snakes and alligators in the water."

He paused, turning toward me with a raised eyebrow. "Seriously? Maybe you should be warning the snakes and alligators that there's a demon in the water."

He had a point.

"Come on. We'll need to be close enough to touch the trees in order to determine what went wrong."

I hesitated. "I'll ruin my shoes."

It was a horrible excuse, and I know it made me sound shallow and vain. In reality, I didn't give a crap about my sneakers, I was just terrified to find out what happened, to confirm that it was all my fault. I didn't want to wade through murky water *and* have my terrible failure right in front of my face.

Irix sighed and came back out of the water, his legs soaked from the knees down, and his shoes squishing out brown water as he walked. He was disappointed, and that was almost as painful as the fact that I'd murdered an entire bayou of cypress trees. I turned to head to the car and squeaked in surprise as he grabbed me from behind, turning me in midair and slinging me like a sack of potatoes across his shoulder. It wasn't the first time he'd done this to me, and I didn't like it any better this time.

"Damn it, Irix! Put me down!"

"But you'll ruin your shoes." He laughed, and I smacked his rear in retaliation. It wasn't a smart move on my part. Irix smacks much harder than I do. My ass was still stinging by the time he dumped me knee-deep into the water next to one of the trees. So much for saving my footwear.

I took a deep breath and turned around to face the tree, or what was left of it. I felt nothing in the way of energy coming from it — just a decaying husk of wood, rotted to the core. The water was littered with brown and black needle-like leaves. I put shaking fingers out to touch the bark and was surprised when Irix put his hand over the top of mine. The warmth of his palm gave me the courage to face what the dead tree told me.

Pain, sharp and sudden, hit the inside of my skull as the

cypress told its tale. There had been a moment of green, a few hours of strength, then everything went black as the life was pulled relentlessly out of the branches, trunk, and roots. It happened fast, tearing through the grove with the strength of a nuclear blast. I curled my fingers into a fist, tears tracking down my cheeks. I could feel the prickle of the Bon Nuit coven's energy from the night before, the heavy sweetness of my own, then a transformation of both into something as bitter as bile.

"I'm so sorry," I whispered to the tree, to the entire bayou. How could something so well intentioned have gone so wrong?

Irix made an odd sound from behind me and took his hand from mine. I felt momentarily bereft, as if he, too, were condemning me, but instead of pulling away, he leaned forward, pressing his palm against the crumbling bark. A crimson glow surrounded the tree, shooting upward into the branches before collapsing back into Irix's hand.

"Fuckers." He muttered. I turned around in shock, knowing he didn't mean me.

"This wasn't an accident from your spell, Amber. Whoever did this wanted to kill these trees."

CHAPTER 18

Jordan frowned, unconcerned that she was knee-deep in murky water, being eaten alive by mosquitoes and other nasty insects. I'd called her immediately, swearing her to secrecy until we determined exactly who was sabotaging our efforts. While we awaited her arrival, Irix and I made a circuit of the bayou groves, checking as many trees as we could. They all told the same tale.

"It's an odd sort of magic," Jordan commented, squinting at the bark. "It looks like a cross between something you do and ours."

My stomach twisted again, and I looked at Irix for confirmation. "You said it was someone that intentionally did this? Not our ritual gone wrong?"

"Yes." Irix's mouth was a grim line. "I've seen this kind of thing in Hel, when Elven kingdoms are fighting. It's a blight spell."

"So you think it's a sorcerer or high-level mage?" My stepsister had told me slaves skilled in magic were afforded privileges in elven society, but were still expected to use their abilities in the service of their master and kingdom.

Irix nodded. "Although it could have been a demon. Pestilence demons have a hard time getting past the gate guardians, but, once here, they get to work killing off plants either through disease or insect infestations. This isn't their usual scale, but with an angel around, he or she would be more discrete than usual."

"A pestilence demon?" Jordan's eyes were huge. "No offence, but if it's a demon, I'm hoping the angel lops his head off before nightfall."

Irix winced, and I rushed to change the topic to the other alternative. "Let's assume it's human. How strong would someone have to be to do something like this?"

Jordan shook her head. "Our entire coven combined doesn't have this sort of power. I can't imagine one mage or sorcerer being able to kill off hundreds of healthy trees — especially magically enhanced, healthy trees."

Irix scooped up a handful of brown leaves from the water and let them slide from his fingers. "If a mage or sorcerer did this, they wouldn't have enough juice to do this on their own. They had help."

That was even more disturbing than the idea of a pestilence demon. Not just one mage, but a group of them? Or a mage and a coven?

"Who could be helping him or her?" I asked, wondering about the seventy coven members who'd declined to join us last night. As much as Bev disliked me, I didn't think she or anyone in Bon Nuit would risk their precious magical energy source just to frame me.

"Crimson Moon," Jordan chimed in softly. "If there was one group in New Orleans big enough to help do this sort of thing, it would be them."

"Why?" That was the big million-dollar question. Jordan

had said that Crimson Moon had philosophical differences with the Wiccan groups and coveted their powerful energy sources, but why in the world would they have escalated dislike to the point where they felt the need to destroy an entire grove of trees?

"They want the ley lines."

So it all came down to territory.

"We lay claim to the spots south of the city, while Crimson Moon taps the Mississippi River and areas to the west. Those are the two most powerful spots in terms of magical energy. But the city has grown, and flooding has been a problem. All the dams and levees that we've put in place to protect communities are blocking the power — particularly the river. The ley lines are shifting, and that puts Crimson Moon in a weakening position."

"But how can killing a bayou forest possibly help them?"

Jordan looked up at the dark gray sky. "All it takes is one good hurricane, unhindered by natural barriers. The levees have failed before; they can fail again. If all the barriers fall like a stack of dominos, the ley lines will re-focus, and the river will once again be a mighty power."

"And how does Bon Nuit feel about that?" What I really meant was 'How does Bev feel about this.

"Most of us are concerned mainly with preserving a balance between nature and human needs, but I won't lie — there are many that like the idea of our coven holding the most powerful energy spots in the state. It doesn't matter the motivation, the entire coven would fight this."

They would — either out of adherence to their creed, or desire to maintain their position as the strongest magical group in the area. I looked at Irix, who was lost in thought as he stared up at the sky. "What do you think?" I asked him.

He shrugged. "We demons get a bad rap, but some of the most destructive acts are caused by the humans themselves."

I thought about the dam, and Darci's claim of sabotage. It was difficult to wrap my head around someone who would deliberately kill both an entire freshwater ecosystem and a bayou forest. If they were so power-driven to do that, who knows what else they had done? I glanced over at the stolen Audi, then back to Irix.

"Are you up for a visit to a dam and an excursion to the less touristy parts of the city?"

It didn't sound like something that would be particularly exciting to a demon, but Irix's eyes twinkled, flecks of silver among the gold. "Sure. I've got nothing to do today except wait for a certain half-elf to *not* have sex and wind up in my bed tonight."

The reminder sent a flare of heat and anxiety through me. Later. Right now I had a mystery to solve, and a few hundred cypress trees to avenge.

"Are you free?" I asked Jordan. "You're the only one who can confirm the energy signatures, and besides, we need a tour guide."

"I'm all yours." Jordan waded purposefully through the water toward our cars, while Irix winked at me behind her back.

"Threesome?" he grinned, teasing. Although I don't think he was truly teasing. I swatted at him, and he easily dodged the blow. "Okay, okay. I'll just watch then."

Demons. They really had a one-track mind. "Focus, Irix. Focus."

"Oh I am. Very focused, indeed."

And he was. Right down the front of my shirt. It was going to be a long day. And, hopefully, a very long night.

CHAPTER 19

$\mathcal{W}$e couldn't get close enough to the dam to do any sort of inspection to the damaged area — physical or magical. Irix and I could have pheromoned our way in, but with an angel prowling around, it wouldn't be wise for either of us to be making that much of a statement. Inspiring sexual activity in a dance club wouldn't be out of the ordinary, but at a work site in the middle of the day, an orgy would cause more notice than either of us was willing to risk. So we were relying on Jordan and her special skills, which we hoped would work through binoculars. Irix had procured the field glasses from somewhere, or more likely someone. I didn't want to inquire too closely.

"Darci said they were blaming it on concrete quality, but she suspected sabotage. Jordan found magical energy when we examined the affected marshes. I'm wondering if this is connected to what happened to the trees. A weakened dam would breach in a storm and severely compromise the downstream areas."

Irix nodded. "It sounds like this Crimson Moon group has the motivation, and if they are the ones who killed those trees, they certainly have the power to do something like this, but don't blind yourself to other causes. Demons love to do this sort of thing. It could be one of us, having a bit of fun, or even a mistake with one of the human contracting companies."

He was right, but I trusted that Darci knew her stuff. And I trusted that Jordan could sense any magical traces, even through a set of binoculars.

"Got it!" Jordan squealed. "Right there, at the base. I was starting to think maybe the spell was on the reservoir water, but it's on the dam."

Magic. But whose?

"It's the same as the cypress grove — a mix of human and something that looks like yours."

"Mine, as in demon?" I frowned. That would blow the whole Crimson Moon theory out of the water. I shuddered at the thought of a powerful demon running amok in the city, the only thing hampering its destruction the presence of a nearby angel.

Jordan lowered the binoculars and gave me a puzzled look. "I don't know. Your energy looks the same when you're doing demon things or elf things. I haven't met any other elves or demons to tell the difference."

She certainly wouldn't have met any elves. None of them had been across the gates from Hel in over two million years. There was a demon right beside me, though.

"How much would I need to do before you could 'see' it?" Irix asked uneasily, obviously thinking about the proximity of an angel.

Jordan shrugged, looking apologetic. "Normally enough to power a charm or ward. I don't know how subtle demon magic is, though."

Subtle was not a word I'd normally associate with demons. Irix must have been thinking the same because he grinned devilishly, and looked around at the sky, his gaze settling on a set of high-tension electrical wires humming about twenty feet to the west of us. I felt the pull, the rush of power through the air, and the transformers sparked, one catching fire. With a completely unnecessary dramatic gesture, Irix flung his hand toward the ground and split a three-foot boulder in half.

"Damn it, would you be more careful," I scolded.

"Another lesson, elf-girl. Always hide in plain sight. Work your succubus magic in the presence of normal human sexual activity and cloak lightning under the shroud of natural storms or the power grid."

"Impressive display." Jordan was all admiration. I was too, but I refused to let Irix know, so I crossed my arms over my chest and muttered "show-off" just loud enough to be sure he heard. He ignored me and watched smugly as Jordan walked over to examine the splintered rock.

"Red and gold, with a swirl of deep brown. Lovely," Jordan commented. Great. As if Irix's ego needed any more stroking. "Makes me think of hot pudding for some bizarre reason — the kind my grandmother used to cook on the stove. I could never wait for it to cool and just ate it straight out of the pan. Almost burned my mouth a few times."

"Yes, but is it like the energy at the trees and the dam?" I interrupted. Sheesh, was she going to go on all afternoon about the wonders of Irix's energy signature? I was on a bit of a tight schedule here.

"No, completely different. It's like nothing I've ever seen before. What else can you do? Besides split rocks in half and make people want to have sex, I mean."

"Lots of things," Irix smiled at her, and Jordan practically glowed. "I can change into one-hundred-and-five human and twenty animal forms — not at the same time, of course. I can create electricity up to the level of lightning."

Yeah, yeah, so could I. The electricity I mean, not changing forms.

"So. Back to the original topic. It doesn't match Irix's energy, so hopefully that rules out the Pestilence demon. I'm only a half-breed, but it can't be elf energy you're seeing. There are no elves here, and I can't imagine their human magic users would leave an elf energy signature."

Irix waved a hand, as though I was disrupting an important conversation with silly questions. "Actually, their humans *do* have an energy signature similar to elves. Elven-schooled mages and sorcerers escape sometimes and bribe their way across the gates. It was a lot more common a few-hundred years ago, when magic was a valuable commodity. Although they had to be careful not to get burned for witchcraft. Now, magic isn't much use outside of children's birthday parties."

That got my attention. "An escaped mage without many career opportunities might be eager to take an offer from an occult group that needed his skills."

"Or she. Lots of mages and sorcerers are female. It's about fifty-fifty, although the men have a tendency to run off more than the women do."

Holy shit, I was learning more about my heritage in one casual afternoon with Irix than a month of sex-demon lessons.

"So we need to track down these Crimson Moon asshats and splatter them across the pavement." Oops, my demon half was getting a bit excited. Maybe we'd just turn them over to law enforcement and save the splattering for another time.

"No," Jordan interjected. "We need to fix the dam and the wetlands. And we need to check the levees. If this is their plan, they probably have some kind of weakening spell on them too — triggered by weather, perhaps. It's hurricane season. It's just a matter of time, and all this is going to come crashing down. We can't go through another Katrina. We haven't fully recovered from that storm. One more like that, and the city is done for."

"There's no bringing those trees back from the dead," I argued. "And judging from last night, these people will undo everything the second we act. It's a waste of our time and resources to run around fixing things that will be broken again by daylight."

Jordan bit her lip, considering my words. "If we're going to barge in and accuse Crimson Moon, we need to have proof. Motive isn't proof. They'll say it could have been anyone."

She was right. But how to prove it was them?

"Let's check the levees," Irix chimed in. "Then we'll think about what we can do to prove it's them. Maybe do another ritual and have a stakeout to see who comes to reverse it?"

Once again I was shocked. This didn't seem like the sort of activity that would interest a demon, let alone a sex demon. Maybe Irix was more than the playboy he'd always seemed.

"Come on, girls." He waved us onward. "Let's hop in the stolen Audi and head out. We've got a lot of ground to cover, and a certain someone still needs to get laid before midnight."

"*Stolen?*" Jordan squeaked as we headed to the car.

* * *

LEVEES WEREN'T LIKE DAMS, and visiting them took considerably more time than I'd expected. They ran the huge length of the Mississippi River, canals, and major lakes all around the city. We made a quick decision and headed toward the levees lining the river.

At some points they were nearly twenty feet high. I'd assumed they'd be large concrete barriers, but, instead, they were tall grassy knolls with a blacktopped path or cement barriers on the wide, flat crown. The land side was steep, terraced with berms and banquettes as we climbed to the top. Once there, the view took my breath away. The Mississippi stretched a mile across, deceptively sluggish as it churned like a brown ribbon to the sea. In between us and the mighty river stood a naturalized flood plain with stands of willow, oak, and cypress. A heron took flight from a small marsh, and I watched him glide down to the riverside.

"Wow." It was all I could manage to say. Behind me was the churn of the city, in front the serenity of nature.

"There's an entire other set of levees on the Lake Pontchartrain side of the city," Jordan said. It had taken her a while to get over her outrage at our stolen conveyance, and I was glad to know she was still speaking to me.

I'd seen Lake Pontchartrain, coming in from the airport, and had been astounded by its size. The only bigger lakes I'd seen had been the Great Lakes along the border with Canada.

"This is going to take us more than one day," I commented, feeling overwhelmed at the sheer distance we'd need to cover. The task was too much, even if we just concentrated on the river side of the city.

"There's a streetcar track along the levee once we get into the French Quarter," Irix suggested. "Can you scan for energy from that distance? Or we could get some bikes and scan from the levee-top until the trail ends."

I got the feeling he didn't mean to "rent" the bicycles and glanced around guiltily at the nearby houses and shops. Irix jacking a car was bad enough. I didn't think I could stomach stealing someone's bike.

Jordan didn't seem to catch the nuance of Irix's comment. She pursed her lips, squinting toward the river.

We'd already looked at the section near Canal Street, eyeballing the stone sea-wall barrier from the winding promenade in front of the aquarium. The streetcar line was a good three-hundred feet from the river's edge. Smart, given the propensity for flooding, but far enough that detecting miniscule spells would be impossible. Jordan confirmed my suspicions with a shake of her head.

"It's the distance plus the speed of the streetcar. They don't go all that fast, but even ten miles per hour at that distance — I'd be lucky to catch anything. I don't think I could manage it while navigating a bike, either."

"We can't walk the whole thing." I voiced what everyone else was surely thinking. The river was like a snake, twisting and turning back on itself as it wound its way toward the gulf. Checking every section of the levee system would take weeks.

"We need to think of where the highest stress points are, and check those areas," Irix said. "Whoever is doing this probably doesn't have the resources to weaken the entire system, so they'll target the areas most likely to be hit hard during a storm."

Both Irix and Jordan turned to me expectantly. "What?" I felt like I was under a microscope.

"Elf." Irix announced, as if that clarified everything.

"Half elf," I replied. Not that I knew what the fuck he was getting at, but it was best to clarify these things.

"Water. Elves have a connection with the elements second only to the angels. You should be able to sense where the surge points would be."

Sheesh, what did they think I was? "Plants. I'm only half elf, and I only do plants. Besides, humans have some of the best data analysis I've ever seen. Why resort to magic when centuries of record keeping have done an accurate job of modeling these sorts of things?"

They both looked at me with blank expressions.

"I've got data on shifts in the Mississippi River delta over the last two-hundred years and changes in the wetlands," Jordan said. "But not storm surge points. I guess I can research it, but it would probably be quicker to use magic."

Oh, for crying out loud. I sighed and took out my cell phone, dialing my brother, Wyatt. He was in San Diego at some kind of internet security conference, which was ironic given that he made a shit ton of money hacking into websites.

"Hey, baby sis." Wyatt's voice was warm over the phone, and I felt a twinge of homesickness. I missed him. I missed my step sister, Nyalla. I missed my mom, who was not really my mom. What a fucked up life I had.

"Hey, bro. Can you do something for me? I need potential breach points in the levee system that protects New Orleans from the Mississippi River. I'm thinking if you check past breaches, and factor in improvements, especially those post Katrina, you'll find the weak spots."

"Sure. I'll bet the Army Corps of Engineers already has that, but I'll pull from some other sources and cross check. When do you need it?"

I winced. "Yesterday?"

Wyatt laughed, and I felt like we were kids again, riding bikes along our gravel driveway, challenging each other to jump homemade ramps and betting on who could clear the most distance. He was five years older than me, but I'd pushed myself to the limit to keep up with Wyatt and his buddies, just to prove I could. And I had kept up, so proud that I could run as fast and climb as high as the big boys. That was when I'd thought I was a human, like my brother —

before I realized that I was nothing more than a beautiful freak.

"Give me an hour, okay? Having fun with Darci?"

"Yeah," I said, reluctant to tell him what was really going on. "How's Nyalla doing, solo at Sam's house?"

"Good." I got the feeling he was also holding back on something. That stung a bit, but I understood. My stepsister had been through a lot. She was entitled to her secrets.

Wyatt promised to text me the results, and I ended the call, turning to face Irix and Jordan.

"Lunch. I'll have the info in an hour, and I'm starving. What's near here?"

"There's a bistro down on the corner." Jordan pointed at a tiny yellow building with not so much as a sign marking its designation. "They make an amazing roast duck sandwich with pepper jelly. Their muffalettas are good too."

"Or Mrs. B's," Irix added. Jordan made an "ooo" sound, her head nodding. "Buttermilk fried chicken and sweet-potato pecan pie."

"Oh yeah." Jordan practically danced. "Mrs. B's gets my vote."

I wondered how Irix knew so much about the city in the short time he'd been here. At two-thousand-years old, he'd probably hung out in New Orleans before, but I doubted Mrs. B's had been around for more than fifty years, max. I was too hungry to waste time grilling Irix about his past travels, so I waved them onward.

"Buttermilk fried chicken it is. I'm in your capable hands — both of you."

Irix grinned, draping an arm across my shoulder. "You'll never go wrong in my capable hands, elf-girl."

Mrs. B's was only a few blocks away. Its brick façade was painted dark mustard and accented with forest-green shutters. The black wrought-iron handrails were less ornate than ones I'd seen in the French Quarter — more in keeping with the sedate air of the building. Mustard paint aside, the place had a severity about it, like an authoritarian aunt who had no problem swatting naughty children with a wooden spoon.

Inside, the place bustled with speedy efficiency. The waitress ushered us to a plain pine table with ladder-back chairs and smoothed her tightly coiffed hair, trying not to stare at Irix as we looked over the menu.

"I've got it, my treat," Irix announced, ordering enough food for a small army. His treat. Right. More like Bank of America's treat.

I forgot the larceny that was procuring my lunch as soon as the food arrived. The signature buttermilk fried chicken smelled heavenly of sage. Beside the platter was another filled with crawfish cakes, a bowl of red beans, and a tray with six broiled oysters — bacon and golden breadcrumbs sprinkled on top.

"Not much on vegetables, are you," I commented, snatching a chicken leg off the platter.

"Life is too short to eat something that can't move of its own volition," Irix teased. "If you must, you can graze on the lawn out back for dessert."

"Hmmm, grass or sweet-potato pecan pie? Such a hard decision."

All conversation was lost as our attention turned to the cornucopia of food. I saved room for a slice of pie and swapped my sweet tea for a hot cup of chicory coffee.

Jordan groaned, scooping up a stray pecan from her plate. "Back to business, now that we're all fat and happy. How are we going to prove any of this is Crimson Moon? I know you suggested fix something and do a stakeout, but I'm not sure I can get Bev to agree to another ritual."

Ugh, that woman hated me, and the feeling was mutual.

"Can you go around her? Ten of your coven were willing to work with me last night, maybe they will agree to again."

Jordan shook her head. "That would get me kicked out of the group. Having a few friends over for a personal working is one thing, assembling a group for a ritual affecting public property is another. I'd be flouting my priestess' authority."

"Then do it yourself," Irix commented, sipping his sweet tea. He'd added sugar. I expected him to go into a diabetic coma at any moment.

"I don't have enough power to do it on my own," Jordan confessed. "Things like this require the energy of a group — the more the better."

"I meant her," he winked at me. "That half-breed elf-girl who hogged all the oysters."

I didn't hog all the oysters. And there is no way I could fix a levee or a dam solo.

"Plants. This half-breed elf-girl doesn't fix dirt, and whatever else that barrier is made of. Point me at a tree, and I'll give it a shot; for a levee or a dam repair, you're going to need to call someone else. And as for the oysters, I seem to recall we each had two."

"Elves must be lacking skills in the basic math department, because you ate four, leaving poor Jordan and me with only one a piece. And yes, you can do dirt. It's part of the earth element. Broaden your horizons, elf-girl."

"I did *not* eat four oysters," I squealed, ignoring the part of our argument that addressed my magical abilities, or lack of. I was far more offended that I'd just been accused of being greedy.

"Umm, you did eat four." Jordan grinned. "Shoveled them down like a woman starved."

Shit. I couldn't control myself when it came to oysters. Those things are like crack. "Okay, okay. I have a thing for oysters. Just make sure you don't have your fingers in the way or you might lose them."

"I'm just hoping to put them to good use tonight."

"My fingers or the oysters?" I couldn't manage to curb my saucy mouth.

"Both."

A faint curl of pheromones caressed me, and I felt myself lean closer to Irix. I wasn't the only one affected. Jordan was forgetting to breathe, and our waitress was stalking over, not-so-subtly undoing a button on her blouse. Time to change the subject before we all wound up naked and on top of the incubus.

"Maybe I can fix another tree grove instead? Or the fresh-water marsh we looked at yesterday?"

Jordan blinked, taking a deep breath as she dragged her eyes away from Irix. "There's a problem with that. We could fix another grove, but who's to say it's one Crimson Moon wants dead? Same with the water. The spell was on the dam, but it looked pretty inaccessible. If we can find a spell on the levee somewhere, that would be our best chance to try and catch these guys."

Damn. How was I supposed to pull this off? My flight left in three days. It's not like I had a lot of opportunity to fail and learn. If I couldn't manage this in the next forty-eight hours, I'd run out of time. I couldn't afford to re-book my flight home, and if I missed it, I'd be stuck hitchhiking, or driving Irix's stolen Audi.

"I'll help you."

I turned to Irix in surprise. He was a sex demon. Outside of energy transference, I had no idea how he was going to help me.

"Sex demons aren't all that great at breaking spells or shuffling atoms around to create molecules, but I know how it's done." He motioned the waitress over for more tea. "I have no idea if elves do these things like we do. They were schooled by the angels, so there's a good chance we have similarities. I'll share what I know, and we'll see if you can make it happen. There's no reason you shouldn't be able to do this sort of thing, elf-girl."

There was an odd sort of warmth in my lower abdomen at his words. He had faith in me to do what I couldn't even imagine. He'd stand by my side, and if I failed, I somehow knew he wouldn't condemn me for it.

"I'll do my best," I vowed.

"I wish I knew more about Crimson Moon," Jordan lamented. "It would help if we knew several of the key players and could put some sort of surveillance on them."

There were four of us, including Darci. Who the hell was supposed to do this surveillance, even if we did know who they were?

"You should call your vampire friend," Irix suggested.

"Ourson? How did you know. . .?" My voice trailed off as I struggled to recall our past conversations. No, I was sure I'd never mentioned Ourson to Irix beyond my running in panic from him after the incident behind the goth club.

"How do you think he got your address to return the boots and your phone?" Irix asked, leaning back in his chair and sipping his overly sweet tea. "I ensured he knew what a poor decision he'd made that evening."

I'd suspected that Irix had been the one that delivered the smack down on Ourson. As unfair as it had been, I felt my heartbeat quicken at the thought that the demon had bothered to avenge me.

"Vampire?" Jordan squeaked. Poor woman. First Irix's stolen car, then this.

"Yeah. The player in the goth club isn't exactly human. Neither are his friends. It's all right. He's harmless."

"Harmless? He takes women out into a back alley and drinks their blood. How is that harmless?"

Shit. How to explain this so Jordan wouldn't totally freak and start roaming dance clubs with Darci's wooden stake and silver coins in tow.

"They only take a small amount — less than you'd give at a blood drive. It doesn't hurt. Actually, it feels pretty good. Think of him as a giant mosquito with a side shot of X."

Jordan regarded me with narrowed eyes. "Easy for you to say. It's not like the vampires are chowing down on your neck."

I swept my hair aside and leaned over to show her my neck. "He did. Didn't hurt any more than a pinch at first, and then all I felt was happy-floaty. You wouldn't even notice the bite afterwards. It's all like a kinky sort of make-out session."

I was stretching the truth a bit, but I trusted that Ourson and his buddies wouldn't actually hurt anyone.

Jordan frowned for a long moment, before giving me a tense nod. "All right, then. How would this Ourson be able to help?"

Irix had been watching our exchange with great amusement. Balancing his chair on the rear two legs, he took a long drink of tea before speaking. "Vampire families are territorial and, unlike the humans they once were, they have a natural life expectancy of thousands of years. Trust me, they know every powerful group in their territory — political or magical. Ask them to find out who these Crimson Moon people are, and what they're doing."

"I'll owe them a favor." I wrinkled my nose, not liking to think of what a vampire might request of me.

Irix waved a dismissive hand. "Pfft. Everyone owes favors. That's the way things work. You just have to word your acceptance correctly so that their request can't go against any previous vow. Otherwise you'll find yourself on someone's bad side."

The thought of owing a vampire a favor filled me with dread. I considered Ourson a friend, but I was still a half-elf, hiding who I was from him. If he knew . . . but there was so much riding on this that it was worth the risk.

I picked up my phone just as it buzzed with an incoming text message. Wyatt, and there was a map attached to his text. Bypassing the message, I scrolled through my contacts and hit dial.

The vampire picked up on the first ring, and I steeled myself for what I was about to do.

"Ourson? It's Amber. I need a big favor."

CHAPTER 20

I should have been exhausted by the time I rocked into Darci's apartment, but I was oddly energized. Each of Wyatt's highlighted spots had revealed some sort of magical spell. They were cleverly worked, according to Irix — just waiting for a trigger to activate a failure. The difficulty was that the levee system stretched for miles, and the spell faults were along huge stretches. It would be quite a challenge to repair them, even if I had the faintest idea how to.

"Grab an umbrella," Darci told me the moment I walked through the door. "Sorry to ruin your vacation, but we're probably going to have rain all the rest of the week."

I felt a fissure of alarm run through me. "Hurricane?" Shit. As if I didn't need any more pressure.

"Oh no. There's a couple of low-grade tropical storms tracking toward the Bahamas. We'll probably just get the spin off. Clouds and light rain off and on."

Thank God. I tore past her, shedding clothes as I went. We were all supposed to go out tonight — Saints and Sinners in the French Quarter. I was hardly party ready with my swamp-stained legs and lank, sweaty hair.

"Give me twenty!" I shouted, racing for the shower.

I was out in ten, hair dried, makeup applied, and flirty blue halter dress on by the time the taxi pulled to the front door. We were meeting Gabriella and Erica there. Jordan had bowed out for the night to research spells. I felt a bit guilty about her absence, but knew she wanted to do everything she could to contribute to our ritual tomorrow. It wouldn't be much of a ritual — me trying to fix a bunch of concrete and earthwork levees with Irix's help. Jordan had volunteered to try and raise as much beneficial energy as possible to assist me. I appreciated her offer, but had a feeling deep in my gut that this was going to all come down to me.

Ourson was hard at work tracking down the members of Crimson Moon, along with their strengths and reputed powers. It left me a bit adrift this evening, nothing to do but wait and try and gather as much energy as possible. I'd have a fun evening with Darci and her friends — nice and relaxing.

Who was I kidding? I was full of nervous anxiety over Irix's ultimatum and the eventual end to this night. Yeah, I had plenty of time to get laid before midnight, but I'd set my course, resolved to have my one night with the demon I'd been craving since the moment I first laid eyes on him.

I was terrified. One night. And after today, it would be even more difficult to let him go. The easy rapport we'd developed, the flirtatious banter, the air of expectation — it was delicious, and I didn't want it to end. Was I making a huge mistake in sleeping with him tonight? Or was this the best I could ever hope for?

"You look hot," Darci pronounced, giving me a quick hug before climbing in the taxi. She was the one who looked hot with her straightened black hair shimmering like a sheet of silk past her shoulders, and an asymmetrical mini dress in tangerine. Not many women could pull off wearing that color, but Darci looked like a long-legged sorbet — good enough to eat.

"Back at cha," I replied, scooting in beside her.

The taxi inched its way through the French Quarter and Bourbon Street, letting us out a few blocks away. We edged through the crowds filling the streets and sidewalks, coming to a creamy yellow, balconied building with patio seating and the ubiquitous green window shutters.

"It's a bit of a tourist trap," Darci warned. "We'll meet the girls, grab a drink and check the place out. Afterwards, if you want, we can head somewhere a bit more off the map."

I *was* a tourist, so I gawked and practically skipped up the sidewalk with excitement. The building had formerly housed a bordello back when the whole area was a red-light district. My kind of place, even if the main draw was a celebrity owner.

Darci pulled open the door. "I'm warning you — it's red. Really, really red."

She wasn't joking. "Holy shit. My eyes hurt just looking at it." I squinted to see if I could locate Gabriella and Erica at the bar.

Wainscoting, trim, leather-inlaid panels, leather seats — all red. The lighting reflected off the walls, bathing all the patrons in a crimson glow. Even the marble bar and table-tops looked faintly pink. It was like an optimist's version of hell — a really garish, horny optimist.

"There!"

Darci grabbed my arm and pulled me to the bar, waving at Gabriella. Erica was beside her, trying to ignore a sunburned man who had white rings around his eyes where his sunglasses had provided more UV protection than whatever he'd applied to the rest of his face. He looked like a reverse raccoon. Turning to speak to Erica, he nearly pitched off the barstool, sloshing half the contents of his margarita onto his lap. He didn't seem to notice.

It was mean, but I left Erica to her inebriated admirer and scooted between her and Gabriella, ordering the most appropriate drink I could think of — a bloody Mary.

Two drinks later, the room seemed a bit less red, and Raccoon Man less annoying. Gavin had arrived, and Darci had moved further down the bar to engage in what appeared to be some very seductive conversation with him. The booze flowed, but no amount of alcohol blinded me to the attractive man in club leather stalking purposefully across the room.

"Coming your way, Amber," Gabriella announced with a nudge. "If you don't want him, toss him my way."

Not happening. "Trust me, you don't want him. He bites, and the whole experience is pretty unsatisfying."

Gabriella ignored me, smiling brightly at Ourson and tossing her dark hair over one shoulder. The vampire's eyes flickered to her, lingering on the bronzed skin at her neck. Oh well. Can't say I didn't warn her.

With a deep breath, Ourson turned to me. "Do you have a moment? Can we talk in private?"

"Sure." We walked closer to the door, while Gabriella pouted prettily and eyed my companion.

"I've got the names for you." Ourson slipped me a folded sheet of paper. "Some of them were quite a surprise. They're a secretive group and include a few bankers and a real estate investor."

"Real estate?" I interjected. "Why would someone who owns property in the city want to see it devalued and destroyed, regardless of ley lines?"

"Insurance, but he's got other reasons too." Ourson waved a dismissive hand. "Anyway, that's not why I'm here. There's someone in their group I can't get an ID on. He's the power behind this. Showed up about a month ago and took control. From what I can tell, he's highly respected and admired."

The mage. If Jordan and Irix were correct, he'd be using magical skills he learned in Hel to assist the group. But what was his motivation? Simple power?

"Can you set up a meeting with their head guy?"

Ourson started. "Why would you want to meet with him?"

I felt stupidly naïve admitting that I hoped there could be some middle ground here. If Crimson Moon wanted power, and I could somehow convince Bon Nuit to share, this whole thing would end. Although, I doubted 'share' was a word in Bev's vocabulary.

"I'm a succubus. Maybe I can convince him to see things my way."

Ourson grinned. "Will do, but the meeting might not be voluntary. You have any problems with that?"

A demon wouldn't, but by this point, Ourson had clearly discovered I was a bit different than the others. "Let's try voluntary first and see how it goes. And thanks for all your help on this."

"I've got backup taken care of, too," Ourson announced.

I'd arranged for a vampire to stake out each section of the levee I fixed, watching and apprehending whoever came to reverse my repair. God only knows what kind of favor the vampires would ask in return, but it's not like the four of us could be everywhere at once. Besides, Darci and Jordan could hardly take down a human who had this kind of magical power at his disposal. Asking them to fire a gun in the city limits was out of the question, so now I had a vampire goon squad.

"You rock, buddy. Can I buy you a drink?" As soon as the words were out of my mouth I regretted it. The vampire's eyes moved past me to fix on Gabriella.

"Your friend?"

It's a free world. And it wasn't like he would harm her any more than the insects that plagued this town in summer.

"Don't let Darci see you picking up our friend or she'll stake you," I warned. "Be respectful. No bashing Gabriella's head against the brick like you did with me. Please, thank you, and ask for her number when you're done. Got it?"

Ourson winked. "Got it."

Five minutes later the pair were out the door, and ten minutes after, Gabriella was staggering back in, a huge grin on her face. Darci had remained oblivious to the whole thing, practically in Gavin's lap at the end of the bar.

"Told you," I said to Gabriella.

She picked up her beer and saluted me with it. "Most fun I've had all week. He asked for my number too."

I bit my snarky tongue and smiled at the girl encouragingly. "Glad you guys hit it off."

I bought the girls another round. Erica scooted further from Raccoon Man, who was nearly facedown on the bar. Darci and Gavin rejoined us, and Gabriella basked in the afterglow of her unwitting encounter with a vampire. I was laughing over some joke Gavin had made when a familiar feeling slid across my skin, like warm silk. I shivered and looked over to see Irix. He was leaning casually against the wall just inside the door, legs and arms both crossed. My time was up.

CHAPTER 21

Irix's eyes met mine, then he deliberately looked down at his watch. For a brief second I wondered who he'd stolen it from.

"Last minute doubts?" Darci whispered in my ear.

More like fears. It was one o'clock, and my time of reckoning had come.

"I don't know whether I'll be home tonight or not." I had no idea how this was going to play out. Would we get a hotel room? Have sex in the stolen Audi? Would he want me gone the moment we'd finished, or would I at least get one night to sleep in his arms?

Darci kissed me on the cheek. "Text me. And stop freaking out."

I gave her hand a quick squeeze and stepped away from the bar, my stomach in knots. Freaking out was a gross understatement. I wondered briefly how sexy Irix would think I was if I puked on his feet.

"A bar full of randy tourists and you still couldn't find anyone?" Irix asked, looking around at the crowded room. "How about that guy?"

Raccoon Man was trying to get Erica's attention by pawing the air beside her. Ugh.

"My friend already staked a claim on that one, and Gabriella scored the only vampire in the bar earlier this evening. Doesn't leave much else. Slim pickings tonight."

Irix tucked my hand in the crook of his arm and led me out onto the sidewalk. "Well, you've got a busy day tomorrow, and I intend to make sure you're successful. Let's get you powered up, and back to full strength."

That was the least romantic thing anyone had ever said to me. Getting "powered up" wasn't the tiniest bit sexy. I guess I needed to get used to this; after tonight, we'd be coolly platonic. My stomach twisted even more.

"Come on, Amber. Where would you prefer we do this?"

He sounded like we were off to sign contracts or conduct a routine business transaction, like it didn't matter at all to him. Irritation, trepidation, and longing all warred within me. I couldn't do this. I couldn't. Not if my one night was going to be all about "powering me up".

"Maui."

There. That should put the whole thing off for quite a while. We'd argue, I'd get another extension and head off to that Bliss club. Irix sighed and gave me an exasperated look.

"How about somewhere within the city limits?"

I tried to think of some place that might have a six-month waiting list, but knowing him, he'd charm his way right in the door.

"Am I not good enough for Maui? Perhaps *you'd* be satisfied to get it on behind a dumpster in some back alley, but I'm not. Maui."

He quickly bit back a smile. "I can see I'm just going to have to take matters into my own hands."

He tightened his hold on my arm and hurried me down the street. I didn't resist, and I'll admit a thrill went through me at his words. This was a bit sexier than "powering up".

"What are you doing? Where are we going?"

"I'm not telling you. You'll just argue and come up with a million reasons why you don't want to go there or do that."

I hesitated a step, and he halted. My uncertainty must have shown in my face, because his gaze softened, and he let go of my arm.

"Trust me, Amber."

I did. It was me I didn't trust. What tonight would bring was inevitable, though. I might as well enjoy it and stop fretting over the aftermath. I nodded and reached out to take his hand. The grin that lit up his face made it all worthwhile.

"Okay. Although I still would prefer Maui."

He laughed, and we strolled down the street hand-in-hand.

"You're a pain in the ass, elf-girl."

I skipped a step to keep up, squeezing his hand. "I can be. If you like that sort of thing, I'd be happy to oblige."

His hand gripped mine back. "Be careful what you offer, little half-breed. You have no idea the things I enjoy."

His tone was light and teasing, but I shivered, reminded that this was a demon I was playing with. Too bad there would only be one night for us, because a part of me really did want to discover all the things he enjoyed.

CHAPTER 22

We walked for a bit through the French Quarter, pausing to listen to a street musician on his horn. After a few blocks, Irix led me to a long, three-story, brick house with flickering natural gas lanterns in wrought-iron hangers at each corner. Forest-green shutters closed the windows off from prying eyes. The long row of fencing matched the shutters and equally ensured privacy in what I assumed was the garden area. In addition to several traditional-style locks, the main entrance had a magical one, opening only when Irix sent a trickle of energy through the metal bolt.

The door opened to a huge foyer with ornate white trim and elegant wood furniture. Off to the right, double-pocket doors showed a room decorated with an eclectic mix of Victorian and modern. Gas light fixtures flanked a small unlit fireplace; leather couches sat on scarlet oriental rugs. The walls were covered with gold brocade wallpaper and dotted with landscape oil paintings.

"Whose house is this?" I was a bit concerned. Irix seemed to make a habit of appropriating things that didn't belong to him. I didn't want the angry owners confronting us with breaking and entering charges, or, worse, discover them butchered in a back closet.

"Mine."

Was he lying, or did he really consider all his stolen goods to be his own? Demons weren't well known for truthfulness. Before I could question him further, Irix walked toward the back of the foyer and into an enormous, modern kitchen. I followed and watched him pull out wine glasses, and a few other items.

"Follow me."

He headed back to the foyer and up the sweeping stairs. I hesitated, realizing what he probably had in mind. He could have been a little more erotic than 'follow me', but at least he intended to give me a glass of wine first. I took a deep breath to strengthen my resolve and followed him up.

By the time we'd reached the end of the hallway on the third floor, I was confused. We'd passed several serviceable-looking bedrooms. Where the heck was he going? Silent, he handed me the wine glasses then made a smooth leap, catching a little knotted rope hanging from the ceiling. A square pulled free, and as he landed, a wooden ladder unfolded. He took the glasses from my hands and climbed.

I waited a second for him to turn on a light, and when none appeared, I followed him up. Hot, humid air hit me as my head popped up above the attic floor.

"Over here."

My eyes adjusted to the dim light, and I realized Irix was standing in front of a large window. The attic had three sets of dormers, giving the roof added height and allowing faint light from outside into the room. With a twist of his wrist, the window opened outward like a small French door.

"Be careful. There's a ridge right in front of the opening, to keep the rain from leaking in. Don't trip."

Jazz music filled my ears, and the tang of the river surrounded me as I carefully made my way through the opening. The incubus' hand found mine, and I heard the glasses clink as he led me across the rooftop terrace to a sofa. The lights of the city spread out to the rear. In front of us churned the Mississippi River, only a half block away, illuminated by lights along the shore and the occasional boat. A breeze lifted my hair, and I realized that the temperature up here was about ten degrees less than at street level. After settling me on the sofa, Irix sat down beside me and opened the top of a small stool to reveal a cooler.

"I can turn on the lights if you like, but it detracts from the view." He opened a bottle of champagne and skillfully poured it into the two glasses, shoving the bottle back into the ice of the cooler before handing me one.

"I like it here in the dark." I did. It was private somehow, like we were invisible to the world. Just a demon and I, drinking champagne and looking out at the city.

"How did you wind up with a house like this?" I was half afraid to know the answer.

"A friend left it to me when she died. It's been interesting juggling the title around since she passed away a century ago, but I wanted to keep it. Lots of good memories here."

"Oh." So nothing nefarious then, unless he was the one who instigated her 'passing away'. I didn't get that from his tone of voice, though.

He turned to face me, putting his drink down. "I thought it a strange coincidence that you chose to run here to escape me, when it's the only place that I own property. New Orleans is like a second home to me."

It was odd. If I'd believed in some kind of divine intervention, in fate, then I would have read all sorts of things into this. I didn't believe in that sort of thing. Or did I?

"Amber, what's wrong? I show up from Hel thinking I'm

just going to help a young half-breed with her skills, and make sure she doesn't kill anyone in the process. Instead, I find a rebellious succubus who refuses to do anything I ask, and is determined to deny, or kill, a portion of who she is."

"I don't want that part of myself. I want to be human, or just a half-elf, but I don't want anything to do with this monster inside me. She hurts people; she uses them. That's not me."

"It *is* you. There is no this half or that half; there is only you. Once you figure that out, you can stop trying to make yourself into something you're not."

There had always been a monster inside me, one who killed the man I'd believed was my father. I thought I'd conquered her, only to have her come roaring to life again a few months ago. But that wasn't my only problem.

"I'll never love. Every man I sleep with becomes uninteresting to me the next day. There will never be a relationship, a marriage with children for me, only a string of one-night stands."

"That's crap, Amber. You love your brother, your sister, your friend Darci. You love plenty of people. You're kind, loyal, and caring. So you'll never have the traditional marriage. How many humans get that anyway? And how many are truly happy with it? Sometimes the life you get isn't the one you wanted. That doesn't make what you have any less wonderful, just different."

I sat in silence, a huge lump in my throat. He couldn't understand. I'd live for thousands of years, watching my friends and family die. I could never have what they had. At least he had other demons back in Hel — a home he belonged in, people just like him to live his life alongside. I had no one. I wasn't an elf, wasn't human, wasn't a full demon — just a beautiful freak; lonely and scared.

I felt his arm around me, his hand rubbing down my back.

"I won't give you my energy if you don't want it. We'll figure out a way to work the magic on the levees tomorrow without it. There are other covens in the city — maybe you can use their energy in a ritual. If you really hate this part of yourself, then I'm not going to try to force you to accept it."

He stood up and walked to the edge of the roof, his shoulders slumped. I felt like shit. Once again I'd hurt some guy — this time a two-thousand-year-old demon. I thought back on what Jordan had said, about my demon energy fueling my elf powers. Maybe that's why the elf in me had always been so silent. I was starving her out too. That part of me I'd always thought was human? Maybe that was the real Amber — the Amber that happened when I stopped thinking of myself as half this and half that, and just *was*.

My eyes drank in the sight of Irix — the way his shirt strained across the muscles of his back and shoulders, the way his pants hugged his backside. The physical attraction I felt for him at that moment had nothing to do with pheromones, nothing to do with any sex-demon magic. It was more than the simple attraction of a woman for a man. I found him irresistible — all of him. The crooked smile, the faint dimple in his left cheek, the way his eyes became molten gold as they looked at me. He was sexy when he was angry, sexy when he was teasing, sexy when he was gentle and caring. I loved his laugh, his quick humor. I loved his sense of honor, so unexpected in a demon. I loved that he was smart, that he could keep up with me, even best me, when it came to knowledge and intelligence.

I loved him.

"Your fichus is dying."

Irix turned around and watched as I stood and walked to the row of plants in a tall box. They served as a nice divider between his terrace and the steeper section of the roof, but the normal deep green of the leaves was spotted with brown, the edges curled inward. I could see this even in the dim light — actually feel the imbalance in the plants. My fingers caressed the leaves, following the stems down to touch the soil. Uneven water supply, excess phosphorus, burning of the leaves from midday watering. I felt Irix move to stand behind me, and I inhaled deep to catch his unusual dark-chocolate scent.

"What should I do?" he asked.

The leaves straightened, brown brightening to lush green. Pink flowers burst from the depths of the foliage, unfolding to drink in the night.

"Fire your gardener." I turned around to face him. "And kiss me."

He leaned close, tracing my bottom lip. "Here?" he whispered. The finger moved to caress my breast, brushing the raised nipple with the lightest of touches. "Here?" His hand smoothed down my waist and stomach, down my thigh then back up the skirt of my dress to rest between my legs. "Or here? Where should I kiss you, Amber?"

Damn. He was just the sexiest thing I'd ever known.

"All of the above."

The playboy façade cracked, and for a brief second I saw the complexity beneath the beautiful face. Lighthearted but intense, dangerous but kind, controlled but wildly abandoned.

Irix wrapped an arm around my waist, but instead of pulling me toward him, he pushed, lifting me upward with a hand cupped around my ass. I gasped, feeling the hard concrete of the roof ledge under me, my back pushing the planter, fichus and all, further back. His mouth crashed over mine, his hands moving upward to keep me from plunging backward off the roof. Nothing was keeping the planter in place, though. I felt it shift, felt the sudden absence of it against me, then heard a splintering crash and several yells.

My chest shook, and I giggled against his lips, the strangeness of laughing while being kissed just as amusing as us nearly braining some poor passerby with a potted plant. Irix began to laugh too. He tilted his head, resting his forehead against mine while still holding me tight on the roof ledge.

The danger of it all — being suspended three stories up with only Irix between me and a nasty death on asphalt and concrete. I trusted him, trusted that he wouldn't let me go.

"You've got a lot of kissing to do. Better get cracking there, demon."

He caught his breath on the exhale, and once again sealed my lips with his. His mouth was just as much of a contradiction as he was — both soft and firm against mine. I opened for him — lips allowing his tongue entry, and legs giving him room to push his thigh through to rub against me.

My hands weren't occupied, so I got to work, pulling his shirt free from his pants, and yanking the buttons loose one by one. Diving under the silk, I ran my hands over his waist and back, feeling the warmth of his skin. God, he felt good. So damned good. My fingers traced every muscle, felt along each rib, and around to the indent of his center back. But touching wasn't enough. I wanted more of him than my fingers could ever know.

Breaking off our kiss, I bent my head and ran my tongue along the firm ridge of his collarbone, nipping and licking my way down the muscles of his chest.

"Fuck! Amber, damn it all, I'm going to drop you."

His skin shivered against my mouth, and I felt his arms grip me tighter, adjusting as I curved my back to go lower.

"Amber. I'm serious. Besides, I'm the one who's supposed to be kissing here."

Spoilsport. He did have a point though, I and really didn't want to test the limits of his demon strength with a long drop at my back. I straightened against him and lifted my mouth to his. One quick, crushing kiss, and then his glorious lips were off to other territory, nibbling along my jaw. He was clearly headed south, although how he was going to accomplish all that other kissing with me arched backwards off a roof was beyond me. Logistics flew right out of my head as he pulled my earlobe between his teeth and whispered his oh-so-indecent intentions.

Images of him licking his way down my body, of my legs over his shoulders, heels against his upper back filled my mind and sent my heart on a wild path. I moved my thigh from between his legs to wrap around his waist, digging a heel into his firm ass. This brought the erection I'd been working on with my leg into optimal position. Right where I wanted it to end up. Later. Much later. After lots and lots of kissing. Anticipation roared through me, and I couldn't help rubbing myself against him, glorying in the shudder that coursed through him at my motion.

"Sofa." The one word was guttural, as if he'd had to force it upward from the depths of his body. I murmured agreement, and he yanked me from the ledge, sitting down on the sofa with me on his lap. My dress was up around my waist, giving me a naughty idea. As Irix moved to push me onto my back, I shifted with a quick twist of my hips, bringing him down on the sofa instead.

"And how exactly am I supposed to do my kissing from underneath you?"

His eyes danced with amusement, and my lips, swollen from his attentions, turned up in response.

"Use your imagination. I'm sure you can figure something out."

Just in case he needed a little inspiration, I lifted the hem of my dress, crossing my arms as I pulled it over my head. With a flick of my wrist it landed half in the open attic window. The cool river air tingled across my skin, tightening my already pebbled nipples. The incubus' golden gaze snagged on them with hunger.

"Come here," he commanded.

I was sitting upright on him, my thighs pinning his arms to his side. He could easily free himself, but I think he was enjoying the illusion of weakness.

"Nope." I rocked against him, feeling his body tense beneath my own. His pants strained with the force of his erection, pushing the zipper against me. The seam of my lacy thong underwear rubbed along my sensitive flesh, enhancing my enjoyment as I ground myself against him. Irix fell into the rhythm, lifting his hips in time to my thrusts. My breathing came hard and fast. I tilted my head backward, feeling the brush of my hair against my naked back. Just a little more. . . .

"Oh no you don't."

Irix slipped his hands free from under my thighs with minimal effort and lifted me against him as he rose to his feet. I wrapped my legs around his waist, protesting in a stream of half-words and curses as he carried me through the open window and down the ladder. I have no idea how the fuck he managed it all. Not once did he stumble, or catch any of my body against the narrow openings. Before I could wonder further, my back was on the softest featherbed I'd ever felt. Irix loomed over me, his eyes stormy, his arms roped with muscles.

"Damn," I whispered, running my hand down his chest and arching my back to resume that lovely contact that had nearly brought me to climax.

He leaned back and placed a hand firmly on my stomach. "Oh no you don't. I'm not done kissing you yet."

"Then hurry the fuck up."

I pushed my body in vain against the hand that held me still. He scowled, eyes betraying the humor beneath the false anger.

"Language, my dear girl. Language."

And that was all he said for quite a while as he bent his head to my breasts.

I closed my eyes and just swam in sensation. His soft hair against my skin, his tongue flicking and sucking then moving to nuzzle the underside of my breasts. The fabric of his pants was harsh against the inside of my thighs, and once again I wrapped my legs tight around him. He murmured something into my skin and leaned his weight on me, pushing me deep into the softness of the feather bed. But there was something more than physical occurring between us.

My hands gripped his shoulders, tracing along his muscles and digging in with my short nails. I'd felt something within the two of us align, like a train preparing to couple. His mouth continued its journey, tickling along my ribs and stomach. Unable to reach his shoulders, I tangled my fingers through his hair, marveling at the softness, at the deep scent of sweet and spice that my hands released.

"Take off your pants." As hot as he was, shirt untucked and sliding half off his shoulders, I really wanted to see him naked. All I had left on was a tiny scrap of lace around my hips. His mostly-dressed state was extremely unfair.

"Not yet." He moved upright, pulling his hair free from my hands and my legs from around his waist.

Terribly unfair, but I forgot all that the moment his hands gripped my knees, pulling them wide as he bent his head between my legs.

There was no way I could think straight. All I could do was swim in the sensation of his lips and tongue on the most sensitive portions of my body. I fisted the sheets, and squirmed against his arms, unable to control my body as it desperately tried to maximize contact. Again and again he teased me, flicking and sucking, biting and kissing, spearing me with his tongue. Each time I hovered on the verge of climax only to have it slide away, until I was pleading incoherently.

Finally he took pity on me, using fingers and mouth to drive me to the edge. My body tensed unbearably, every muscle tight and quivering, then I relaxed in abandonment a second before the wave rocked me. It was like a slow-moving jolt of electricity spreading from my sex out to the very tips of my fingers. Waves receding and advancing. Crashing across me then slipping gently out to sea.

I opened my eyes, feeling exposed and vulnerable as my body poured out all my secrets along with my passion. Irix watched me, and his expression was something I'd carry in my memories forever. No matter what tomorrow morning brought, I could always close my eyes, see his face and know this one moment was worth a lifetime of loneliness.

"Amber, I . . . you are . . . beautiful."

What had he meant to say? Something about himself? I didn't have a chance to ask before he again covered my body with his own. His hands, his mouth, I felt as though he were all over me, deep inside me, although we hadn't yet joined.

"Pants. Off. Now." I panted, tugging at his dark brown hair.

"All right. All right." He laughed, and stood up, performing the most unselfconsciously erotic strip show I'd ever seen. The silk shirt slid from his shoulders onto the floor, and his hands unbuckled the belt, leaving it attached to the pants as he slid them down. Naked underneath. I caught my breath at his beauty. Thick and long, curving upward and begging for my hand. He slid the scrap of lace from my hips, then climbed up on the bed — on his knees and towering over me. Unable to resist, I reached out a finger and traced it along his length, feeling him pulse and jerk as I worked my way slowly forward. Reaching the end, I collected the pearl at the tip of his sex and brought it to my mouth.

"I can't wait any longer." His voice was desperate.

"Then don't."

He crawled over the top of me, arms supporting his weight as I reached down to position him at my core. For a demon who couldn't wait any longer, he was surprisingly restrained, easing into me as I tilted my hips upward. My body stretched around him, tight but yielding as he pressed forward. His pelvis touched mine, and we both hesitated, as if frozen in time. Then he bent his head, licking along my bottom lip as he moved his hips.

I gasped, and he took that opportunity to fuse his mouth to mine, increasing his rhythm. I mirrored his movements with my own thrusts. Faster. Deeper. We gained momentum, and our kisses grew frenzied. The slide of our bodies against the sheets was deafening to my ears, accompanied by the occasional moan. Lifting himself upright on his forearms, Irix adjusted his angle, and our rhythm broke into a chaotic, wild series of deep thrusts. I opened my eyes as the tension built deep within me, wanting to see Irix above me as I came.

The orgasm rocked me, as powerful as the first. As I clenched tight along his length, I felt him thicken, his body shuddering as he followed me over the edge. His face was naked with hunger, the teasing playboy gone and someone raw and primal in his place. Jaw locked tight, eyes shut with his head dropped back, he shuddered, pouring himself into me, and I felt a surge of energy lighting me up from the inside. Irix's energy. I'd forgotten the purpose of our joining — I'd been so focused on the pleasure our bodies brought to each other.

His eyes met mine, slightly unfocused, but more open

than I'd ever seen. For another second, I saw the real Irix in all his complexity, and then he grinned down at me, pulling out as he collapsed beside me on the bed.

I closed my eyes and floated in the gently ebbing tide of our passion. The warmth of Irix's body, the weight of his arm across my waist, the feel of his leg entwined with mine — it all surrounded me, cradled me. The mingled scent of us filled my nose. I wanted time to freeze, to preserve forever a feeling so precious. Worries about what tomorrow might bring were shoved aside so they wouldn't mar the beauty of something that, for me, was beyond the physical, beyond 'powering me up' for my work tomorrow.

"Hmmm." I couldn't help the soft noise of contentment that spilled from my lips.

Lips caressed my shoulder. Irix chuckled against my ear, pulled me tight against him. And I floated in the perfection of the moment.

* * *

I woke with the gentle breeze from the ceiling fan caressing my skin. Rolling over, I knew Irix was still beside me before I even saw him. I could actually feel his presence. We'd somehow pushed the sheets off the end of the bed in our sleep, and he sprawled naked across the mattress. The glory of his olive-skinned body made me catch my breath, but it was his face that entranced me. He seemed so innocent in sleep, like a child without a care in the world. Dark lashes brushed their tips against high cheekbones, and his lips were soft and open as he breathed. Unexpectedly, his eyes popped open, and I found myself drowning in their pools of amber.

Something odd flashed across his face, an unusual second of vulnerability before he closed in to kiss me. I pulled back in alarm, and the walls came down.

"Morning breath," I muttered, covering my mouth with my hand. Mine, not his. Of course, leave it to an incubus to *not* have morning breath.

His eyes warmed, and he grinned as he snatched me and pulled me to him. Before I could protest, he'd yanked my hand aside and kissed me. Anxiety fled and desire took its place as his tongue explored my mouth. Demons. Kinky pervs all of them, me included.

"Elves do not have 'morning breath', he told me, allowing me a moment to drag much-needed air into my lungs. "They always smell of trees or the sun or rain — whatever their environment."

"And what do I smell like? Bed sheets?" I asked, tracing the lines of muscles on his chest with my fingers. He shivered under my caress.

"Sex." His grin was downright wolfish. "Sex and me."

All ability to communicate fled as he bent his head toward mine to reclaim my lips. Meanwhile, his hands wandered lower — one busy rolling and flicking a nipple, while the other tickled along the side of my other breast. I arched my back; he knew right where to touch me to bring me to the edge. We were going to be late to meet Ourson at the levees, but none of that mattered. It was morning, and Irix still clearly wanted me. My heart sang, and I pushed him onto his back, rolling on top of him.

"My turn for the kissing," I told him. "But I'm going to start low and work my way up."

$\mathcal{W}$e *were* late — even more so because I'd insisted we stop at Darci's so I could change into jeans and a t-shirt. I refused to perform magic wearing last-night's crumpled dress. The morning walk of shame was awkward enough without sweating along the Mississippi River wearing blue silk and five inch heels.

Since we were already late, we swung by a nearby bakery to pick up beignets and coffee. By the time we arrived, I was flushed with embarrassment over our tardiness. I hated being late. It was so disrespectful. And, of course, Ourson had already arrived, surrounded by five of his vampire family, all trying to look inconspicuous and failing miserably.

"I'm sorry," I told him, feeling my face heat up as I remembered exactly why I was late. Honestly, I would have rather spent the whole day in bed with Irix, but we had a city to save.

"No problem, we weren't here long." Ourson snagged a coffee cup out of my hand and passed the stack around while I sat the carafe on a nearby bench. "And you look especially beautiful this morning. Too bad you're not a vampire."

"I could be," I teased. "Just say the word."

I felt great. Funny how I'd grown so accustomed to being depleted of energy that I'd forgotten how incredible it felt to be . . . full. The morning rain had tapered off, and the sun breaking free of the clouds heated the pavement. Mist curled upward in the rays of light — evaporating from the puddles on the black asphalt. A gentle breeze swept in from the river, lifting my hair and stirring the tree leaves. It was like a Disney movie. All I needed was for the whole lot of us to break into song.

"We haven't had any luck setting up that meeting you wanted," Ourson said in between sips of coffee. "They're refusing to meet with us. Do you want me to grab the head guy in a dark alley and force the issue?"

So much for happy Disney song. An image of the vampires dragging a middle-aged banker through the streets of New Orleans crossed my mind. Somehow I doubted that would engender the spirit of peace I hoped to establish.

"No. Let's see if they change their minds tonight." Maybe our work at the levees would force them to the negotiation table, especially if we caught them red-handed trying to reverse my spells.

"Sorry, sorry. Hope you all weren't waiting too long."

A flustered Jordan hurried toward me, a man and two women in tow. Good thing I brought extra coffee and pastries.

"Irix and I just got here." I handed her a bag of beignets and pulled one from a second bag.

"This is Evie, Kristin, and Stu. They've offered to help."

Kristin. The name bounced around in my head for a few moments before I placed it. "I've heard about you," I told the woman, reaching out to shake her hand.

She blushed, turning her sunburned skin even brighter pink. What a contrast with the severe Bev. Kristin looked to be late twenties with generous curves beneath the faded Grateful Dead t-shirt and khaki cut-offs. Her round face was accented by strawberry-blond frizz that had escaped her braid. She might be a powerful witch, but the woman looked more likely to be relaxing at a clambake than leading the largest coven in New Orleans. I could see why Bev had retained control of Bon Nuit.

"Whatever you need. We can watch for the bad guys or help you set up the ritual. Anything." Kristin enthusiastically pumped my hand, bypassing the bag of fried dough.

"Yeah," Evie chimed in, pulling a pastry from the bag and handing it to Stu. "I'm very excited to be working with you again. Bev can stuff it." She was a short, thin woman a few years older than me with a thick mass of brown hair and eyes the color of chestnuts.

I liked them immediately. Anyone who was willing to take my side over Bev was a good way toward becoming a friend. I turned to Stu, who had managed to hold three beignets in one hand while passing the bag to me with the other. He probably could have managed six with the length of his fingers. The man's whole body was thin and elongated like a stork's, but it was his long, narrow hands that drew my attention. I found myself glancing down at his feet and wondering if other parts of his anatomy were equally as long.

"Thanks for the breakfast," he said, a shy smile on his face. "And yeah, Bev can stuff it. We don't believe you had anything to do with the dead trees in the bayous."

Bayous? As in plural? And Bev could do more than stuff it if she was spreading rumors around that I was killing trees. Them's fighting words.

Jordan must have seen the look on my face because she seized my arm and pulled me off to the side.

"I didn't want to upset you, but during the night another bayou suffered the loss of its cypress trees. We're now hugely vulnerable in any good-sized storm." She took a deep breath and winced. "Bev has accused you of foul plague magic. She said you used their energy to curse the whole area. And she blames me for bringing a demon into their fold."

The fury I initially felt disappeared in a wave of guilt. "*Their* fold". Jordan had been ousted from her coven, and even though I hadn't been responsible for the death of the trees, her situation was completely my fault. I hugged her, crushing the bag of beignets between us.

"It's okay." Tears choked her voice. "Stu, Kristin, and Evie walked out with me. Bev *can* stuff it."

"She's a nasty bitch." I stroked Jordan's burgundy ringlets and hugged her tight before pulling away to look into her dark eyes. "And I'd be honored to assist you and your new coven with your Beltane ritual next year."

Heaven knows how I'd raise the plane fare to fly down here, let alone get off school at end-term of my senior year, but I knew I'd somehow make it happen when I saw the excitement in Jordan's eyes. A half-succubus at Beltane would be quite a draw. Bon Nuit could suck eggs; Jordan's little group would draw pagans from all across the state if she chose to open the Sabbat to guests. It would be sweet revenge to have a bigger, better celebration than the largest coven in New Orleans. Take that, bitch.

"I feel bad that I've thrown you in the middle of all this," she said, wiping her eyes with her forearm. "Here you are on vacation; I pressure you into doing this ritual, and it all blows up in your face."

"Pfft." I waved a hand and dug in the bag for a beignet. "This is a whole lot more exciting than getting drunk on Bourbon Street every night. "Come on. Let's meet Ourson's crew and get started."

Her eyes widened when she laid eyes on the vampire. "So he's really. . .?"

"Yeah." I took a nibble from the pastry, spilling powdered sugar onto my t-shirt in the process. "We're all friends. Just don't let him pick you up at a club. He bites."

"I have no intention of letting him pick me up anywhere, and if he tries to bite me, I'll hex him."

Now *that* I wanted to see.

"Beignet?" I held the bag out to Ourson. He declined, but the sandy-haired vampire next to him looked at the white paper bag with interest. "Here. Before I eat them all myself," I told him.

Jordan laughed. "She will too. You should see her with a plate of oysters. She's like a piranha with legs."

Half-breed, thy name is Gluttony. I took another bite from my pastry and extended my hand — the one not covered in powdered sugar. If Ourson wasn't going to do the honors, I'd just introduce myself. "I'm Amber, and this is my friend Jordan. She and her friends are witches, and they'll be assisting us today."

The vampires had originally ignored Jordan, but when I mentioned the word "witch", their heads pivoted to her, wary respect in their eyes.

"Raol, Frederick, and Guy," Ourson said, pointing to each in turn. I was amused to hear the sandy-haired man's name was Guy. That made him the Guy guy.

"No women?" Jordan, and the predominance of women in her group evened things out a bit, but it was strange that Ourson hadn't brought any female vampires.

"There are a few taking the night shift on the stakeout." The vampire and his crew exchanged grins. "We're the low men on the totem pole, so we get the joy of the day shift."

I briefly wondered about Eloise and Helen. How high up in their society were they?

"What kind of witchcraft do you practice?" Ourson asked Jordan.

She glared at him. "The kind that shrivels a man's testicles to the size of raisins."

The four men winced, and Guy actually took a step back.

"We've got a long day ahead of us. Let's save any potential genital mutilation for later." I hastily grabbed Jordan's arm and pulled her aside.

That snapped Jordan out of her hostile mood. "What do you want us to do?" she asked.

I had no idea. I didn't even know what the heck *I* was supposed to do. I looked around for Irix and found him holding court with Jordan's friends, all of whom looked ready to get naughty behind the bushes with him without a moment's notice. I squashed down an ugly jealous thought. This was what he was — an incubus. I couldn't fault him for that. It's not like I could ever expect fidelity from him.

At that moment Irix looked up at me and smiled. My whole world brightened. He jogged toward me, leaving the others mid-conversation.

"You ready to get started?" His voice was rough, like velvet rubbed against the nap. I couldn't help but step closer to him.

"I don't know what I'm supposed to do."

He grinned again, and my heart thudded. "You're going to get a feel for the atoms and molecular structure that make up the barrier, and then identify the magic surrounding the weakened area. I can blast the spell with raw energy and destroy it, but there might be an explosion. You'll need to contain it, and re-create the levee molecules."

What the fuck was he talking about?

"Explosion?" Forget all the molecule stuff, I was absolutely not comfortable with the idea of a magical spell detonating right in my face.

"Sure," Irix sounded casual, like we were discussing the fact that water was wet. "Breaking magic always results in some kind of explosion. Not on an atomic level, mind you. I doubt whoever put this down has that sort of power. Angels, now, those bastards can really pack a wallop of power. You don't want to go about breaking one of their spells."

"I don't intend to," I hastily assured him. "How big of an explosion are we talking about?" It better be less than a street-legal firecracker, or I was calling the whole thing off.

Irix shrugged. "We won't know until we get in there."

This endeavor was beginning to sound like a bad idea. I looked around at my interested audience, worried that I'd wasted everyone's time coming here on a demon's assurances that I could do these impossible things.

"And you said I was supposed to contain this explosion? At risk of repeating myself *again*, I'm a half-elf. I heal plants, make things bloom. I'm like a ramped-up version of Miracle-Gro, not Superman."

"You got this, elf-girl. It's energy absorption, just like you do with your sexual partners. Just like you did at the Wiccan ritual. Easy peasy."

Yeah, but if I fucked it up. . .. I crammed the remainder of the beignet in my mouth and motioned for everyone to stand back. They complied hastily, having overheard my entire conversation with Irix. With that amazing lack of confidence from my new friends, I turned to face the levee. My heart in my throat, I took a hesitant step forward.

"Wait."

Didn't have to ask me twice. I spun around and nearly collided with Irix. He loomed over me, the warm smell of chocolate and spiced rum twining around my flesh and filling my senses. His eyes danced as he raised a finger and traced it along the edge of my mouth.

"Powdered sugar."

I froze, transfixed by his touch, by the heat in his golden eyes. Slowly he bent his head toward me. I closed my eyes and felt the tip of his tongue licking the sweetness from my lips. I caught my breath and opened my mouth to him — inviting, pleading silently for him to give me more. Muscled arms encircled me, pulling me tight against his chest as our lips merged into a kiss.

Energy filled me like a sparkling stream dancing across the rocks. We weren't even having sex and there was a transfer. That had never happened when we'd kissed before. I wondered for a fraction of a second about the unusual exchange then lost myself in a slow wave of passion. My hands gripped his ass, drawing him even tighter to me. I felt the hardness of him through his jeans and rocked against him. There was a strange sensation of merging, as if our very souls entwined together in the fraction of space between our bodies.

He pulled away with a quick caress that clearly said "later". I panted, dazed and rather uncertain what it was I was supposed to be doing. We had an audience, staring at us openmouthed. A soft "wow" came from Jordan.

"Do you trust me, my elven princess?"

"Yes." I did. As much as I trusted my own brother. Probably even more.

He smiled, obviously pleased at my response, and led me up the bank of the levee to the paved path on top.

"Touch the grass. What does it tell you?"

I knelt down and placed my palms on the neatly manicured strip of green bordering the bicycle path. It was cynodon dactylon, better known as Bermuda grass. The rough, coarse blades were a thick mat under my hands.

"It's healthy. Plenty of sunlight and lots of nutrients from the soil. Flooding doesn't normally get this high, but they put down a nice layer of topsoil and apply compost regularly. It's an ideal grass for this sort of thing — hardy, withstands lots of traffic and high heat. It doesn't mind a saline environment.

Best of all, it has a very dense, deep network of roots that prohibit soil erosion. That's critical on a slope like this where soil can be lost due to rain."

"And under? Where the roots are?"

I closed my eyes, feeling the wind on my face and reaching with an inner part of myself down through the plant into the dirt below.

"The grass has taken hold nicely. These roots have been known to reach two meters down into the soil, but the deepest I feel here is about ninety centimeters. Most of the root bed is half a meter deep."

"Further."

I hesitated. It was like jumping off a cliff at midnight into the unknown. Tentatively I felt the soil around the roots, noting the phosphorous and nitrogen levels. Sensing Irix's eyes on me, I took a deep breath and reached further.

Dark and shifting. The sweet smell of decay. There was nothing to hold onto and I fell, my insides lurching like the downward plunge of a rollercoaster. Then I felt a hand on my shoulder, and everything within me snapped into place.

"Topsoil, then sand and a crushed rock mixture. Alternating stone and sediment layers. There's a synthetic mesh. I think it's to anchor the levee foundation in case of severe flooding. There's some kind of baked clay, tiles maybe, at the riverside edges about two feet in. To divert water from the foundation? Under the levee . . . holy shit! Mud. And water. This whole fucking city is built on water!"

"Language," Irix scolded. I could hear the amusement in his voice. It's not like he hadn't been flinging the curse words around lately. Pot and kettle, baby.

I pulled up from the water table and extended my awareness out along the stretch of earth and stone. It was cleverly constructed and stable enough to withstand a sizable storm. The only way this levee could be breached would be if the floods from the river topped it. Not impossible, but the river at that level would be a once-in-five-thousand-years event.

Nothing. Nothing. I kept reaching, grounded by Irix's touch. What had Jordan seen yesterday? Maybe it wasn't the levee, but something else that had been spelled. Just to make sure, I continued searching and smacked into something that felt like a thousand nettles against my skin. I gasped and pulled back, hesitating when Irix squeezed my shoulder reassuringly.

"Easy there, elf-girl. That's the spell you've been looking for."

It was unnerving enough venturing out into unknown territory like this, but actually coming up against the spell brought it home to me that I was absolutely not prepared to do this sort of thing. All I knew was that it hurt. I hadn't the foggiest idea how strong it was, what it was meant to do, or how to go about containing the explosion Irix was about to cause.

"Ready?"

"No." Fear and uncertainty made me a little snappish. "Just give me a second. I've got to figure out what I need to do once you remove it, or we're going to be totally fucked."

To give Irix credit, he didn't get on my case again about my potty mouth. I carefully reached out, examining the area surrounding the spell to try and learn what I could without getting zapped. I could see a network of links, like little feeder roots, from the magicked area into the levee, ten feet in diameter. The links were dormant, invisible unless traced backward from the spell. As I dove down, I saw a column of magic, held in stasis. It reached all the way through the levee, deep into the water table below.

"I can't really tell what the trigger is, so I'm thinking it has to be something external, perhaps from the magician? I do know what it does, though. When triggered, ten feet of the levee drops like a sink hole."

I heard someone behind me inhale sharply. "If there's a flood, the water will rush right through into lower ground." It was Jordan, her voice pitched high with anxiety. "The pressure will erode the surrounding walls of the levee and huge sections will collapse. This whole district would be underwater in no time."

"That's not all. There's a significant part of the spell driven down into the water table. It acts like a water spout, pulling everything up and sending it like a geyser into the air."

"Erosion of the foundation," Jordan added. "It's not just the geyser of water, but the sudden fast flow underneath that's a danger. There'll be a chain reaction of sinkholes all along the levee. I saw twenty along the portions we looked at yesterday. The whole thing would come down if that happened."

And a failure like that would make the damage from hurricane Katrina look like a rainstorm puddle.

"Ready now?" Irix asked, his hands on his hips.

"Hold on there, cowboy. Let me figure out what I need to replace before you start blowing us all up."

"No."

That was the only warning I got before everything went to shit.

I felt the prickly, forbidding area of the spell collapse upon itself, leaving a vacuum of space that tried to suck in all the matter around it. I panicked, holding onto the structure of the levee with every ounce of magical might I possessed. A full demon would have quickly created additional dirt and rock to fill the hole, but I had no practice with that skill. Sweat trickled down the sides of my face and between my breasts as I struggled to hold on. I wanted to tell Irix to hurry, but couldn't even spare the concentration to speak, I was so intent on holding the barrier together. Just as I thought I could hold on no more, the vacuum that had been the spell blew apart in a burst of energy.

I heard myself scream, and I pulled. It was like yanking on the end of cooling taffy. The energy spun into me, too much to handle. I didn't know what to do with it all, and it burned through my nerve endings. My muscles spasmed and pushed against my skin. I struggled to hold it, juggling it around like a hot potato while simultaneously supporting the fragile edges of the levee. My body shook with the effort, and I felt myself begin to lose control. Damn Irix for putting me in this position! Everyone around me was going to die, and there was nothing I could do to stop it. Jordan, Ourson, all their friends. Irix.

This time my scream was in rage and frustration. I summoned every ounce of control and turned the energy searing its way through me outward, driving it into the empty hole in the barrier that had once held the spell. Like pieces of a puzzle, the energy slotted into place. I directed its formation, mindlessly deciding what atoms and molecules it should take. When the last piece of explosive energy trans-formed, I opened my eyes and swayed. A hand reached out to steady me, strong and firm against my shoulder. Irix.

I turned toward the incubus and, without a word, punched his jaw as hard as I could.

His head rocked to the side, and I cradled my hand, winc-ing. Our audience of witches and vampires stared with round eyes at the pair of us. I wasn't sure whether they were speechless from the miracle I'd just pulled off, or from my assault upon a demon nearly two-thousand years my senior. It didn't matter. The only thoughts in my mind were relief that we all weren't dead, and fury at Irix for nearly killing us all.

"You fucking asshole!" I hissed, hitting him once more, this time in the chest. "I. Wasn't. Ready. What part of 'wait' did you not understand?"

My breath came in fast gasps, and I noticed my hands were shaking. Hell, my legs were shaking too. It was all I could do to remain standing. We'd all nearly died. The realization of my mortality, of the fragile lives surrounding me, crashed through my mind. I felt shaken to the very core, but Irix stood before me, calm, his eyes like crystallized honey.

"Do you want to do this or not?" His voice was as cold as dry ice, freezing its way through to my heart. This incubus was nothing like the passionate man of this morning. Gone was the irreverent playboy, the unexpectedly gallant hedonist. Instead, I faced a harsh, powerful demon — a being to be feared and respected.

"I wasn't ready," I repeated, but this time my voice trembled, rising into a fearful soprano at the end. Irix's stern countenance didn't betray an ounce of sympathy. His hard eyes traveled down my length and up again, clearly finding something in me that was lacking. I ached from the inside out, hurt and confused over his unyielding attitude, and feeling a twinge of sorrow that I'd let him down, that I wasn't the demon he'd thought I was.

"I understand that." His eyes softened slightly, only to retreat into fossilized amber again. "But this is your venture, not mine. I care not one whit about human losses, or petty power struggles among their magical groups. I'll be irked if my beloved home here is destroyed, but such is the fate of all things physical. We have nineteen more spells to break, nineteen more sections of the levee system to rebuild. If you're not up to the task, stop leading your friends on and tell them. We'll pack up and be on the next plane back to Maryland."

I gasped like he'd thrown ice water in my face. His honesty was brutal, and I wasn't sure what to say. I *wasn't* up to the task. I hadn't realized what I'd needed to do when I'd committed to this thing, and I was in way over my head.

"I can't. . . ." I'd barely held on this time. The thought of going through this nineteen more times filled me with fear. This was an impossible task — one that I had rashly taken on without understanding the demands it would place on me. There was a tiny part of my mind that was still angry with Irix — angry with him for assuring me I was up to this, and for throwing me into the deep end by breaking the spell before I had determined what I needed to do.

There was a flash of disappointment on his face, a moment of sorrow. "You're so young. There's no shame in recognizing your limitations. We'll leave the humans to deal with this themselves and return to Maryland where we can continue your training."

I felt a horrible twisting in my gut. Irix was speaking to me as though I was a schoolgirl unable to pass her finals and being held back a grade. I wanted to be more than that to him. I wasn't addled enough to think I'd ever be his equal, but somehow I wanted his respect. I wanted him to see me as an adult.

"Maybe we can help," Jordan interjected hesitantly. "A spell to contain the area, or to help with channeling the energy from the spell dissolution, perhaps."

I appreciated her offer. It made me realize there were people here who depended on me, who would give me any assistance necessary to help protect their livelihoods and their city. If only I knew what I needed.

"This is going to kill me." I ran a hand through my hair. "I'll eventually slip up and we'll all die."

He shrugged. "So give up."

I'll be damned. Something of the Lowry stubbornness must have worked its way into me through my upbringing, because I'd seen Wyatt and Nyalla assume the same immovable stance that I now took.

"Everyone needs to stay at least a hundred feet away until I've completed the repair. We'll take this slow and get as many in as we can before nightfall. If we don't get the rest done, I'll come back tomorrow and finish. There's no imminent danger from any storm, so we've got some time."

I heard voices behind me agreeing. My eyes were fixated upon the demon. Irix nodded, a sharp, quick jerk, before he motioned for us to move on. His expression was guarded, but for a second I thought I saw a glimmer of pride.

I was practically face down in my muffaletta, conversation an indistinct buzz around me. Nine. All I'd managed was nine of the twenty spots of the levee that we'd identified as being magically compromised. The smoked meat, cheese, and olive-pepper relish filling the sandwich were the perfect choices to refuel my body, but something deep inside me remained drained and numb.

"You okay?" Darci's hand rubbed my back, her dark eyes peering up at me as she bent her head low to see my down-turned face. She'd brought us all lunch. I'd barely managed to extract my sandwich from the waxed paper bag. Even simple tasks were becoming beyond my capability.

"Just tired."

Understatement of the year. There's no way I could finish this thing, no way I could even manage one more. The next one would kill us all — or at least Irix and me. I'd been ensuring the others stayed well back from us as we worked. The vampires didn't mind, but Jordan and her friends were frustrated with their inability to help. They saw me struggle, knew the risks I was taking, and kept proposing ways they could assist. I probably could have used a few of their ideas, but I was too worried about their safety to try any.

"Finish up your sandwich, and let's get going." Irix's voice was measured and calm. He'd driven me along with a combination of encouragement and insults all day. In spite of my exhaustion, if he snapped at me one more time I was going to yank his head off and toss it into the Mississippi.

"I can't do any more." I'd said that before the last one, but this time I really, really meant it. Staring at his knees, I refused to raise my gaze any higher and see the inevitable look of disappointment in his face. I already felt like enough of a failure.

"I know. I'll take you back to my place or to Darci's for some sleep then we'll go out tonight to recharge. You can come back tomorrow and finish up."

A long nap sounded good. I was too exhausted to worry over what Irix's idea of recharge might mean and the expected conflict it might cause with my ethics. And I was too exhausted to think about the daunting task of repairing eleven spell-weakened areas tomorrow when today's nine had just about put me in my grave.

"Your place." I didn't want to hurt Darci's feelings, after all I was supposed to be here visiting her and not shacking up with some demon, but I longed to doze off in Irix's bed with his scent all around me. Yeah, I was pissed that he'd driven me like a mule today, but he'd pushed me to do things I'd never thought possible. Without him, I'd have given up at the first spell.

A strong hand brushed along the top of my head with tenderness. That did more than any words could to let me know how much my decision had meant to the demon.

"Text me later and let me know your plans." Darci gave a short snort of laughter. "Unless you intend on spending the evening on your backside, I'll join you."

"Dinner, maybe?" I'd probably need to spend a good bit of the evening recharging through sexual activity, but unless Irix was into sploshing, dinner should be at maximum an R-rated event.

"Deal."

Sandwich consumed, I pulled myself to my feet and sought out Ourson and his vampire buddies. We'd need to set up some sort of watch schedule along the levee before I went to take my big nap. The vampire was, surprisingly, talking with Jordan, his buddies milling about with the other witches as they finished their lunch. From the last few days, I'd discovered vampires generally regarded humans as no more than inanimate bags of blood and seldom bothered to interact with them. The fact that Ourson was chatting with Jordan and she wasn't trying to stake him or lop his head off was odd.

"Umm, sorry to interrupt, but we need to figure out who's going to watch which site, and some kind of rotation."

Ourson turned to me, a happy smile lighting up his face. "We were just discussing that. There's nine locations and only eight of us. Jordan said she can put alarm traps on the remaining one, but I'm worried we wouldn't get here in time to catch him or her. Or them."

"Ourson is going to ask his family to send another vampire," Jordan chimed in. "I've had three more of my former coven members call me to express support. They said they'd take a shift. Leaves us a bit short-handed, but we'll make it work."

"Irix and I can take a shift too," I volunteered.

Ourson shook his head. "Better not. After what happened at the bayou, they may have spells that detect demon presence. We don't want to scare them off."

"But won't they detect Jordan's spells, too?" I turned to her, eyebrows raised. If the Crimson Moon guys were detecting for demons, I'd assume they'd be scanning for other magic. We weren't exactly stealthy at the bayou. We didn't think we needed to be.

"Probably," she replied. "These guys are pretty arrogant. I'm doing some basic spells. They'll think we're a bunch of amateurs, disable it and head on in."

"Then we'll grab them." Ourson grinned, gleaming white teeth contrasting with his dark skin. "They won't be expecting a vampire. We don't broadcast our presence, and with all the human vampire-wannabes in New Orleans, our activities go very much unnoticed."

Seemed my friends had everything worked out. Warmth ran through me as I looked at the vampire and witch. How wonderful it was to be working with such intelligent and capable people.

"You guys are awesome." Jordan beamed at my compliment. "I'm leaving it all in your hands. Text me any time, day or night, if you need me."

"Got it."

Jordan jogged off to consult with her friends, leaving me with Ourson. I narrowed my eyes as I gave him the stare-down.

"Okay, spill it. You don't look twice at a human unless it's to check their blood type, *never* speak to them beyond persuading them into a back alley — why the sudden buddy-buddy with Jordan?"

The vampire shuffled his feet, looking sheepish. "Well . . . she's a witch."

"And?"

"We have a long history of working with witches and magicians. They provide us with valuable services, and we partner with them in business or provide support to them in other ways."

I took a deep breath, wondering exactly what "services"

Jordan would be expected to provide, and what exactly a *vampire* could offer a group of Wiccans. I might be half demon, but I was very protective of my friends, and I absolutely counted Jordan in my inner circle of protectiveness.

"What would you want her and her friends to do?"

Ourson's eyes widened in alarm. "Things like camouflage and look-away spells, or attraction charms. Some of our family aren't physically appealing, and they have difficulty attracting humans. We don't condone forced feedings. A good witch or coven can make all the difference to these vampires."

Okay, that wasn't so bad. I glared at Ourson, just to make sure, and got the feeling from his expression that he was being honest with me. Biting me aside, he'd always seemed like an upfront kind of guy.

"And what sort of support would you provide to them?" I forced my voice into a neutral tone, to prevent my disbelief from showing. Slight distrust aside, Ourson was my friend, and I didn't want to insult him or his family.

"We can assist them in funding business ventures, or in funds for coven activities. It's not just money, though. There have been times in the past when being a witch or a magician was dangerous. We'll protect them, shield them from groups or individuals who may do them harm."

This didn't sound too bad. My fears laid to rest, I gave Ourson an impulsive hug. Surprisingly, he returned it, ruffling my blond hair as we parted.

"I'd rather work with witches," he confessed with a quick glance at Jordan and her friends. "Mages are powerful, but they tend to be self-serving. Modern witches have more honor, especially those that follow the Wiccan path." He frowned. "You do think this Jordan witch is honorable, don't you? I trust your opinion. Succubi are good judges of character."

I bit back a laugh. I'd never thought myself particularly skilled at determining motive or the character of anyone — human or otherwise. Ever since I'd found out what I really was, I'd swam in a sea of suspicion. Still, I trusted Jordan, and if *I* did, then a vampire could certainly trust her too — as long as they didn't get bitey.

"She's honorable, but if she suspects you're not, all deals are off. Got it?"

Ourson's eyes were serious as they met mine. "Got it."

Everyone quickly scattered to their various posts after exchanging cell phone numbers, and Irix drove me back to his beautiful brick house. We didn't exchange so much as a single word the entire way there, and it was bliss. I nearly dozed off in the passenger seat, my head against the cool glass of the window, feeling the soothing rumble of the Audi through my tired muscles. Once there, I staggered up the steps, shedding clothes as I climbed.

After freshening up in the little hallway bathroom, I headed straight for the bed. Irix was there, putting a bottle of water and what looked like a plate of cookies on the night-stand. I swear, this guy was better than the service at the Hilton.

"I've got to run out for a few hours," he said, his back to me. "I'll make reservations for tonight and text Darci the details. Call me if you need anything."

Yep, definitely better than the Hilton. Something in me twinged with disappointment that he wasn't going to curl up with me in bed. I yearned to feel the strength of his arms around me, the long length of his thigh draped across my legs, the brush of his hair against my shoulder. It was probably for the best, though. I doubted we'd get much sleep if we fell into bed together, and I desperately needed rest.

"Thank you."

He turned, his eyes shadowed and somber. "After dinner,

we're going to find you someone. I won't take 'no' for an answer, Amber."

I knew exactly what he meant, and my stomach plunged. This thing between us was so new, and I wasn't sure what would happen introducing our demonic needs into the relationship this early. Somehow I had hoped it could just be the two of us, no matter how impractical and impossible that situation would be. We needed others, the pair of us. Monogamy would never be part of our lives.

"You can't exist solely on the energy I transfer to you, elf-girl." He smiled, but it was a tight, grim sort of smile.

"I know." My mouth was like dried cotton as I replied. I did know, but the reality of our situation didn't make me feel any better.

He was in front of me in two quick paces, kissing me quickly on the forehead. "Sleep. We've got a busy night ahead, and eleven more spots to repair tomorrow."

I watched him leave, closing the door behind him. His parting words were like a shot of adrenaline, leaving me exhausted yet filled with restless insomnia as I crawled between the cool, soft sheets. Eleven more. Shit, how was I going to do that?

CHAPTER 25

$\mathcal{I}$ floated into consciousness with the warmth of skin pressed along my backside. An arm curled around my waist, angling upward to cup my breast with a long-fingered hand. I rubbed along Irix's body like a cat, purring as sleep fell from my mind.

"Better?"

The hand at my breast slid gently around the base, a finger flicking lightly at my nipple. My breath hitched, and I leaned into his hand, enjoying the languorous feeling of waking in a man's arms.

Irix chuckled. "I take that as a yes."

His lips trailed down my neck and across my shoulder as his fingers tortured my breast with feather-light touches. I reached a hand behind me, trying desperately to reach an equally sensitive part of his anatomy, but my position only allowed me to stroke along the lower part of his waist and across the hard planes of his hips to the powerful thighs pressed against mine. He murmured in appreciation, and I caressed the length of his leg, feeling the springy roughness of sparse dark hair and taut muscle.

"Ah, my elf-girl, you tempt a demon beyond every rational thought. I'd love to spend the evening driving you to the edge so you make that little squeaking noise, but we have dinner reservations."

Only one thing penetrated my fog of sleepy desire. "I do *not* make squeaky noises!"

"You're right." His fingers stroked the sensitive flesh on the side of my breast, and a serpentine shift of his body brought the firmness of his erection against my ass. "It's more like a whimper. The kind of noise a little puppy makes when it's rooting for its mother's milk."

That wasn't much better, but by this point I didn't care. He could have compared me to a shrieking harpy and I would have ignored it.

"Of course *I* look and sound like I'm having some kind of cardiac event. Or possibly being eviscerated by another demon with horns. Did I ever tell you how much I hate horns?"

It was hard for me to reconcile the sultry demon who drove me to orgasmic insanity and this playful, funny one. He seemed to be both at once right now, his hand roving lower to stroke tantalizingly close to where I really wanted it to be. My body lit up with sensation like a sparkler on the Fourth of July, and I struggled to keep my mind on his words.

"How do you know what you look and sound like?" I couldn't imagine one of his entranced humans would have had the nerve to make such an unflattering observation of the incubus.

"Oh, I know. Some demons are very fond of mirrors — humans too. Walls of them, sometimes on the floors and ceilings. It's rather a mood breaker to watch yourself during *la petite mort*, let me tell you."

My laugh came out as a very unsexy snort, and we both

snickered.

"Oh, I like that as much as the puppy noises," Irix teased, tickling me lightly across the stomach. "But we need to get going. Darci will be there soon, and you're leaving in a few days. I know you want to spend time with her."

I did. Sighing, I pulled myself away from his warmth and slide out of bed, looking for my clothing. Crap. I should have gone to Darci's. None of my clothes were here besides the jeans and t-shirt I'd worn all day. With the heat, I'm sure they were a bit ripe.

"No, in the closet. While you were playing Sleeping Beauty, I picked up a few things."

I opened the closet door, convinced there would be a miniscule black dress, or a skin-tight backless number in fire-engine red. Instead, beside a row of shirts and pants, hung a flowing white dress. It seemed to be one long, thin piece of fabric, wrapped halter-style across the bodice, cinching the waist, then widening into a knee-length skirt that slit up the side to where my hip would be.

"Ooo, pretty!"

"It's as close as I could come to what elven women wear in Hel without causing you to be arrested for indecent exposure. Not that you couldn't smile your way out of that."

I'd been told that the elves generally felt more skin should show than cloth. My stepsister had to be strongly persuaded to cover her breasts and rear end after spending her entire life among the elves.

I slid into the dress after searching in vain for clean undergarments. There was no way to wear my bra with the backless style, but a pair of panties would have been welcome. I eyed the ones crumpled on the floor with my dirty jeans and wondered if I had time to wash them in the bathroom sink and blast them with the blow dryer.

"Oh no you don't." Irix watched me intently from the bed,

the sheets a tangle around his legs, his chest bare in the orange glow of sunlight streaming through the windows. "It's commando for you tonight, my elven princess."

I stuck my tongue out at him and sashayed into the bathroom, fully aware that his eyes followed every move of my hips. A spare hair tie from my purse gave me a tousled up do, but I'd have to go without makeup. I glanced in the mirror, thankful I'd always had a clear complexion and that my eyelashes were a few shades darker than my golden hair.

Irix was shrugging into a shirt when I walked back into the bedroom, his pants unfortunately already on.

"Well, this is as good as it's going to get." I announced.

He glanced up, his eyes warm as they did a slow tour of my form. "Good thing, or you'd be leaving a trail of dead bodies in your wake. You're beautiful enough to stop a man's heart, little half breed."

I laughed, flattered and a bit embarrassed. "Well, the sneakers are going to ruin the effect, unless you intend for me to go both commando and barefoot?"

"Dear girl, never doubt my attention to every detail."

The demon grinned as he lifted a shoe box from the end of the bed and handed it to me. Inside was a gorgeous pair of peep-toe pumps — cream with gold soles and heels. I slipped them on, marveling at the comfort even though I stood on my tiptoes, a good three inches taller than I had been.

We stood for a moment, admiring each other. The incubus was breathtaking in simple slacks and shirt, his sable hair loose and brushing his shoulder. Even in jeans, he looked like he should be standing on his yacht as it drifted on a turquoise sea. The perfect fit and high quality of his clothes emphasized that air of casual wealth. But it was his face that really captivated me. A wayward lock curled from his forehead along sculpted cheekbones to tease the corner of his mouth, and I could hardly tear my eyes away. Part of me wanted to bail on Darci and have Irix slowly slide the dress from my body. A vision of him on top of me, my legs around his waist, gold heels digging into his hips flashed across my mind. Delayed gratification always made sex all the better, and we had all evening to let the tension build to its crescendo. With a little luck, we'd be so frenzied we'd never make it to the bed. Sex on the staircase was one of my favorites.

"We better go." My voice husky with desire.

Irix extended his arm gallantly, one corner of his mouth quirking up in a lopsided smile. "Only if you promise to tell me all those naughty thoughts going through your mind just now. I nearly changed my mind watching the look on your face."

I snaked my hand inside the crook of his arm, laying it lightly on his hard bicep. "Tell you? I plan to show you."

Lust danced in his golden eyes. "Oh, even better!"

"There's a storm alert." Darci's tone was excessively casual as she popped a shrimp into her mouth. A drop of garlic butter hovered for a second on her full lower lip before she licked it off with a sexy swipe of her tongue.

Gavin's eyes snagged on his girlfriend's mouth before he reluctantly tore his gaze away to his own meal. He'd gotten off work early and joined us to make the evening a couples' date. "No worry. It's just a tropical storm, and it looks like it's going to clip southwest Florida and peter out in the Gulf."

"Wasn't this one of the tropical depressions over the Bahamas yesterday?" I didn't know much about hurricanes, but something moving that fast seemed a bit concerning to me.

Gavin shrugged. "It's hurricane season. This kind of thing is regular as rain. Unless there's a change in the storm track, or an upgrade in status, it's just business as usual for us."

Darci and I exchanged a quick glance. Something about this storm bothered me — badly.

"That is fast." Darci stiffened, lowering her voice. "Katrina went from a tropical storm to a category three in one day, then four the next. This could be nothing, but we should be prepared in case there's an evacuation announcement. Even if this turns out to be nothing, there's another one right behind it."

She was skirting the issue because Gavin didn't know about our paranormal status, or the magical sabotage of the bayous, the levees, and at least one dam. I ran the numbers in my head. A tropical storm near southwest Florida could easily veer into Mexico, die in the Gulf, or slam into Galveston or Louisiana. My skills were in plants, not weather. I was totally out of my element.

"Fifty-miles-per-hour winds with gusts at seventy-five around Key West," Darci commented, her mouth a grim line. "As Gavin said, nothing to worry about. Now."

I read between the lines. It was a lot to worry about. With everything we'd seen, these Crimson Moon folks were primed for a hurricane to reach New Orleans. Who's to say they'd leave it all up to fate? They could negate my healing of the cypress trees, implement devastating spells in both dams and levees. Would it be beyond their abilities to influence weather? It wouldn't take much to grow a tropical storm to a hurricane, and change the trajectory toward New Orleans. If they were truly powerful. . . .

My mind raced through various environmental classes to remember historical typhoons and hurricanes. A category six in the Philippines not so long ago had losses of over six-thousand lives with massive property damages. New Orleans was still fragile from recent storms. That along with the magical compromises of their defenses could result in even greater losses. My stomach twisted. If these people had the ability to control weather, the entire city could be leveled — with damage that wouldn't be easy to recover from. The population hadn't yet recuperated to pre-Katrina levels. This kind of disaster might mean the end of the city. Surely that wasn't what Crimson Moon wanted? They just wanted to change the course of the ley lines, not destroy the town. But if the ley lines were their only goal, why did their preparation seem excessive?

Irix reached out a hand and ran his fingers along the bare skin of my thigh, squeezing my knee. In spite of the location of his hand, his touch wasn't seductive. The warmth of his fingers rubbing gently across my knee was reassuring. I could count on him to protect me, to keep me safe, but it wasn't me I was worried about. In spite of his surprising tenderness, he was still a demon. He might care for me, but I couldn't expect him to care about any of the humans in the city, or their property. Hopefully I wouldn't have to test his morality. With any luck, we'd catch the people responsible and strengthen the city's defenses before the storm came anywhere near us.

I struggled to turn my mind away from topics we couldn't discuss in front of Gavin, longing to ask Darci how the vampires and Jordan's crew were doing. This was a double date. What topics would be safe, non-paranormal ones?

"What does your school schedule look like this fall?"

Darci grinned. "Cake walk. Senior year, girlfriend. I've got a few core credits then my independent study. I've applied for an internship with the mayor that would be twenty hours per week, then full time after graduation. Keep your fingers crossed for me."

Irix leaned forward. "Amber said you were planning a career in public service. Are you looking to get into the city council, mayoral, state rep/senate, or the federal level?"

I gave him a suspicious look. With demons, there are no innocent questions. I doubted Irix was making small talk. Why was he so interested in Darci's career plans?

"If I can manage to get this internship, then I'd like to stay at the mayor's office for a few years to make connections and learn the ropes." Darci glowed at the prospect. "When the timing's right, I'll start out with city council, delegate, or board of education, then with some luck be elected mayor. My end goal is governor. I'm not interested in a federal position at the moment. I'd like to influence grass roots changes right now, and then move into higher-level politics. My ultimate goal is to advocate for Louisiana and New Orleans."

I felt a twinge of envy. Darci had always had her future mapped out — driven and ambitious since the first moment I'd walked into that dorm room and laid eyes on her. Me? I had no idea what the heck I was going to do with my life. A year younger than Darci, I'd be graduating this coming year too, after leapfrogging my way through high school and college. It was a little late to still be waffling on a career, but I'd never been able to see past graduation. I liked plants, but could hardly make a career out of going to people's houses and causing their tulips to bloom.

"It all hinges on this internship then?" Irix asked.

I pulled my attention from my own career, or lack of, and concentrated on Darci. My friend had a happy, eager grin that creased the dark skin of her cheeks. She only got that look when she was in love, or discussing her political aspirations.

"I've got some other alternatives, but it *would* really jump-start my future. These positions are super competitive, though, and it takes more than just good grades and a background in leadership to get them. My family isn't well connected, even though we've been in the city for generations. I've got a good shot at it, but I'm not going to give up if someone else gets the position."

Darci was always pragmatic. She might not get the internship. It meant so much to her, and she'd give it her heart and soul. It killed me to think that some snot whose parents wrote big campaign contribution checks might win out over my friend. Irix rubbed his hand along my thigh, and a feeling of peace warred with my anxieties about Darci's chances at her dream job, and the unfairness of the world.

"Even if you don't get the internship, you'll find something promising," Gavin said, giving Darci a quick kiss on the cheek. "You're not a woman who gives up easily."

My friend exchanged a glance with me, communicating everything in a brief look, the way best friends do. Yes, Darci wasn't a woman who gave up easy — on boyfriends, on her career, or on weird half-demon-half-elf friends.

"I'm sure you'll get the job, and you'll be running the city in no time." Irix saluted Darci with his wine glass.

"Thanks for the vote of confidence, but it's a long shot." Darci shrugged.

"Nah." Irix leaned back in his chair, taking a sip of wine. "I know these things. You'll get that internship, guaranteed."

I kicked him under the table and gave him a squinty-eyed glare. I wasn't sure what he was intending, but I hoped he wasn't leading my friend on. I had every confidence in Darci's smarts and ambition, but Irix had no right to make pronouncements he didn't intend to follow up on. Irix winced, pinching my leg in retaliation. He was saved from further damage by the arrival of our dinner.

After we'd finished, and Darci and Gavin had left, I rounded on Irix, finally free to chew him out. "How could you guarantee Darci that internship? She's got her heart set on it, and now she'll be completely crushed if it doesn't happen. I know how these things work. It takes connections and money to get these jobs — things her family doesn't have. She deserves it, and it sucks, but you raising her hopes like that is horrible."

Irix looked perplexed, taking my arm as we went to leave the restaurant. I pulled out of his grasp, and he sighed, looking heavenward.

"I don't promise what I can't deliver, half-breed. I'll take care of it. She'll get the job."

My mind raced through the possibilities. Did he intend on seducing the Mayor and somehow compelling him to hire Darci? Would he make a huge campaign contribution with stolen money? I remembered Irix paying for our dinner tonight in cash. Crap, how much *had* he stolen from that ATM?

"Why? Why would you do this for someone who means nothing to you, for a human?"

The shutters came down over his eyes, and he shrugged. "It amuses me. I always enjoy a good seduction, and the prospect of blackmail is quite exciting."

Shit. Darci would have a fit if she knew how her internship had been earned. "You can't set up the mayor of the city and blackmail him! That's wrong."

Irix's face was set in hard lines as he stopped and turned to face me. "Darci is your friend. You know that she's the best candidate and how much good she'll do the city. Others are using underhanded methods to gain the advantage. I'm offering you a level playing field."

"That's not a level playing field. What you're proposing is illegal and completely immoral. Darci doesn't want to win that way, and I'd never condone that sort of thing. I'd never do that myself."

"Really? If someone's life depended on the mayor's decision, would you? If breaking the law and bending your ethics saved others, or a bayou full of cypress trees, would you? Morality is a surprisingly malleable concept."

I felt a storm of indecision at his questions, but he was missing the point. "This internship isn't a life-or-death event. Darci will succeed without it — she's that driven, that good."

I felt the weight of his stare in my bones. People edged

past us on the sidewalk, and a breeze came down the cross street, pressing my skirt against my legs.

"I won't interfere if you don't want me to."

There was something odd in his voice, something that made me think he wasn't telling the truth.

"Swear it."

His lip twitched into a half smile, although his eyes remained solemn. "I swear on all the souls that I Own that I will not personally interfere with Darci's internship candidacy."

I wracked my brain trying to find the loophole in his vow, frustrated that I hadn't taken more interest in debate or law classes in my studies. "Okay."

"So, we're good?" Irix extended a hand.

"Good." I went to shake his hand, and he held on, tucking it into his arm as he turned and began walking once again.

"Your friends are your household, Amber. You need to give serious consideration to how you support them and nurture their loyalty. The day might come when you need to smash what you consider your ethics, or risk losing them."

What the hell was he talking about?

"Household?" I struggled to keep up with him in my high heels as we strolled down the sidewalk.

Irix's lips turned up in a crooked smile. "Household. It's the people you consider yours, the ones that belong to you. Demons, elves, humans — anyone."

"Darci doesn't belong to me!" My voice was an outraged squeak.

"Of course she does. You lived with her at your university. You live at her apartment when you are in her town. If she needed your help, you would risk your personal safety to come to her, and she you. She's yours."

"No," I argued. "That's friendship. Darci is my best friend. I don't 'own' her."

Irix made a noise that sounded suspiciously like a snort. "Silly. Half-breeds can't 'Own'. And I doubt your incredibly strict ethical standards would allow you to seize and hold anyone's soul. Your household are not those you 'Own', they're those that belong to you."

I frowned. Clearly there were some communication issues between Irix and me, and the definition of the word 'belong' seemed to be one of them. I saw it as slavery, but from what he was saying, it seemed to be something different in Hel.

"Who do you have in your household? Are they free to leave and go elsewhere?"

Irix turned into a side street, tugging me along. "Of course they're free to leave. Household members choose to be with you, in fact, they often beg to be with you. You protect them, raise their status through association. Most of my household members are demons, although incubi and succubi don't have the large households that other demons do. I often have humans in my household. Colette, who willed me my New Orleans home, was one of my household members."

His face tightened in grief as he mentioned her name. I had wondered about their association, but now I felt a sympathetic tug toward him at this sign of caring.

"Tell me about Colette." I was surprised Irix showed such feelings toward another — especially a human, and I wanted to know more.

"I met her just after New Orleans was captured by the Union Army. The early conflict was military, but as it moved into the city, there were specific punishments against women who protested against the occupation. Colette was the mistress of a man who died at Fort St. Phillip. He'd given her the house early in their relationship, and she managed to keep it by being savvy enough to walk the tightrope between Union and Confederate forces."

"What did she look like?" I don't know why that was so important to me, but I wanted to get a visual of the woman that Irix spoke of with longing and grief.

"She was a mulatto — not so light that she'd be passe blanc, but lighter than your friend Darci. She was tall and a bit thinner than the fashion when I first met her, although you would consider her curvy now. She curled her hair into long ringlets, but with the humidity, little wisps would spiral up tight against her scalp."

His voice softened with nostalgia, and I felt an unwelcome pang of jealousy.

"Had she been a prostitute? A madam?" I don't know why I cared, but I did.

"No. She gave her favors to whom she pleased. Prostitution would have probably been in her future after the demise of her lover, but as part of my household, she had other choices. That's what ownership means, Amber. I shielded her, protected her — just as you would with Darci."

I was getting a better idea on the concept, even though the thought of his feelings for Colette still were like a blow to my stomach. "Did you protect her from actions from the Union army? Keep her safe?"

A haunted look flashed across Irix's face. "As much as I could. Demons can't stay here long, and there were times when I needed to go back to Hel. Colette was tough. She could take care of herself, but I always felt guilty when she was alone."

"How did she die?" I couldn't help asking, even though I knew the question would cause him pain.

"Colette loved her food and drink. She'd indulged quite a bit through the decades and eventually succumbed to her excesses."

"You couldn't help her?" It seemed impossible to me that a demon found any physical problem beyond their abilities.

Irix shook his head. "Demons aren't good at healing. That's an angel thing. We can fix our own injuries, but when it comes to another, we're pretty helpless."

I halted at a street corner, staring at him. "I'm so sorry."

We continued in silence while I tried to reconcile my preconceptions of demons with this man that cared enough about a human to protect her, to mourn her for over a century.

"Did you love her?" It was the question I was terrified to ask, but I needed to know the answer, no matter how much it might pain me.

Irix gave me a quizzical look. "There are many different kinds of love, little half-breed. Demons can care deeply for most-favored humans. Sometimes that emotion comes close to what you would think of as love." He sighed. "It's painful to have feelings for a being that has such a short life. Many demons find it easier to put humans in the same category as lesser life forms. Others are simply incapable of caring for any who are not beings of spirit."

That seemed kind of snobby, but as I thought of all my friends and family that would die long before me, I began to understand. How many times could someone say 'goodbye' before their heart hardened into a self-defensive rock?

"Do demons ever fall in love with demons?" *Or half-demons?* I added silently.

That got a short laugh that didn't seem to stem from any sort of amusement. "Sometimes. It's an intense ride that always ends up with one or both demons dead."

"Always?" Surely there had to be some demon partner-ships that stood the test of time.

"Eventually yes. Immortality probably contributes a bit to the violence of our affairs, but mostly it's just that we're demons. Selfish, amoral beings don't tend to form solid relationships. Two selfish, amoral beings are pretty much doomed."

Something inside me twisted at his words. Doomed. I didn't want to explore this any further, and Irix hadn't completely answered my earlier question.

"Were your feelings for Colette what humans would call love?"

He hesitated a moment. "Yes."

I wondered how they'd worked that out with his incubus needs, if they'd even had sex. I couldn't see Irix having a platonic relationship with anyone who was willing to have sex with him — and they were all willing. Would he have tied her to him, leaving her longing as he dashed back and forth to Hel and satisfied his hunger with other humans? I thought of the man in the hotel room and wondered how desperate Colette had been if Irix had left her for years at a time. A decade is nothing to a demon, but it's a painful eternity to a human.

Irix put his arm around my shoulder and drew me close. "I don't want tonight to be filled with ghosts of the past. You did amazing magic today, far above what others of your age would be capable of. I'm proud of you, Amber. I want to celebrate your intellect, and your power. Let's do something special."

We were only a few blocks from his house, I realized. My heart sped up at the thought of what special things Irix and I could do. My earlier fantasy of the stairway loomed in my mind, and I picked up the pace.

"Grab some champagne and head back to your place?"

His hand caressed my shoulder. "Ah, my elven princess, the champagne is already on ice."

Imagine my shock when we rounded the corner and I saw the dark brick of his house in sharp contrast to the golden light pouring out the open shutters of every window. A party?

Irix followed me up the front steps, his hand dropping from my shoulder to cup my ass and urge me forward. As I neared, I could hear the music through the thick, centuries-old walls. It wasn't the thumping base of the college parties I usually attended; this was low and deep, with a middle-eastern flavor. As I opened the door, a cloud wafted toward me — sweet and heavy, the scent swirled through my brain, slowing my thoughts and sending the nerve endings across my skin into overdrive.

"What is that?" The music was thankfully low enough that I didn't have to shout.

He sniffed. "Cannabis."

I raised my eyebrows. I'd smelled plenty of pot in my life, and none of it had this peculiar aroma.

"And opium. Mostly opium."

He grinned sheepishly, while my mouth dropped open in horror. "You rob a bank, steal a car, and now you have a bunch of people doing hard-core drugs in your house?"

"Well, I hope to be doing them too. If you don't like opium, you can always do hash instead."

I made a series of incoherent noises while he grabbed my arm and led me through the narrow hallway into the room with golden-papered walls, an excess of dark mahogany trim, and naked people. Naked people smoking drugs from elaborate bejeweled glass bongs that looked like they cost more than my car.

"I think I'm overdressed for the occasion." It was the only thing I could think of to say as I watched one man lean over and exhale smoke seductively into another's mouth before closing the distance with a passionate kiss.

"Easily remedied."

Before I realized what was happening, Irix had lowered

the zipper on the back of my dress with a quick, smooth movement, sliding the thin silk from my shoulders to puddle at my feet. I opened my mouth to protest, but forgot my objections as the demon's hands skimmed my waist. He kissed along the top of my shoulder, into the hollow of my collarbone, and my little purse hit the floor.

I knew the combination of Irix and second-hand opium smoke was blurring my judgment, but I didn't care. Turning to face him, I unbuttoned the front of his shirt by feel as our mouths merged. Before his shirt joined my dress on the floor, I felt the hands of others on me, caressing my calves and back. Someone nibbled their way up the sensitive skin of my waist, licking along the side of my breast.

I didn't care. Actually, I cared a lot, and it was all good.

"They're all yours," Irix murmured in my ear. "Six to do with what you want, and not a single one of them wearing socks."

My monster purred, pleased at his gift and basking in the energy already flowing into me. I struggled to find some part of me still rational enough to insist that these people could hardly be considered consenting. Yeah, they'd willingly come to a drug-fueled orgy, but I doubt they'd agreed to be sexually tied to me for life.

"I can't do it." My voice trembled with the half-hearted protest.

"A feather light tie." Irix's voice was as silken as the shirt I'd just stripped off him. "Or no tie at all. You choose, and I will make sure you maintain control."

I practically collapsed in relief. The sensation of six people caressing me with hands and mouths was more than I could withstand. I wanted to turn to them, feel their flesh against mine, and fulfill their greatest fantasies.

"No tie. Just tonight, and nothing more."

My monster screamed in protest, but this was a test. If I

could manage to do this, even with Irix's help, then maybe I could trust myself to hold back. Next time, a light tie, then next time a bit more. If I promised the monster what she wanted in the future, maybe I could extend that future out another century or so. Maybe forever.

For now, six humans in one night should be enough to sustain me for what I needed to do tomorrow. In addition, I felt a steady flow of energy from Irix, his continued gift to me. I appreciated it. Without his energy, I would be too hungry to maintain any sort of self-control.

"I promise," he told me.

I wasn't sure whether I truly believed him, or was so desperate for what those around me were so willing to give. I had no choice but to trust him. Taking a deep breath and squeezing my eyes shut, I turned around, giving myself over to the press of flesh.

They surrounded me, and under the onslaught of sensation, I was dimly aware of Irix moving a few feet away to watch. I sensed his pleasure — as great as my own, and wondered if he was as aroused as I was.

"Take out your cock," I commanded, opening my eyes to meet his golden ones. He was leaning against a tall table, watching me intently. Never taking his eyes from mine, he slowly lowered his hands to his pants and released the top button. A hand skimmed along the bulge tenting his pants, while the other slowly eased down the zipper. With a twist of his hips, the pants whispered to the floor, leaving him gloriously naked . . . and very, very hard.

"Kiss that doe-eyed beauty beside you," he instructed, taking himself in hand with a slow, firm slide. "I want to see how wide her brown eyes become when you take her over the edge."

I'm not often attracted to women, but I turned to the cocoa-skinned woman to my left without a second thought.

Her skin was soft as my hands smoothed down her back to cup her ass. I met her gaze briefly before pulling her toward me and merging her full lips with mine. She tasted of peaches and honey, and my tongue explored her mouth as my hands learned their way around her body. The others stroked me encouragingly, allowing me to give all my attention to the sweet woman before me.

Her breasts were full and heavy in my hands, and she made small whimpering noises into my mouth as she fisted my hair. Breaking off the kiss, I lowered my head, dropping down to flick a dark nipple with my tongue.

She gasped. And something quacked. *Quack, quack, quack. Quack, quack, quack.* What the fuck? It was coming from somewhere near my feet. Had someone let a duck in the house? I was kinky, but I wasn't *that* kinky.

Quack, quack, quack.

My phone. And I knew exactly what that ring-tone meant. "Sorry, so sorry," I said as I shimmied free from all the hands so I could drop to the floor and scrabble for my purse.

"Amber." Irix's voice carried a stern warning along with the promise of punishment. I shivered in anticipation, but we'd have no time for that sort of fun. No time for fun with the woman I'd been kissing either. I planted a long kiss on the inside of her thigh in apology as I yanked my phone from the purse.

"Amber! If you don't put that phone down right now, I'm going to take you over my knee and smack you so hard you won't be able to sit for a week."

So tempting. I stood and waved the phone at him. "It's Ourson. They've caught someone."

CHAPTER 27

The light rain dampened my hair and caused my silk dress to cling to my body as we dashed from our street-side parking spot to the sex club. I hadn't expected the vampires to take their captive to Bliss. Honestly, I hadn't given much thought to what they'd do if and when they actually caught someone. I guess this was more private than questioning someone along the riverfront, and he or she would hardly be likely to escape from the vampire-owned establishment.

What I wasn't prepared for was the scene that met my eyes when Eloise led us up a set of private stairs and into a room behind a heavy metal door. Ourson and Guy the Vampire Guy stood on either side of a bald, middle-aged man who looked like he'd been dragged through a field of sticker bushes behind a fast-moving pick-up truck. He didn't seem very dangerous at the moment, duct-taped as he was to a chair. As a matter of fact, he kind of reminded me of my high school chemistry teacher, Mr. Wilcox. I felt rather sorry for him until I noticed the blood covering the front of Ourson's shirt.

"Oh my God! Are you okay?"

"Stabbed me with a spelled athame." The vampire shifted his weight and winced. "Another half an inch and you'd be scraping my remains off the levee path."

My mouth felt dry, realizing how close my new friend had come to death. I was a college student, a botany major, and I was obviously in way over my head. How had this whole thing gotten so dangerous? What if someone had been killed?

"Jordan and her friends, Raol and Frederick — are they all okay?"

Ourson's lips twisted with grim humor. "They're fine. I'm the only one who got skewered."

"But it will all be for nothing if we can't get this piece of trash to talk." Guy the Vampire Guy smacked Chemistry Teacher across the side of the face, raising a red welt on the man's pale skin and rocking his head to the side. Mr. Wilcox clamped his lips together. He glared at the vampire, but his bound hands trembled.

"Here's what we found when we searched him," Eloise chimed in, motioning toward a stack of boxes that served as a makeshift table.

I shook my head as I surveyed the odd collection of items, hoping someone else knew what they were.

"Blessed chalk, holy water, and a stone of invisibility." Irix looked thoughtful as he sorted through the items. Unrolling a sheet of paper crammed with squiggly lines in some kind of dark-red ink, he raised his eyebrows. "Doorway to Hel scroll. That's . . . odd."

The tone of his voice indicated that a scroll opening a gate to the realm of the demons was far more than odd. I pushed aside a small, round, button-shaped item and picked up a polished six-inch dowel inscribed with more of the squiggly lines, this time burned down the side. "What's this?"

Irix glanced at it briefly before returning his attention to the scroll. "Chicken wand — the smaller, more portable version. I know someone who would pay dearly for that. You might want to keep it."

I wasn't sure what the protocol was on who owned these items. Did we give them back to Mr. Wilcox? Were they the property of the vampires? Irix had a bent towards larceny, but I didn't exactly want to follow in his footsteps when it came to that particular sin.

Eloise shrugged. "Keep the wand if you like."

I nodded my thanks and tucked the small dowel into my purse. How did one go about brokering the sale of a chicken wand? And what the fuck did a chicken wand even do?

"It's one way for one being," Irix mused, still looking at the scroll. "I could see where this man may have one going the opposite way — for summoning a demon he'd contracted for a job, but no human would want a fast, portable exit to Hel."

"You can have that one," Eloise said, peering over his shoulder. "Not like any of us would want to go there."

Probably not. Demons made unreliable allies, and Hel was filled with elves — their mortal enemies. "Maybe he stole it off a demon," I suggested, thinking again of Irix's bad habits.

Irix shot a quick look at the human in question. "He wouldn't be the first, although humans who steal from demons usually have very short lives." With a quick movement, he rolled the scroll and tucked it in the waistband of his pants. "Shall we help the vampires question their guest?"

We wandered over to Mr. Wilcox, who was looking worse for wear. A thin line of blood trailed from the corner of his mouth. All three vampires eyed it with interest, and I swear I saw Eloise lick her lips. Shit, we better get this show on the road before they got any hungrier.

"Who are you, and what were you doing at the levee?" I asked, unsure where to begin.

Mr. Wilcox swallowed hard a few times, his face white as the wall behind him. "John Smith. I'm a tourist from New Jersey. I was just taking a walk along the river."

I sucked at this whole interrogation thing. Still, everyone seemed to be waiting for me to do something, to direct them. Even Irix held back, watching as if the whole scenario bored him. I'm sure he'd rather be back at his party. Heck, I'd rather be back at his party.

"At two in the morning?"

"I was out on Bourbon Street and wanted to sober up before going back to my hotel."

He didn't seem particularly drunk, although he did look like he was going to vomit any minute. "Carrying a bunch of magical items?"

"Like I said — I'm a tourist. I got them at one of the voodoo shops as souvenirs."

"Right. Holy water, maybe, but the tourist shops don't have scrolls to Hel, spelled athames or chicken wands." Whatever the heck chicken wands were.

He looked up, eyes darting between me and the vampires. "I dabble in the occult. Last time I checked, freedom of religion was in the Bill of Rights."

What should have been a wise-guy show of confidence was rendered null by a terrified stutter and short panicked breaths.

"Last time I checked, sabotaging the city's flood defenses isn't in the Bill of Rights."

Mr. Wilcox dropped his gaze to stare at his lap. "I have no idea what you're talking about."

Three sets of fangs came out, and Eloise glided toward the man, making clear her carnivorous intentions. Mr.

Wilcox cringed, straining away as far as his bonds would allow.

"Go ahead. I'm not afraid of a little blood loss."

The poor man could hardly get the words out, he shook so badly. He may have stabbed Ourson, but I still felt sorry for him. Heck, I'd shot the vampire in the balls with a jolt of electricity. Maybe there were extenuating circumstances here.

"A little blood loss?" Eloise drawled, her child-like voice somewhat lisping with her sharp fangs exposed. "There are three of us, and I'm particularly hungry. By the time we're done, there won't be a drop of blood in your body."

"I'm not afraid of death either." He clearly *was* afraid of death, but Mr. Wilcox lifted his chin defiantly. I could see that he intended to stand his ground, in spite of the vampire's threats. A dead mage wouldn't do us any good. He'd called Eloise's bluff.

"Perhaps eternal life would motivate you to talk?" Irix asked softly.

It hardly sounded like a threat to me, but our captive gasped, struggling frantically against the duct tape that held him to the chair.

Irix stalked toward the man like a cat creeping up on a mouse. "I'll take my time, rip your soul from your flesh over the next few hours while the vampires lap up your blood."

The vampires seemed in favor of this idea. I held perfectly still, wondering what Irix was talking about. How could the torture he was proposing have anything to do with eternal life?

"What is it you fear, human?" The incubus leaned over the chair, tracing a long finger across the man's cheekbone. Mr. Wilcox shook, shutting his eyes tightly, but still not saying a thing.

"No matter. No need to tell me a thing. I'll take your soul

with all your thoughts and memories. Your secrets, the plans of your group, it will all be revealed."

Irix placed a hand on the man's cheek, and another against his chest. A glow surrounded his fingers. Mr. Wilcox cried out, and Irix gave a low laugh that held pure evil in its tone. Now it was my turn to shudder, reminded that the sexy, playful incubus had a dark side that made my own monster seem like a saint.

"I will know all — everything you fear, the nightmares that cause you to wake screaming, but there will be no more awakenings, no more relief from the terror. For all eternity, you will suffer with no hope of salvation."

I watched in horror as drops of blood began to bead on the man's skin. He screamed, convulsing, as Irix's hands glowed with light.

"One more chance to change your mind, my friend," Irix purred. "Are your friends really worth the torture you'll suffer in my hands?"

The demon must have let up on what he was doing, because Mr. Wilcox's eyes flew open with a gasp. "Stop. I'll talk. I'll tell you everything if you promise not to Own me."

Irix smiled. It was one of the cruelest smiles I'd ever witnessed, and my stomach lurched at the sight. "I swear on all the souls that I Own, I will not claim you if you tell us everything. The truth — otherwise I am relieved from my vow."

The man nodded, a drop of blood rolling down his forehead to hover at the tip of his nose. The glow around Irix's hands faded. He stepped back, and Mr. Wilcox promptly puked.

Being duct-taped to a chair doesn't give a person much room to maneuver, and our captive now had vomit down the front of his shirt and in a puddle on his crotch. Eloise wrinkled her nose in disgust, clearly put off her dinner by the sight.

"My name is Steve Mulligan," the man said, spitting to clear his mouth. That wound up along with the vomit in his lap. "I'm an apprentice with the Great Order of Crimson Moon, New Orleans Chapter."

Mulligan. I liked Wilcox better.

In spite of the fancy title of his magical order, apprentice didn't sound very impressive. This guy had to know something, though, or he wouldn't have been nosing around the levees loaded for bear with magical weapons.

"What was your purpose at the levee tonight?"

Mr. Wilcox hesitated, as though he was about to refuse to answer, but a quick motion from Irix wiped the color from his face.

"I make the rounds each night. A bunch of Wiccans messed up something we did in a bayou south of the city a few nights back. My job tonight was to check our spells along the levee, and report if any had been tampered with."

"Are you the only one doing this?"

The man shook his head. "Three, sometimes four. There are a lot of spots, and they're spread out. It would take too long for one person to check them all."

"Where are all the spelled locations?"

He shot a nervous look at Irix and swallowed hard a few times before reciting a long list of locations. Three bayous, five sections of wetland closer to the gulf, the twenty spots along the levee we'd found, as well as twelve additional ones on levees along the canals and the lake, the dam, and two sea walls further south of the city.

Shit, that was a lot of locations.

"How long have you all been doing this?" There is no way any group, even with a sorcerer or mage helping, could spell all that in a few weeks. Crimson Moon must have been working on this project for a long time. And there was no way we could fix all that in the next few days. My heart sank. Even if we managed to capture all of Crimson Moon and their mage, the city would remain compromised until the spells were broken. I might need to miss my flight and drive home in Irix's stolen Audi after all.

"Six months, although we began testing last year. The first spells weren't very stable, like the one at the dam. They either went off early, or didn't have the range of effect we'd hoped."

From the twenty spells we'd found at the levee, and the damage to the cypresses, I hadn't thought this was a casual endeavor, but I'd never envisioned the extent of their plot. The careful planning, the numerous locations — these people were serious about ensuring the success of their scheme.

"Who do you report back to?" I had the list that Ourson had given me and was hoping the name he gave me would match one on that list.

"Adelphia," he replied promptly.

I wasn't sure if he was lying or not. Who the fuck names their kid "Adelphia?"

"What's their real name?"

He cast a nervous look at Irix. "All I know is that she's a woman. None of them use their real names with me. Anyone initiate and above is robed or hooded in ceremony, and I've never met any of them outside our meetings that I'm aware of."

How in the world were we supposed to crack a secret society if nobody knew each other's names or appearance? Frustrated, I figured I'd at least ask the million-dollar question, although this guy was so low in their organization that he wasn't likely to know.

"Why? Why would you want the city to suffer such

destruction in a storm that you would spend huge resources and a year or more in planning?"

"We used to control the most powerful ley line in North America, but all the dams and levees have dispersed and weakened the energy. Nature and the ley line will recover if allowed to take their course. We have the skills to do great good with that power restored. It's all for a greater good."

Easy for him to say. I fumed, unable to imagine how anyone could justify the destruction of a major metropolitan area, including significant loss of lives, with some nebulous "greater good". Plus the whole thing was breathtakingly overkill.

"That's a lot of damage just to yank the ley line power away from another group."

Wilcox shifted in his seat and dropped his chin to his chest. "Some of the spells might not work. We need to make sure the first hurricane brings success, or Bon Nuit will find a way to block future attempts."

It still didn't make sense. I could see them targeting a few bayous and the river levees to free up the Mississippi River, but what about all the other spots?

"Why put spells on the lake and canal levees? And the wetlands to the east of the river?" None of those breaches would affect the ley lines.

His gaze was just as puzzled as I'm sure mine was. "I don't know. Maybe for diversions? All I know is that we want to get control of the ley line energy."

What a bunch of assholes. They were willing to destroy property and risk people's lives as a diversion? I was so lost in my angry thoughts, that I almost missed Mr. Wilcox's next words.

"I've got no idea what the foreign guy wants though. We're not paying him for his help. Personally, I think he's got a different motive than the rest of us."

"What foreign guy?"

"I don't know who he is, but he's the only one who doesn't wear a hood or mask. Blond hair, almost white, with green eyes. He's pretty tan, but, with that hair, I'm sure it's spray-on. He's a real jerk. Orders everyone around like we're all slaves. I don't think the elders would put up with him except he's the most amazing magician we've ever seen. He's truly gifted."

Or truly elven trained, and doing it since before he was out of diapers. "What's *his* name?"

"I don't know. Everyone calls him 'Weaver' because of the way his magic meshes everything together."

I walked over to Irix. "A mage from Hel?"

He shrugged. "Or a demon. A mage would probably have the usual mercenary motivations, but many classes of demons simply enjoy destruction and death and wouldn't ask for payment."

"But Jordan said the magic didn't match," I argued.

"Maybe she was wrong. Maybe other demon's energy doesn't look the same as mine does. I just think we should keep all our options open."

We. I really liked that I wasn't in this alone, that Irix might consider this project to be just as much his as mine.

"I hope it's a mage," I muttered. "Although if it's a demon, that angel might do the work for us."

"Maybe. Angels sometimes arrive too late." He fingered the scroll in his waistband. "And if Weaver has another of these, he may intend to be across the gates before the shit hits the fan."

I looked at Mr. Wilcox, slumped in the chair, and wasn't sure what to do next. "I don't think he knows anything else. What should we do with him?"

It was a perplexing problem. I doubted the police would lock him up for checking magical spells. How loyal was he to

Crimson Moon? If he told them about us, about the vampires and Bliss, all my friends would be at risk. This Weaver guy might not be above blowing up the club, or hunting down Ourson and his friends. Normally, I'd bet on Irix in a fight with just about anyone, but I didn't know how powerful mages from Hel were, and if Weaver was even a mage. Incubi and succubi weren't all that powerful compared to other demons.

"The vampires will take care of him." Irix replied, already taking my arm as if to lead me from the room.

I didn't like the sound of that one bit. I pulled away and turned suspiciously toward Eloise. "Take care of him how?"

Everyone in the room seemed confused by my question.

"What would you prefer?" Eloise asked, as if she were treading on landmines. She clearly didn't want to offend me, but had no idea where I was going with my question.

"Well, I'd *prefer* we let him go."

Mr. Wilcox seemed in favor of that too. His eyes darted to me with a tiny glimmer of hope. The vampires stared at me as if I'd gone insane. Irix put a reassuring arm around my shoulder.

"Darling, we can't let him go. You must put your household ahead of this stranger's life. Besides, he said he wasn't afraid to die, and all I vowed was that I wouldn't Own him."

Irix sounded eerily regretful at the prospect of not Owning the man. I shivered, moving out from under his arm with the pretense of examining the man closer.

"We can just drain him," Eloise added cheerfully, looking like a young child eager to head off to the circus. "We've got a gland that activates when we feed that makes the process enjoyable for the human. He'd die without pain."

Mr. Wilcox didn't look any happier at that prospect, but he stiffened his shoulders in a show of courage.

"Are you kidding," Guy argued. "The nasty bag of blood

nearly killed Ourson with a spelled athame. I say we take our time and pull him apart over the next few days."

My stomach turned, and I struggled to think of some alternative that would make sense to them, that they'd respect as more than the sentimental emotion of a young succubus.

"He's . . . mine. I want him."

Eloise's lovely violet eyes widened in shock. "Of course. Would you like a private room to enjoy your captive?"

"Amber, perhaps you should allow the vampires to have this one. I don't think he's a good candidate for you to Own."

Irix came closer but didn't touch me. I knew what he meant. Half-breeds couldn't Own, and I didn't have a really good idea what it entailed anyway. I just figured claiming the man would give me the opportunity to get him out of here and time to figure out what to do with him. I turned to face Irix and saw the table with the human's belongings strewn across it. In two steps I was there, picking up a rectangular object.

"You'll call your contact." I waved the phone at him. "And tell her that all was clear on your rounds, but you had a sudden death in the family and had to leave town for a few days. If you cooperate, you'll have your freedom by next week. If not, then I'll give you to the vampires and let them do as they please."

Mr. Wilcox nodded enthusiastically. "Deal. Everyone knows my mother in New Jersey has been ill, so it won't be suspicious if I suddenly have to go away."

We watched as the human made his call. Irix leaned over me, his lips nearly touching my ear. He was so close, I could smell the warmth of his skin.

"And where do you intend to keep your new pet, darling?" His voice was full of amusement, and his hand skimmed my lower back. "Chain him to our bed, perhaps? He already views you as his savior. He'll happily tie to you as deep as you wish."

Ew. The very thought of having sex with a guy that reminded me of my high school chemistry teach was repellant. I had a better idea. Hopefully I could trust the vampires to go along with it.

"Ourson, I will leave Mr. Wilcox in your care for the next few days. You'll be allowed to drink from him as much as you want, in compensation for your injury. Just don't take so much blood you endanger his life."

The vampire's brow wrinkled as he looked around the room. "You mean the human? I thought his name was Mullins or something."

Oops. He'd forever become Mr. Wilcox in my mind. "Yeah, him. Can you vow to me that you'll not mistreat him? That you'll keep him safe from harm until I reclaim him?"

Ourson cast a disappointed look at the bound man. "Okay, but you owe me big time, Amber. Babysitting your pet, a man who stabbed me with intent to kill, isn't high on my list of fun activities."

The other vampires started at his familiar tone toward me, but I smiled, giving my friend a quick hug. "Done. I appreciate it, buddy. And coffee is on me tomorrow."

Irix and I left, assured by Ourson that no harm would come to Mr. Wilcox beyond a slight bit of anemia. Eloise led us through the security into the club and left us with the groups of beribboned, mostly-naked people, gyrating on the dance floor.

"Do you want to stay here, or go back to the house?" Irix asked, looking around with interest at the dancers.

I hesitated, not sure how to voice my thoughts without offending him. "If you could drop me off at Darci's, I'd really appreciate it."

The whole interrogation of Mr. Wilcox had unsettled me,

and the side of Irix I'd seen had more than unsettled me. I'd imagined him as a powerful and stern incubus with a sexy, playful side, but I'd somehow ignored the fact that under it all he *was* a demon. Irix wasn't human, and part of him gloried in the ultimate control of others, in pain and pleasure that he could dish out as he wished. I hadn't quite come to terms with my own monster. Irix's sent a spike of fear through my heart.

"You are not going back to Darci's," the demon snarled. My blood ran cold, and the perverted monster in me was even more attracted to him.

"I don't need sex, I just need sleep." I stuttered, backing away a few steps. His hand shot out and grabbed my upper arm with a vice-like grip.

"Fucking hell you don't need sex. And I'm not letting you go back to Darci's tonight. You're mine, and you'll sleep in my bed. Do I make myself clear?"

How could I want someone so much and be so terrified at the same time? "I don't think. . . ."

Irix yanked me toward him before I could finish my sentence and tossed me over his shoulder. His arm clamped my hips against his body. I felt like a dead deer being hauled out of the forest as he strode through the crowd of dancers, pushing them out of the way with his shoulders. A few cheered, giving him a thumbs-up, and I felt my temper flare.

"Put me the fuck down!"

None of my protests or attempts to kick and hit did any good. Once we reached the stolen Audi, Irix paused. The second he put me in the car and let go, I'd turn into a ferocious hellion. He could hardly drive with me biting and punching him the whole way. I squirmed against his grasp, confident that in a few seconds I'd be able to either make a break for it or defend myself appropriately.

Imagine my surprise when he turned away from the car

and strode down the street with me over his shoulder. The asshole meant to walk ten blocks through the busy city with me like this. I screamed in frustration and kicked, managing to land one square to his balls.

Irix hesitated, and I felt his entire body tense with pain. His grasp on my legs became excruciatingly tight. After a few seconds, he continued walking.

"I told you once, little half breed, that if you did that again, you'd suffer the consequences. Never let it be said that I'm not a man of my word."

Pheromones flowed from the incubus in a thick wave, coating me and filling all my senses. My struggles halted, and I was embarrassed to find myself arching against him, trying to maximize our contact.

The next ten blocks were a blur. I rubbed myself along Irix's muscular shoulders, kissed down his bicep as far as I could reach and inhaled deeply, taking in every bit of him that I could. I was wet, and I knew he was fully aware of that fact. By the time he lowered me down in front of his door, it was all I could do to keep from dropping to my knees and taking him in my mouth.

"Wait." His voice was husky and raw with need as he unlocked the door with a shaking hand. It seemed my staircase fantasy was going to become reality because we'd hardly gone two steps through the doorway before our mouths sealed together, and hands gripped each other with frenzied hunger.

Somehow we managed to make it up the stairs and to his bedroom. I had no idea if any of the orgy crowd were still in the house or not. The faint aroma of opium and cannabis lingered, but all I knew was Irix. I half tore the clothes from his body, and he did the same. Before I could take a breath, I was naked on the bed with him on top of me. His amber eyes met mine, and I gasped, desperate with hunger. I needed him inside me, all around me. I needed his hands on my breasts, his mouth on my skin. I wanted him to possess every inch of me, and I wanted it now.

"No."

I could hardly believe my ears. I arched my back, bringing my pelvis against his erection to show him how much I wanted this to be a "yes".

"No." He pulled away, looking down at me with stormy eyes, his mouth a tight line. The level of pheromones dropped like a stone, and I found my thoughts muddled — desire fading into confusion. Was this his revenge for my kicking him in the balls? He'd threatened the first day I'd met him that if I did it again, he'd chain me to the wall and leave me unfulfilled, tortured by his pheromones, but from our staircase ascent, I'd gotten the idea he was just as crazed with lust as I was.

"I need to go out for a while. Please stay here, at least until I return?"

He was definitely leaving me frustrated, but "please" was a far cry from chaining me to the wall. And what in hell did he have to do in the early hours of the morning with a willing half-succubus in his bed? I swallowed hard and nodded. He rewarded me with a charming, crooked smile, and a brief kiss on the forehead. I pulled the rumpled comforter over my naked body and watched him dress, dozing off as he shut the bedroom door behind him.

It became crystal clear what Irix had been up to as soon as he crawled naked back into bed and pulled me to him. Energy flowed into me with every stroke, lighting me up as much as his caresses. Sleepy sex made everything seem so much more intimate, and when we came, I held his hips to me, refusing to let him withdraw, wanting to prolong that feeling of union as long as possible.

The thought of how many humans he must have fucked

sent a spike of jealousy and fear through my heart. Had his activity put him at risk of being detected by the angel? At least he had that scroll with him in case he needed to get away quickly, although I'd freak not knowing what happened to Irix until he managed to get a message back to me. It scared me that he'd taken this chance, and I felt guilty that I hadn't remained with him at Bliss and picked a partner or two.

Finally he rolled to the side, adjusting my position and holding me against his warm chest. I felt his breath stir my hair and kissed right where his heart beat. He smoothed my blond locks from my face and murmured a short phrase in another language before kissing the top of my head.

"Sleep well, my elf-girl."

And I did.

CHAPTER 28

Only one thing could have gotten me up at six in the morning and forced me to drag my butt to a graveyard. I'd woken to the 'quack quack' of my cell phone and nearly flew from the bed when I read that Ourson had finally scored a meeting with Nathanial Basteau of Crimson Moon.

"I gotta run," I shouted to Irix as I scrambled around looking for clothing.

Damn, it looked like my choices were sweaty, dirty shorts and t-shirt from yesterday, and half-ripped silk dress from last night. If only I had time to swing by Darci's.

"Make sure Ourson sticks with you." Irix was reading the text and climbing out of bed at a more leisurely pace than I'd managed. "This could be a trap."

That slowed me.

"Do you think they suspect we have Wilcox?"

"That, or they discovered we disabled the levee spells. You'll find out when you get there."

'*You*'? I paused, holding up my filthy t-shirt. "Aren't you coming with me?"

"You may only be twenty, but you're a grown woman, and this is your project. You can handle a human mage."

He turned to rifle through the endless array of shirts hanging in his closet.

"Which is why you want Ourson to stick with me?"

"It's always good to have a vampire at your back."

His words were light and casual, but there was something tense lurking behind them. I watched as he pulled out two shirts, tossing them onto the bed.

"I'll meet you at the levee when you're done." He shrugged into one of the shirts.

It hurt that he wasn't coming. I really didn't want to do this without him by my side, but I was too rushed to argue. Instead, I pulled on my dirty shorts, wincing at the thought of wearing them another day.

"Okay. Text me and let me know which location you're at, and Ourson and I will meet you there."

In the end I wound up wearing the dirty shorts sans underwear, and one of Irix's shirts knotted at my waist. It smelled like him, even though it had been freshly laundered. I wondered if I could steal it.

Ourson met me right outside Irix's house and drove me there, unlocking the cemetery gates with a large metal key. This wasn't one of the old graveyards, but a newer one up by the lake. Instead of tall tombs, these interments were buried partially underground with a raised slab. Step tombs, Ourson called them. I followed the vampire along the pathways, weaving down the rows to a spot at the rear of the cemetery. There stood a man, face hidden by a wide-brimmed hat. Nathanial Basteau. I wondered how he'd managed to get past the locked gate. Did he too have a key, or a more magical means of entry?

We stood beside him for a few long moments before he

acknowledged our presence. Ice-blue eyes skimmed over Ourson dismissively before Basteau turned to face me.

"Whatever they're paying you and the other demon, I'll double it."

The man didn't beat around the bush, which was fine with me. We had eleven more spells to break before nightfall. I hardly wanted to waste the entire morning in a cemetery making small talk.

"They're not paying us. Look, I understand why you're doing this, but there has to be another way."

"They've summoned you and demanded service? I had no idea Wiccans would do such things. They've always turned up their noses at our path and methods."

I hesitated, not sure how to explain our cooperation to Basteau. Full demons wouldn't selflessly volunteer to help a bunch of humans. "All that matters is we can't leave until this is resolved. None of us want to spend the next few decades making and breaking spells. Surely there can be some compromise?"

Basteau pushed his hat backward with an index finger, giving me a hard look. "So Bev is willing to talk?"

Not likely. I'd hoped I could find out how much Crimson Moon was willing to budge on this, and then go back to Bev with a proposal. Half a loaf had to be better than none at all — which was what she was facing if that storm coming up the gulf hit the shore with any force.

"Would you agree to a schedule where Crimson Moon and Bon Nuit share access to the ley line?" It still left out all the smaller groups in New Orleans, but it was a start.

The man laughed. "That old harpy must be really scared if she's proposing a share, and sending one of her summoned demons to meet me instead of coming herself. Tell you what, let Bon Nuit know that we want full and exclusive access by midnight, or we move forward."

Shit, this whole thing had gone nowhere. "And what would that leave them? They'd have nothing at all."

Basteau shook his head, smiling. "They'd have the satisfaction of knowing their actions saved lives, prevented damage to the city. That should be enough for those tree-huggers."

"It wouldn't be enough for Bev," I retorted. Sad, but true. Control of the ley line would come before protecting the city. It didn't escape my notice that Bev and this man shared several moral defects.

He shrugged. "Oh well."

"We can break your spells faster than you can replace them. Any advantage you have now will soon be gone. I'd suggest you reconsider negotiating." I was so pissed off that I could hardly keep my voice calm and steady. The monster inside me really wanted to kill both Basteau and Bev and be done with it, but I pushed her back.

The man gave me a sharp look, tilting his hat forward again. "We'll see about that."

I watched him walk away. Basteau's last words sent an uneasy chill down my spine, and I was grateful that Ourson was by my side. "This meeting was a bad idea. I think I may have made things worse."

Ourson shook his head. "No. Whatever they have planned, you didn't contribute to it. The reason they agreed to this wasn't to negotiate, it was to show us their power and issue a threat."

"Well, I got the threat loud and clear."

"Me too." The vampire grimaced. "I'm going to suggest we either double up a vampire and witch at each site, or pull the witches off watch tonight."

Jordan would have a cow. I winced, thinking of what she was going to say when I told her. I couldn't help but agree with Ourson, though.

"I'm also going to ask if Eloise will take a shift. She's powerful, and if she thinks our magic-user liaisons are in danger, she'll step in."

I nodded then remembered something I'd been meaning to ask the vampire. "I don't mean to be rude or anything, but what is her story? She seems to be very young for a vampire."

Ourson laughed. "Her human appearance is child-like, but, as a vampire, she's a mature woman. She's actually over six-hundred-and-fifty-years old. Her father was an alchemist and had business interests with a prominent vampire family in France. When Eloise contracted the plague, he asked to have her turned."

I let out a breath I hadn't realized I'd been holding. "That's pretty much what I'd thought. She must have been ten or twelve?"

"Eight. Far younger than we usually consider for candidates, even back then. It's a miracle she survived. The process of becoming a vampire is very taxing physically, and her body was still fighting the plague at the same time."

I made a mental note to tell Darci and put her mind to rest. The ride back to the river was uneventful, but I kept thinking of Basteau's vague threat. What did Crimson Moon have planned? I was relieved to pull up to the grassy knoll and see Jordan and her friends standing with the group of vampires.

"Where's Irix?" I asked her, gratefully taking the coffee she offered me. We'd been so rushed to get to our meeting at the cemetery, that neither Ourson nor I had been able to stop for a cup.

"He's not here yet." My Wiccan friend was practically hopping with excitement. "Fifteen more people have left Bon Nuit in support of us. Isn't that awesome news?"

It was, although I really didn't want their first task to be as dangerous as this. Before I could tell Jordan about the need to partner one-on-one with a vampire, she continued happily. "Do you think we can finish the other eleven spells by the end of today? It will be great to put this all behind us."

"I'm afraid it's going to be a while before we can put this all behind us." I went on to tell her about the capture of Wilcox, what he revealed, and the meeting with Basteau. By the time I'd finished, Jordan's shoulders were slumped and her coffee cooled, forgotten in her hand.

"What do you think they'll do?" Jordan's voice was barely a whisper. "Kill another bayou forest? Disrupt one of the Bon Nuit rituals? Come after us personally? Are we going to be safe in our own homes, or should I alert the others to put up wards?"

Crap, I hadn't even thought about the last one. Crimson Moon wouldn't go that far — to attack people in their own home, would they? I looked around for Irix, relieved to see the black Audi pulling up to the curb. It was silly to worry over a powerful demon, but Basteau seemed pretty knowledgeable about summoning and demonology — far more knowledgeable than I was.

"Ourson offered to partner a vampire with each witch tonight, but I'm beginning to think it might be safer for you all to remain home and take any precautions you need to ensure your safety."

I could see the struggle in Jordan's expressive face. It had to hurt her pride to consider this.

"Okay. We'll help out today, then sit tonight out."

Part of me wanted to send them home now, but I couldn't deny her this little thing. After all, this was *their* city, not mine. I gave Jordan a hug, and she headed off to tell the others about this new development.

"Ready to work, elf-girl?"

Irix's arm encircled my shoulders, and he bent his head to

give me a kiss. My heart lurched at his show of human affection.

"Yes. We've got a lot to do, and. . . ." I halted, frowning at the incubus.

"What's wrong?"

There was a lot wrong. Not just the meeting with Basteau, either.

"Where did you get all that energy? You're practically humming with it."

He shrugged, but I saw tension around his mouth that belied the casual gesture. "Breakfast. I've got a big appetite, remember?"

Sexual innuendo, but I wasn't amused. He'd put himself at risk to gather all this in such a short time. It's a miracle that angel hadn't gotten a lock on him with his activity last night and this morning. I caught my breath at the thought that Irix may have been discovered and killed. It would have been all my fault too. My fault for being stupid, and stubborn.

"Here you are warning me to be careful, and you go and do this both last night and this morning? And you'll be helping me today with the levees? That's way too much of your energy signature flying around with an angel this close."

"I haven't managed to survive two-thousand years by being stupid. I know what I'm doing, little elf-girl. You've got enough to obsess about. I'll be just fine."

He seemed the usual Irix — carefree and relaxed, but over the last two days I'd somehow gotten the ability to see beyond the mask he wore. He was worried — about me and himself. I couldn't let this go on.

"You should have realized by now that I freak out about everything — you included. Please promise me you won't do this again? You need to lay low. Tonight I'll go out and have sex. You can watch if it will convince you that I can do this on my own."

He grinned, and this time it was genuine. "You swear on all the souls that you Own?"

"Absolutely." I linked my arm in his and headed toward the others.

"Well then, I am *definitely* going to watch."

CHAPTER 29

We were three spells broken, eight to go when I got the text from Jordan. Rather than have everyone follow me around, risking their lives while I struggled to contain explosions, I'd sent the vampires to check out the areas Mr. Wilcox had listed as having other spell work. Jordan had spent the night creating detection charms for her team of witches and the vampires. They had taken off to check the locations we repaired yesterday.

Kristin found four of your fixes reversed. Spells for damage are back in place. Meet you by the Aquarium.

Twelve more to go instead of eight. I felt exhausted just thinking about it. These assholes were putting stuff back almost as quick as Irix and I were removing it. We needed to stop them sooner rather than later.

Worse, this meant Crimson Moon hadn't taken Mr. Wilcox's word for it that he'd checked all the levee spots. We'd been found out. Now they knew what we were up to and that we had their colleague. They'd be even more vigilant about checking their spots and probably speed up the timing of their planned disaster. I looked at the dark grey sky, at the swirl of clouds moving in from the south, and worried. That wasn't the only thing I worried about. Basteau's threat still loomed darker than the rain clouds over my mind.

Call everyone in. I'll be right there.

Irix had been reading over my shoulder. As I typed, he looked around at the joggers, the tourists walking by, at the vagrant woman dozing on the grass beside her shopping cart.

"I don't know how many are in Crimson Moon," he said, his voice low, "but there's a good chance they've positioned people to watch the locations during the day."

"Do you think they'll attack us?" I had a vision of people shooting me, or trapping Irix in a circle. Or banishing the pair of us to Hel. Worse, images of my friends shot or stabbed were also crowding my mind.

"Not in a busy park like this." Irix put a hand on my shoulder and gave it a reassuring squeeze. "In the lesser populated areas, they might try to stop us."

Thankfully most of the places Mr. Wilcox had listed were in the city, and even with the threatening clouds, people were still out and about.

"So that means we should probably give up on the bayous for now." I'd hoped to try my hand at doing something to help the cypresses. Their dead silhouettes haunted me, even though I worried there was nothing I could do.

"There's plenty to do in the city without you trying to resurrect the dead — even plant dead."

He was right, but it still broke my heart to leave New Orleans without even trying.

Finished, we headed to meet Kristin, Irix weaving the black Audi through the streets to park a block from his house. We walked past Café du Monde, with its seductive smell of frying beignets, and up to the brick-topped seawall that kept the Mississippi River from the city's historic French Quarter. The red-headed witch sat on a bench overlooking a huge riverboat casino, docked and awaiting passengers. She had a familiar white bag beside her.

"Here. I felt bad about being the bearer of bad news, so I bought you a treat."

I am so going to miss this city, I thought as I dug a pastry from the bag, spilling white powdered sugar down the front of my borrowed shirt and shorts.

"The homeless lady has been watching me for the last half an hour," Kristin whispered, busying herself with the bag of beignets. "How do you want to play this?"

"Well, if they're watching all their locations, then they probably already recognize Irix and me. And now you, too."

"And probably the rest of us if they were there when we first met this morning," Kristin interjected. "It's a good thing we're all regrouping."

Once again I thought of Basteau's threat. "Everyone needs to make sure they stay in the well-populated areas. Tell them to stay aware and take note of anyone paying a lot of attention to them, or who they suspect is watching the area."

Irix reached over to help himself to a pastry. "Do you want to power through today and fix as much as you can, or spend some time strategizing? You do realize they're going to reverse as much of your work as they can, and tonight there's most likely going to be a fight."

My heart lurched at his words. Beyond electricity, I had nothing to bring to a fight. I doubted this would be the sort of thing where hair-pulling and scratching would make any difference. Plus, I was worried about my friends. Mr. Wilcox had nearly killed Ourson with a spelled athame. What weapons would the rest of Crimson Moon and this mage have at their disposal? I doubted the scroll and chicken wand we recovered were the extent of their magical items.

And magical items aside, I wasn't going to rule out that Crimson Moon might use a pistol or a knife in the back to stop us. "Let's fix as much as we can today to try and get ahead of the game. They can't repair them all."

Irix reached out and ran a hand down my shoulder to cup my elbow. "And tonight? The vampires managed to catch the guy last night. I doubt it will be as easy now."

I bit my lip and gave voice to my thoughts. "I don't want any of my friends to be hurt or killed. Maybe if we just watch which ones they tamper with and don't engage them, we can come back tomorrow."

I knew it was a lie. "*We'll see about that.*" They were going to attack us. If it came to a fight I would defend my friends, but the thought of killing set my heart racing. An image flashed before me of my father convulsing on the garage floor. I'd always hoped I wouldn't have to face that side of my monster again.

"What happens the next day, and the next?" Irix's hand on my arm was gentle, but his tone had a steely note to it. "This can't go on forever, Amber. Eventually this is going to turn violent — probably sooner than you think. It's better that you do it on your own terms."

Strike first. It was one thing to take a life when I was five years old and didn't realize the finality of my actions, it was another to stand here and coldly plot an attack on living human beings — people who had wives and children, mothers and brothers, people who felt what they were doing was right, no matter how twisted their logic. People that looked like my high school chemistry teacher. I was facing a hard decision, and there was only one choice I could allow myself to make.

"I'll do what needs to be done," I whispered to him, hoping he'd somehow understand.

"Me too," Kristin said. "I might be a transplant, but I still consider this my city. I won't let these people be the cause of widespread death and destruction. I can kill if I have to."

Easy for someone to say when they'd never done it — never seen the light fade in another's eyes, hear their screams, smell the burning of their flesh. . . .

I looked from Irix to Kristin and swallowed hard before nodding. I didn't want to be this person, but this was about survival, this was a time when I needed to do hard things to protect others.

"I'll call the vampires, if you call Jordan and the rest of the witches," I told Kristin. "Ask them if they have anything defensive, like a magical binding spell, or a freeze spell, or something they can use tonight."

I had no idea if those things were possible, or even if Jordan's group could create them before tonight. Remembering past conversations with Wiccan friends, I seemed to recall certain spells required specific moon phases and ingredients that might not be available on the fly. This *was* New Orleans though — home of the occult. If something like this could be purchased, it would be here. And where was Jordan, anyway? She'd told me in her text she'd meet us here.

Kristin nodded and moved off to make her calls while I turned to Irix. "Part of me wants to fix as much as possible, especially with a storm moving up the gulf, but we can't spread ourselves too thin tonight by watching every single spot. What do you suggest?"

The incubus looked across to the other bank of the Mississippi, the breeze ruffling the dark hair around his face. He looked oddly noble, like a warrior planning a battle strategy — so at odds with the amoral demon that hid beneath the surface.

"They'll want to engage us. Our activities are going to lessen the impact they want — perhaps even negate it, given time. They'll want to take us out just as much as we do them.

I say let's fix everything we can — show them just who they're messing with. We'll pick a spot that suits us best and do something really flashy there, and then wait. They'll come."

"I'll be too weak to do much at the actual battle." So would he. It made me feel guilty to know my abstinence had drained him, weakened him. If he was hurt, if *any* of us was hurt, it would be my fault. "I'm a pretty decent shot, so maybe I can get a gun. Or if I can find enough sexual partners I can use electricity."

"I don't want you to fight. Your job is to fix as much of these magical faults as possible, then stay safe."

His words . . . stung.

"Amber, I haven't been able to persuade you to have sex with anyone but me, your vow a few moments ago aside. I know I'm not going to sway you into actions that most likely will kill a human being." He caressed my arm as if he understood and forgave me my inability to come to terms with the demon inside me. "I'll fight in your stead."

A vision of him dead and bleeding on the top of the seawall rocked me. I could never stand by while my friends died before my eyes. I could never stay safe and watch him die.

"I'll fight. And I'll do whatever I need to prepare for it. Women, married people, guys with sandals and socks."

He didn't even crack a smile. "I'd rather you stay safe. It's okay, Amber. You don't have to do this."

"Yes, I do. How am I going to live for ten-thousand years knowing that I hid while those I cared about died? That I could have made a difference and chose not to?"

"You'd rather live with the guilt that you tied unwilling humans to you? That you killed?"

His voice was as soft and gentle as his hand on my arm.

"Yes. I'll live with that guilt. These people are relying on me to help them. A whole city of people, their livelihoods as well as their lives, rest in our hands. My ethics are fucked either way. I'm choosing the path I'll best be able to live with — the one that will let me sleep at night."

His eyes met mine, warm with a note of concern. I thought he was about to say something, but a shout from Kristin took our attention.

"Guys! Jordan isn't answering her phone or texts."

CHAPTER 30

We were all clustered in Irix's house. The faint scent of opium lingered from the night before, but no one remarked on it. We were all too concerned about Jordan. Irix leaned against the leather-inlaid hunt table, arms crossed as he watched us with hooded eyes. I wished he'd take control of this. I hadn't the foggiest idea what to do. All I could think of was Jordan's burgundy hair in the sunshine as we broke the spells along the levee. She was smart, cautious, a skilled witch. Where was she?

The front door slammed, and footsteps sounded in the hallway. "Not at her house," Ourson announced almost before he'd turned the corner to enter the living room. "Nothing to indicate a struggle."

"This isn't like her," Stu insisted. "She'd have checked in by now, even if her phone died."

What should I do? I looked at Irix imploringly, but he refused to rescue me.

"We've got a list with the names of some of their members," Ourson said. "They take one of ours, we take five of theirs. Maybe even that Basteau guy."

We already had one of theirs, and I doubted Basteau was defenseless against vampires or demons. There wasn't enough proof that Crimson Moon was to blame for Kristin's disappearance to go to the police. I doubted they'd take a vague threat from a man at a cemetery to be substantial evidence of foul play or intent to harm.

"What if they kill her in retaliation?" Kristin's sunburned face was pinched with fear.

They all turned to me for guidance, and I scrambled to come up with a plan.

"They haven't contacted us yet to make any demands. Let's continue to break the spells on the levee until they do. We'll stick together so they won't be able to take anyone else."

The demand came late afternoon. We'd just finished with the last of the spells on the levee when I got a text from Jordan's phone. My initial excitement fell abruptly as I saw the message. We were to cease all magical activity on the levees and bayous, and let Mr. Wilcox go. I was instructed to banish the two demons to Hel in Mr. Wilcox's presence. If he returned and reported this was done, they would release Jordan unharmed. If not, she would be killed.

Odd. They seemed to think I was one of the Wiccans and not one of the demons. That gave me hope that Jordan was okay and had some kind of plan in place.

"I don't know how to banish demons," Kristin said, tears in her eyes. "I explored some other paths in my past, but I've been Wiccan for years now. I've never summoned a demon before. We don't do that sort of thing."

Evie and Stu both nodded, adding that none of the now twenty defected members of Bon Nuit knew anything about summoning or banishing demons.

"Why did they send this to me?" I mused. "Why not send

it to Bev or Jason? *They're* the leaders of Bon Nuit, and as far as they know, the coven is the one doing this."

Stu looked thoughtful. "It's late. I wonder if they sent it to Bev and she told them to stuff it. Jordan may have convinced them that you were a witch with enough power in the coven to put together a coup over this."

"If so, maybe we can fake it," Evie interjected. "Somehow lie that you both were banished and that Bon Nuit has backed off."

It was a good idea, but as much as Mr. Wilcox seemed to appreciate my intervening on his behalf with the vampires, I couldn't trust him to lie to his own order about our banishment. I turned to Irix and saw the scroll in his waistband. It only transported one to Hel, but maybe we could work some kind of sleight of hand and make them think we were banished.

"Kristin can you make up a fake ritual? Maybe with enough smoke and mirrors, they'll think both of us were truly banished. People believe that David Copperfield and Criss Angel guy. No reason Mr. Wilcox won't believe us if we plan it right."

Kristin's pink skin turned ghostly pale. "I can do a fake ritual, but I'm not an illusionist. If we screw it up and their guy doesn't believe us, then Jordan is dead."

I eyed the scroll again, wishing we had another.

"The button," Irix announced. His eyes were hard topaz and his mouth tight. I had no idea what this button was, but the incubus clearly didn't like the idea of using it one bit. "The man captured by the vampires last night had an elf button. It transports one and any other being or thing that is touching him or her. Kristin can do her fake ritual, and I'll secretly activate the button. As far as the human is concerned, we were banished."

"But we'll be in Hel," I protested. The thought of leaving

the witches and vampires behind to deal with the Crimson Moon group and their elven-taught mage sent ice through my veins. Jordan was already in danger. How many more of my household would suffer without my protection?

"Not for long." Irix smiled, although his eyes remained cold and hard. "Banishment would mean we couldn't return here unless summoned. The gates would no longer work for us. Utilizing a button means we can find the nearest gate and be back here in record time."

I opened my mouth to protest and snapped it shut. We had no idea where the button would take us, and the nearest gate back from Hel could put us halfway across the world from New Orleans. By the time we managed to convince a Korean airline to fly two people without passports seven-thousand miles, New Orleans could already be underwater.

This was the best option on the table, the only one that would keep Jordan alive. I had to trust Irix, put myself and the fate of all those I cared about in a demon's hands.

Mr. Wilcox was once again duct-taped to a chair. He was looking slightly better than the last time I'd seen him, although his pallor led me to believe that Ourson had taken more than his usual pint of blood.

Our spectator was against a brick wall, well away from the chalk circle and runes that covered the cement floor. Bliss hadn't been appropriate for our theatrical deception, so the vampires had arranged for us to use an old warehouse in the commercial district. Kristin, Evie, Stu, and five other Wiccans were busy getting candles and incense in order while we stood by. I walked over to Mr. Wilcox, who was regarding it all with bewilderment.

"They have one of our friends," I told him. "They've threatened to kill her unless the Wiccans back off. You're to witness our banishment then report back to your order that we've complied so they let Jordan go unharmed."

Mr. Wilcox had the grace to look ashamed. "I'm sorry. I know I owe you my life, and hate that it's come to this."

"You can repay me by making sure Jordan comes out of this alive." The thought that we'd be unable to help from

Hel was more worrisome than my journeying to that dangerous place. I was a half-elf — an abomination in the eyes of my kin. If any of them knew I was still alive, the death sentence I'd once had on my head would be renewed. Still, none of that weighed as heavy in my mind as Jordan's safety.

"I will." The man seemed to wrestle with something then looked up at me, his eyes earnest. "Tell me your names, and I will summon you back as soon as I am able. Maybe in a few decades, I'll be able to call you back and negate the banishment."

I only had the one name, and I wasn't sure how summoning and banishing would work with me as a half-demon. Besides, Irix and I intended to be back here tomorrow.

I shook my head. "I appreciate the offer, but I'll be okay."

He laughed. "Yeah, I guess so. Sex demons — someone's always summoning you. Other demons can grant riches, power, and revenge, but everyone wants to summon the demon that will give them passion."

"That passion comes with a hefty price," I reminded him.

"Every demon's gift comes with a hefty price." He looked up at me, a sheepish smile on his face. "Some things are worth the price. One night of mind-blowing sex is definitely worth it."

I felt the trickle of attraction, the curl of pheromones that slid seductively toward Mr. Wilcox. It was kind of creepy, given how much he looked like my high-school chemistry teacher, but my monster was willing to overlook that.

"Amber. We're ready."

I reached out a hand and cupped the man's face, my thumb caressing his cheekbone. "What was your name again?"

"Steve. Steve Mulligan." His voice was a whisper. I moved

my hand to trace the corner of his mouth with the tips of my fingers.

"Goodbye, Steve Mulligan. I hope to see you again, preferably under better circumstances."

His eyes flashed, and I could tell he was imagining all those 'better circumstances'. "Me too. Me too."

I reluctantly dropped my hand to my side and turned to join Irix in the circle, careful not to smudge any of the runes around the edge of the line.

"You okay?" he asked, taking my hand.

I looked at Kristin carefully placing candles at the four quarters "I'm worried about them. What if Crimson Moon doesn't keep their end of the bargain?"

"Eloise said the vampires will keep an eye on things and step in if they don't let Jordan go as promised. Remember, they have that list of names and won't be shy about using it."

Ourson and his group were interested in a mutually beneficial relationship with the Wiccans, but I couldn't imagine the potential of a few spells in the future would equal their sticking their necks out like this. I glanced over at Irix's shadowed face and wondered if he'd offered Eloise a favor in return. It would be unlike a demon to do that to protect a human he hardly knew, but Irix seemed to be full of un-demon-like behavior lately.

"Besides," he continued, "we'll be back by tomorrow. As soon as we land in Hel, I'll transform into my winged form. Once we figure out where we are, I can fly us to the nearest gate. Then it's just a matter of catching a plane back to New Orleans."

I hoped it all went as smoothly as he thought. We fell silent as Kristin began the ritual. It all followed the structure of what we'd done in the swamp, except instead of the raspy scrape of Wiccan energy, I felt nothing. It was like watching it all unfold on a movie screen. Kristin gave us a discrete nod and Irix gathered me to him, burying my face against his chest. His chin rested on top of my head. I heard Kristin intone the words that would supposedly banish us back to Hel until summoned.

"*Glah ham, shoceacan,*" Irix whispered into my hair, and I heard a faint 'snick'.

My stomach lurched, and I felt like I was tossed into the center of a tornado. I clung to Irix, digging my face into the softness of his shirt and breathing deep. It was over in a fraction of a second, but the vertigo continued to spin me around for minutes after my feet were on solid ground. My body felt odd. It stretched and pulled, as if my skin were accommodating changing bone structure.

"You eventually get used to it," Irix murmured, stroking my back and holding me upright against him. "The first time's a real bitch, though."

Indeed. I reached a hand up to rub against my tingling face and felt the ridge of cheekbones and elongated ears that rose through my long hair into unfamiliar points.

"You truly look full elf now, little half-breed." Irix reached out to run a finger along the point of an ear, and I caught my breath at the sensation. "Your demon half might not have a huge range of forms, but you are very skilled at blending into your surroundings."

Great. I was the half-breed chameleon. Well, at least with the pointy ears, I wouldn't be mistaken for a human and enslaved, or discovered for the half-breed I was and murdered.

I breathed deep, lifting my head from the safety of Irix's chest and looked over his shoulder. We were in a surreal woodland, an unbelievable mix of rainforest and northern-European plants living side by side. The bird song was accompanied by a harmonious mix of what sounded to be insects and amphibians. The brush beside us rustled. I tensed, relaxing as a small, furry animal darted out. It paused a few feet from us, short nose twitching under luminous brown eyes.

"Durft," Irix said. "They're pretty tasty if you can catch them."

I couldn't imagine killing something so cute. Extending my fingers, I made kissy noises at the fluff ball. Its jaw unhinged, and fangs the size of my pinkie extended down as it hissed. I snatched my fingers back.

I felt the demon's chest rumble against me with laughter. "I was two hundred when I caught my first one, and he tore me up something fierce. Got away, too. Left me bleeding and missing half my toes, and I didn't even get to eat the little monster."

Two hundred. And I was a few weeks shy of twenty-one.

"Where are we?" I asked, feeling secure enough to step out of Irix's embrace and turn around to survey the rest of the forest. The air felt comfortably warm, but something in the atmosphere lifted my skin with a strange tingling sensation. It was as if a low-level electric current constantly ran through me.

"One of the elven kingdoms." Irix walked to a tree and ran a hand down the bluish-gray bark. "It's hard to tell which one since they tend to favor similar styles in their created landscapes. I'll be able to better get my bearings once we're airborne."

My mind halted at created landscapes. "This . . . the elves *made* this? Trees, plants, and wildlife?"

"Well, not the wildlife. All the plants, and the general environment. You'll see once we cross the border into the demon sections. None of this is indigenous to Hel. It's all a reproduction of how the Elven homeland was before their sun went nova."

This was a far cry from reviving wilted begonias. I forgot to breathe as I stared around in renewed amazement.

"Although they didn't create any of the animals — elves can't do that sort of thing, they did a program of selective breeding over the last several-million years and have been able to approximate many of the animal species they once had."

"It's a shame they couldn't find a planet where the plants and animals were more similar to their homeland," I commented, still amazed they'd accomplished so much, even in millions of years.

"Well, your planet is actually nearly identical to theirs. They had the opportunity to share it with you, but during the war between the angels and demons, they chose to come to Hel rather than remain under the angels' thumb. It was the lesser of two evils, in my opinion. I can only imagine how their lives would have been with the angels breathing down their necks all the time. We pretty much leave them alone, other than the occasional trespass."

I wandered over toward a thorny shrub that had dark purple berries nestled among the green-gold leaves. Were they edible? If I had created this paradise of flora and fauna, I'd make them edible. I reached out toward the leaves and heard a thrumming noise, barely audible, beneath the bird-song. Instinctively I shot out my hand and grabbed the arrow mid-flight, snapping the shaft in two as I whirled about to block the archer's aim.

It hadn't been meant for me. The arrow had been shot straight toward Irix.

"Amber! Get down!" Irix shouted.

No fucking way. Stupid, I know, since Irix could quickly heal any wound, where I was more vulnerable to injury. A flurry of arrows came at me, too many to catch. As one ripped through the flesh along my arm, something huge knocked me to the ground from behind, driving the breath from my lungs. I heard the thud of arrows into solid flesh, felt the massive form on my back relax, squashing me further into the dirt.

"Get. Off. Can't. Breathe."

The pressure lifted, and the weight slid to the side of me. I rolled over and stared into a narrow bird-face, complete with sharp beak and a scaled head. My terror vanished the moment I met its golden eyes and recognized Irix. My gaze traveled from the freaky pterodactyl head, down an over-sized human torso, to scaled arms and legs that ended in talons the size of my forearm. Pinned tight to his back by arrows were huge leathery wings. He looked like a pincush-ion, bristling with the feathered shafts.

A voice shouted something in a language I didn't under-stand, and Irix tried to move his arm protectively over me. Whatever was on the arrows must have had a numbing effect, because his arm twitched, and he collapsed into a heap beside me. Seeing him like this, a mighty demon brought down, snapped something inside me, and I shrieked in fury, jumping to my feet and spinning to face the two men behind me.

Judging from their pointed ears, they were elves. Blond and fair-skinned with chameleon-like clothing that shifted and changed to blend with their background. They were holding a net of sparkling silver between them, and their mouths dropped open as they saw me.

Again with the sing-song language. The only word I understood from the handful Nyalla had taught me was "elf". Yeah, assholes. But I'm only half an elf, and one-hundred percent of me was pissed. Before they could recover from their shock, I launched a lightning bolt at one of them, frying him to a blackened lump of flesh. I'd never channeled such power before. I wasn't sure if it was my anger or the weird tingling feeling I got from the air in Hel, but what was supposed to knock him down cooked him on the spot. I didn't have much chance to register dismay at the over-the-top effect of my powers, though. The remaining elf dropped his half of the scorched net and screamed a word I recognized as "demon" before taking off through the woods.

I hated to leave Irix numb on the forest floor, but I knew I couldn't let this elf get away. I dashed through the forest after him, following the shifting colors of his clothing — a shimmer against a green and brown backdrop. He knew his surroundings, but my speed was equal to his. I shot the occasional burst of electricity, setting brush ablaze and crashing limbs to the ground. One blast overshot my mark, passing the flashing form of the elf and exploding a tree in front of us. It was just the break I needed. The elf paused enough for me to plow into him, knocking him into the dirt where we tumbled through smoldering leaves and twigs into a painfully thorny sticker bush.

I'm not much at hand-to-hand combat, and that last blast of lightning seemed to have depleted my powers. I shocked him with what little I had remaining, and he squealed, punching me and squirming to free himself from my grasp. My hands slipped, and he pulled something shiny from his belt, driving a knife toward my chest.

I did what all good women do when facing death. I kneed the guy in the balls. Elves must have testicles of steel. My blow didn't drop him, but it did cause him to flinch enough that the knife heading for my heart nailed me in the shoulder instead.

It hurt like fuck. I'd never been stabbed before, but I didn't think it was supposed to burn like a red hot poker through my flesh. The elf pulled the knife free, and with a snarl, clearly planned to attempt a more deadly strike. Before he'd began his downward thrust, I did my second girly thing.

I grabbed him by the long blond hair and pulled with all my might.

Evidently, elven scalps are more sensitive than their genitals. A high-pitched scream rent the air, and I rolled to narrowly avoid a second stab. The elf's weapon plunged deep into the ground, half an inch from my armpit.

This had to stop. Now.

Twisting the silky hair in a fist, I yanked toward the ground, turning the elf's head and jerking his body sideways. His movement gave me enough room to pull my upper body upright and sink my teeth into the nearest visible flesh. Which happened to be his stupidly big, pointed ear.

Elven ears seemed to be even more sensitive than their scalps. Given that this was a significant erogenous zone for me, I kind of expected the blood-curdling scream that poured from my opponent. He let go the knife, sacrificing both his weapon and his balance to use both hands to pry my teeth from his ear. I let him. Then I snatched the knife from the loamy ground and drove it into his back.

It was like riding the mechanical bull at the rodeo, except from the bottom. One hand in his hair, the other gripping the knife, and my teeth firmly clamped on his ear, I wrapped my legs tight around him and held on like the good 'ole country gal I was. He screamed and thrashed. Bits of foliage magically grew and twined around my body, trying to yank me from him like ropey hands. I wanted to pull the knife out to stab him again, but was afraid of losing my grip and slim advantage. My arms shook with the effort to hold on, vines digging into the flesh of my back and stomach. The wound in my shoulder burned and throbbed, and I felt my hold on the knife slip.

The elf lurched free. Everything went blurry as my injured shoulder slammed into the ground, and I was vaguely aware of the elf jumping away in preparation for a mad dash through the woods. I'd never catch him this time. I was spent. Hooking a leg around his, I managed to trip him and send him sprawling backward. The knife hilt protruding from his back slammed against a tree. The elf paled in agony as the weapon flew from his flesh, ripping out a chunk of skin and muscle.

Shaking off my dizziness, I dove for him, but my arms closed around nothing but air. I wasn't sure if the elf had found an inner reserve and managed to run for freedom, or had somehow teleported. The amount of blood on the ground would normally have signified a mortal wound, but Irix had told me that elves had the power to heal themselves. If so, this guy would soon have reinforcements heading our way, and they would probably be better armed.

I wiped my bloodied hands onto a patch of moss and pocketed the knife. I needed to find Irix and get us the fuck out of here, and back to New Orleans. Only one problem. With my mad dash through the forest, I hadn't paid enough attention to my surroundings. I had no idea how to find Irix.

I was lost. In Hel.

CHAPTER 32

I read somewhere that whenever you're lost in the wilderness, you should stay put so rescuers can find you. I was pretty sure there weren't any search parties in Hel — at least none I wanted to encounter. Staying put seemed especially hazardous given that the elf-that-got-away was probably going to direct his buddies to this location. Facing vengeful elves was about as high on my wish list as facing a firing squad.

Thankfully I'd left a trail of scorched earth in my wake. There were trampled briars and moss where I'd wrestled with the elf, and the smoking remains of a tree lay to my left. I'd tackled my foe before he'd reached it, so I turned my back on the blackened trunk and headed in the opposite direction, pausing occasionally to note broken branches and crushed ground cover. Birds chirped cheerfully overhead, but I was tense, straining my ears to hear anything that might indicate pursuit of the two-legged kind.

There were a few times I had to backtrack after I'd taken a wrong trail. Two things I was putting on my to-do list — some kind of martial arts class, and an orienteering class. If I ever got back home, that is. There was a horrible fear edging in at the back of my mind, no matter how I tried to stomp it down. Elves were all about the purity of their race, and to them I was an abomination. They'd thought I was dead, killed in infancy by my mother, but now they'd know the truth. If I didn't get out of here, if they managed to catch me, I'd be a dead half-breed.

Finally I saw the clearing ahead of me, saw a large reptilian bird-like creature thrashing around on the ground with arrows protruding from its back. My heart raced as I ran toward him.

"Irix!"

He turned his beaked head toward me, eyes full of relief.

"Pull out the arrows." His voice was guttural, raspy as sandpaper on glass.

I didn't hesitate, yanking the barbed shafts from his back and wings, tearing chunks of flesh with each pull. I had to brace my foot on his back to remove several of them. He never made a noise, never even flinched. Finally the last arrow was out, and Irix lay panting and bleeding black all over the leaf-covered ground. His eyes met mine for a fraction of a second, then a flash of light blinded me. When my eyesight cleared, I saw Irix in the form I knew, stark naked. He sprang from the ground and grabbed me in a crushing embrace.

"Arm. Shoulder," I gasped into his chest, trying to keep from screaming in pain as he pressed against my wounds. He loosened his grip, but his hands were still tight on my waist.

"Sorry. I thought . . . I worried. . . ." he buried his face in my hair and breathed deep, shuddering on the exhale.

"I chased the other elf, but he got away, and it took me a while to find my way back. Why were they shooting at us? I thought you said I looked like an elf. Surely they don't just go slaughtering each other in forests."

"They probably didn't see you at first. And elves do go slaughtering each other in forests. We're in Wythyn. They're at war with pretty much everyone right now. You're dressed like a human. They might have thought you were a spy from another kingdom." He glanced at the blackened elf a few yards away. "Of course, once you did that, they pegged you right away as a demon."

"But I thought demons got along with elves. Would they really kill you over something so minor as trespass?"

"Those arrows wouldn't have killed a full demon, just incapacitated one long enough to secure and interrogate. But that's not the problem." He pulled away and looked around, his posture tense and wary. "They know what you are. Amber, you're in great danger. We need to get out of here fast."

He stepped back, and with a blinding flash, resumed his bird-like form. Wings spread like a reddish-gold canvas and flexed, stirring the tree limbs with their movement. I hesitated, uncertain how this was going to work. I really didn't want to ride on his back. Given the numbness and pain in my arm and shoulder, there was no way I could hold on for any distance. A vision of me falling off Irix and crashing through the trees to my death churned my stomach.

"Is there a way you can carry me and not be gripping my shoulder?"

Irix looked down at his scaled arms and wiggled the huge talons that took the place of fingers. Ouch. They weren't exactly designed for gripping something you didn't intend on eviscerating.

"Sorry," he hissed. I swear I saw the edges of his beaked mouth turn up in a devilish grin.

In a blink, I was over his shoulder, face pressed against the ridge where his wings joined in a mesh of sinewy muscles. My shoulder screamed in agony. A mist of white briefly closed in on my vision.

"No. This won't work," I gasped. Bouncing along his back with every beat of his wings would surely be the death of me.

"How about this?"

He swung me around in a fireman carry, and this time I did scream, my voice echoing through the trees. Irix made a clucking sound and darted out a two-foot-long forked tongue to lick along my shoulder and arm. Before I could protest the inappropriate timing and let him know that huge forked tongues didn't exactly do it for me, my arm grew blissfully numb.

"Contact poison to disable prey. It has other uses too." He chuckled, which sounded like a guttural cough ending with a series of clicks. I laughed too, feeling strangely at peace with the world. He could have torn his sharp beak through my belly at the moment and I wouldn't have felt a thing. Say what you will about sex demons, but they did have some rather pleasant ways of killing a person.

I especially was grateful for my delirious state as we began a stomach-clenching ascent through the trees and into a red-gold sky. A sharp tingle hit my skin as we rose through the canopy, and heat hit me in a blistering wave. The air shimmered around us. I risked a quick look down before turning my face to Irix's scaled chest. It was a long way down.

"We set off the alarm," Irix said, his beak brushing my ear. "I've got to get high enough that I can get my bearings and see where Wythyn ends and the demon lands begin."

How in the heck could we get any higher? I risked another quick look and saw a cloudless sky, a red sun pulsing in the air, and little green textured bits below.

"Surely their arrows can't reach us up here." My voice was

slurred and low. I felt his beak rub against the side of my head, his talons reassuringly tight on my arms and legs.

"Elves have more than arrows at their command. Their magic combined with the humans is a mighty force. Up higher we'll be safe from elven weapons. The air is thin. You'll be light headed, but I won't let you fall."

I wasn't afraid, and I wasn't sure whether it was the happy-place effect of his saliva, or trust in Irix himself. His wings beat faster, stirring the wind around us to a gale-force gust. I felt the muscles in his body tense, scales flexing in a smooth wave against my body. The whole thing was strangely erotic.

Although, sex was an odd thing to have on my mind, considering I was clutched in the arms of a giant, scaled, flying lizard-bird thingie with a beak full of sharp teeth.

"Ah. There." I could feel Irix's relief and peeked down. The swaying spirals of green ended in a sharp line. Red stretched like a sheet of glass toward the horizon, darker than the sky and tinged with brown instead of gold. Irix banked sharply right. I gasped, squeezing my eyes tight and holding my breath to keep my insides from exiting violently.

He chuckled. Asshole. "We're in the border lands now. I'll drop down a bit lower."

Thankfully the decline was accomplished without vertigo-inducing suddenness, and I once again looked, eager to see the place Irix called home.

Outside the lush elven forests, Hel appeared barren. The red dirt rose in little clouds at each beat of Irix's wings, making the ground a blur of fog in our wake. Ahead, thorny bushes rolled about. No wind beyond what we created stirred the oppressive heat, and I wondered if the tumble-weeds were some kind of sentient, mobile being.

"All of Hel isn't quite so desolate," Irix commented, his eyes fixed on something far out of range of my sight. "To the west are swamps and great seas. To the north, towering mountains and ice."

"Where is your home?" I saw a vague outline of grey shapes against the sharp line of the horizon and wondered if those, too, were mountains.

He pointed his beak ahead, nodding at the tall grey things outlined on the red sand and sky. "Dis. There's a minor gate there, but it goes to a remote location in Germany. We'll stop briefly, and then head west into the swamplands. The gate there comes out in Maryland. It's the closest we can get to New Orleans with the least amount of risk."

Sounded good to me. I'd lost track of time, but hopefully we'd be back on the human side of the gates by morning, and in New Orleans in a few hours. Sooner if we weren't making this side trip. Maybe he needed to swing by his place and pick something up. It sounded kind of weird, but remembering his naked, human form in the elven forest, I figured he might need clothing. It's not like he could run around New Orleans with a beak and wings. Although he could probably steal something to wear. It's not like he didn't steal stuff all the time.

"Why are we going to Dis? Can't we just head straight for the gate? That was our original plan."

"It was our original plan before you got stabbed and shot with an arrow. I'm taking you to Dis to get fixed up." He tilted his head and met my eyes with a golden eye, twinkling with amusement. "See, I know a guy...."

CHAPTER 33

The thick-walled stone building was bursting at the seams with barrels, sticks, and basket after basket filled with pungent herbs and spices, but I couldn't keep my eyes off the bald, robed man. Likewise, he couldn't seem to tear his gaze from me. It was a mutual staring contest.

"He doesn't understand why you don't speak Elvish," Irix interpreted. "And he claims not to have any healing scrolls."

"Then let's go." The delay was annoying me. This bald guy dissecting me with his eyes was annoying. And my wounds were more than annoying me — especially now that Irix's lovely numbing venom stuff was wearing off.

Irix ignored me and launched into a back-and-forth singsong with Bald Guy. I reached up a hand to press against my shoulder, and it came away streaked with red and thick yellow. Okay. Maybe I did need a healing scroll. Or a serious shot of antibiotics.

"Show him the knife."

Irix's tone was bossy, but I could hear the underlying worry. What the fuck was on this knife anyway? I shouldn't have a raging infection an hour after getting stabbed.

Shaking off thoughts of losing a limb, or my life, I pulled the elven knife from my belt loop and extended it toward the bald guy. He took it tentatively, with two dainty fingers, and held it as far from his body as possible.

There was more back and forth between the two of them. Tired of being a third wheel in an indecipherable conversation, and trying to keep my mind off my throbbing arm, I walked around the shop, examining the trays of stuff. The dried and fresh plants were surprisingly like those at home. Portulaca grandiflora, rhamnus frangula, long poles of birch. I walked to the other side of the room, and what I saw there had me eyeing Bald Guy with wary suspicion. Digitalis purpurea, amanita muscaria, ruta graveolens – all toxic plants, at least to humans. Who knows what kind of purpose they had when ingested by demons or elves. I wasn't about to try one and find out.

"He says he has something to help you."

I spun about to see the bald guy disappearing through a back door, and Irix regarding me with concern. I'm sure he had to pay dearly for whatever help I was about to receive. Once more, the demon had stuck his neck out for me.

"You don't have to do this, you know. We can pop through the gate, you can steal a bottle of Amoxicillin from a CVS, and I'll be good to go."

"It's a spelled dagger." Irix's voice was hushed, and he glanced toward the back door to ensure Bald Guy hadn't returned before speaking. "I can't guarantee the human medicines will work, and once we go through the gates, these sorts of remedies won't be easily available."

Good point. Irix seemed about to elaborate, but at that moment, Bald Guy came back into the room, bearing a bag full of herbs and a rolled up piece of parchment. There was more arguing, and Irix turned to me, his gold-colored eyes furious.

"I need to step outside. Evidently I'm not trusted to witness the incantation."

Strange that I, a total stranger, was. I nodded, convinced that even with a bum shoulder, I could take this dude. He might have magic on his side, but I wasn't without skills, and after frying an elf like a campfire marshmallow, I was feeling confident.

Irix walked out the front door, and Bald Guy motioned for me to take my shirt off. I'm half succubus, so it didn't really phase me to stand before him in my bra. Examining my arm and my shoulder, he made a 'tsk-tsk' noise and placed the bag of herbs against the knife wound, indicating I should hold it in place.

Unrolling the scroll, he said a few unrecognizable words. The parchment vanished in a puff of dust, and the herbs against my shoulder grew hot and began to smoke.

"Uhh, is this supposed to happen? I'm not going to burst into flames or anything, am I?"

Imagine my shock when he replied.

"No. Hold tight against skin and stay strong with pain."

I forgot the pain, ignored the stench of burning infection, and just stared at the man while he busied himself pulling what seemed to be lengths of gauze off a roll.

"Terrible danger will follow you home," he continued.

I was still amazed that he knew English, so it took a few moments for his words to sink in. "Who will follow me home?"

"Demons. Mages. Elves. Be wary." He cut the gauze and walked to me, examining the smoke coming off the herbs pressed against my knife wound. "Take off now. Poison gone."

I pulled the netted bag away, gagging at the horrible yellow goo that covered it. The bald guy began to bind my shoulder with the gauze.

"Elves? Where would I run into an elf?" Elves didn't cross the gates from Hel. Ever. And I had no intention of returning to Hel in the foreseeable future.

He secured the gauze and took the now-disgusting bag of herbs from me before meeting my eyes with a stern gaze. "Anywhere. Elves leave because angels are too strict, but life with demons is bad too. If angels and demons busy fighting, elves can take home from humans. Maybe not today, but elves are patient and live long."

Great. Now I didn't just have to worry about demons and sorcerers who might want to profit from a bounty on my head, but also elves sneaking through the gates and measuring my world for new drapes and carpet.

I thanked the man and walked out. Irix immediately inspected my shoulder.

"Looks good. Let's get going." I was still preoccupied with the bald guy's words as Irix flew me to the gate. Although my shoulder felt as good as new, he still insisted on the undignified fireman carry. I didn't protest too much, since I figured my priority should be not getting dropped and less about how I looked.

Red sand gave way to colorful grassy plains dotted with twisted trees, and then to patches of marsh. To my right stood a forest of autumn-like red — our destination. As I slid off Irix's shoulders, I saw the gate, a shimmer of prismatic light just inside the tree line.

"Ready?" Irix asked, his beak snapping. He changed form and yanked the pants and shirt from the bag he'd had looped over his head during flight.

Not really. I looked at the shimmer, wondering whether it would feel as horrible as transportation via the elf button had. I was nervous about the gate guardian, too. They were some kind of minor angels, and fully capable of taking out demons that crossed out of Hel. What he or she would do to me, I didn't know. Then there was the little issue of my blood-stained, filthy clothing. If I survived the gate, and the guardian, I'd most likely be hauled off by mall security.

I took a deep breath. There was no time for my angst. We had to get back to New Orleans.

"So, you open the gate, distract the guardian, and I slip through? Where do I meet you?"

Irix shook his head. "No. I activate the gate, and you go through first. I'll be right behind you."

I looked with dread at the shimmering gate. "And what do I do when the guardian tries to rip my head off?"

"I've got an idea. After seeing you like this, seeing how the elves reacted to you, I'm thinking the guardian is going to do the same."

I scowled. "Same what? Shoot me full of arrows and stab me?"

Irix walked forward, hand outstretched. "No. Just trust me."

I did. And even if I didn't, I really didn't have any other choice if I wanted to get back in time to help my friends.

With a sweep of his hand, the demon opened the gate. It was like a rip in the air, revealing row upon row of colorful displays and shoppers with tiny baskets. I recognized the store right away.

"Go," Irix urged.

I clenched my jaw and walked through.

Nothing. One moment I was at the edge of a forest, the next I was looking at an array of Urban Decay cosmetics. Irix walked through right behind me, bumping me as he entered the store. I stepped to the right and accidently plowed into a young woman about my age. I heard her basket hit the floor, lip gloss and little jars of moisturizer rolling across the carpet.

"Oh, sorry!" I turned toward her to apologize further.

She was staring at me, her eyes practically out of their sockets, and her mouth gaped open, moving as if she wanted to say something.

"Are you okay?" I asked. Maybe she'd swallowed something when I'd bumped into her. My mind raced trying to remember the steps to the Heimlich maneuver.

The woman made a choking sound and waved her hands around, pointing at me, then at the demon beside me. Had she seen us come through the gate? Irix grabbed my arm and yanked me toward the exit.

"Let's go. Now!"

I struggled, but finally had to move to keep from falling. I looked bad enough without being dragged through Sephora on my ass.

"That's the gate guardian," Irix hissed once we were clear of the store.

Holy shit. She looked just like a human. How could the demons tell? And why the heck wasn't she trying to kill us? I thought she'd do something more lethal than gasp wordlessly.

"What happened to her?" I asked as we practically ran through the mall.

"Just what I thought would happen." Irix's voice was smug. "After two-and-a-half-million years, she finally saw an elf cross through the gates."

Great. My cover was blown with the elves, and now the angels would know about me. The only difference was that the elves would hunt me down as a half-breed, while the angels would be ready to kill the fatted calf for the return of the prodigal elves.

CHAPTER 34

The LED battery graphic on my dead phone was taking forever to turn green, and the "I heart Baltimore" shirt I'd just yanked over my head was big enough for two. Worse, the woman in the bathroom stall next to me was clearly having a gastrointestinal problem.

Irix had jacked someone's BMW from the Columbia Mall parking lot and had driven top speed to the airport, abandoning it in the drop-off area. We'd split up outside the ticket counters, and I'd thrown all my ethical objections out the window, promptly stealing this t-shirt and a battery-operated quick-charge for my phone.

I didn't really want to know what Irix was doing. We needed plane tickets on the next flight to New Orleans, which I'm sure he could manage. I had no idea how much money he had left from his bank robbery, but I'm sure he had plenty of credit cards in other people's names to use. All I could think about right now was getting my damned phone to work so I could call Kristin or Ourson and get a status. That and the woman's pained noises from next door.

Shoving the phone into my pocket with an irritated

growl, I exited the restroom and looked for Irix. He was already in the security line, holding two tickets and a pair of duffle bags.

"We've got a problem." He handed me a ticket for Amber Shania Lowry.

My mind screeched to an abrupt halt. "How the fuck do you know my middle name?"

I told no one my middle name. It wasn't on my driver's license, on any of my documentation. It was bad enough sharing the same first name with a gazillion other women my age, but to have my middle name inspired by a country music singer . . . times like this, I wanted to string my mother up.

"It's on your birth certificate. Why? It's a pretty name. Sounds very elvish."

How did he ever see my birth certificate? I frowned, recalling what he'd said before I had a fit over my middle name. "What problem? You said there was a problem?"

We inched forward in the security line. "That storm is hitting New Orleans now. It's not bad, but the one on its heels is gaining force. All the flights have been cancelled, so we're going to Houston."

My jaw dropped. "That's nearly seven hours to New Orleans! Couldn't we fly to Baton Rouge, or Mobile?"

"No direct flights, and given the weather issues, I was seriously concerned we'd wind up trying to drive in from Atlanta. Houston was the closest I felt we could realistically expect to arrive without a cancellation."

I felt tears sting my eye, and glanced at my phone. Still not charged enough to power on. Damn the stupid gate from Hel that had drained every drop from my cell-phone battery.

We continued to the security checkpoint, Irix charming the TSA inspector who was scrutinizing our ID and tickets.

Once clear, we headed toward our gate. I felt numb. Hopeless. Depressed.

"Hungry?"

"Oh hell no. If you'd been in the bathroom with me, you'd understand why. I may not eat for a week." That was the closest I could come to joking. I thought I was going to rupture from anxiety. Stupid phone, and now we had to drive nearly seven hours into a storm to reach our friends. If I couldn't contact them before we had to shut down our phones for the flight, I was going to go crazy.

An arm went around my shoulder, and Irix gathered me close to him. "Amber, please stop with the worry. You're driving me crazy. I can't stand to see you like this. Please."

"I can't help it. I don't know what's going on — whether Jordan is safe, or if the Crimson Moon group has replaced all the spells we broke."

He kissed the side of my head, giving me a quick hug. "The vampires are on it. Crimson Moon may have a mage on their staff, but Ourson has a whole family on his side. You've no idea how dedicated a pissed-off vampire can be. Plus, Kristin and the other Wiccans shouldn't be discounted. You gathered these people into your household for a reason. Trust that they'll do what needs to be done."

Trust. That word again. I'd spent my life trusting everyone I encountered, but ever since I'd learned what I was, I doubted everyone and everything. Maybe it was time to go back to the Amber I used to be. I returned Irix's hug and glanced at my ticket. D9. We had another ten minutes before boarding, and I really wanted to drag Irix into a bathroom stall for a quickie. That idea went right out of my mind as I checked my phone and realized it had enough juice to power on. Seconds later I was dialing Kristin as Irix steered me through the crowd and toward the gate.

"Amber!"

Relief flooded me at Kristin's voice. "Did they let Jordan go? Is she okay?"

"We have her. They let her go this morning. She's okay physically, just really weak."

"Can I talk to her?" I really wanted to hear her voice, just to convince myself she was truly all right.

There was a muffled noise over the phone. I got in line with Irix to board, hoping I had time to talk to Jordan and make another call before I had to shut the phone off. We were heading down the jetway when I heard Jordan's voice.

"Amber, they put all the spells back in place on the levees. There's a storm hitting the city now, and another right behind it."

Jordan sounded terrible. Her voice was faint and raspy, and she sounded out of breath.

"We're on our way, but need to drive in from Houston because of the storm. We'll be there by nightfall," I promised.

"You need to know. . . ." Jordan paused for a few loud breaths. "They called Bev first, and she told them I was no longer Bon Nuit, that I was acting alone. They were going to kill me, but I convinced them to call you. Told them you were a powerful witch who had divided the coven. That the group was split and Bev was on her way out. They don't know you're one of the demons."

I could barely hear Jordan. Her words were coming in little gasps. "Rest. I'll be there as soon as I can."

I'd take care of those Crimson Moon assholes, protect the city, then I was going after Bev. I felt the rage bubble up inside me — a deadly anger I hadn't felt since I was five. I had desperately wanted to put this part of myself away forever, but some actions could not go unpunished. And some people just needed killing.

"Wait," Jordan croaked. "Basteau. He is their mage. White-haired guy is like you."

There was an alarming series of coughs from the other end of the phone. I begged Jordan to take care of herself, again reassuring her I was on the way. As soon as I hung up, I dialed Ourson. We were already in our seats. I only had a few more minutes.

"Amber!"

I buckled the seat belt one handed and saw Irix talking to a flight attendant out of the corner of my eye.

"Ourson, I can't talk. We're taking off in just a few moments and flying to Houston. Once we land, we'll drive to New Orleans."

"What do you want me to do?"

I loved this vampire. He understood urgency better than anyone.

"That list of Crimson Moon members you had? They're all yours. Go get em. I'll owe you a favor, whatever. I really need your help with this."

There was a few seconds of silence, then Ourson's voice, full of affection. "Amber, this is our city too. We're just as concerned with this problem as you are. There's no need for favors. Plus, you're my friend. That's good enough for me."

I was going to start crying. He was more than a friend: he was part of my household. "Thanks, Ourson."

"No problem. Call me when you land."

I turned off the phone and gratefully took the coffee and granola bar Irix handed me.

"Jordan says the white-haired guy, Weaver, is a demon," I said, stuffing bits of the granola bar in my mouth. "Basteau is the mage."

Irix frowned. "I wonder if Basteau bound the demon into service, or if it's working for them on its own."

"Would it matter?" I mumbled, my mouth full. Either way, the thought that we may have to face a demon once we got back to New Orleans was daunting.

"It matters a lot. A bound demon is compelled into service. Once you kill the summoner, it's free. And it's often very grateful to those who have freed it. One working voluntarily won't be as easy to deal with. Depending on what level it is, we may not be able to defeat it."

Shit. Wondering what we might be facing tonight, I took a sip of my coffee and just about choked to death.

"Holy shit! What's in here? It tastes like a pint of whiskey with a teaspoonful of coffee."

"Drink it," Irix instructed, quickly kissing my cheek. "You need to sleep if you're going to be at all functional tonight."

He was right. I'd been up for over twenty-four hours. Three hours on the plane, and another few while Irix drove, would really help. I eyed him, hoping he'd do the same. I would need his strength tonight.

"Bottoms up." I drained the coffee-flavored whisky in a long gulp, shuddering as the alcohol hit my senses.

"Mmmm. I truly love it when your 'bottom's up'," Irix teased.

I smiled and rested my head on his shoulder, drifting into sleep as the plane pulled away from the gate.

CHAPTER 35

The bump of our plane touching down awoke me. My head still rested on Irix's shoulder, but the demon had clearly been up to something, or someone, while I'd been sleeping. My hair practically stood on end from all the energy he held.

"Mile-high club?" I wasn't exactly jealous. Sex in a tiny plane bathroom was no picnic. There would have been no room for me to join in, even if I had been awake.

"About half the plane can now cross that one off their bucket list," he said cheerfully.

Shit. Half the plane? There wasn't likely to be an angel nearby, but I couldn't help glancing out the window as we taxied to the gate. I was glad he had the extra energy to handle whatever we'd face tonight. If only I had time for a sex-spree, but we'd need to bolt out of the airport, steal a car and drive like crazy if we were going to make it to New Orleans before nightfall.

Powering on my phone, I saw a text from Ourson and one from an unknown number.

We have three. Rest are in hiding. Wiccans all together for their safety.

Three out of our hair was better than none, and I was glad Kristin and her crew were taking precautions. Without looking at the other message, I dialed the witch.

"Sixty!" she squealed without preamble.

Huh? What a weird greeting.

"Forty more have left Bon Nuit and come to us showing support." Kristin was breathless with excitement. "It got around that Bev refused to help Jordan, and people are ditching her left and right. Sixty of us with the vampires and you two — we'll win this thing! We're already setting up for a ritual to try and turn the storm away from us and back into the gulf."

"That's awesome news." We were parked at the gate, and I juggled the phone as I grabbed one of the duffle bags Irix had brought on board. What the hell did he have in these things, anyway? "We're deplaning now. Keep me in the loop, and we'll be there as quick as we can."

I hung up and looked at the text from the unknown number.

CB

Okay, but call back whom? I stuck the phone in my pocket, thinking it was probably a wrong number, or someone trying to sell me a home protection system. There was no time to be polite, and I could hardly manage a call while Irix and I half-jogged through the airport and into the parking lot.

Once there, Irix became a demon on a mission. We swooped down aisle after aisle as his head swiveled from side to side. Finally he stopped in front of a Cadillac sedan.

"Seriously?" I asked as Irix magically unlocked the door, disabling the alarm system as he slid into the driver's seat. We'd passed up several Mercedes and BMWs for a Cadillac?

"Five-hundred-and-fifty-six horsepower V8." He motioned me to hurry and get in. "Zero to sixty in three-point-nine and one-ninety-eight top speed. Plus it has a full tank of gas. We'd get there quicker on a bike, but I didn't think you wanted to travel three-hundred-and-fifty miles on the back of a motorcycle."

Most definitely not. I buckled in as Irix placed his thumb against the ignition. The engine roared to life. About halfway into our drive, I picked up my phone and saw another text from "unknown".

CB

All right, dammit. But if this was a telemarketer, I was going to hunt him down and make him pay. I dialed the number, tapping my foot impatiently as it rang.

"Meet me at the warehouse in an hour," a hushed voice announced.

Huh? This was clearly a wrong number. Although my succubus half was very intrigued at the idea of meeting some man at a warehouse for what sounded like a clandestine affair.

"Who are you calling?"

"Amber. The demon. It's me, Steve."

His voice was low, but I made the connection as soon as he said the name. It was the human formerly known as Wilcox, the doppelganger to my high school chemistry teacher. My blood froze in my veins. As far as he knew, I'd been banished, never to return unless summoned. Now that he knew I was back in this realm, all of Crimson Moon would be ready and waiting. I shot a warning glance at Irix and put the phone on speaker.

"You must have the wrong number." I tried to keep my voice as casual as possible. "There's no Amber here."

I heard him take a deep breath, practically felt the tension through the phone. "I know a bogus banishing ritual when I see one, and I know what I had on my person when that vampire grabbed me. I kept your secret, made sure your friend was released. Please. I need your help."

I looked over at Irix for guidance, and he nodded. Strange how such a simple gesture could convey such content.

"I'm five-plus hours out of New Orleans. What's happening? Can you wait, or do you need protection?"

Not that I had much to offer him in way of protection. I'm sure he wouldn't welcome Ourson and the vampires, and I was wary of bringing him to Jordan after her experience at the hands of Crimson Moon.

"I . . . I can wait. Can you text me when you're close? I have information for you in return for your assistance. I want to leave Crimson Moon, but I'd prefer to not wind up dead or Owned because of it."

He sounded so desperate that my heart went out to him. "I'll personally ensure your safety. Sit tight, and I'll let you know when we're coming into town. I'll meet you at the warehouse where we had the banishing ceremony."

"Thank you." His voice was saturated with gratitude. "Please hurry. They're conducting magic to upgrade the storm, and I'm worried the city is in danger."

I hung up and turned to Irix.

"Pedal to the metal," he quoted, accelerating with a speed that pinned me to the back of my seat. "City to save, alliances to forge, a household to protect. Plus there's the promise of a kick-ass battle tonight. Could be my personal best-night-ever."

CHAPTER 36

*E*very careful footstep was magnified in the warehouse, echoing off the metal containers and steel girders. Heavy doors shut the storm firmly outside, leaving me in an eerily silent building.

"Did you come alone?"

I jumped, my heart racing. The whispered words seemed to come from nowhere. I hadn't heard any footsteps besides my own, hadn't seen any shadows in the dimly lit building.

I spread my arms. "No vampires, no witches, no demons, except for me."

They were all outside, checking for spells and guarding against attack. I was still as tense as wire about to break. If Steve were pulling a complicated double-cross, I was wide open and vulnerable. Hopefully as a half-demon, whatever magic he'd use on me would only be half as effective.

The apprentice appeared from behind a brown container, walking toward me in silence.

"I was afraid to contact the vampires or the witches," he said, eyes darting here and there. "I know where they're conducting the ceremony. All of Crimson Moon will be there. I'll tell you and let you know what wards they have in place."

For a price, of course. "What do you want in return?"

"A guarantee of my safety."

Of course, but there had to be more. I nodded.

"The others . . . it's Basteau and that white-haired foreigner you need to take out. Yeah, we all want use of the ley line energy, but we're willing to come to a peaceful solution." He squirmed, looking around the warehouse then down at his feet.

It was a relief to know that the entire group wasn't set on a course of violence and destruction. "I'm sure once this is all over there will be a way everyone can share the ley line."

"One more thing. You spared my life when the vampires wanted to tear me apart. I know I'm stupid asking this of a demon, but can you make sure you don't kill my colleagues?"

I had no desire to kill them, but we'd be storming into a magical ceremony. I couldn't guarantee there wouldn't be collateral damage. "We'll do our best, but if they attack us, we're not going to hold back. Is there a way to get a message to them so they'll stand down, or even fight against Basteau and the other guy?"

Steve shook his head. "I can't. It's too risky. These guys are powerful, and everyone is afraid to go against them. I don't know what they'll do in a fight, but I can't take the chance that any warning I give them would be leaked."

"Okay. Deal." Sparks danced along my fingers as I readied a low-voltage strike, just in case. "You do understand that we can't allow you to leave. Just in case this is a trap."

He eyed my fingers and backed up a few steps. "I'll tell you the location and the wards, but then I'm out of here. I'm not risking my life further."

I hated to zap the guy, so, instead, I poured on the pheromones, matching each of his backward steps with a forward one of my own. His eyes widened then he shook his head, pulling a small metal charm from under his shirt. The sparks against my hands sputtered and fizzled out, refusing to return. The tendrils of my sex magic swirled a foot from him, unable to penetrate the invisible barrier. He'd prepared for this meeting.

"I'm leaving. They're at sixteen-forty St. Charles Avenue. There are alarm wards on the doors and windows, and a keep-away spell surrounding the grounds. Good luck."

"Not so fast, Dumbledore."

I'd prepared for this meeting, too. Steve spun around and looked down the barrel of a shotgun held in the steady hands of my best friend.

"But you said you came alone," he sputtered. "I have a truth amulet. You didn't lie."

"I said there were no witches, vampires or other demons," I corrected. "Darci is human and doesn't practice magic. She is, however, a damned good shot, so you might want to hold very still and keep your hands where we can see them."

I pulled out my cell phone and sent Ourson a quick text. Seconds later, the doors opened, and Irix entered, Kristin by his side.

"Kristin, would you please search Steve here and confiscate all his magical items? Be careful, I'm not sure what he's got on him."

I turned to Irix, wrapping an arm around his waist. It felt good just to be next to him again.

"Ready to fight?" I relayed what I'd learned from the apprentice.

"What about him?" Irix nodded toward Steve. There was an amazing pile of charms, amulets and little colored bags at the apprentice's feet.

"I'm thinking of asking one of the vampires to watch him.

I don't really want to drag him along with us, but I don't trust that he won't tip them off that we're coming."

"I'll just take a few of these things with me then." Kristin had finished her thorough pat-down and stuffed two amulets, a scroll, and several of the colored bags into the pockets of her cargo pants.

"I'd watch him, but I've got to get this shotgun back to my Dad," Darci commented. "The storm's picking up, so I'll probably just stay there."

Irix nodded. "Let's get moving then, before the storm worsens."

Inexplicably, the storm had dramatically increased since I had entered the warehouse. Gusts yanked my hair from its barrette and tangled wet strands around my face. The rain pelted us with cold hard drops as we raced to the car. Thankfully the Cadillac had good handling in bad weather. We crammed as many witches and vampires as we could into the sedan, while others did the same with their cars and trucks. It wasn't the most dignified way to travel, but it was the most efficient.

Stealth wasn't necessary as we pulled up and parked across the street from the St. Charles Avenue house. The rain had begun to flood the road, and several inches of standing water, plus the weather forecast, meant that we were the only ones out. The huge Pepto-pink Victorian house seemed like an unlikely spot to hold a magical ceremony. I checked the address, just to make sure.

"It's the right place," Kristin whispered, holding up an amulet. It glowed green. "There's a ton of magical energy going on in there."

We climbed from the cars like clowns at a circus, some circling around to the back of the house, as we'd agreed earlier. The rain had tapered off to a drizzle, like it was gathering strength for one massive strike. Grateful for the reprieve, Kristin, Ourson, and I stood by the black wrought-iron fencing that surrounded the house lawn.

"It's all spelled, just as that guy said." Kristin once again held the amulet in front of the iron gate.

I held out a hand, wondering what a keep-away spell did, and was immediately seized with a massive headache and an urge to puke. Fighting against it, I touched the iron and found myself across the street, climbing into the passenger seat of the Cadillac. So *that's* what it did. How the heck were we going to break that? I couldn't even touch it. Then there was the alarm function on the doors and windows that Kristin explained wouldn't just let Crimson Moon know we were trying to get in, but would prevent any kind of lock picking — magical or physical.

I crossed the street to where Ourson and Kristin stood. Everyone was in place awaiting our signal, and we didn't have time to sit around and brainstorm options. I needed to decide what to do, and decide it fast. As I always did when faced with a huge decision, I looked around for Irix and real-ized I hadn't seen him since we'd gotten out of the car.

What I did see was headlights from something big headed towards us. Given that we were standing in front of a house, I acted.

"Get out of the way!"

Ourson grabbed Kristin and moved with a blur of speed to the corner. I followed, nearly as fast. There was a huge crash, and the iron gate, along with three sections of fencing, went flying as a delivery truck smashed through it and into the front yard. Not stopping, the truck sped ahead, avoiding the steps to the front door and driving straight into the front of the house.

Irix had taken care of the wards, in what I was coming to learn was typical demon style. "Tell the others to move in," I instructed Kristin, rushing forward.

There was just enough room between the truck and the jagged edges of smashed siding and drywall for me to squeeze through. Irix was punching his way through on the other side.

"Hurry!"

I hurried. We may not have set off the alarm spell, since Irix had avoided the doors and windows, but I was pretty sure everyone had heard a huge truck smashing through the house.

"To the left!" Kristin shouted, holding the amulet in one hand as she tried in vain to squeeze through the tight opening into the house. I paused just long enough to see Ourson smash his fist through the drywall, widening the space, before I took off.

A narrow hall led to a set of double doors with elegant brass handles. Irix lowered his shoulder and crashed through them in a remarkable imitation of the delivery truck. The room was huge, and in the center was a group of robed figures standing inside a series of circles and pentagrams etched into the floor.

"Hold steady!" A man shouted. I recognized his voice.

The casters returned to their positions, taking up a chant. I ran forward, unsure whether I'd be able to enter their circle or not.

Not. I bounced off what seemed to be an invisible wall and flew backwards to plow into Irix. We sprawled on the floor in a heap.

"Curtain!" Basteau called out.

Blackness fell over the room, so dark that I truly couldn't see my hand in front of my face. The chanting seemed to come from the left, then the right. I was sightless and couldn't even use my hearing to pinpoint their location. Not that I could do much with the magical wall that surrounded them.

Orange orbs glowed in front of me, and I jumped. Irix was underneath me on the floor, so it wasn't the demon with the freaky eyes. My hands crackled with electricity, but I held back, waiting for the monster to attack.

"Cool stuff these Crimson Moon people have," Kristin said cheerfully. "Watch this."

I couldn't watch anything. All I could see were her weird eyes, blinking in and out. Something came in front of them, blocking them from my view momentarily, and then I heard a series of screams disrupt the chant. With a 'whoosh' the blackness fell, and I blinked as my eyes adjusted to the sudden return of light.

Inside the circle people frantically shed robes that seemed to be dissolving right off their bodies. Basteau screamed for them to resume, but no one listened. That's when I noticed that their clothing wasn't the only thing disappearing. The etchings on the floor smoked, huge gashes burning their way through the marble.

"Now!" I shouted.

The other witches and vampires had made it into the room and had been equally blind, but now everyone ran forward, dragging various members of Crimson Moon out by their shredded robes. Irix and I ignored them and headed for Basteau.

His eyes widened when he saw me, and then narrowed. I braced myself, thinking he would launch some magical attack at us, but, instead, he turned and ran. I could have easily caught him, but I didn't want to put on the elven speed and leave Irix in the dust. Catching Basteau wasn't the problem, it was what I was supposed to do once I had him. Electricity was pretty much all I had. I didn't want to kill him, and ever since I'd incinerated that elf in Hel, I was reluctant to produce anything stronger than a static shock.

Irix might not be as fast as I was, but he was certainly

quicker than a middle-aged mage who had been posing as a banker. We gained on Basteau, following him through the connecting rooms of the vast house. As we neared what had to be the rear room, I put on a burst of speed, unwilling to let him escape outside.

"Amber, no!"

Irix knocked me aside with his arm, sending me into a round table. Pain lanced through my side, and I gasped, trying to regain my balance. Instead of me, Irix had gone through the doorway, unable to stop his momentum. He now stood frozen inside an inscribed series of triangles. I heard a mocking laugh, then a series of words in a language I recognized but couldn't speak.

I had no idea what Basteau was casting, but it most certainly wasn't good. The triangles crossed the threshold. I'd be unable to enter the room without stepping into the same trap as Irix. There might be another way in, but I had no time to search for it. I wished I had the delivery truck to crash through the walls. The flimsy round table I'd whacked my side on probably wouldn't make a dent in the dry wall. There was only one way in. If I failed, at least I'd suffer the same fate as Irix — whether that be banishment or a fiery death.

I walked forward and felt a sharp jolt as I entered the center of the triangle.

And then I walked right out to the other side.

Basteau abruptly stopped chanting, his mouth wide open. "How . . . why? What *are* you?"

I wasn't about to tell *him*. Instead I said one of the few phrases I knew in Elvish. "Feallendlith gal-moed."

Nyalla told me it meant something like 'rotted whore' and was considered a terrible insult to both genders. She must have spoken true, because Basteau recoiled, and his face grew ashen.

"Stay right where you are, or I'll fry you." I didn't want to kill him. Well, I *did* want to kill him, but none of the robed individuals in the other room had white hair, and we needed to find Weaver.

Basteau raised his hands in that universal gesture of surrender. Then he spun around and bolted.

Before I could think, I'd launched something at him. Whatever it was, it wasn't my standard stream of electricity. The blast left my hand and hit the mage, blowing him into a spray of red chunks that decorated walls, ceiling, floor, and me. The only one spared was Irix, who was in the spelled triangle. I shook the blood and bits of flesh off my hands, looking for something reasonably clean with which to wipe my face.

"Elf-girl, when you stepped into this banishing ward, I was ready to kill you myself. What were you thinking?"

I had no time for Irix's scolding. I'd blown up the only man who probably knew Weaver's whereabouts. Even if he'd been a summoned demon, there was no guarantee he wouldn't go on with death and destruction. Hopefully an angel would get him. In the meantime, I was covered with gore, and my own demon was still trapped.

"How do I get you out of there?"

Irix pivoted around, looking down at the floor. "Does Kristin have any more of those acid spells? We need something to break the lines, and since they're drawn into the floor they'll need to be dug across or burned out."

I walked through, trying to ignore the sting of the barrier as I crossed. In the other room, the witches and vampires had corralled the half-naked Crimson Moon members into a corner. Kristin gasped when she saw me, bringing a hand to her chest.

"I'm okay. This isn't my blood — It's Basteau's. I accidently blew him up."

That didn't seem to faze the witch one bit.

"Irix?" Her voice trembled.

"He's fine too, just trapped in a bunch of triangles. You wouldn't happen to have any more of that acid stuff, would you?"

She strode past me, red-blond curls bouncing on her shoulders. I followed her and watched as she traced the lines of the triangle with her finger.

"Amazing. Usually crossing it or breaking it with a touch will allow the entrapped being to escape. There must be some sort of incantation needed to open the barrier."

I watched her in amazement. "How do you know all this? I mean, you're Wiccan."

Kristin brushed the red curls from her forehead and gave me an embarrassed smile. "I've path hopped a lot in my life. Golden Dawn, Voodoo, Shamanism, Wicca — I've dabbled in it all."

She seemed to have done more than dabble, but I held my tongue. She turned back and touched the outer line of the series of triangles once more.

"Salt."

I spread my hands and looked to either side of me. Table, lamp, chair, sofa, and a bookshelf.

"I don't usually carry it with me. Should I go search for the kitchen?"

"No need." Kristin reached into one of the pockets of her cargo pants and pulled out a plastic bag full of white grains. "Girl's gotta be prepared for anything, you know?"

Yes I did. Kristin spread the salt on the portions of the triangle lines that crossed the threshold, and then rubbed it in, as if she were scrubbing the floors. Sitting back, she surveyed the mess of gritty white on the oak floors.

"There. Come on out, you sexy beast."

Irix winked at the redhead and stepped through the barrier. I let out the breath I hadn't realized I'd been holding.

Then I grabbed him and held him like I never wanted to let him go. I'd been so scared, so worried that he would be banished, killed, trapped in this pink Victorian house forever. His arms came around me, and for a few moments all I knew was his scent, the warmth of his flesh against mine. I wanted to stay wrapped in his arms for all eternity, but our job wasn't finished.

"Weaver is still out there somewhere." I said, pulling back from our embrace.

"Demon or not, we've got a city threatened by this storm," Kristin chimed in. "Those Crimson Moon folks agreed to work with us to try and diffuse it, but I'm still worried about the levee spells."

I looked up at Irix, into his golden eyes. "To the levees?"

His face was all hard angles as he met my gaze, looking every inch the two-thousand-year-old demon. "Yes, but we take Ourson to stand guard as we work. Just in case."

CHAPTER 37

The Cadillac felt like a paper boat tossed in the ocean as we drove through the flooded streets toward the Mississippi River. Rain pelted down in hard sheets, breaking every few seconds to take a breath. I clutched the seat, grinding my teeth as we hydroplaned our way along the roadway.

Irix had insisted that Ourson ride shotgun, which pissed me off to no end. I was safely in the back like precious china, wrapped in the leather coat the incubus had insisted I take from him. I seethed until we pulled up to the curb.

"Lights, camera, action, elf-girl. Let's get a move on."

Ourson stood guard as Irix and I staggered our way through the wind and rain to the levee. The process of breaking the spells was second nature to me by this point. We worked our way through three of the spells as the storm gained ferocity. Whatever Kristin and the others were doing, it didn't seem to be working. We were on the edge of a hurricane, and if we couldn't break these spells, the city would be in danger. It was a race against time, and even with Irix's huge store of energy fueling me, I worried we'd be too little, too late.

As we pulled up to the aquarium, parking on Canal Street. I had a moment of nostalgia for Café du Monde beignets and Irix's house just a few blocks away. Opening the car door, I stepped out into the wind and rain. Not that it mattered. I was already soaked from the last four locations.

I'd barely taken four steps before a weight hit me from behind, knocking me into the sodden grass. My nose and mouth filled with cold, damp dirt, but I felt heat across my back.

"Mage," Ourson shouted.

I heard the splash of running through the flooded grasses, and Irix's weight lifted off me. I rolled over, smelling the distinctive aroma of burnt fiber and flesh. The demon had burns across one side of his face. Half of his shirt and pants had been singed and partially melted to his body. Polyester really sucked when it came to fire.

"Holy shit. Are you okay?" I reached up to touch Irix's blistered face.

He jerked his head at my touch. "Fine. Ourson has got this guy. Come on, we've got to get moving. Sixteen more spells to go."

I got it. He didn't want to expend energy on fixing his injuries when we had work to do, and a potential demon on the loose. I gripped his chin in my hand and ran my fingers gently over his burn. "Then let's go, sweetheart."

We fought against the wind gusts, past the aquarium and down the riverside path. Once in place, I reached down into the seawall, deep below to where the spell had its roots. It was hard to concentrate with my soaked clothes plastered to my skin, shivering as the rain and wind lashed against me. Even the leather jacket was drenched. A gust of wind tossed my wet hair to the side, and out of the corner of my eye I saw a figure cresting the top of the levee. In spite of the dark and the rain, I knew it wasn't Ourson.

"Wait." I said, grabbing Irix's arm.

He followed my gaze and instantly moved to stand in front of me. It was too late. The flickering light from the aquarium patio had caught the man, and I saw his white hair. Worse, he saw me.

Weaver spat out a stream of Elvish. Irix tensed, his hands curling into fists. The white-haired man wasn't a demon; he was an elf. *He's like you,* Jordan had said, and I'd never considered the possibility that she meant Weaver was like my elven half.

Two-and-a-half-million years, and one had finally crossed the gates from Hel. I didn't have time to ponder the implications of an elven presence among the humans.

"*Yf e-lyffel.*"

The words rolled from Weaver with a burst of power, and the ground beneath me shook. He'd activated the spells — all of them. Trusting Irix to shield me from any attack, I dropped to the ground and pulled, trying to re-direct as much of the spell energy into me as possible. The asphalt moved like living sand under my hands. I felt the supporting rocks and rebar begin to loosen, molecules separating and dissolving.

Oh no you don't. Now I wasn't just trying to absorb the spell, but desperately solidifying the structures beneath me. And it wasn't just the one spot, it was twenty locations along several miles. I felt like a pulled piece of elastic, stretched and on the edge of coming apart. I couldn't continue like this. I'd need to make a hard decision to either let some of the spells activate, or leave the barriers weakened and vulnerable to the storm. I just didn't have enough power, not enough juice to pull this one off.

Irix's hands rested on my shoulders. I felt his face press

against the side of my head. Energy flooded me, saturating every pore and slamming through me into the seawall and beyond. I opened myself wide and took everything he could give, channeling it into the structures across the miles. Cutting through my concentration, I heard Ourson in the distance, shouting something about angels. Angels were the least of my problem right now. If I couldn't contain these spells, keep the storm barriers intact, there wouldn't be enough of either of us for the angels to kill.

Stone, sediment, concrete, tiles, complicated polyester netting, sand — my lungs burned, and my head pounded with pain as I recreated everything, right down to the lush Bermuda grass and asphalt on the crown. When it was all over I collapsed, shaking against the ground. Irix's arms went around me, drawing me backward onto his lap, against the warmth of his body.

"You okay?"

I nodded, my cheek rubbing against his wet shirt. "Did you get the elf?"

"No." I heard the bitter regret in his voice. "He ran for it, and it was more important that I help you. I'm sure that's what he was banking on when he activated all the spells at once."

As much as I wanted to stay and ride out the storm in Irix's arms, we had a problem. Such a massive display of demon energy wouldn't have gone unnoticed. And I was willing to bet angels wouldn't mind a bit of rain if they were hot on the trail of a demon.

CHAPTER 38

"Υou've got to get out of here." I stood, feeling the cold cut through my damp clothes as soon as I was out of Irix's arms. He still had the scroll. A few words, and he'd be safe from the angels.

The wind had loosened the incubus' dark hair from its tie and whipped it around his face in wet strands. He looked like a pirate with his soaked, translucent shirt and rain-drenched face — a very sexy pirate.

"I'm not leaving you, Amber. That elf knew what you were."

"What did he say?" I'd heard the anger under the fast-paced words.

"You don't want to know. It doesn't matter, because I'm not leaving you."

He needed to leave. The nearest gate was hundreds of miles away, and the scroll only transported one. The elf might be a threat to me, but the angels bearing down on us were a huge threat to Irix. I'd rather wait thousands of years for him to return from Hel than see an angel take his head off.

"The elf ran away. His mage, all his supporters are dead. He's probably already back in Hel. Get out of here."

Irix frowned. "Even so, I can't run off and leave you here to face an angel alone."

I loved him even more. How un-demonic of him to risk his personal safety over and over again to protect me.

"I'm fine. Ourson and the vampires will protect me. I'm only a half-breed, and besides, that gate-guardian seemed to think I was full elf." Sure enough, Ourson was waving frantically, calling my name and urging me to come with him.

Irix's mouth thinned into a tight line, his eyes like yellowed stone. "Fooling a gate guardian is one thing, an enforcer angel another. Besides, what kind of demon am I to run away and leave my protégé in the care of vampires?"

"One who stays alive." I pulled him into my arms and kissed him, loving the taste of rain on his lips. The trickle of energy he'd been transferring to me turned into a river. I gasped against his mouth, feeling as if I'd been lit up from the inside. When we pulled apart, I noticed how tired he looked. Had he given me everything he had, knowing that I would probably need it more than him?

"Please, Irix." I ran a gentle hand over his burned cheek, touching the muscle that twitched in his jaw. "I'm begging you; use the scroll and go. If you stay and fight this angel, I'll help you, and we both know how that would turn out."

I could tell Irix didn't like this one bit, but it was the only option we had. "Promise me you won't do anything stupid," he said. "That you'll stay with Ourson and let the vampires protect you."

"I promise."

Ourson had run over to me and was tugging my arm. I turned from Irix to follow the vampire, letting my hand linger against him as long as I could. "Call me!" I shouted over my shoulder, unable to resist teasing him even while my heart broke.

He laughed, and when I turned around before climbing into Ourson's car, he was gone.

* * *

THE WINDSHIELD WIPERS on the vampire's blue Corolla beat a frantic tempo as we crawled through the empty streets. Traffic lights flashed red, and water pooled on the asphalt, overwhelming the street gutters. With every gust of wind, the rain sheeted, blurring the world before us into gray.

"Don't be afraid." Ourson took one hand off the steering wheel to give my hand a reassuring squeeze before quickly placing it back.

"I'm not."

We'd had storms like this up in Maryland, just not for as prolonged a period. With the mage dead and Kristin's group working to downgrade the storm, the rain and wind should have lessened. Instead, the sky seemed to have been whipped into a fury. How bad was this going to get? With a bad storm, the city would be pummeled, but the levees would hold, and we'd all dry out in a few days. But a hurricane?

If only I'd had the time to fix the wetlands and bayous. An image of the dead cypresses reared in my mind, and I felt a slow burn of fury. What kind of elf could possibly do such a thing? A pestilence demon, yes. A selfish, power-hungry human, yes. But this was not what I'd ever thought of when I contemplated my elven half. Maybe the demon inside me wasn't the only one capable of being a monster.

"I hope this storm dies down soon. Even if it doesn't, there's no need to worry. Bliss is stocked with lots of food and fresh water, and we've got generators in case we lose power. We'll keep you safe, Amber. As your friend, I promise it."

I heard the unsaid portion — that he'd protect me from the angel, protect me as Irix had done. Ourson was a good friend. I glanced at him and saw the lines around his eyes as he stared out the windshield. A huge piece of metal sheeting blew across the road in front of us, and the vampire swerved to avoid it. How terrible would it be if this continued increasing, with the city already weakened by hours of onslaught? Kristin and her group were giving this their all, but their magic may not be enough. I felt the hum of Irix's energy coursing through me and made a decision.

"Can I borrow your car?"

The vampire slowed to ease through a deep section of water. In a few hours, most of these streets would probably be impassable.

"Uh, yeah. Sure. As soon as the storm passes."

"No. I mean now. I'll drop you off at Bliss then I've got something to do."

Ourson risked a quick look at me. "You're joking. There is no way I'm letting a Yankee tourist run around the city in the middle of a hurricane."

"Maryland is south of the Mason Dixon line, and, at this point, I think I'm more than a tourist. I'm a demon. I'll be fine, even in a hurricane. If you don't want to loan me your car, it's okay. I'll just steal one."

Not that I really could steal a car. Even if I'd been able to overcome that moral barrier, I had no idea how to hot-wire the thing with either human or demon skills.

I could hear his teeth grind through the noise of the storm. "I promised Irix I'd keep you safe. That doesn't include loaning you my car so you can drown, or get squashed by a falling tree."

"I'll be back in a few hours, and then I'll stay at Bliss until you tell me it's safe to leave. Promise."

His knuckles whitened on the steering wheel, and I remembered that demons lied.

"I swear on all the souls I Own that I will return to Bliss in no more than two hours and remain there until the storm passes."

Not that I Owned any souls, but that vow seemed to satisfy Ourson. He pulled up outside the nightclub and put the Corolla in park, opening the door to the downpour.

"Be careful, Amber," he shouted over the noise of wind and rain.

I scooted over, waving at him as I shut the door. I was drenched, as was the seat, and the car's dash and steering wheel. Ourson waited in the rain, a vertical slash of darkness in gray as I pulled the car back into the flooded street and eased my way south of the city, towards the marshes and bayous.

CHAPTER 39

Instinct alone got me to the site of the dead cypresses. I hadn't seen a car since I'd left the city, and the swamp water lapped up over the edges of the bridged roadway, flooding it over a foot in many areas. I'd needed to detour several times to avoid roads flooded beyond the Corolla's ability to ford. Once at the bayou, I parked smack dab in the center of the street, figuring that no one else would be foolish enough to be driving around in the middle of this mess.

Within seconds of exiting the car, I was soaked. Eyelashes and eyebrows simply weren't enough to hold back the rain that dripped into my eyes and stung my skin. I shivered at the cold after a week of intolerable heat and waded out toward the dark shapes that I knew were the dead trees.

It wasn't just the need to protect the city and my friends that made me come here. I felt a sense of outrage at the elf who'd killed these trees. In my eyes, he'd betrayed his kind. To destroy a healthy, natural ecosystem for selfish gain was abhorrent. If it was the last thing I did, I'd undo the damage he'd done — I'd at least leave this state no worse than the humans had made it over the centuries.

Finally I saw the trees; blackened trunks with branches that drooped naked stems into the rising waters. Reaching out, I touched the bark and thought of the trees they'd once been, the trees they'd become after the Bon Nuit ritual.

Anger, and a sense of injustice, unlocked the store of Irix's energy I'd held within, powering it beyond even what I'd done at the levees. I felt the ground shudder, the tree twist against my hand. As I opened my eyes, I saw the trees shimmer with golden light, visible even through the driving storm. Golden, like the color of Irix's eyes.

I thought of him, the passion in his kisses, the way his eyes devoured me. He'd more than met me halfway, going far beyond a demon's nature to help me save the city. I hoped I'd see him again, that he'd still care for me when I did. I hoped he'd be proud of what I was doing now, even if he beat me senseless for disobeying him and putting myself at such risk.

The forest exploded in green and growth, limp branches launching upward and sprouting needles, new trunks rising from the waters to thicken before me. They rose, firm and proud, enveloping the dark sky and easing the wind that drove against them from the south. I smiled, rubbing the rain-blackened bark of the tree. Then I looked up.

The mage had been the one with the weather magic, but Irix had once told me elves were masters of weather. They created seasons at their whim, rain and sun as they pleased. I was only a half-breed, but I'd *felt* the spell Basteau had cast. The pattern of energy, the incantations and symbols spun across my mind, forever committed to memory as if they'd been etched there. Maybe, just maybe, I could do something to downgrade this storm.

Summoning every last bit of energy within myself, I raised my arms to the heavens. As I felt the storm, experienced its power and force, I sensed something familiar — something prickly, like static against my skin. The witches. Their spell was full of power, but it just couldn't seem to take hold. Like I'd done in the Bon Nuit ritual, I gathered their power to me, held it tightly inside, then launched it in a blast toward the storm.

Riding the surge of energy into the huge swirl of cloud and wind above, I slowed the storm. It felt like turning off a faucet that had long been rusted. My legs shook, and I sank to my knees in the murky water. The rain still fell, but steady instead of driving. The wind's roar quieted. The sky lightened enough to see the trees silhouetted against it. My ears rang, unaccustomed to the relative silence. And I heard a shout.

The angry expletives were in a language I didn't speak, but having had them shouted at me earlier today, I recognized the voice and dove face down into the swamp water. I just missed being cooked by the fireball that skimmed the bayou's surface.

The water warmed around me, and the first thing that went through my mind was that someone had peed in the swamp. Funny as that was, it wasn't the appropriate time for humor with an elf launching fireballs at me. I felt a surge of energy as I resurfaced above the water and realized the elf was trying to stir up the storm again and reverse what I'd done to dampen it.

A sort of tug-of-war ensued between us. I was drained of energy, barely able to stand, but in the face of his onslaught, something clicked within, and power rushed through my very bones. It was as if a door opened and a huge conduit began funneling energy into me. My skin prickled with it, and I felt like my hair was standing on end. Realizing that we were at an impasse, the elf gave up, and, with a scream of frustration, launched another fireball at me.

This one was smaller than the last, and I managed to avoid it. Thankfully, Irix's leather jacket shielded me from the heat. Another followed that one, and I began wading as quick as I could through the water, trying to evade the elf and head toward the road. My only defense was electricity, but I was reluctant to toss a lightning bolt at this guy with us both standing in two feet of water.

The elf must have ran out of fireballs, because the next thing I felt was roots emerging from the murky soil beneath my feet to wrap around my legs. I could hear him splashing after me and assumed he meant to hold me in place until he could catch up. I might not be a master of weather, or have any idea how to create a fireball, but plants were *mine*. I easily stepped free of the roots and played his trick back at him.

Through the dark and rain, I saw the bold horizontal lines of the roadway ahead. The elf was still pursuing me, but hadn't gained any. When it came to control of plant life, we were evenly matched. Not bad for a half-breed barely twenty-one years old. My surge of pride was short lived, though, as I realized I'd not have time to get in the Corolla, start it, and get out of range before the elf caught up.

I was scrambling up the rise to the roadway, still fighting off grasping roots, when I saw a faint flash of light up the road. It couldn't have been lightning. Was some idiot walking around in a hurricane with a flashlight? Or worse, driving in this downpour? I thought I was the only fool heading into the eye of the storm in a car tonight.

My run through the swamp had brought me out somewhere else on the roadway, and the Corolla was nowhere in sight. Taking a gamble, I ran south. If I didn't find the car, maybe I could outrun the elf and manage to lose him at some crossroad, or another bayou. Deep in my heart, I worried I was facing my death. I was only a half-breed, and the man behind me could most likely outrun me on the flat. Giving up wasn't an option, though, so I poured on the speed and raced in a straight line down the roadway, rain stinging my skin.

I saw that flash of dim light again as I rounded a corner and wondered if it really was lightning. I didn't have any experience with tropical storms or hurricanes. The light worried me less than the thud of footsteps, audible over the pouring rain. The elf was gaining on me. I could practically feel him behind me, his breath on my neck, the brush of his hand against my arm.

Something grabbed my shoulder, spinning me to the side. I felt a body thud into mine, and I twisted frantically. His hand slipped on the rain-soaked jacket, and a sharp, hot pain lanced my side. The fucker had stabbed me.

Luckily, Irix's coat had concealed my form, and the knife missed its mark, tearing through leather and my shirt to skim the skin of my waist. I panicked, realizing how close I'd come to dying. Screaming, I twisted and slipped the leather coat off one shoulder, knotting it around the knife blade that the elf was trying to tug loose.

The beam swept across us, like a spotlight. Not lightning, but I didn't have a spare moment to wonder what the hell it was when I was fighting for my life. If this elf got the knife loose, I wouldn't be so lucky the second strike. There were no plants nearby for me to utilize, and my human fighting skills were next to nil. I'd never taken martial arts, or even been in a cat fight. I'd always been the peacemaker and found myself relying on instincts alone, hoping that the slim chance I had of surviving would roll to my advantage.

I was yanked to the side with the elf, before falling to the pavement as his hands loosened. Rolling for some much-needed distance and springing to my feet, I took a quick glance behind me to assess the situation before I took off again. What I saw rooted me in place, my mouth open in amazement.

Irix. He'd stayed. He'd come after me. He was wrestling the elf, pounding him with some kind of energy.

After the first few hits, Irix began to falter. He'd always been so strong, but right now he seemed exhausted. The elf absorbed his lightning bolts, lashed him with wind and rain, and stabbed him repeatedly with the knife he'd managed to free from my leather jacket. I wasn't sure what to do. Lightning didn't seem to affect this elf, and there wasn't anything else offensive I knew how to do.

I watched, helpless, as Irix fought, absorbing the elf's blows and fixing his own wounds as he tried to gain the advantage. The surge of adrenaline I'd felt earlier left me in a rush, and I felt even weaker, dropping again to the pavement. Frantically, I ran through my inventory of skills, and for the first time in my life I'd wished I was more demon than elf. Maybe then I'd be able to help Irix.

Electricity. Plant growth. Minor control over weather. Nothing useful, and I had no weapons on me. I crawled toward the pair, now rolling across the roadway, and managed to grab a thrashing foot. I hoped it was the elf's. A flash lit the sky, and I saw that I held a booted foot that clearly wasn't Irix's

Fear for Irix sent me beyond all rational thought, and I acted on instinct. Rot. Disease. Death. I poured every hateful thought I had into that foot I held. That dreadful day I'd killed my father — the day that haunted my dreams, came to mind. The anger, the resentment. He'd feared me for as long as I could remember, but he had been hateful to Wyatt. I'd seen him beat my beloved brother, say cruel things to him. I'd seen Wyatt cringe, enduring his blows and curses. I'd snapped, in defense of the brother I adored. I protected those I loved — then and now.

The shoe I held blackened, and so did the few inches of flesh above it. I wasn't especially strong, but the pain of necrotic tissue distracted the elf enough for Irix to get hold of his neck. With a flash of gold and a twist, the elf's head popped off, like the cork from a bottle of champagne, and rolled with a spray of blood across the rain-soaked road.

Irix and I stared breathlessly at each other, emotions jumbled as we crouched over the headless body of the elf. Without a word, I launched myself at him, plastering my body against his to knock him flat against the pavement. My lips met his in hunger, desperation, need.

"Amber," he gasped when he'd finally come up for air. "Are you hurt? I saw him stab you."

"Flesh wound. But why are you here? You're supposed to be safely back in Hel."

Even in the darkness I could see his stern look. It filled me with a sense of belonging. Weird, I know, but the thought that someone cared enough about me to be pissed at my actions filled me with a surge of emotion. So far, only my brother, Wyatt, and the woman I'd always called my mother had loved me enough to reprimand me.

"Why are *you* not with Ourson and the vampires at Bliss?"

I squirmed, as much to feel him against me as in embarrassment. "I wanted to repair the trees, to protect the city, so I came out here. I didn't know the elf would come here too."

"You lied to me." Irix's voice was soft, and there was a note of pride mixed with the anger.

"Yeah, I did." Might as well be honest about it. Not like he'd believe me if I tried to make up some excuse. I'd known from the moment we fixed the levees that I was going to come here and do what I could to repair the southern barriers.

"You've got a lot of demon in you for a half breed." He

kissed me, his mouth warm in contrast with the cold rain. I relished every moment, knowing he needed to go.

I rolled off as he broke the kiss and extended a hand to help him to his feet. He grabbed it, but didn't put any weight against me as he rose. I saw the dark shape of a vehicle off to the side, half submerged in the swamp with headlights reflecting in the water. The stolen Cadillac, no doubt.

"You need to go." I hated this second goodbye even more than the first.

"Yes."

Hopefully in a few decades, or centuries, he'd be able to cross back over from Hel. My heart ached with the thought. Decades was far too long to wait to see him again. A year was far too long to wait. I'd be miserable without him, counting the hours until I could see him again.

"Make sure you get rid of the head and that body." Irix motioned toward the elf corpse. "You don't want the vampires to find it and make the connection between this elf and you."

"I'll take care of it."

Irix took the scroll from his waistband and unrolled the parchment. Surprisingly, the paper and the ink were unaffected by the pounding rain. "Swear to me you'll go back to safety with the vampires, and keep yourself well-fed and healthy until I see you again."

I couldn't help but laugh. "I swear on all the souls I Own that I'll keep myself safe and healthy until I see you again."

He laughed, knowing full well how meaningless the oath was. Even so, this affirmation of my demon-half pleased him, and his smile warmed my heart. "Until later, my little half-breed."

"Until later."

He spoke the words of the scroll, and disappeared in a flash of light. I felt oddly bereft, standing in the rain with

only the water-logged headlights of the Cadillac for illumi-
nation. Shrugging the torn leather jacket back over my
soaked shoulder, I located the elf's head and threw it into the
swamp along with his body. The alligators would find it long
before any human, let alone vampire, did. That done, I left
the Cadillac and jogged down the roadway to find Ourson's
Corolla.

Following a sharp bend in the road, I saw the shape of it
ahead, along with something else that glowed like a thousand
spotlights. Between me and my getaway car stood an angel.

CHAPTER 40

I froze, unable to even breathe. Part of my brain had decided that if I held very still, like a rabbit, the angel wouldn't see me. The figure of light wasn't myopic enough to miss a drenched, muddy woman standing in the middle of a roadway. With a flash, she was before me, thankfully dimming her wincingly bright glow to something just a few degrees beyond a night-light.

Still, my feet refused to move. My heart beat frantically, and I waited for my death to come. Would she blast me apart with some kind of energy? Lop off my head as I'd heard they always did to demons?

"*Gothnel daega fae-linna y willenthall.*"

Huh? Her words weren't the scratchy hum that Irix sometimes spoke. This sounded like the Elven language I'd heard so much of this week. Could this angel possibly have mistaken me for a full elf as the gate guardian had done? As bedraggled and dirty as I was?

It was time to wing it.

"We should speak English out of courtesy for the humans that claim this land."

My voice chimed out low and melodic, in harmony with the soft rain. The angel tilted her head, silvery curls swinging low over her shoulder.

"But there are no humans hereabouts. They are all safely in their homes, hiding from the rain and wind as they always do."

True. I scrambled to come up with some other plausible reason for keeping the conversation in English.

"This is my custom. I'd be deeply grateful if you would humor me."

The angel nodded respectfully, blue eyes wide as they stared unnervingly into mine. "Of course. Dearest *fae-linna*, on behalf of the angelic host, I welcome you. We have longed for the day that you would return to our fold. The humans here will benefit greatly from the presence of elves, and we will guide you in your path to higher vibration."

She didn't make any more sense in English than she did in Elven. All I knew was that the humans would *not* have benefited from the presence of that elf asshole I'd just served up to the alligators, and I truly didn't want to be on this woman's path to higher vibration — whatever that meant.

I inclined my head in a gracious nod and frantically wondered when this angel was going to leave so I could get in Ourson's car and hightail it back to Bliss as fast as I could. Thankfully, I didn't have to reply.

"I so dislike to bother you while you are restoring balance to this portion of the land, but I am seeking a demon who has violated the terms of our treaty and befouled this realm with his disgusting and base energy."

Yeah. I was fucking that demon yesterday morning. That response was likely to get me killed, though. Besides, I wanted to know how much of a fix she had on Irix's energy. Too much and he might never be able to return.

"I have sensed some disturbing energy in this area and the

nearby city." I waved my hand vaguely toward the bayou. "What sort of demon are you seeking?"

The angel sighed, giving me a charming, self-deprecating smile. "I'm afraid all the human technology and the storm have masked his classification and identity."

I carefully let out the breath I'd been holding. "I'm so sorry. I must ask for your forgiveness. No doubt my own magic also hindered your ability to identify this trespasser."

"Oh, no need to apologize. Correcting imbalance and bringing about right order is always a priority. We will find the trespasser and bring him to justice in due time."

Hopefully not. I looked around at the trees and smiled apologetically at the angel. "I wouldn't want to keep you from your duties any longer."

"Oh! And you, yours. Lovely work you've done here with these trees. Such harmony, such beauty of purpose. You and your brethren are always welcome. I hope to encounter you again."

As flattering as it was to have an angel praise my work, I was eager to get away from her.

"Thank you." I waited for her to disappear and grew increasingly anxious as she remained, staring at me with those fathomless, blue eyes.

"The wind and rain is invigorating. I'm glad to encounter another who respects the power of the storm and does not hide in some flimsy dwelling."

I held my breath again as her gaze roved over me.

"But why would you wish to remain muddy, with torn clothing and damage to your body."

Fuck. I remembered Irix telling me that elves never smelled, never had a hair out of place, that they could heal their injuries with a few words. I panicked briefly, and then I remembered something my stepsister, Nyalla, had told me.

"The human technology is out of harmony with my abilities, and I have yet to adjust. I would rather exert my energies on the trees than on the vanity of my personal appearance and clothing."

The angel reached out a hand to me, and my heart nearly stopped. Her touch was cold, like marble. A white glow streamed into me, like a shot of ice through my veins. Without looking, I knew the knife wound along my side had been healed.

"Travel well, my little sister," she said with a warm smile.

"Travel well." I managed to choke the words out as my heart thumped.

With a flash of light, the angel vanished, leaving me momentarily night blind on the deserted road. My knees quivered with the ebb of adrenaline as I staggered to the Corolla and crawled in, sagging with relief against the steering wheel. I wasn't dead. I'd done magic that an angel thought worthy. And Irix could return — just as soon as he could make it across the gates from Hel safely. Now the only thing left to do was keep my promise to the incubus and return to the safety of the vampires and Bliss.

The car started with a turn of the key. The storm eased from moderate rain to a light drizzle, and I felt the air warm as I turned the car around to head back into the city.

CHAPTER 41

I still hadn't gotten over how weird it felt to be back in Maryland. This had always been my home, but one week away had changed all that. There had been no word from Irix, and I desperately wanted to return to New Orleans, to close my eyes and remember our time together, to curl up in his bed and try to catch his scent.

All I had were memories and a torn leather jacket. Even the energy he'd shared with me was gone, used on the bayou and in fighting the elf. The small amount I had now was what I'd gathered on my own through carefully chosen encounters.

I felt like another person masquerading as myself. Three weeks had seemed like a lifetime as I numbly went through the motions. My twenty-first birthday, all the joint celebrations with Nyalla, preparations for my senior year — none of it seemed to matter anymore. All I could think about was that week in New Orleans. Irix. Would he ever return? What danger could I be in from the elves who now seemed to have no problem crossing the gates from Hel?

"Can you translate something for me?" I asked Nyalla. My

stepsister was curled up on my bed as I packed my bags for college, a stack of mail beside her. Most of it appeared to be travel brochures.

"Sure. What do you think about Aruba?" She waved a glossy tri-fold of aquamarine sea and white beach at me. I couldn't help but smile; the girl was obsessed with the ocean after her vacation on the Eastern Shore.

"Looks beautiful. I hear there's some great diving, too."

She pursed her lips, looking adorably pensive as she contemplated the brochure. "Hmmm. Maybe. So . . . what did you want me to translate?"

Nyalla had been helping me learn Elvish the past few weeks. I didn't have much skill with languages, but this one I was willing to put in extra effort to learn. I hadn't been able to work up the nerve to ask her until now. *You don't want to know,* Irix had said, and I wasn't sure I did want to know. But it was better to face my enemies with as much knowledge as I could, no matter how much it frightened me.

"What does this mean?" I repeated what the elf had shouted at me at the seawall levee, trying to recreate the pronunciation as best as I could. My sister frowned, repeating a few words for clarification.

"It sounds like 'Traitor, betrayer of your people and harlot to the demons. You will be lower than the buried corpse in our new world, cursed by all your kind.'" Nyalla's eyes grew big. "What did you do? I've never heard an elf say that kind of thing before, and, trust me, I made them plenty angry when I was a slave there."

So this was worse than 'rotted whore'. At least it seemed the elf didn't realize I was a half-breed. I was being cursed for siding with others against my own kind, and having sex with Irix. As bad as it sounded, being mistaken for a full elf might just be the thing that saved my life. Again.

"Oh, and I almost forgot — this came for you this morning."

Nyalla handed me an overnight mail envelope. Weird that someone would send something to me at my brother's girlfriend's house. I'd never lived there. Wyatt didn't receive his mail there. As far as I knew, Nyalla and Sam were the only ones who did. I didn't recognize the scrawl of handwriting on the label, and the return address was indecipherable. Huh.

I tore open the top of the envelope, dumping the contents into my lap. Inside was a sheet of paper and a note. My heart beat out of control as I recognized the bold, dark script.

See you soon.

Unless he was standing in the doorway, it wouldn't be soon enough. Still, tears sprang to my eyes. He was thinking of me, planning on returning. I'd wait; I'd wait forever. Opening the other sheet of paper, I realized I wouldn't have to wait forever, only until March, because it wasn't a sheet of paper — it was an airline ticket.

An airline ticket to Maui.

ACKNOWLEDGMENTS

A huge thanks to my copyeditors Dionne Lister and Jennifer Cosham whose eagle eyes catch all my typos and keep my comma problem in line, to Meredith Bond at Anessa Books for her formatting expertise, and to Damonza, for cover design.

Most of all, thanks to my children, who have suffered many nights of microwaved chicken nuggets and take-out pizza so that Mommy can follow her dream.

ABOUT THE AUTHOR

Debra lives in a little house in the woods of Maryland with her sons and two slobbery bloodhounds. On a good day, she jogs and horseback rides, hopefully managing to keep the horse between herself and the ground. Her only known super power is 'Identify Roadkill'.

For more information:
www.debradunbar.com